Hand-Me-Downs

Rhea Kohan

HAND-ME-DOWNS

Random House New York

*Grateful acknowledgment is made to the following for
permission to reprint previously published material:*

Holt, Rinehart and Winston: "Fire and Ice" from *The Poetry of
Robert Frost,* edited by Edward Connery Lathem. Copyright 1923,
© 1969 by Holt, Rinehart and Winston. Copyright 1951 by
Robert Frost. Reprinted by permission of
Holt, Rinehart and Winston, Publishers.
United Artists Music: Lyrics from "Hi-Lili, Hi-Lo" by
Bronislau Kaper & Helen Deutsch. Copyright © 1952,
renewed 1980 Metro-Goldwyn-Mayer Inc. All rights
administered and controlled by Robbins Music Corporation.
All rights reserved.

Library of Congress Cataloging in Publication Data

Kohan, Rhea.
Hand-me-downs.

I. Title.
PL4.K786Han [PS3561.O37]   813'.54   80-5285
ISBN 0-394-51161-1

Manufactured in the United States of America

First Edition

24689753

For the woman I most love and admire
in all the world:
my mother,
CLAIRE ARNOLD

Hand-Me-Downs

Prologue

As a young child, in the small town of Visoka where she was born, Malka early learned to despise her contemporaries. Instead of wanting friendship and to be like everyone else, as most youngsters do, Malka wanted only to be different. In no manner did she wish to be one of the others, for she considered them all stupid, narrow, dull peasants. She had no friends. She was certain that association with ordinary, uninspired people would make her become like them. She was positive that mediocrity was contagious. So anxious was she to differentiate herself from those around her, that whatever they did, she did the opposite. It was then that she realized the extent of her ill luck—for instead of being admired for her uncommonness, she was shunned. Instead of being considered original, she was considered odd.

People began to whisper that she was possessed. Her parents were bewildered and wondered what they had done to deserve such an affliction. They were frightened by her strangeness, by her flagrant disregard for customary and expected behavior. Most of all, they were frightened by the intense, piercing anger in her eyes. They, too, began to believe she was possessed and approached the rabbi for advice.

"She must be married," he told them. "When she is married, she will be as other women."

Malka, when she heard what was in store for her, went into a towering rage. She shrieked and cursed her parents. She ran around and around the room, stopping only to pound her head on the wooden table. She carried on all night, disturbing the sleep of the entire village with her cries. In the morning, she told her parents that although she was only fifteen, although men were fools and children burdens, although she wanted more out of life than the privilege of washing her husband's feet, she would do as they wished. Stunned by her unexpected acquiescence, her parents stared at her. After a moment, her mother smiled: "You will see, Malka," she said softly. "When you are married, you will be happy."

"No, I won't," Malka said bitterly. "What I will be is away from you. That is what will make me happy."

After her father had beaten her for her disrespect, he began his search for a bridegroom. Since word of Malka's unfortunate reputation had spread far and wide, he found it impossible to obtain anyone desirable for her. Forced to settle, he settled for Joseph Blazyk. Joseph was poor, Joseph was uneducated. Joseph was all he could get. Joseph was also imperfectly formed. On one hand he had six fingers, on the other hand also six. "How fitting," murmured the inhabitants of Visoka righteously, "for one freak to be matched with another. See how wonderful and just are the workings of the Lord."

For her part, Malka was strangely docile. She sat quietly with her mother and sewed her bridal gown. She helped prepare the food for the guests and cleaned the house. Her mother, believing at last that her daughter was normal, kissed the rabbi's hands and blessed him for his wisdom.

Four months before her sixteenth birthday, Malka was married to Joseph Blazyk. It took her only a few days to realize that instead of freeing her from the domination of her parents and permitting the fire and energy that bubbled within her to explode and expose her as a passionate and extraordinary being, marriage had merely bound her forever to a man with ugly, deformed hands. Furious at having deceived herself into believing that with wedlock would come liberation, appalled at the realization that she had aided in the destruction of all her dreams, depressed by visions of her miserable future, Malka reverted to her former behavior.

She vented her rage and disappointment on poor, bewildered Joseph. Almost beside herself over the enormity of the tragedy that had befallen her, she became worse than ever. She refused to cook or keep house for her husband. She refused to allow him into her bed. When, as a last resort, he beat her for her unwifely behavior, she spit in his beard and raked her nails across his face. Ashamed at his inability to control his wife and not knowing what else to do, Joseph took his paltry dowry, bought up pots and pans and sundries, and went out on the road.

Surprisingly, he did very well. When he had sold all his stock, he purchased more and better merchandise. People at first bought out of pity, but after a while, won over by his soft voice and wonderfully humorous stories, they bought because they liked him. "Where did you get such a humor?" they would ask. "Misery makes me funny," he would reply, selling them pots and ribbons.

After five weeks Joseph returned to his home and knocked timidly on the door. Malka opened it and gaped in angry dismay at her husband. She had believed that Joseph was gone for good. For the past five weeks she had lived alone, hungry but happy for the first time in her life. Before she could slam the door in his face, Joseph held out to her the pile of coins he had earned. She stared at the money and then looked up at him. Slowly she opened the door and stood aside for him to enter. They sat down at the table, and Joseph watched while Malka counted the coins. She counted them four times and put all but two into a drawstring bag, which she hid under the floor in a dark corner of the room. Then she put on her shawl, picked up the two remaining coins and left the house. When she returned, she cooked the food she had bought and set it before Joseph, who was still sitting at the table.

Since his homecoming not a word had been exchanged between them. Now Malka looked at her husband and spoke: "Wash yourself before you eat," she said. "Bring me some water," Joseph ordered. Malka sat very still and stared at the floor. Then she got up and brought him some water. While he ate, Malka made up his bed. Two days later he was back on the road.

Little by little they prospered. Joseph worked very hard, having discovered that Malka's ardor grew in direct proportion to the pile of coins they were amassing. The greater the amount of coins he brought home, the greater was her passion. He knew then that money made Malka hot. He knew then that his unfathomable wife had the soul of a whore. She would wait impatiently for him to finish his meal and then begin her ritual. First she would bathe, slowly and thoroughly, and then unbind the long chestnut hair she had refused to cut off before their wedding. Initially, Joseph had been greatly disturbed at her lack of modesty, but now, enormously aroused by the sight of her large naked breasts and the realization that he would soon be bedding this whore, he sat gripping the arms of his chair, white-knuckled, red-faced and breathing rapidly.

In nine years they had six children, all of whom survived infancy, all of whom were born with the normal number of fingers. Malka, secure in the knowledge that under her kitchen floor was a huge and ever-increasing pile of coins, felt certain that her luck had changed. As her family grew, she hired workmen to enlarge her house. Although she was still regarded with suspicion, people no longer averted their eyes when she passed. Some even nodded to her.

Malka surprised herself by becoming fiercely devoted to her children. More content than she could ever recall being, Malka, suspicious and restless, still could not relax enough to take pleasure in her good fortune. She was constantly on guard against the fickle demons of destiny who could, with the flick of a finger, turn a dream into a nightmare. Basically she was an unlucky woman and had been given a twelve-fingered man to keep her ever mindful of that fact. Underneath her apron lay an unspoken wish: More than anything else, Malka Blazyk yearned for the ability to do one thing perfectly; only one thing, O Lord. What that one thing was wasn't important. But she wanted to be able to do it better than anyone else in the world. And she knew it would never happen. She was unlucky, and no one would ever know her essence.

Only through her children could she achieve personal glory. Only through them could she hope to discover the key to the thick and heavy gates that kept her penned inside the prison of obscurity. She seethed and boiled with frustration, knowing that inside of her lived an extraordinary person—and no one would ever know.

She pored over her children and studied them constantly, searching for the one who would free her. Of the six, she selected three possibilities and was eagerly awaiting the imminent birth of her seventh child and, she hoped, fourth possibility. Her seventh child was a mongoloid idiot. In horror and disgust, Malka turned her face to the wall and refused to look at the baby, who was fat, healthy and useless. She refused to feed it. She had been cursed again. Her husband and mother pleaded with her to relent.

"Malka, this child is God's will. You cannot let him starve to death."

"Then I will drown it."

Malka's mother tried to take the child to a wet nurse, but Malka refused to allow it. Terrified, her mother fled to her bed and went into a decline, positive that Malka was insane. Joseph, desperate, went with his six children to the house of his brother, Gershon. Two weeks later, they returned. They found the baby gone without a trace and Malka sitting alone. Her face was stony and set, and her eyes were as hard and as empty as the eyes of a corpse.

Joseph never asked about the baby and Malka never told him. However, he heard from the rabbi that the screams of the starving infant were heartrending and lasted for six days and nights. During all that time, said the rabbi, Malka just sat and waited for it to die. From then on Malka, who had always been difficult, became impossible. She sat for hours staring into space. She removed her head covering and walked bareheaded to the market place. She refused ever again to observe the Sabbath, light the candles or set foot in the synagogue. She let it be known that, for her, God did not exist.

The townspeople called her a murderess and resurrected their long-buried fears and suspicions. Parents cautioned their children against going near the house of the Blazyks or associating with its residents. They averted their heads and refused to look at Malka, lest she give them the evil eye. If, despite all their efforts, they were unable to avoid her, the villagers protected themselves against her wickedness by spitting three times and tying red ribbons on their bodies.

Malka ignored all of this. She remained at home, filled with bitterness and grieving over what would never be hers. In the night she would fling herself at Joseph in shameless, ravenous abandon, and he, incapable of resisting her breasts, her thighs, her fevered eyes, and inflamed by the realization that he was now penetrating a murderess, wept as he thrust himself inside her.

In the spring she gave birth to her eighth child, aided in the delivery by her five-year-old daughter, Helen, and an old woman who, in sixteen pregnancies, had never borne a living child and was therefore immune to Malka's malignity, having already been sufficiently afflicted. The child was born blue and dead, strangled by its own cord. It had six fingers on the right hand and a great red birthmark on its face.

The people of Visoka now rose up in wrath and terror, absolutely convinced by this irrefutable evidence that the devil's daughter was dwelling among them. In a frenzy, they stoned the house and threatened the lives of all the Blazyks. Malka's mother, already ill, managed with her dying breath to accuse Malka of having killed her. The mother's death was the final straw. The sages of the village held a secret meeting and recalled every instance of what they now realized was Malka's demonic behavior. Unless they rid themselves of this evil and accursed creature who had killed not only her own child but her own mother as well, a great calamity was certain to be visited upon them. Harboring this abomination, this handmaiden of Satan, would surely bring down the wrath of God upon them all.

They decided to burn out the Blazyks, and a week later, having received permission from the reluctant rabbi who, being a nonviolent liberal, would have much preferred to run them out of town by pursuing them with rocks and sticks, set out for the Blazyk house armed with torches. They arrived to find the house deserted and the Blazyks gone. Fearing for the safety of their children, Joseph and Malka had dug up their coins, sewn them into the lining of their clothes, packed up the family and departed Visoka forever.

Somewhat disappointed but undaunted, the elders of the village burned down the house anyway. During the year that followed, strange happenings were said to be taking place among the charred ruins. The baker's wife, out on an errand, walked too close to the house and not five minutes later slipped and broke her ankle. A dead cat was found where the door used to be. A couple from another town, en route to Warsaw, camped there for the night, unaware of what they were doing. The next morning, they came into the village for supplies. The townspeople eyed them curiously and fearfully, but the couple appeared fine. However, a few months later, when they had a child, word filtered back to Visoka that the child could not hear—nor, it was later discovered, could it speak.

It was obvious that something must be done. True, Malka was gone, but her evil miasma lingered on. They decided to clean up the area and change it from a place of doom to a place of hope and growth. Since no one in town would go near the place, they hired two peasants to clear away the burnt remains and to till the soil and make it arable. In the spring, seeds were planted. All this Gershon wrote in a letter to his brother. He told Joseph that although they tended and cared for the farm diligently, although the weather was perfect and the rain ample, nothing ever grew on the land, not even a potato.

On the ship to America, Bella Blazyk, age two years, ten months, sickened and died. Rigid with grief, Joseph looked on as his youngest child was buried at sea. Malka sat dry-eyed. She mourned the passing of the child without any outward show of emotion. She was used to heartache and loss. She was used to getting kicked in the face. She was unlucky and always had been so. Although Bella's death was not an auspicious beginning for a new life in a new land, as far as Malka was concerned, it could have been worse. Bella had been a sweet child, but she did not possess the seeds of specialness. She was not a possibility.

Feeling Joseph's eyes upon her, Malka looked into his stricken face. Joseph had adored his Bella. Therefore, for his sake, and because he was a good man, Malka put her hands over her face and tried to weep. But what she never got over, what finished her for good, what dried up and desiccated the little that was left of her ability to feel, was what happened to Benjamin.

Of her five remaining children only two were extraordinary, Max and Celia. Benjamin could have been extraordinary too, the best of all of them, but now, instead, he was merely crippled. Benjamin's condition so infuriated Malka that she could barely stand to look at him and would sometimes forget to give him lunch. Before the accident she had believed that she had overcome her unfortunate destiny and in the night would cautiously whisper to Joseph: "I have a lucky son. I have a son, Benjamin, who has the power to change bad into good. He has the power to make people believe him. Could it be that I have overcome my destiny?"

Before Benjamin's gift became obvious to her, Malka had believed in nothing, not in God, not in religion, nothing. All she knew was that despite her desperate efforts, she had been cursed from birth. She had been cursed by being born with fierce ambition—but without luck. And if Malka believed in anything, it was in luck and the importance of having it. She had believed in Benjamin, but now, since he had embarrassed her by becoming a cripple, she realized that nothing had really changed at all.

Her son Max was brilliant. He had an amazing affinity for numbers and words. In only two months he had learned English. Her daughter Celia was beautiful. It was as if an angel had touched her face and given her what she needed to survive in America—a lovely skin, a lovely body, a sweet smell and blue eyes. Helen and Murray were ignored and scorned by their mother. They were what Malka knew was the worst thing to be next to unlucky. They were ordinary, merely ordinary. Their function was simply to take up space—to eat, to drink, to live and die in unsavory anonymity. To them she served only the back of the chicken and the bones of the fish. No soup, no salt, no tomatoes. But, ah, Benjamin. He had been the one, and now look at him! Had Malka been capable of weeping, she could have drowned the world.

When she and Joseph and the five children had arrived in America, Malka became uncomfortable. She was not afraid; people who believe in nothing are afraid of nothing. But there was something restless here, an atmosphere of instability, of capriciousness. Like the citizens, the imps of fate were also free, free to mock, free to spite, free of the constraints of custom.

Malka knew immediately that America was a dangerous place. Always wary, always suspicious, Malka became paranoiac. She warned her children to be careful, to keep their eyes open and their mouths closed. She cautioned them against letting their guard down and developing trust in anything human and therefore inconstant. Malka trusted only things mathematical and immutable and never permitted her children out of the house except for purposes of education. She allowed them to go to school and to take music lessons. Every morning she told them the same thing: "I bore you against my better judgment and in great pain. I did not suffer in order to see you become damaged in the hands of hoodlums or under the wheels of a moving vehicle. Mind what I say. Be ready to run if you have to, and always look both ways when you cross the street." Despite her admonitions, Benjamin, en route to his violin lesson, managed to get run over anyway.

At the sight of her favorite child lying in the street under the wheels of a delivery van, Malka began to shriek and rip her hair and clothes. It wasn't grief she felt, she was long beyond grief. It was rage. It was a fury so intense and so primitive that had she not been restrained, she would have murdered the driver of the van, as well as her wounded son. To Malka the sight of Benjamin lying torn and bleeding on a public thoroughfare, in full view of strangers and neighbors, was a monumental humiliation. To Malka, getting run over was common. All the way to the hospital she berated him: "See?" she ranted. "See what happens to a stupid boy who doesn't listen to his mother? Now look at you."

Benjamin remained in the hospital for twenty-seven days. So offended, so insulted, so ashamed was Malka over Benjamin's carelessness that not once in all that time did she visit him. Her husband and children were horrified. Joseph told her that her behavior was unmotherly and not normal. "Malka," he pleaded, "the boy is asking for you. Visit him, comfort him."

"No," said Malka, in an icy voice. "He is no good to me now."

"Malka, he is your child. You are his mother."

"I will never forgive him. Never."

Joseph stared at his wife. He had never understood her, but this attitude frightened him. "Malka," he said gravely, "the child is blameless. I have overlooked many things, *many* things. This I cannot overlook."

Malka sat stonily in her chair. Her eyes were steel. "He was what was left of my hope," she said expressionlessly. "Through him I could have achieved greatness. His accomplishments would have been my accomplishments. People would admire him. They would say, 'Only an amazing woman could have grown this amazing man. Who was the mother?'" She raised her eyes to Joseph's face. "What good is he to me now?" she asked him.

For a long time Joseph sat staring at the hands that had forced him to marry this woman. Then, without a word, he stood up and left the room. He went to the hospital and visited Benjamin. When he returned home, he packed a few belongings and moved to a small apartment three tenements away. He saw his children daily and his apartment became their second home, their refuge from Malka's relentless supervision. Joseph never spoke to Malka again and crossed the street to avoid her whenever he spied her outside. In a letter to his brother, Gershon, back in Poland, he told of the separation. "I have left my wife of nineteen years, Malka Blazyk," he wrote. "I did this because she is not human."

Joseph's departure left Malka unmoved, although she had, in her way, loved him. She had already suffered so grievously that this latest agony was merely another gash in an already lacerated soul, merely another indication of her cursed, miserable, unlucky destiny.

One by one all the children, the extraordinary and the ordinary, grew up and left. Benjamin, stunned and damaged, more by his mother's savage rejection than by his accident, became a psychiatrist, moved to California and married an actress. Beautiful Celia, while working as a counselor in Camp Takawanda, got hit in the face with a volleyball and had her nose badly broken. She brooded over this for two years and then flew out to California where her brother Benjamin arranged for her to be operated on by a colleague in reconstructive surgery. Celia later married the colleague.

Max and Murray Blazyk together established Blaze Lighting Company. Max handled the business end; Murray, with Joseph peering over his shoulder, handled the sales. Helen worked for them as receptionist-bookkeeper until her marriage to Leonard Ritter in 1947. Shortly thereafter, Blaze Lighting, including Joseph, also moved out to California, where they supplied kliegs and spotlights to movie and television studios.

Malka sat at her window and grew old alone in her apartment. The neighborhood children were afraid of her and called her a witch. None of it made any difference. Malka cared about nothing, was attached to nothing, and felt affection for nothing. Because of this, she was happy. She had discovered, finally, that the roots of pain are embedded in love. Since loss of what one loves unleashes that pain to wreak havoc and misery, it clearly follows that when you love nothing, nothing can hurt you. She was free and at peace at last.

Helen, the only one now left in New York, worshiped her mother, as children who are neglected tend to do. She found Malka fascinating and visited her every Tuesday without fail. Malka was not a cordial hostess. While Helen made instant coffee and cheerful conversation, Malka sat and looked out her window, ignoring Helen as she had always done. One day Helen brought her husband to meet Malka, who had refused to attend the weddings of any of her children.

"Mama," she said, "this is Lenny, my husband." Malka, ignoring the introduction, sat at the window and watched a Buick make a right turn. Helen and Lenny looked at each other. Lenny held up his hand to forestall the remark Helen was about to make and walked over to Malka. Smiling gamely, he leaned over and spoke loudly into her ear. "It's a pleasure to meet you, Mother Blazyk." Malka turned her head and looked at him with her cold, dead eyes. "Ged adda fin here," she said, and went back to her perusal of the street.

The following Tuesday, Helen let herself into the apartment and, as usual, found her mother in the chair by the window. "Ma," she told her, "I got a letter from Celia today." Expecting no answer and receiving none, she went on: "Celia says we should move out to California. She says it's a paradise out there. What do you say, Ma, should we move to California? Huh? You, me and Lenny?" Silence from Malka. Helen put on the coffee and picked up around the apartment. About a half hour later, when she went over to offer her mother "a nice hot cup of coffee and a prune Danish," she saw that Malka was dead, and had probably been so for several days. She died, Helen realized sadly, as she had lived, looking out on an alien world that had neither recognized nor had a place for her. The family was shocked to discover that, at her death, Malka was only fifty-one years old.

With nothing left to keep them in New York, Helen and Leonard moved out to California, where Leonard went to work as a sales representative for Blaze Lighting. Helen became pregnant and gave birth to the first of her three daughters. Her second child she called Natalie; her third was Phyllis. But the first, even over Lenny's strong objections, she named Marilyn, in honor of her mother, Malka.

Chapter 1

FROM THE VERY BEGINNING, Marilyn was Daddy's girl. Helen did not know how this happened but always blamed it on the colic. She had conceived quickly and from that day on until Marilyn's birth had been sicker and more uncomfortable than ever before in her life. She had morning sickness morning, noon and night. She was always exhausted. By her fourth month, she had lost six pounds. Assured by the doctor that the second trimester would bring an end to the nausea and propel her into what he called "the beautiful bloom of pregnancy," she waited, weakly counting the days and throwing up. In the middle of her seventh month, she knew it was hopeless. Her stomach was huge, her face broken out, her hair stringy and oily. She had what the doctor called a "pregnancy mask," huge dark circles under her eyes and little red blebs all over her body. Her skin, shiny, stretched and pulled taut over her belly, itched maddeningly. Her fingers and ankles swelled, her back ached, her breasts hurt and the nausea continued unabated.

When at last her water broke and she went into labor, she welcomed the pain—but not for long. Fourteen hours of labor dimmed her enthusiasm, and she never again wanted to hear the word "push." At birth Marilyn weighed seven/eleven, how lucky. She was born screaming and didn't stop for four and a half months. Helen wearily offered her breast, which Marilyn furiously spurned. At this rejection, Helen, who had suffered for so long only to be angrily repudiated by the cause of it, dissolved into depression. Lenny and two doctors swore that the baby's tantrums were the result of colic, and begged her not to take them personally, but Helen couldn't help feeling that the baby didn't like her. Eventually Marilyn got over her colic, but Helen never got over her feeling.

Concerned for his wife, Lenny sent for his recently widowed mother, Yuspeh. She arrived, examined the infant, made Helen a cup of tea, told her that worrying about children made lines in the face, unpacked her one trunk and two shopping bags and settled in—permanently.

Marilyn's first smile was for her father. Her first word was "Papa." And Lenny adored his firstborn. He thought the moon shone in her smile and was eclipsed by her tears. There were days when he came home at lunchtime just to see the baby. He complied with her every demand and denied her nothing. She was the apple of his eye, the salt of his earth, the sun in his heaven, the money in his bank. She was his absolutely most favorite thing in the world, and he was hers.

Helen, forced to stand apart, watched disbelieving as her life grew cold. She was amazed at the far-reaching ramifications of colic.

She tried to love Marilyn, tried to put aside her daughter's indifference, tried to deny this disdain and dismissal by yet another Malka. And yet the mere sight of the child would unleash her anger. She ached to love Marilyn—after all, she was her child—but could never seem to summon up the tenderness necessary to overcome the inordinate rage she felt at her daughter's rejection. Marilyn, tiny as she was, appeared to sense her mother's attitude and reacted to it with increased negativism.

Still Helen took good, albeit impersonal care of Marilyn. She bathed, dressed, and fed her. She read her *Mother Goose* to get her to eat. But she never kissed a little foot, or buried her nose in the warm, sweet neck, or held her baby close in her arms to whisper loving nonsense and gently nibble an earlobe. She rarely played with her, not only because she had no inclination to, but also because Marilyn's response to her seemed so grudging. It appeared to Helen that the child merely tolerated her while she waited for her Papa to return home.

When it was time for toilet training, Marilyn refused to "squeeze hard" for lollipops or red balloons. It was only when Helen told her to "make a wet for Papa" or "make a poo-poo for Papa because he will be soooo happy" that the training was successfully completed. To her sister, Celia, Helen confided that she had "found the key to Marilyn. What it is," she said to Celia, "is that child will do anything for Lenny. She won't go to sleep, so I tell her that Papa will be angry with her, and she's off to bed like a lamb. For me," Helen said bitterly, "she could not care less, but for Lenny, she would learn Latin."

By her third year, Marilyn was "independent," as her father called her, "headstrong, cold and demanding," as her mother called her, and "a spoiled brat from the first water," as her grandmother Yuspeh called her. And yet, as confused and dismayed by the effect that Marilyn was having on her life as Helen was, she never, even at the height of what she called Marilyn's "obnoxiousness," ever laid a hand on her. And Marilyn, already aware that her Papa would *never* get really angry with her, rose to ever-increasing heights of naughtiness. When she deliberately and despite repeated warnings not to touch, broke every knick-knack on the coffee table, and her grandmother Yuspeh, armed with dustpan and broom, demanded that Helen give "that terrible spoiledness a good smack, look what she on purpose did," Helen refused—aware perhaps that were she to chastise Marilyn physically, she would be incapable of stopping. Instead, she threw the child into her room and kept her there, despite Yuspeh's pleading to "let her out already, Helen, the child could die in there and I could lose an eardrum, how can you stand that crying, where is your heart?" until Lenny returned and sprung his daughter, who had been screaming steadily for over three hours and was now beyond hysteria. It took Lenny an eternity of holding, rocking, crooning and kissing to soothe Marilyn, and was also the basis for the first serious argument that Helen and Lenny ever had. "She did it to spite me," Helen declared, "she knew how I loved those things." And Lenny, glaring at his wife, pounded his fist on the table and thundered, "Are you crazy? The child is only three years old. What can she know of spite?"

Yuspeh, too, scolded her. "I told you you should give her a smack. A smack is over in a minute and the hollering is over in two—look what a trouble you made—everybody upset—my son is beside himself—the baby is hoarse—I myself got a headache, a migraine from such a behavior."

Helen, alarmed by Lenny's fury as well as her own, redoubled her efforts to achieve a better relationship with her daughter, or at least establish some sort of détente. She vowed that the next time it became necessary to discipline Marilyn she would be smarter about it, and either release the child earlier or time the punishment more conveniently. Because Marilyn was bright as well as difficult, she soon learned to put herself into her room immediately after a crime was committed, a maneuver calculated to avoid being dragged and thrown in by a livid mother, and one that also disarmed Helen, rendering her impotent and unable to vent her anger. Almost despite herself Helen admired the child's intelligence and her spirit.

Marilyn, for her part, was awed by her mother, by her power and by her own inability to manipulate Helen. In fact, she much preferred Helen to Yuspeh. Helen was rough, but both mother and daughter had drawn the lines that neither cared to step over. Yuspeh was another story. Helen suffered, but Yuspeh didn't give a damn. Helen still tried to do her motherly duty and on the surface at least keep up normal appearances. Marilyn and Helen, when they collided, clashed head on, but Marilyn never quite knew where she stood with her grandmother. She and Marilyn were wary of each other.

One evening Helen and Lenny went over to Celia and Jack's for dinner. When Marilyn awoke from her nap, she discovered to her horror that she had been left alone with Grandma. For dinner, Grandma gave her a nice broiled lamb chop, cut up, with mashed potatoes and broccoli. Marilyn pushed it away. "No," she said angrily. Now, had Papa been home he would have said, "The child doesn't like lamb chops, give her something else." Her mother, who was fanatic about feedings, would have irritably and reluctantly read her "Little Red Riding Hood," and gotten her so engrossed that she wouldn't realize she was being fed. But Grandma only looked at her and frowned. "What is this 'no'?" she asked and pushed the plate right back in front of her. "No," Marilyn repeated even more angrily and gave the plate such a push that two pieces of lamb chop fell off onto the table. Grandma drew her brows together in a fearful frown and put the pieces of lamb chop back on the plate.

"Look, you," she said, "listen on me what I tell you. You eat the supper like a nice girl and nothing happens. You don't eat the supper like a spoiled brat from the first water and also nothing happens, except you go to bed a hungry girl. Me, I don't care you eat or you don't eat. To me it's all the same. But one more time you push away the plate and it falls on the table lamb chops, I take mine hand and give you such a smack you wouldn't sit for three days, maybe even a week." Then she pushed the plate back in front of Marilyn and the two of them sat there at the table looking at each other.

Marilyn took her forefinger and gave the plate a little push. Nothing fell off. She gave it another little push and again nothing fell off. "Hah!" said the grandmother, "push harder. You could use a good licking." Marilyn's hand flew back into her lap. "I want Poppy and Mommy," she whimpered, her eyes beginning to fill. The grandmother shrugged. "You want so you want. Everybody wants. Who doesn't want? I had a friend, may she rest in peace, Fannie Bogotch. Everything she saw she wanted. Eat your supper. I'll tell you a story about mine friend, Fannie Bogotch, who even when she didn't see it, she wanted it." She pushed the plate back in front of Marilyn, who picked up her fork and, enthralled by the story, finished her food.

During her bath, while her grandmother was washing her hair

and Marilyn was yowling that there was soap in her eyes, Lenny and Helen came home. Yuspeh looked up at them from her kneeling position beside the tub. "Helen," she said, firmly gripping Marilyn by the hair, "God should only give you strength. From this one you will have your hands full." She looked meaningfully at Helen's stomach, swollen in pregnancy once again. "Maybe," she said, "the new one will be easier, because harder it couldn't be."

She took a cup of vinegar and began to rinse Marilyn's hair.

Natalie was born in three hours. By two months of age she was sleeping through the night. Helen had been disappointed because the baby wasn't a boy, but her dissatisfaction vanished in a glow of love and gratitude for her new daughter's splendid behavior. Natalie rarely cried. She nursed happily and never spit up. She lay quietly in her crib, even with a full diaper. Best of all, she didn't have colic. Helen knew immediately that although she hadn't given birth to a son, she had provided herself with a friend.

Marilyn was enchanted by the baby. She pinched her every now and then because her grandmother kept warning her not to, but soon, seeing that Natalie posed no threat to her position as her Papa's best-beloved, she was free to enjoy her—and she did. By the time Natalie was able to fetch and carry, she was happily and gratefully fetching and carrying for her sister. Helen, who strongly resented Marilyn's use of her little sister, pressed her lips together and let it go by because Natalie seemed so delighted to serve.

Phyllis was born when Marilyn was six and Natalie three. She was a sunny child and never bothered anybody who didn't bother her. Marilyn, secure in her father's totally accepting adoration, had by now isolated her main source of competition. It wasn't either of her sisters. She began looking at her mother with narrowed eyes. Every time Lenny would put his arm around Helen, Marilyn would thrust herself between them, throw her arms around her father's waist, look defiantly up at her mother and say, *"Mine."* Occasionally she would tell Helen to go away. This made Lenny roar with delighted laughter, but Helen was not amused. One night she told him so.

"You know something, Lenny?" she said bitterly.

"What?"

"Sometimes I think that child hates me."

"What child?"

"Marilyn."

Lenny lowered his paper and looked at his wife. "Don't be ridiculous," he said. "How can a six-year-old child hate anybody?"

"I can't help it. That's what I feel."

"It's your imagination," Lenny said, eyes glued to the sports page.

Yuspeh, who had been listening avidly, turned to her son. "You're a dumbbell," she told him.

Lenny carefully folded the newspaper and put it down. "What's that supposed to mean?" he demanded.

"It means you're a dumbbell. Any man who treats a daughter like a wife and a wife like a daughter is in mine opinion a dumbbell."

"Ma, what are you saying? Helen, what is she saying?"

"I'm saying you should kiss more the wife and less the daughter; and when the daughter pushes in, a smart father should push her out, because if he don't, he's a dumbbell who will ruin his own daughter."

"What do you mean 'ruin'?"

The old woman got out of her chair, crossed the room and stood in front of her son. "A daughter who loves too much the father, loves too little the husband," she said quietly, and left the room.

Lenny sat back in his chair and sighed in confusion. "Do you know what she's talking about?" he asked his wife.

"Yes."

"Well," said an irritated Lenny, "will you be kind enough to let me in on it?"

Helen stood up and gave her husband a disgusted look. "Your mother was right," she said. "You *are* a dumbbell." Then she

turned abruptly and walked up the stairs to the bedroom. Lenny
looked after her. He picked up his newspaper and began to read.
After about five minutes he got up and went upstairs. He found
Helen turning down the bed. He took the bedspread from her
hand and turned her around.

"Helen," he said quietly, "you can't really believe that . . .
that I love Marilyn more than you . . . do you?"

"No," she answered, "but Lenny, it doesn't matter what *I*
think, it matters what *she* thinks . . . and *she* thinks you do."
Helen finished turning down the bed and walked into the bathroom. She began to fill the tub. After a moment, Lenny followed
her in and sat down on the closed toilet.

"So?" he said.

"I'm going to tell you something, Lenny, a little story. The
day we brought Phyllis home from the hospital, Marilyn came
over to me. 'Are you happy about the baby?' she asked. 'Of course
I am,' I told her. 'But,' she says to me, 'Papa told me you wanted
a boy.' 'I wanted a healthy baby and that's what I got,' I said."
Lenny nodded. "So?"

"So then she says, 'Papa says you were a little disappointed;
are you?' So I smiled at her: 'Well,' I said, 'I *did* want a boy.'
'Are you disappointed?' she asked me again. 'Well, a little,' I
said. And then she gives me this big smile. 'I'm not,' she says.
'I'm *glad* it's a girl.' Lenny, you should have seen her eyes. They
were full of triumph. She was happy that I didn't get what I
wanted. I tell you, Lenny, that child doesn't like me. And what's
worse," she added quietly, "there are plenty of times that I don't
like *her*." Helen leaned over and shut off the water. She heard
Lenny exhale loudly.

"All right," he said, "I won't pay her so much attention."

"Do what you want."

Lenny stood up and walked to the door. "Maybe you're right,"
he said. "Maybe it's no good for her. All right, I won't pay so
much attention to her."

Later that night, Lenny held and kissed his wife. He told her
how much he loved her. He told her how very dear she was to

him. "I know, Lenny, I know, sweetheart," Helen murmured into his neck. Lenny thought for a moment. "Marilyn is too spoiled. She shouldn't talk like that to you. From now on," he said, holding her tighter, "there's going to be a new regime around here. From now on I'm not going to give her so much attention." They smiled sleepily at each other. "I think that's a good idea," Helen said. "You have two other children, you know. They deserve some attention also." "So does my wife. Starting tomorrow, there's going to be a new regime around here." They kissed goodnight and then turned over and went to sleep.

Lenny's brave and sincere resolution lasted exactly one day. It was the shortest regime in history. Marilyn, in a brilliant burst of statesmanship, managed to execute the coup d'état by catching chicken pox from her classmate, Cindy Rubin. She broke out over every inch of her body, ran a fever of 104.5°, and scared her parents, especially her father, half to death. When Helen reminded her husband of his new regime, he threw up his hands in disbelief.

"How," he asked incredulously, "do you deny a little special attention to such a sick child?" He took days off from work to be with her and heaped her bed with books and toys. Tenderly he smeared her with calamine lotion. While Helen ran to the pediatrician with Natalie and Phyllis for gamma globulin shots, Lenny sat at Marilyn's bedside, praying that the pox on her face wouldn't leave scars. After two weeks, Marilyn began to mend.

Helen, who had not been able to comb her daughter's hair because of all the oozing scabs on Marilyn's scalp, now armed herself with comb and brush and tried to get the tangles and knots out of her hair. As she pulled at it, it occurred to her that it was exactly the same color her mother Malka's had been. She looked up from the braid she was plaiting and found Marilyn staring at her. The child's eyes were full of tears.

"Marilyn, what's the matter?" Helen asked, concerned.

"You're hurting me," she said.

It was only then that Helen became aware that she was pulling her daughter's hair so tightly that her head was practically at right angles to her shoulder. Several scabs on her scalp had been combed or pulled off and were bleeding. In horror, Helen dropped the braid as though it were the thorny stem of a rose, and burst into tears. Marilyn watched her cry for a while and then put her hand on her mother's shoulder.

"It's all right," she said. "I won't tell Papa."

Helen wiped her eyes and finished braiding her daughter's long, red-brown hair. She picked up the comb and brush and rose from the bed. "I love you, Marilyn," she insisted unsteadily, "of course I love you. I named you for my mother." Then she ran out of the room and into the kitchen. She sat down on a chair, holding the hairbrush so tightly that her knuckles whitened and her nails dug into her palm. She recalled all the little "accidents" that had befallen Marilyn. The times when she had reached for Marilyn's hand and scratched her arm. The time she zipped up her dress and caught her daughter's skin in the zipper. The times Marilyn had tripped over her mother's feet. The time she had put her into the bath and almost scalded her because she had "forgotten" to turn on the cold water. All the little accidents that at this moment she realized were, perhaps, not accidents at all.

Even years later, she would sometimes, in the night, tightly squeeze her eyes shut and shudder in dismay and disbelief, not over what she had done to her own child, but over what it signified. She knew absolutely that she would be as separated, as alien, as apart from Marilyn as she had been from her namesake, Malka.

Marilyn had, in the meanwhile, allied herself with a less threatening mother figure. As Malka had favored Celia, so did Marilyn. Helen accepted their relationship with relief and regret. She released her daughter, fully aware that they were forever bound together by their devotion to Lenny and by what they knew of each other. Neither wanted a confrontation because both were certain that it would be impossible for Lenny to choose between them. Both loved him too much to make him choose. In the meantime Helen took pride in her daughter's beauty and academic accomplishments. Marilyn was an excellent student and was, after all, half hers. Marilyn grudgingly respected her mother for her formidable position and her awareness of the situation. On the surface all remained as it had been. Sometimes they would forget themselves and talk to each other as though no unbridgeable moat existed between them. The underlying confusion and anger came to the surface disguised as ordinary, unimportant skirmishes—over Marilyn's messy room, over Helen's old-fashioned discipline and taste, over common, everyday things like that. They hollered at each other the way mothers and daughters do and formed an unspoken but very necessary alliance, a pact, a silent promise, never to expose what lay buried behind their eyes. Or at least to try not to.

But still Helen suffered. She didn't want this feeling. It was all wrong, and she wanted it to go away. Marilyn was her flesh and blood, her child. Helen had had an unnatural mother. She didn't want to be one herself. So she tried to smother the feeling. She did all the things she thought a mother should do, all the things she did for Natalie and Phyllis. She tried to convince herself that everything was as it should be instead of as it was. But despite her efforts, sometimes a glimmer would be seen, a bubble would escape and rise to the surface, and the curtain would part just a little—like the time Marilyn, aged fifteen, came raging downstairs, screaming that she had no clean underwear or blouses. "Why didn't you do a wash?" she cried.

"I did a wash yesterday," Helen said calmly.

"So where are all my things?" demanded Marilyn.

"I washed everything that was in the hampers. If your laundry was in your hamper, it was washed; if your laundry wasn't in your hamper, it wasn't washed."

Marilyn stood in front of her mother, seething. "Where are my things?" she asked through tight lips.

"Wherever you left them."

"I left them in my room."

"So look in your room. I certainly didn't take them out."

"Goddamn you!" Marilyn exploded.

At that, Yuspeh looked up from her mending. "Feh!" she said.

"What kind of talk is that? Maybe if you cleaned up your room once in a while instead of leaving it for your mother and me, you would know where your things are."

"You mind your business, Grandma."

"I know where they are," sang ten-year-old Phyllis.

"Where?"

"Mommy cleaned up your room and threw everything under the bed," laughed Phyllis, delighted.

Marilyn, shaking, turned to face her mother.

Helen looked straight into her eyes. "I am not your maid," she said.

"I hate you," Marilyn whispered and ran up the stairs.

Helen looked after her, and Yuspeh thought she saw her mouth moving. Whether or not Helen whispered, "The feeling is mutual," she never knew for sure. Marilyn got even with her mother later on, however, by getting Natalie not only to do her wash, but also to fold it when it came out of the dryer.

Helen, skilled in patience, pressed her lips together and waited. She knew that some day, one way or another, Lenny or no Lenny, she would be rid of Marilyn. It took several years, but God in His infinite mercy, just at the point where she could bear Marilyn no longer, sent her Ira Stillman.

Chapter 2

THEY MET when Marilyn was in her last year of graduate school, completing her master's degree in American history. Although it was not her main area of interest, Marilyn had always been fascinated by ancient European history. Even the names of the various populations, many of which no longer existed, sparked her imagination. Her head was full of strange nations—the Khazars, the Rus, the Bulgars, the Magyars, the Ghuz, the Petchenegs.

Ira was across the hall, teaching a course in accounting, or applied economics, as it was listed in the brochure. Actually, he was instructing his students in "How to pass your CPA exam the first time."

Ira was an orphan—a word, a sound as exotic to Marilyn as "Hun," "Pict," "Polan" or "Cherkassian." She had never met an orphan before. When she told her father about meeting this instructor named Ira Stillman, and he said, "So, he sounds nice, what is he?" Marilyn answered, "An orphan."

Ira's parents had perished in their sleep in a freak accident involving a gas heater and the family dog, a mixed breed named Discount. Ira, who had spent the night at his friend Ritchie's house, had returned the following afternoon to find the milk still on the doorstep and the newspaper still in the driveway. Seeing a morning scene at two-thirty in the afternoon confused Ira. He stood there, looking at his house, bewilderment and cautious curiosity soon giving way to panic and dread-filled suspicion.

He ran to a neighbor's and called his home. When he received no answer, he called the police, who, after sniffing around, broke every window in the house. Even so, it was many hours before the gas fumes dissipated and it was safe to enter. Ira raced in, before well-meaning hands could restrain him, and found his parents as though asleep, looking perfectly normal, except for the bright-red color of their skin—as if blushing for abandoning their fourteen-and-a-half-year-old son and causing him such ill-deserved and untimely grief. Discount lay under the gas heater, his tongue hanging out, looking thirsty and disappointed.

Ira was taken in by his mother's sister, who did it only because it wouldn't look nice if she didn't. His uncle, who worked as a bookkeeper in the business office of RCA in the Valley, sold Ira's parents' house and withdrew Ira's bar-mitzvah money from the bank, putting it in his name, in trust for Ira. He put Ira's mother's wedding and engagement rings in a safe-deposit box. He told Ira that this would pay for his education—and room and board, since they weren't rich people. Ira, perhaps sensing something, perhaps recalling that his parents never got along all that well with his aunt and uncle, or perhaps just because he was Ira, kept a meticulous financial record of all monies due his relatives, as well as, in neat black-and-white columns, all the amounts, plus interest, less taxes, due him.

When, three years later, Ira was accepted at UCLA and asked for his inheritance, he proved to be a better bookkeeper than his uncle, who had somehow not accounted for over twenty thousand dollars and had somehow misplaced the key to the safe-deposit box.

"Let's forget about all this," soothed his uncle. "You are our only nephew, we took you into our home and hearts, a frightened orphan with nowhere else to go. That ought to be worth *some-*

thing, shouldn't it? Why make a big deal out of this?" And when Ira remained silent, his uncle went on, "You're not gonna make a big deal out of this, are you?"

"Yes, Uncle Manny, I am. I'm gonna make a *very* big deal out of this." And he did.

In college, Ira decided to major in business administration and accounting, since it had already proved so profitable for him. He took a two-bedroom apartment in West Los Angeles with three other accounting majors, even though he preferred, and could have afforded, to live alone. He reasoned that he would be less inclined to weep in his bed at night with someone else in the same room. Ira missed his mother and father unceasingly. An only child, he had worshiped and been worshiped by his parents. Since their death, hardly a night went by that never-forgotten and happy memories had not reduced him to tears. He missed them so, the closeness, the caring, the caresses. Ira wanted to get married, so that he could be part of a family again. He wanted children so that he would have blood relatives that he loved who would love him in return. He wanted posterity. He made himself into the type of person his parents would have been proud of—a law-abiding citizen.

When he graduated from college and passed his CPA exam, he began actively looking for a wife. His father had been a gentleman, considerate, affectionate and temperate, and Ira modeled himself after the memory of his father. Girls liked him and so did their parents. When Ira became engaged to Marilyn, two mothers who had never before lifted a hand to their children slapped their daughters on the side of the head and called them fools.

Ira and Marilyn used to joke about their meeting, which occurred one day when both walked out of their classrooms simultaneously. Ira told Marilyn that he always knew there were benefits to higher education. Marilyn called him the boy next door. On their first date, when Ira arrived to pick her up, he walked into her house and felt as though he had come home. Ira was so happy in Marilyn's house that he would drop over even when she was out or studying for exams and couldn't see him.

Once, while discussing his former lawsuit against his Uncle Manny and Aunt Gussie, he slipped and called Marilyn's father "Dad." He even risked the wrath of his best friend, Artie, by fixing him up with Natalie. But it was Helen whom he adored. They would spend hours together in the kitchen, where she would feed him, pat his arm and talk. They were both alarmed at Marilyn's recent decision to take her own apartment. Ira was upset because he would miss the family, Lenny was upset because he would miss his daughter, and Helen was upset because she would miss Ira. Only Grandma agreed that it was a good idea. She wasn't upset in the least. If she were, she would be upset that Marilyn might change her mind.

"It's a good idea," she insisted, "and also it's good for me. Mine back hurts already from always bending and picking up her mess. Everywhere in her room is mess. In her own apartment she'll have to clean up her dirty bloomers herself. Let her go. Let her see what it's like to wash a dish and change a bed." She would pull Marilyn into a corner and whisper to her, "Don't let them they should make you change your mind. A girl needs to be independent. A girl from your age needs to make up her *own* mind. Go, Momeleh, before it's too late."

Two days before Marilyn was to sign the lease on a one-room-plus-alcove-and-terrace "studio" apartment in Santa Monica, Ira proposed. They were standing on the apartment's terrace, or "ledge" as Ira called it, looking at the view—an unobstructed panorama consisting of the back alley of the house next door. On a clear day, the parking lot of Von's Supermarket could be seen in all its black-topped splendor. Ira had his arm around Marilyn's shoulder and she was telling him how she could turn the alcove into a bedroom by hanging multicolored beads across the entry.

"But, honey, that alcove is tiny, there's not even a window in it."

"I know," Marilyn sighed. "That's why I decided on beads instead of a louver door."

"There's no kitchen, unless you call a wall with a sink, stove and minifridge hanging on it a kitchen."

Marilyn laughed. "C'mon, Ira. I don't give a shit." Ira winced.

"I'll buy a couch, a table, some pillows and a bunch of plants, and the place will be adorable." She looked up into Ira's skeptical face. "Look," she said, "I'm not going to be cooking all that much anyway. For one thing, I don't cook; for another, you'll be taking me out for dinner. I won't even know I *have* a kitchen."

Ira smiled. "You can hang beads across it," he said. They turned and walked back inside. Through the thin walls, they heard the blare of an unseen neighbor's stereo. Ira walked over and began knocking on the walls, testing the construction. From the other side of the wall came an answering knock.

"It doesn't bother me," Marilyn said defensively, before Ira could protest about the noise. "I won't be here during the day."

"I don't want you to be here at all."

Marilyn looked up at him. "Tough," she said, "I like it. I'm getting enough opposition from my parents. I don't need you to add to it."

Ira walked over and stared down at one of the two bridge chairs that decorated the empty room. He took a handkerchief out of his pocket and wiped off the seat of the chair. He sat down and crossed his legs. "There *is* another alternative," he said.

"There are a *number* of alternatives," Marilyn answered, pulling over the other chair and flopping down on it before Ira had a chance to whip out his handkerchief. "I can stay at home; I can move in with a friend; or I can fuck a millionaire and let him keep me in a penthouse at the Beverly Wilshire." She waited for Ira's wince and when it came added: "But I don't want to. I want to live here."

Ira leaned over and took her hand. "As I said before, there is another alternative." Marilyn reached into her bag with her free hand and pulled out a cigarette and a book of matches. "That other alternative is marrying me." He took the matches from her and struck one, holding it to the tip of her cigarette. Marilyn stared at him in astonishment.

"I wish you wouldn't smoke so much," he said.

Unable to move, Marilyn watched the match burn down. Ira blew it out and lit another. She inhaled nervously.

"Ira," she whispered, "you're complicating my life."

"On the contrary," said Ira, "not only am I simplifying it, I'm also improving it. I have a *two*-bedroom apartment, a full kitchen, a terrace the size of this living room and walls you couldn't hear Ethel Merman through." As Marilyn continued staring at him, he said, "Think about it."

"But I sign the lease in two days," she moaned.

"So, think fast," he said, standing up and pulling her up with him. "You're a smart girl." He kissed her lightly on the forehead. "I'm making you an offer you shouldn't refuse, dummy. I'm extraordinary husband material and your family is greatly in favor of the alliance. I asked them for your lovely hand last night," he said, lifting her hand to his lips.

"You asked them . . . ?"

Ira put a gentle finger to her mouth. "I love you, Marilyn. I'll always value and care for you. Marry me, Dolly," he said, throwing out his arm and indicating the empty room, "and let me take you away from all this."

Marilyn looked into his smiling face. Only her father called her "Dolly."

"Don't call me Dolly," she said crossly.

"Shall we pick out the ring?" asked Ira.

"No. I haven't accepted your proposal yet. Maybe my family has, but *I* haven't."

"Your mother was so happy, she cried. She said, 'I'm getting the son I always wanted.' "

"I don't care what she said."

Ira grinned. "Your father said, 'Ira, you're the one I want for my Dolly. Having you for a son-in-law would make me the happiest father in the world.' "

"He said that?"

"Close enough. He said, 'Tell my Dolly that for her to marry you is my dearest wish. Tell her that she couldn't give me a better gift.'"

"He did?"

"Well, close enough."

Marilyn sat down abruptly. "I know he likes you."

"*Loves* me," laughed Ira, sitting down also. Marilyn threw her cigarette butt on the floor; Ira checked to make sure it was out.

"You're not being fair," she said.

"All's fair in love and war."

Marilyn made a face. "What did my sisters say?"

"Nothing. They were upstairs."

"Oh. What about my grandmother?"

"I don't think she said anything."

"*My grandmother?* C'mon, Ira. What did she say?"

"Really," said Ira, wrinkling his brow. "I don't think she said a word."

"I don't believe it."

"In fact, she never talks to me. She just looks."

Marilyn sighed. "Consider yourself lucky."

Ira stood up and looked at his watch. "In exactly forty-eight hours I hope to be a happy man—and a lucky one."

"Oh, fuck off, Ira," Marilyn said and waited for the wince. When it came, she reached for another cigarette and turned away to light it herself. Ira watched her and shook his head in disapproval. "That's a dangerous habit."

"Why would I want to get married?" she asked him. "What do I need it for? Women don't have to get married nowadays."

"Because you want to be a lawyer, and I'm on my way to becoming a business manager. Because I'll be a *good* business manager, one with a long list of wealthy show-business clients. My assets will be your assets, my contacts will be your contacts, my list will be your list . . . and, of course, because you love me."

"Do I love you? How do you know I love you?" Marilyn asked, puffing furiously on her cigarette.

"Because I'm wonderful," smiled Ira. "Ask anybody. Ask your father."

During their honeymoon, while they were sunbathing on the beach, Marilyn sat up, leaned on her elbows and squinted over at her new husband, who, despite liberal and repeated applications of Coppertone, lay burning in the sun instead of tanning. At that precise moment she realized with a sickening, stomach-lurching certainty that she had married a schmuck. Ira lay there with his eyes closed, smiling slightly. The sparse hair on his chest was matted with perspiration and clots of suntan lotion. His wrists dangled limply over the arms of the beach chair, and his thin, hairy legs were spread apart, toes turned in, almost touching. His new Laguna bathing trunks were crumpled and damp, standing slightly up from his thighs, the white drawstring hanging out of the elastic waistband.

The Hawaiian sun beat down; through the shimmering heat waves Marilyn saw that her husband's hairline was receding and his large-lobed ears didn't match. A huge drop of sweat was making its way down the side of his body and across his rounded stomach. Stopped by the elastic of his trunks, it slowly flattened out, changed direction and eased across his ribs to disappear between his back and the striped terrycloth towel on the chair. Marilyn followed its course, mesmerized, and then in disgust turned away to stare at the vast blue undulating ocean.

She watched as a surfboarder rode a foam-crested wave triumphantly into shore, where he stood silhouetted against the white sky, tanned, tight-muscled and smiling. She glanced again at Ira, lying loose and slack-lipped beside her. She picked up some sand and dribbled it over his faintly pulsing stomach, where it stuck and clung to the oil and sweat. Slowly she sank back into her chair and reached under it, groping for her can of 7Up. She gulped the tepid, bland, now fizzless liquid, desperately trying to drown her depression. She visualized her future stretching ahead as endless, as alien, as arid as the beach.

To add to her upset, Marilyn remembered when she had

looked at Ira differently. When she had looked at him with her father's eyes and shared his opinion. On her first date with Ira, he and her father had talked in the living room for about twenty minutes, and later Papa had taken her aside and whispered, "You sure know how to pick 'em, Dolly." She wondered if she had married Ira because her father had fallen in love with him, or because her mother had said shrewdly, knowing her adversary, "Let go of him. He's too nice a boy to have his life ruined."

Whatever the reason, Ira had given her the same feeling she had always gotten from her father—the feeling that she was a precious and valuable something. With her father, and now with Ira, she felt cared for, protected, perfect and faultless. They loved her unconditionally, and because Marilyn needed that so very much from her Papa, she had believed it was also necessary from her husband.

She heard the reason for her present misery groan and turn over onto his stomach. Again, and with frightened, angry, sun-bleached eyes, she looked at him. His back was crisscrossed and lined with the imprint of the creased towel on which he had been lying. She felt suddenly nauseated. Today was Tuesday. She had married him three days ago, and already she was sick of him. She wanted to call her father in Los Angeles and tell him that she knew Ira too well, that she didn't need him and didn't want him —that Ira would erode her as surely and inexorably as water did land. But she was heavy and weighted down by heat and despair, and she lay inert.

The sun had baked away the foggy illusion of love and now the blazing reality of her enormous folly lay exposed. On Saturday night she had married a schmuck, and now she was lying next to him on a beach in Hawaii. Now she was Mrs. Schmuck.

"Ira," she said, leaning over and shaking his shoulder. Ira stirred but didn't open his eyes. Marilyn took the can of 7Up and dumped what was left of it over his sun-reddened back.

"Umm," he said, smiling, "that feels good. What time is it?"

"Ira, you schmuck," she whispered, "I want a divorce." Ira yawned, stretched and sat up. He picked up his shoe and peered into it. "Did I put my watch in your beachbag?" He took the bag and began to paw through it. "Ah," he said, holding up the watch, "seek and ye shall find." He noted the time, carefully replaced the watch and held both hands out to his wife. "Will the loveliest lady on the beach take a swim with me?"

Ignoring his hands, Marilyn nodded and stood up. She felt Ira's eyes caress her body, and she shuddered. "I love you," he whispered in her ear. "I love you more than I've ever loved anyone."

Marilyn turned and looked at him. "Ira . . ."

"I love you, Mrs. Stillman."

Marilyn got her bathing cap from the foot of the chair and started toward the water. She knew that after his swim Ira would stand for a moment, tilt his head first to one side, then to the other, and bang the water out of his ears. She leafed through the years ahead of her as Mrs. Stillman and every night saw Ira neatly fold his pants along the crease and carefully hang them in the closet. She saw him putting shoe trees in all of his highly shined shoes and placing them side by side exactly where they belonged. She saw him comb the hair out of his hairbrush, shake his head in disapproval, and then comb the hair out of hers. She saw him driving the family car, sitting straight up with both hands gripping the wheel and never ever exceeding the speed limit.

While they were dating, Marilyn was charmed by Ira's habit of helping her into the car, waiting while she settled herself, and then fastening the seatbelt for her. After adjusting it, he would straighten up, smile and say, "There, it's always better to be safe than sorry." She had felt treasured. Now she knew that if he ever belted her in again, she would take great pleasure in belting *him*, in savagely smacking away his pale, freckled hand. Even at two in the morning with no moving traffic, Ira never walked when the sign said "Don't Walk." He kept off the grass and never trespassed. He never pushed when he was directed to pull. He respected and obeyed authority, the law, any written instruction. Not once had he ever gotten the urge to litter, or run down an up escalator. Ira was perfect. He would take out the garbage without a murmur and say with great understanding, "Don't cook if you feel tired, honey. I'll just go and rustle up something for the two of us."

How could she ever have thought him marvelous? How could she ever have mistaken whatever it was she felt for love? Watching him dive into a wave, Marilyn stood rigid with anger at herself, at Ira, at the world. Three days ago she had married a man who would never write where it said "print," who would.hold every package "this side up," who would never forget to "wait for the tone before dialing." She was gripped with an over-powering urge to fold, spindle and mutilate Ira Stillman.

"Oh, my God," she moaned softly, watching her husband splash in the ocean, "what the hell have I done?" How could she return from her honeymoon and inform her parents that she wanted a divorce? What would she tell them when they asked, ashen with shock, "Why? Are you crazy? Why?" They loved Ira. They thought he was wonderful. She could hear her mother as clearly as if she were an arm's length away. "What's the matter with you? Ira worships you . . . he's ambitious. When he opens his own office, he'll be able to give you the moon. Does a normal woman take a Certified Public Accountant and throw him out like a used Kleenex?" How could she explain what would happen to her if she were forced to live with a man who would sooner die than allow his wife to hear him belch or fart? A man who after years of marriage would still turn on the water in the bath-room sink so as not to insult the ears of his wife with the sound of his peeing. A man who would religiously brush, floss and rinse after every meal, including snacks. A man whose dirty un-derwear would always be clean.

Her father—who thought that everything she did was fine, even when it wasn't—would be devastated. He would take her aside and in a low, concerned voice ask her, "What happened in Hawaii? Did he make you do, you know, anything funny? Tell Papa." Both he and her mother would insist that she had not given herself enough time in which to make such an important decision. Both would assure her that lots of girls get the jitters, and she would be fine as soon as she settled down. Both would inform her that as far back as they could remember, there had never been a divorce in the family. They would find it impossible to understand that she wanted to divorce Ira Stillman for the very same reasons for which she had married him.

Marilyn, standing on a beach, making holes with her nails in her rubber bathing cap, hardly understood it herself. The fact that a man who had always wanted to own and drive a Jaguar XJ had instead bought a Pontiac Firebird, because it got 3.6 miles more to the gallon, hardly constituted grounds for divorce.

Ira was now standing waist-deep in the Pacific, energetically waving to her. She put on her bathing cap, one side of which looked like Swiss cheese, and slowly waded in. The water was cold on her solar-heated body, and she shivered. Ira took her hand and told her that the water temperature was seventy-two degrees, and she would soon get used to it. Marilyn held her arms up as a wave broke over her, and then settled into the water, lifting her feet and floating with the current. She loved the ocean and believed implicitly that salt-water bathing prolonged life and promoted health. Whenever her family took a vacation, it was always to the beach. She felt Ira's hands encircle her waist as he lifted her over a wave. He pulled her toward him and kissed her salty mouth, pressing his body against hers. Her breasts flattened against his chest as he held her tightly, one hand on her back, the other on her bottom. She closed her eyes as they went underwater, mouth to mouth, belly to belly, bodies glued together. She felt him stir and harden and she moved even closer, parting her legs until she could hold him between the vise of her thighs. He moaned deep in his throat and Marilyn surprised herself by feeling enormously aroused. She yearned to be in bed with him, to spread herself for him, to force her breasts into his mouth. She reached under his bathing suit and groped for him, gripped him fiercely and heard him moan again.

She shook with passion, intensely excited by her ability to make Ira lose sight of the fact that he was engaged in a public display of activities that he had always insisted should be conducted only in private. She trembled with the knowledge that by the simple act of sliding her tongue between his lips she could cause him to forget, not to give a damn, about the fact that it was stupid to travel first class on an airplane because what it really boiled down to was that you were paying an extra hundred and ten dollars just for a meal.

"Let's go back to the room," he murmured, but it took twenty minutes before he was in any condition to emerge from the water. Marilyn told him she'd wait for him in the hotel, knowing that her passion would be doused by the sight of Ira hosing the sand off his feet.

Back in the room, she quickly showered and perfumed herself before slipping nude into bed. She waited impatiently for his return, inordinately stimulated, moist and ready, aching with the need to make him moan, to make him groan, to make him oblivious to all rules and regulations, to make him, if only for the moment, uncaring about what was sensible and what wasn't. She wanted to fuck him into spontaneity, and to be fucked, if possible, into forgetting that three days ago she had married a CPA with a CPA soul, and by so doing had doomed herself to years and years and unending years of devotion, protection, insulation and boredom.

After two weeks in Hawaii, they returned to Los Angeles, Ira with a red nose, a peeling back and a broad smile; Marilyn with an even tan, a case of honeymoon cystitis and a compelling determination to obtain a divorce.

On the first Friday night after their return, they went to Marilyn's parents' house for dinner, setting a precedent that continued for years. Her parents and sisters fussed over the newlyweds, and Ira fussed over her. Her grandmother stared at Ira all through the soup and roast chicken. By dessert she was nodding and smiling at every word he uttered. When her sisters excused themselves to get ready for their dates, Ira stood up politely and remained standing until they left the room. This gesture so impressed her grandmother that she broke her night-long silence in order to express her approval. "You a nice boy," she said.

After dinner, over coffee in the living room, her father beamed upon them with such happy satisfaction that Marilyn didn't have the heart to destroy his pleasure by confessing to him her lack of it. When her father asked how they had liked Hawaii, she smiled and told him it was glorious.

Chapter 3

IRA SPENT THE FIRST YEAR of their married life building up his clientele in the hope of opening up his own office; Marilyn, applying to law schools, doing and redoing the apartment, shopping, lunching with her father, sisters and friends, trying desperately to submerge her ever-growing discontent with her life. She was grateful for Ira's ambition, serving as it did both to keep him away from home and to pay for the hordes of interior decorators she kept hiring and firing. Their apartment was on North Palm Drive in Beverly Hills—new, secure, expensive. It had wood-burning fireplaces in three of the five and a half rooms, and two bars. The living room opened onto a nice-sized patio that overlooked the street and was shaded by two huge palm trees, which regularly dropped long, pointed brown leaves onto the chaise longues and built-in gas barbecue. Ira told her to spare no expense in decorating it—he had clients to entice and entertain. She had already been through six decorators by the time she met Rex Bonhomme, né Ronald Birnbaum. Observing his blond perfection, Marilyn hired him instantly, declaring that if he did as good a job on the apartment as he had on himself, he would indeed be worth his ridiculously exorbitant fee.

"I want," she told him, "an open, muted, elegant look."

"But of course, Madame," he replied. "Only elegance would suit you."

Marilyn looked down at her scuffed clogs and rumpled jeans, one size too large. She pulled a cigarette from the torn breast pocket of her unpressed plaid shirt, lit it and grinned.

"You're a discerning fellow, Rex," she said, "and I appreciate your keen eye. What have you in mind?"

Rex pursed his pretty lips and ran his long-lashed eyes appraisingly over the apartment. "I see pale yellow, pale green and white," he said at last.

"No."

"No?"

"No."

"You have another suggestion, Madame?"

"I'm not a pale-yellow person, Rex. If I went color, it would be red, black, silver."

"Ah," he breathed, "drama, sensuality."

"Ah," replied Marilyn.

"White carpeting, white couches, red-and-black-patterned chairs, silver-lamé draperies—perhaps an ebony piano in that nook there," suggested Rex, gesturing toward the nook with a graceful arm movement worthy of Nureyev. He smiled down at Marilyn and questioningly raised a plucked and perfectly arched eyebrow.

"Yes?"

"No."

"No?"

"Yes."

Rex furrowed his brow in concentration. "Let us consider, then, the living room/dining room area."

"Let us, indeed."

"Will you accept off-white carpets—pale beiges, accents of green—by that I mean plants—glass tables—touches of chrome?"

"Yes."

"At last a meeting of minds," smiled Rex.

"And the bedrooms?"

"The same."

"And the den?"

"The same."

"And the kitchen?"

"White, white, white—plants—off-white and beige tiled floor."

"Rex," she said, "I have the nagging suspicion that every room I walk into will be just like the room I walked out of."

"We call that coordination, Madame."

" 'We' may call that coordination—*I* call it monotony."

Rex heaved a huge sigh. "You must trust me, Madame. I have done many of the finest homes in Beverly Hills. Stars' homes, sheiks' homes, the homes of millionaires—and all, may I add, have been greatly satisfied with the results."

"They all trusted you?"

"Totally."

"They gave you carte blanche?"

"Absolutely."

"Rex," said Marilyn, "I'm going to confide to you an intimate secret about myself, something I've confided to very few people, maybe ten at the most. Come here."

Rex walked over, bent down and put his ear close to Marilyn's lips.

"You told me to trust you," she whispered. Rex nodded solemnly. "Well, here's the secret. Call me silly, call me goofy, but I never trust anyone I have to pay."

The next day he sent her a little note regretting that due to the demands on his time he could not participate in the decoration of her apartment. Note in hand, Marilyn called her Aunt Celia.

"Do you want to hear rejection?" she asked. "I just got fired by an interior decorator."

"How crushing," laughed Celia, "but do you want to hear *real* rejection? My friend Vivian, after a thorough internal examination, got fired by a gynecologist."

"Ouch," grinned Marilyn, and with Celia's decorator's card and help, did the apartment herself, down to the last ashtray—which she carefully positioned on the coffee table. She stepped back and looked around her, studying the results of the work that had taken a year of her life and 50,000 of Ira's dollars to achieve. She sat down on the new couch, dug her toes into the new carpet, ran her hand over the smooth surface of the new side table. Everything looked nice—open, muted, elegant. So what.

The depression of anticlimax began to flow through her bones and Marilyn leaned her head on the back of the couch and closed her eyes. She had, she reflected, done a super job of sprucing up her prison. A breeze wafted in through the screened sliding door of the patio, fluttering the palm fronds of the large standing plant in the corner. Ira lived here, too. Marilyn pushed herself up and plodded to the den. Seating herself at Ira's desk, she picked up the phone.

"Papa?"

"Dolly! How nice."

"Are you busy, Papa?"

"Never for you, Dolly."

"Can you come over?"

"That's my pleasure. Is everything all right?"

"So-so."

"I'll bring some Chinese, we'll have lunch."

Instantly Marilyn became more cheerful and busied herself setting the table, pleased now in anticipation of her father's reaction to the apartment.

As a child, Marilyn had felt secure only in a room which contained her father. She still did. She could sit with him for hours, peaceful, free of the fears that haunt and hover over children, free of the tension her mother's presence instilled. The sight of him made her feel good. Lenny entered, laden with packages.

"This is the food," he said, placing a container-filled brown paper bag on the table. "This is for a housewarming." He handed her a check. "This is for my Dolly." He laid a large,

beribboned white box in her arms. "This is also for my Dolly."
He hugged her, kissing her on both cheeks.

Marilyn quickly undid the bows, pushing them over the sharp
edge of the box. Inside, beneath layers of tissue paper, was an
exquisite blue lace-trimmed satin bedjacket.

"For when you have visitors after the baby is born," said
Lenny.

Marilyn held the jacket at arm's length and admired it. "But
Papa," she smiled, "I'm not having a baby."

Lenny began taking containers out of the bag. He arranged
them in a row on the table and as he opened each one, stuck a
serving spoon into the contents.

"Not tomorrow, maybe, but soon, right? Ira tells me he wants
to start a family."

"Ira," said Marilyn disgustedly.

"It's not a bad idea, Dolly," Lenny said, pushing a container
of shrimp in lobster sauce toward his daughter. "The apartment
is finished—beautiful, a palace, but finished. You got something
better to do?"

"Yes."

"What?"

"Law school, Papa," said Marilyn earnestly. "You know that."

"After the baby—first things first."

Marilyn picked up the container and spooned shrimp and
lobster sauce onto the fried rice on her father's plate, then served
herself.

"Papa, Ira and I, we're not exactly ecstatic."

"So who is?" asked Lenny, taking a mouthful of food.

"What I mean," she said quietly, "is that I'm not certain about
our future as a couple."

Lenny turned quickly toward his daughter, looking, thought
Marilyn, suddenly pale. "What are you saying, Dolly?" he asked,
alarmed. "Are you and Ira having trouble?"

His distress was so apparent that Marilyn, upset and annoyed
with herself at having caused it, tried to drop the subject. "Your
food is getting cold, Papa," she said, pointing at his plate. "Here,

have a sparerib." She dipped into the container and plucked out a sticky rib, which she put on his plate.

"If you're having problems, Dolly, tell me."

"It's nothing, Papa—we'll work it out."

Lenny took a deep breath, relieved. He picked up the rib and began to chew. "Every young married couple needs to work things out. Nothing is perfect. When you have a baby, it keeps you so busy, you have no time to dwell on little annoyances."

"Would you like a grandchild, Papa?" teased Marilyn.

"Would I like a grandchild!" he beamed. He was silent for a moment, just smiling and smiling and shaking his head up and down. Then he held the rib out and looked at it. "Would I like a grandchild, she asks me," he informed the rib, waving it and beaming.

He stayed with Marilyn until about four-thirty, and the afterglow of delight and contentment, the feeling of safety that always filled her after seeing her father lingered on, reaping benefits for Ira, who returned home to an unusually civil wife. The wary look that had become habitual before his encounters with Marilyn faded into one of pleased and grateful surprise. She had even fixed drinks.

"Your father was here," Ira observed.

"Yes. You got lucky today—" And as Ira tightened his lips and took a deep breath, she went on. "Please, Ira—no long-suffering sighs." She looked at him and pitied them both. "I'm truly sorry, Ira," said Marilyn. "I know I'm not easy, and you try very hard."

She put her index finger into her glass and turned the ice cubes around. Some vodka and tonic splashed into her lap. Ira leaned over and offered her a mixer. With his napkin, he began wiping up the spill.

"Too hard," she murmured, drawing back and pushing his hand away. They sat silently for a moment, both staring into their drinks. Then Ira straightened up.

"Bob Bedford was in today," he said. "His last two films grossed sixty-seven and seventy-two million dollars, respectively. He owns ten points per film, netting him something like five million dollars. The man's affairs were in such chaos that he found himself barely able to pay his bills."

Marilyn smiled. "Why am I finding it so difficult to feel compassion for him?" she asked.

"He practically pleaded with me to take him on and bail him out—one of the biggest stars in the world."

"And a God-fearing man," added Marilyn, "a backbone of his church—but short."

" 'Relax, Bob,' I told him. 'I'll take care of you.' "

"And?"

"And I *will* take care of him."

"And the point of this little story?"

"Anything can be worked out, Marilyn," Ira said quietly, "even us."

"Mr. Fix-it."

"I do my best," said Ira.

Marilyn took Ira's glass, walked over to the bar and freshened both their drinks. She felt Ira's eyes on her back and was again flooded with pity.

"I know you do," she whispered, and her eyes filled with tears.

"Why isn't it enough?" he asked. "What do you want from me?"

Marilyn blinked rapidly, not wanting Ira to see her cry. Even as a child, she had preferred either to sob out her sorrow on her father's chest or to creep off and cry alone. She hated especially for her mother to see her cry, because Helen seemed so gratified whenever Marilyn, despite desperate efforts, would finally break down. And Helen always made the same smug, it seemed to Marilyn, comment.

"Well, since animals don't cry, perhaps you are human after all. Your Grandma Malka never cried. I never saw her cry, not once. Maybe there's some hope for you, but not if you don't change your ways. You keep on like this—" And then her voice would ominously trail off, leaving Marilyn to ponder fearfully the dire possibilities and make the dread comparisons between herself and the evidently inhuman Malka for whom she had been named and to whom she was obviously so similar. She remembered the way her mother's lips would whiten, her nostrils flare, her eyes grow clouded, almost opaque, when a transgression of Marilyn's—and there were many—brought Malka to mind. And after each scene, both Helen and Marilyn would wait for Lenny to return—Marilyn to burrow into her father's arms and weep, Helen to pull him off into their bedroom to inform him of Marilyn's latest horrendousness and shrilly demand over and over, "What does she want from me? What does she want from me?"

Dry-eyed once more, Marilyn turned around and, carrying the two drinks, walked over to Ira and handed him one.

"There's nothing I need from you, Ira," she said, and as she saw his eyes widen, added hastily, "You give me all you can, I know that."

They sipped their drinks silently, and after a few moments Ira lifted his head and looked appreciatively around the room. "You've done a wonderful job with the apartment," he said. "It looks lovely."

"Thank you."

Again they lapsed into silence. Marilyn, aware of Ira's scrutiny, averted her eyes. That was another thing her mother used to bitch about. "Look at me when I talk to you," she would scream. Naturally, Marilyn would immediately make it a point to look everywhere but at her mother's face, not understanding why Helen felt it so imperative that Marilyn look at her when that angry face was the last thing she wanted to see. Deliberately, she would turn her head and gaze at the window, at the wall, anywhere but into those seething eyes. She remembered feeling very frightened, yet at the same time triumphant, almost gleeful, at her ability to goad her mother into near hysteria by merely refusing to meet her glance.

"Marilyn? Hello?"

Startled, she jerked her head up, and the ice cubes rattled in her glass.

"Where were you?" Ira asked with a strained smile.

"In your many conversations, has my mother ever mentioned her mother, Malka, to you?"

"Many times."

"What did she say?"

"That she was a fascinating woman—not like the other mothers. She showed me a picture of her once—not just of her, but of the whole family."

Marilyn nodded. She knew the photograph, even had a copy of it. It had been taken by a professional photographer shortly after the family had immigrated to the United States. In it Malka and Joseph were seated side by side on a narrow bench. Joseph sat with his feet solidly planted on the floor, his legs wide apart. Celia, sitting on the right side of his lap, leaned against his shoulder, with Helen standing on his left, her hand resting on his thigh. Max, Ben and Murray stood behind their parents and all, even little Celia, stared solemn-faced, directly into the camera. All but Malka and Helen. Helen's head was half-turned, looking at her mother. Malka looked at nothing. She sat with her hands clasped in her lap, and her eyes, slightly lowered, gazed off to the side, away from Helen, away from the inquisitive, meddlesome lens. Marilyn would pore over the picture, and it seemed to her that Malka disdained even to glance at the snooping camera, almost daring it to pry into and forever capture whatever personal and singular visions or phantoms or demons might be lying behind her eyes, or worse, foolishly peering out.

Marilyn applied to UCLA's law school the following week, but her application was late, the class was filled and she was put on the waiting list. She moped, she read, she moved crystal ashtrays and lamps from this table to that and back again. When the wallpaper in the powder room began to displease her, she considered redoing it and submerged herself in samples and swatches. At last, bored beyond tears, depressed and disgusted with herself, she removed her IUD and put her future in the firm but fickle hands of Mother Nature. Ira, delighted by visions of pudgy little fingers and toothless smiles, spent weekends in the company of real estate brokers and agents. He bought a house in the flats of

Beverly Hills, with acres of back yard and a fence-enclosed swimming pool. Marilyn, terrified by her own decision to relinquish control over her life, roamed through the large, empty rooms of the new house like a robot, turning here, turning there, directed by stronger forces than she.

"Do what you want," she said to Rex Bonhomme. "I don't give a damn."

Chapter 4

WHEN IT ACTUALLY HAPPENED, Marilyn was pleased by her pregnancy, and interested in observing the physical and hormonal alterations that took place in her body and its chemistry. She looked forward to reproducing herself, as though Ira had had nothing to do with the process, as though her unborn child were a clone of herself. The birth itself was uncomplicated, the pain of labor not unbearable. Her child was brought to her clean and sweet-smelling by a smiling nurse.

Marilyn took one look, and her fantasy was shattered. The baby was a boy. It was the image of Ira. Even after holding and feeding it, she felt no kinship with the infant whatever. She had conceived it, she had carried it, she had birthed it and bled for it. And now, looking at it, she was appalled—this wasn't her child at all; it was Ira's.

Ira named the baby Todd, after his father. Marilyn, aloof and disinterested, wouldn't have cared if he had named him after Attila the Hun—most of the time she referred to the baby as "it" anyway. But there was something educational about motherhood. Marilyn became aware of certain predilections, unsettling tendencies, surprising reactions, of which she had previously been ignorant. She learned something about herself and was horrified.

Once, years before, when she was a child playing in the back yard, she had discovered a baby bird lying in the grass. It was a very young bird, newly hatched in fact, looking almost embryonic. It had no feathers, only a soft, damp fuzz, and its whole body seemed to shake with each rapid heartbeat. Marilyn stood there staring down at her discovery, feeling a strange and irritating discomfort. Even then, as a child, she remembered thinking that if it was her destiny to find a little bird, she would have much preferred finding a dead little bird. Because it was alive, it had now become an obligation that was forced upon her. Where was a cat when you needed one? She watched it for a while, hoping that the bird's peeps would grow even weaker and finally cease altogether. She knew it couldn't last long, lying there and baking in the hot, dry California sun. She wondered if the mother bird was grieving. After about five minutes, she moved over and, using her body to shield it from the sun, she hollered loudly for Natalie and Phyllis, who in a moment came bounding around the side of the house to stand beside her and gaze in delight at the tiny, fuzzy, half-dead creature lying in the grass.

Natalie gently lifted it up and held it carefully in the palm of her hand, while Phyllis, chattering like a squirrel in her excitement, ran into the house to line a shoe box with cotton to make a bed for it. Natalie brought it into the house and tenderly placed it on the bed of cotton. The bright black eyes stared unblinkingly, and whether it was terrified or dying or grateful or bewildered, it gave no sign. Helen called a local pet shop and was given directions for its care as well as an unoptimistic prognosis for its survival.

Patiently, Natalie and Phyllis fed it, one drop at a time, with an eyedropper, but the man in the pet shop had been right. The bird lived for two more days and, at some point in the night, peeped its last little peep. When, in the morning, Natalie and Phyllis ran eagerly to check on their new pet, they found it stiff and still, the black eyes open, the little bird claws rigid and extended. They buried it in the back yard with the whole family in attendance. An hour after the funeral, Marilyn dug it up again to see if it had begun to rot and left the shoe box sitting on top of the grave, the cover off, when she lost interest and decided to go to her friend's house.

Natalie and Phyllis wept when they found the body covered with ants and flies, and Helen had to shove the whole mess into a plastic bag which she sealed with a twister and threw into the garbage pail. Her sisters looked reproachfully at Marilyn, cried and told her they hated her. Her mother called her inconsiderate, unfeeling, and looked at her in disgust. Marilyn didn't care a bit. Her father soothed her by telling her privately that what she did merely indicated an intelligent curiosity. Yuspeh was angry because Marilyn hadn't had respect enough to have reburied the deceased and had left it instead to gather flies, some of which got into the house. Even as a child, Marilyn had never cared for anyone or anything that was forced upon her peremptorily. She much preferred her obligations to be self-imposed.

And here was another imposition—but Marilyn had expected to love this one. The contrast between the anticipation and the actuality stunned her.

Badly shaken by her inability to relate to her own child, Marilyn hired a housekeeper as soon as the baby nurse left. She screened the applicants carefully, judging them on warmth and motherliness, patience and calm. Unhappily aware that she had unwillingly cheated her poor baby out of what was rightfully his —a loving and involved mother—Marilyn was determined that her proxy be as close to the real thing as possible. After two weeks of intensive interviewing and scrupulous checking of references, she hired Ophelia Pineda.

In the meantime, she mourned for the lost joys of mother love. She was haunted by the tales Helen had told her of her grandmother Malka, whose brand of mothering was also, to say the least, peculiar. She began passionately to tell herself that her unnatural attitude was not inherent, that it was merely triggered by this particular child and would not apply to subsequent offspring.

Largely to reassure herself, she yielded to Ira's urging and became pregnant with her second child when Todd was a year and a half. This one was also a boy. It also looked like Ira. Marilyn tried, but after three feedings she asked the nurse to see to the baby's needs in the hospital nursery.

Ira named the baby Jeremy, after Helen's father, Joseph, and Marilyn, three days later, placed Jeremy into Ophelia's outstretched arms and resubmitted her law school application. While waiting for her records to be processed and her acceptance to be approved, she spent days at the library reading books on child development, boning up on psychological case histories of notorious mothers and brooding about her indifference to her children. She vowed over and over again to become more involved in their care, to take a greater interest in their achievements, to clap her hands in delight over a new tooth, a first step, a baby chuckle. Instead, she shopped for them, never missed an appointment at the pediatrician's, repapered the nursery.

Ira, a devoted father, noted her efforts and also noted her failure. He spent hours with the children, not only because it gave him pleasure, but to make up for their lack of a mother as well. He assured himself that Marilyn's love would grow and develop along with the babies; that very young children were not everyone's cup of tea. He tried to convince Marilyn of this and to comfort her when she cried, which she did often. Sometimes he would come across her sitting in the nursery, staring at the children, her eyes wet.

"What's wrong with me?" she would whisper in a voice filled with pain.

"Give it time, Marilyn."

"I'd give a million minutes if it would help. Let me go, Ira. You'll all be better off."

"Give it time, Marilyn."

Todd and Jeremy were quiet, placid children. They were bright and alert and reacted to Marilyn as they would to a visitor, friendly but wary. They seemed to sense her duplicity, to realize that her attentions and intentions were well-meaning but forced and insincere.

It tortured Marilyn to hear them laughing and playing and then see them fall silent when she walked into their room.

It was with great relief that she entered law school. All the loving energy that she yearned to put into her children but couldn't, she put instead into her studies. She made law review after her first year, a distinction which should have given her great gratification. Her father made a fuss over her, took her for Chinese food and never once said, as her mother did constantly, "What kind of mother sits all day in school while a stranger raises her children?" If her father noticed that she was not as uplifted over her academic achievements as she should have been, no doubt he attributed it to the stresses of hard work.

"Top of the world, Dolly," he said, toasting her with his cup of oolong tea. "I'm so proud of you I could bust. But I think you're working too hard. You look peaky."

"Guilty would be more accurate."

Lenny put down his teacup and took both her hands in his. "Your mother is an old-fashioned woman," he comforted. "She doesn't understand that not everyone can stay home and take care of children. It's a new world now and not like it used to be with women. She doesn't understand that."

"But she's right, Papa. I see the children very little, and I can't seem to—I don't—" Marilyn's voice faded out, and she gazed wet-eyed at her father. "I'm so guilty," she repeated, needing yet unable to tell even him the truth.

Later that night she tiptoed into the nursery and gazed at her sleeping children. She bent over them, these two little Iras, and studied the rise and fall of their chests, the shadow of their lashes on their cheeks. She gently pulled thumbs out of mouths and adjusted the bedclothes. They were sweet, good children who didn't deserve to be abused and neglected by an uninterested, unloving mother.

"Dear God," she whimpered, "what's wrong with me?"

Standing in the quiet, dim room, lit only by a Raggedy Andy nightlight, Marilyn acknowledged that there was indeed something wrong with her. She was an emotional freak. Some people were born armless or legless or mindless—deformed. She, Marilyn, had also been born with an imperfection, perhaps even more crippling than those: a short circuit in her emotional switchboard. The little lights for fear, pain, hate, indifference and anger flashed and blinked, emitting and receiving appropriate signals. But those for love, joy, empathy, warmth and acceptance were dim, glowing feebly at best, gleaming only for her father, flickering for her sisters, glimmering for her Aunt Celia.

She ached to divorce Ira and finally do right by her children by placing them away from her in the custody of their father. Several days ago, in a forensic law seminar dealing with the legal rights of parents and children, the question of child abuse and its definition had arisen. Marilyn stood up and informed the class that in her opinion the reason that so many people reacted so strongly to the subject of child abuse was that so many people, so many parents, came so very close to being abusers themselves.

If she divorced Ira, her children would be safe, thought Marilyn. She would move out, away from them and their father, away from the agonizing guilt they inspired.

She cried now, her arms crossed over her stomach, shoulders bent. "I wanted to love you," she wept. "I wanted so to love holding you. I wanted to be a devoted daughter, a loving wife, a tender mother." She lifted her face, crying open-eyed in her sons' bedroom. "I never wanted to be what I am," she sobbed brokenly. "I wanted to be a good girl." She looked up at the ceiling, straining to find the compassionate, forgiving eyes of God, and saw instead the face of her mother, closed, hard and accusing.

Chapter 5

CELIA SMILED OVER HER EMPTY WINEGLASS at her niece. "Dear heart," she said, "please shut up." She lifted a perfectly manicured hand and waved at the waiter, who was instantly bowing deferentially over the table. "André," she said, "do be a love and bring us some more wine." Marilyn reached into the silver bread basket for a roll and began to butter it. "I really mean it this time, Aunt Celia. This time it's for real. I'm divorcing Ira."

André arrived with the wine and poured some for Celia. She tasted it, smiled her approval, and he filled both glasses. When he was gone, she lifted her glass. "To a new and I hope more interesting topic of conversation."

Marilyn took a bite of her roll. "You'll see," she said.

Celia rolled her eyes. "I don't need it," she said, "but I'd love a dollar for every time you've told me that. As far as I'm concerned, you've long passed the point of boring me. I am, by now, in very real danger of becoming comatose."

Marilyn smiled. "I'm telling the family next Friday."

"Why not," sighed Celia. "Hasn't that been your opening line every Friday night for the past eight years?" She handed Marilyn a menu. "Shut up and read."

Actually it was six years, not eight, thought Marilyn. The first time she had announced to her parents her intention to divorce Ira, had been exactly three weeks before her second anniversary. She had wanted to tell only her father, but it hadn't worked out that way and she was forced to break the news not just to him but to her mother and grandmother and sisters as well. Naturally, all hell broke loose, with her mother becoming furious and her father pleading with her not to rush into anything. Her grandmother had sat clicking her teeth, her eyes bright, asking over and over, "Did you hear that? And this is supposed to be the smart one?"

Their reaction was, of course, no surprise. Her whole family was crazy about Ira.

The second time she told them was about six months later, and again they let her have it. This time, her grandmother was fierce. "What do you expect from a girl who never cleaned her room?" she asked. "What do you expect from a slob who left her dirty bloomers lying around for other people to pick up? Hah?"

She had repeated the performance over and over, at least three or four times a year, and by now, after eight years of marriage, a law degree, and two little boys, they were used to it. As the years passed, her family found more and better reasons to be disgusted with her. Now she had two children who were exactly like Ira and in whom she had no interest, now Ira had opened his own office and was no longer merely a CPA but a successful business manager. Now she had a nine-room house on Maple Drive in Beverly Hills, complete with housekeeper, weekly poolman and gardener, and a new Seville in the three-car garage.

But Marilyn knew that marriage to Ira and everything that came along with it, including motherhood, was killing her. Her secretary, Ginger, would sit patiently while Marilyn told her, for want of anyone else who seemed able to understand, about her unhappiness. "Everyone else in the world has difficulty making decisions," Marilyn told her, "but not Marilyn Stillman. Oh, no. Marilyn Stillman makes wonderful decisions. But can she act on them? Look at me, Ginger. I decided to divorce Ira years ago, and look at me. Why can't I move? Why am I still here? I handle other people's divorce cases every day—there's not an attorney in town who wouldn't handle mine—and still I sit, immobilized."

Ginger thought for a while. "Well," she said, "maybe you should force *Ira* into divorcing *you*."

That night Marilyn told Ira he was an inept lover. She told him she was going to have an affair. Ira thanked her for being so honest. He told her that he could not help being aware of her discontent. He told her that he was not exactly thrilled with their marriage either, but he had no intention of putting himself or his children through a divorce. He told her all of this in a calm and reasonable voice.

"If you want to divorce me, Marilyn, go right ahead. Just know that I will oppose it vigorously. Would you consider a marriage counselor?"

"For what? I don't want to fix this marriage, I want to end it. I have for years."

"Go right ahead," said Ira, and picking up his attaché case, he sat down at his desk and began looking into the purchase of municipal bonds for one of his clients.

"You'll hear from my attorney, Ira," she said. But since she never called an attorney, he never did.

They had very little to do with each other now. Occasionally they fought, but rarely. Occasionally they slept together, but also rarely.

Terrified and bewildered at her inability to extricate herself from her unbearable situation, she called her Uncle Benjamin.

"I'm afraid, Uncle Ben," she wept into the phone. "You're a psychiatrist. What's wrong with me? Why can't I get out? I think I'm going crazy." She began to sob even harder. "Please help me."

"Marilyn, I gave you a prescription for Valium. Have you filled it?"

"Yes."

"I want you to take ten milligrams," he said. "That's two of the little yellow tablets. Will you do that?"

"Yes."

"Good. After you have taken them, lie down and at ten minutes to the hour, I want you to call me. I will instruct the service to let you ring through."

"Okay," she whispered.

"Good. I'll wait for your call."

"Thank you, Uncle Ben."

When she called back, he told her that for obvious reasons, he could not treat her, but since he felt that therapy would be beneficial, he wished to refer her to a colleague in Beverly Hills. "Do you know of a Dr. Sanford Leventhal?" he asked.

"I think so. Is his wife's name Bobbi?"

"Yes."

"I know her."

"Well, give him a call and make an appointment. My nurse will give you his number."

"Thank you, Uncle Ben."

"Marilyn, I want you to feel free to call me whenever you think it's necessary."

"Thank you, I will."

"Good. How are your parents?"

"Fine."

"Good. Send them my love."

And that's how she got into group therapy.

"Marilyn?" said Celia sharply.

Startled, Marilyn looked up and into the eyes of a politely smiling André, small gold pencil poised over his pad, patiently waiting.

"Marilyn," said her aunt, "André is ready to take your order."

"Oh, I'm sorry. I'll have the salade Niçoise, André, and your wonderful herb dressing."

"Well," said Celia, when André went off, "what else is new?"

"I called Uncle Ben."

"Oh?"

"I'm starting group therapy."

Celia nodded and took another sip of her wine. "I think that's a *won*derful idea. Who's your doctor?"

"Leventhal. I know his wife."

"I suppose that's as good a basis for selecting a psychiatrist as any."

Marilyn smiled. "Do you know him?"

"Is there a doctor in this town I *don't* know? My brother is a doctor, my husband is a doctor, your cousin Matthew is a doctor, and Kenneth is in medical school. And you know something? They all stink."

"Thank you. Now I feel better about going."

André arrived with the food and served it quietly and efficiently. "Will there be anything else?" he asked. Celia shook her head and André glided off.

"When is your first session?" asked Celia.

"Wednesday, and every Wednesday thereafter, until such time as I am finally capable of moving my ass and dumping Ira." Marilyn reached for another roll.

"Put that down," ordered Celia. "You've had two already."

"I don't care," said Marilyn and began to butter it.

"So why are you once again announcing your eternally impending divorce next Friday?" asked Celia. "It takes less time to make the Grand Canyon than it does to complete therapy."

"Just keeping in practice."

Celia laughed. "That's the best-rehearsed line in history. Well, I suppose they expect it by now. How are the children?"

"Fine."

Celia pushed her plate away and looked at her niece. She had always wanted a daughter, but as luck would have it, it was her sister, Helen, who got the girls and she the boys. She lit a cigarette and inhaled deeply. "Marilyn," she said in a puff of smoke, "if you do, by some psychoanalytic miracle, become capable of, as you put it, dumping Ira, what then?"

Marilyn picked up her wineglass and drained it. She looked around for André and seeing him at another table took the wine bottle from the cooler. "Some wine?" she asked her aunt. Celia held out her glass and Marilyn filled it, then filled her own. She put the now-empty bottle back into the cooler. "I'll start to live," she told her aunt, taking a long sip of wine.

"On what, dear heart? You barely make enough to pay your secretary."

"Not alimony. I don't want a penny from him."

"That's the dumbest thing I ever heard."

"Look, he put me through law school. I'm grateful, Celia, but I don't need him anymore."

"I repeat, on what do you intend to live?"

Marilyn lit another cigarette. "I'm young," she said, "I'm smart, and I'm on my way to becoming a successful attorney—something will turn up."

Celia smiled. "When you say that, you remind me of your Uncle Murray. When he and Max came out here, business was lousy. Everything seemed to be going wrong. Max would sit for hours juggling the books and swallowing Gelusil. Murray would smile, put his feet up on the desk, and make grand plans for the future. 'I don't understand you, Murray,' Max would cry, tearing his hair out. 'The business is going in the toilet and you sit here like you don't have a care in the world. Are you made of plastic? Don't you know we owe three hundred thousand dollars?' And my brother, your Uncle Murray, would walk over, throw his arm around Max's shoulder and say, 'Max, Max, stop worrying. God will provide.' 'God will give us three hundred thousand dollars?' Max would ask. 'Of course,' Murray would say, 'you'll see, something will happen good.' 'Are you saying God gives money to people who need it?' 'I am.' At that Max pops another Gelusil and chases it with an Alka-Seltzer. He looks at Murray, whose feet are now back on the desk, as though he's lost his mind. 'In that case, you imbecile, explain to me why India is still a poor country. In that case, you moron, why were Jews starving in concentration camps? Why didn't God give *them* money?' And Murray would look at Max and say: 'I don't know about Jews and I don't know about India, but I know that for you and me, Max, *some*thing will turn up.'"

"And did it?" asked Marilyn.

"Oh, yes."

"They got the money?"

"Nope—they got an arsonist."

"An *arsonist*? What arsonist?" Marilyn looked flabbergasted.

"Your father," said Celia and laughed out loud. "Why else do you think they gave him a piece of the business?"

"Jesus H. Christ," Marilyn gasped.

"Well," said Celia, smiling broadly, "now you've got something else to discuss in therapy."

They both looked up as André materialized at the table, holding a tray of French pastries. As Marilyn eyed the tray with interest, Celia said, "Just coffee, André," and added in a stern voice, "Neither of us needs any of that, especially those of us who have pigged out on three rolls." She looked up at the waiter. "Two coffees, André, and the check, please."

Marilyn looked fondly at her aunt. The three regrets of her life were her marriage to Ira, her two whiny and uninteresting sons, and that she was Helen's daughter instead of Celia's. Helen and Celia, two years apart in age, were two hundred years apart in attitude. Marilyn even looked like Celia. When she was a little girl, it was Aunt Celia who took her shopping for clothes, Aunt Celia who styled her hair, Aunt Celia who had gotten her to stop biting her nails. She had spent more time at Aunt Celia's house, playing with Matthew and Kenneth, than she had at home. The whole thing was a mistake. She should have been Celia's daughter. Marilyn believed in the law of compensation. She believed that Newton's third law of gravity also applied to life: for every "force" there was an equal but opposite "force"— or should be. She knew from personal experience that life, like an algebraic equation, balanced out. She had a lousy marriage but was still young enough to find alternatives; she had a fledgling career but plenty of potential; she had Helen for a mother but Celia was her aunt. Best of all, she had her father, and he made up for everything. Marilyn picked up a packet of Sweet 'n Low and poured it into her coffee.

"Celia?"

"Yes, dear heart?"

"Do you remember when I was a little girl you said you wanted to adopt me?"

Celia smiled. "The offer is still open."

"We were in Saks, and I was trying on a dress for Matt's bar mitzvah. I must have been about seven."

"That dress cost me forty-two dollars, but it was worth every sou—it even looked good on Natalie when you outgrew it."

Marilyn added cream to her coffee and stirred it slowly.

"I tried it on, and you looked me over," mused Marilyn. "You made me turn around and around. You looked at me for what seemed like an hour, and then you said, 'I always wanted a daughter, and instead I got two jocks—so, if it's okay with you, I'm adopting you, kiddo.' "

Celia smiled at her niece. "Did I say that, honey?"

Marilyn nodded. "Yes, you said that. And I remember crying and crying all the way home."

"So you did," said Celia. "It almost made me change my mind."

"Do you know why I cried?"

"I don't know why anyone cries."

"I cried because the choice was so painful. It was my first sacrifice. I had to give you up in order to keep my father."

"You gave me up?"

Marilyn nodded.

"Well," said Celia, taking a sip of her black coffee, "in that case, dear heart, you can pay the check."

Chapter

6

HELEN RITTER NEVER HAD to buy a plant because she saved pits and made them grow. The kitchen in her Encino home gleamed greenly with avocado plants, grapefruit plants, mango plants. Every morning she turned the soil and watered her plants with great care, never too much or too little. She fed them with crushed eggshells, cigarette ashes, coffee grounds and the blood from defrosted New York steaks. She polished the leaves with a paper towel dipped in milk. She felt that her plants knew her and waited for her to tend them. They liked it when she hummed and put her face close to their beckoning, welcoming branches. On nice days they would all be put outside, and when it rained, Helen collected the rainwater in plastic pails for a special treat. If they had to be pinched off or pruned, she would apologize for any pain she might be causing them and assure them that what she was doing was for their own good.

On Fridays, when the whole family came for dinner, she would caution her children and grandchildren to be careful and not brush against or knock over her plants. She would gaze at all the things she had grown, the plants decorating her kitchen and the children, sitting like flowers around her table, and marvel at what could come out of a seed. Helen's plants gave her great pleasure. She wished she could say the same about her children. For one thing, she knew she could be a much happier woman if only her daughter, Natalie, would find a nice boy and settle down. Of her three daughters, it was Natalie she pitied most—stoop-shouldered, heavy-breasted, near-sighted, kind-hearted Natalie. Of all of them, only Natalie had inherited her green thumb.

Sometimes Helen would stare at her daughter and instead of seeing a round-shouldered, bespectacled, twenty-nine-year-old woman with skinny legs and sad, squinting eyes, she would see a ripe, rich, black-loamed field, tilled, turned and ready to receive pits and seeds that could burst and bloom and flourish —if only she could find a nice boy to plant them. Sighing, Helen began to peel an onion for the soup. Her family would be here in two hours. The kitchen smelled good, the clock ticked loudly, the soup bubbled and steamed. The plants waved their leaves gently and, aided by the sunlight streaming through the windows, cast odd, moving shadows over the clean white-and-green vinyl floor.

Helen lowered the flame under the soup and turned toward the chickens that were waiting in aluminum-foiled roasting pans to be seasoned. Her mother-in-law hovered over them, searching for pinfeathers. She was eighty-two years old and knew enough to mistrust a chicken that came home covered with plastic wrap. She called them "dead chickens," positive that they had been mass-produced by a huge, hen-shaped machine. She herself had never bought such a chicken. *Her* chickens had been alive and cackling with tousled feathers and beady, stupid eyes. Slowly she would walk past the noisy, smelly wooden coops, ignoring the feathers that floated down onto her coat and head, until she spied the one. Then she would beckon to the man who would come over and peer with her into the coop. She would point and say, "That one," and he would reach in, grab the chicken of her choice by the legs, and hold the hysterical bird up in front of her for a closer examination. Eyeing it critically, she would blow on its breast to part the feathers and check the skin color. When positively

satisfied, she would nod her head and he would take the squawk-
ing, flailing bird into the back. He returned it to her, wrapped
in bloody newspaper, inside a brown bag, intact except for the
head and feathers.

She would take it home, disembowel it herself, clean it, scrape
it and flame it. She saved the giblets and eggs, if any. She
removed the fat for rendering and cut the bird into quarters.
Then she would boil it. *That* was a chicken, not a dead piece
of rubber like these. Helen was a good girl, except she didn't
know her chickens. Plants she knew, but not chickens.

Yuspeh clicked her dentures in regret for all the good things
that were forever gone, that her grandchildren would never
know or see or taste. She bent lower and put her nose to the
smooth, shiny breast of what Helen called a chicken. She
smelled it. Nothing.

"Mom," Helen yelled in annoyance, "stop doing that." She
hurried over to the counter, laden with jars, tins and packets
of seasoning. The old woman straightened up and moved aside.
Helen began to sprinkle salt, pepper, garlic powder and onion
powder over the birds. Her mother-in-law clicked her disapproval. "A real chicken should have its own taste," she said.
Helen opened a packet of G. Washington seasoning and shook
it carefully over the chickens. "That's enough poison," Yuspeh
said. "Stop already."

"Ma," sighed Helen, "please sit down." Helen watched her
mother-in-law carefully lower herself into a chair, and then
picked up the paprika and finished off her birds. The old woman
stared unblinking at the quivering underside of her daughter-
in-law's upper arm. She had been living with Helen and Lenny
for thirty-two years and knew all their secrets. She had watched
her grandchildren unfold and had known all their secrets, too.
She was a great-grandmother. She had the feeling that she
would live forever, growing steadily older and stronger, shaking
off illness and stiffness the way a dog sheds water, the way
Helen was shaking the paprika. She wondered whom she
would live with and learn things about when Helen and

Lenny were gone. She hoped it wouldn't be Natalie—Natalie who was carried along through life like a dry leaf in rushing water. With Natalie, there would be nothing to spy on or guess at. Natalie went to work every day and came home to knit sweaters for her relatives. She spent all her money on wool. She begged to do favors for people. Her big secret was that she had never been loved by anyone outside her family. Her big fear was that she never would be. Her large, round, rarely touched breasts seemed to be too heavy for her spine and dragged her down, rounding her shoulders and bowing her head so that it jutted forward, like a turtle's. Her stomach protruded, making a shelf to support those breasts, while her lower back curved inward. Some beauty. The pity was that all this could be changed in a minute if only the girl would stand up straight. But telling her this was like knocking your head against the wall.

The old woman sighed. Natalie, Natalie. Helen should have thrown her out years ago, forced her to make her own way. Yuspeh shook her head. She had neither patience nor sympathy for people like Natalie. Opening her eyes, she watched Helen wipe down the counter. "With those *tsitskes,* she could have maybe seven, eight nice boys crazy to put their faces there. But she don't stand up straight." Helen shrugged, knowing instantly to whom Yuspeh was referring. She rinsed out the wash cloth and hung it over the center divider of her sink.

"She's maybe not such a beauty, but believe me, there are plenty worse," said Yuspeh.

"Do you want a cup of tea?"

The old woman nodded and continued, "She's too much in the house. Outside she could maybe find somebody. For every pot there's a cover . . . except she don't stand up straight."

Helen filled the teapot and put it on the stove. Opening the cabinet, she took out two glass mugs with handles and one tea bag.

"Yetta Press had a daughter uglier than Natalie. She had a face like a pinch with no lips and hair in the nose. Yetta was crazy from pain from looking on her. So, one day, I said to Yetta, 'Yetta . . .' "

"You want honey or sugar?" Helen asked, interrupting.

"I'm living with you thirty-two years and still you ask me?"

Helen filled the two mugs with hot water and dipped the tea bag first in one and then in the other. "Have the honey."

"So give me the honey. So I say to Yetta, 'Yetta, you got to watch that girl. She don't look where she's going. She could hurt herself good.' So Yetta says to me, she says, 'Yuspeh, don't worry about that girl. Nothing will ever happen to that girl, because I will be stuck with that girl for the rest of mine life.' "

Helen brought the tea to the table and sat down with her mother-in-law. "So?" she asked.

"So, that ugly girl her name was Faye, got married, not only once, but twice. Go explain it."

Helen smiled and sipped her tea. "One day someone will come along who will see Natalie for the wonderful girl she is."

Yuspeh looked at her daughter-in-law in surprise. "You believe that?"

"I do."

"You believe that life is a supermarket and people go shopping until they see a box of prunes they like? You believe a girl is like a prune? Hah!" she snorted. "You believe that, you believe baloney."

"Natalie is a wonderful girl," Helen protested.

"You know that, we all know that, but that's all what knows that. You want a nice boy to know that? Paint it on her head."

"Mama," Helen said sharply, "drink your tea."

The old woman obediently picked up her tea and blew on it. Cautiously she stretched her lips to the glass and took a tiny sip. "Maybe you should fix by her the nose."

"There's nothing wrong with her nose," Helen said angrily.

"Who is blind like a mother?"

Helen stared moodily into her tea. She would be a happy woman if only Natalie could find a nice boy and settle down. Neither Phyllis nor Marilyn had had any problem in that department. They both married wonderful boys. They both married young. They both stood up straight and had nice noses.

"You've got to have luck," she said. "Everything in life is luck."

Her mother-in-law took a noisy sip of tea and wiped her mouth on her apron. "You also got to make your luck," she said. "Natalie don't do anything to make her own luck. She sits all the time and knits. When she don't knit, she sews. When she don't sew, she makes needlepoints. What kind of business is that for a girl? Sitting in the house you don't find boys. She got to go out from the house to a dance—to a trip—to a movies. She got to stand up straight and make her own luck." The old woman nodded righteously and took another noisy sip of tea. "A lot is your fault," she said.

Helen looked up. "What do you mean, my fault?" she asked sharply.

"You never say nothing. You let her knit and never say not one word." Yuspeh put down her glass and straightened up. She looked accusingly at her daughter-in-law. "You should say, 'Put away the wool and go out. Stop sitting in the house!' That girl makes a million excuses, and you take all her excuses and never say nothing." Her voice shook in indignation. "She says her back hurts, you tell her, 'Lie down.' She says she's tired, you say, 'Lie down.' What is she tired from? From what does her back hurt? She's a secretary for Lenny's business, not a digger from ditches." The old woman's voice rose angrily. "Even her job she didn't get herself. You told Lenny to make her a job."

"Don't get so excited," Helen said wearily.

"I'm not excited."

Helen went over to the wall oven and opened the door. She began to baste the chickens. "All she needs is for her luck to change."

"All she needs is for her mother to change," Yuspeh retorted.

Helen closed the oven door and picked up the used tea bag. She tore it open and pushed the wet leaves into the soil around a newly potted grapefruit plant. Gently she stroked a rich, green leaf. Of all her daughters, Natalie would have been the best wife and mother. She would have been satisfied, not like Marilyn. At the thought of Marilyn, Helen's lips curved into an angry frown. Marilyn. "There is no justice in this world," she said quietly.

"You just now learned this?" asked Yuspeh.

Helen looked up at the clock. She went to the refrigerator, got the vegetable crisper and began to wash lettuce leaves. She dried them in paper towels, and taking out her large salad bowl, started ripping the cold, crunchy leaves.

"You want I should help you?"

"No."

Helen, who grew up with a woman who spoke so infrequently her mouth seemed to creak like a rusty hinge on those rare occasions when speech became necessary, had eagerly welcomed the constant stream of words that flowed like tap water from the lips of her mother-in-law. Once Yuspeh got started, she couldn't seem to turn herself off. She more than made up for all those years of heavy and oppressive silence. Thinking back, Helen couldn't recall ever having had a conversation with her own mother. Malka communicated through tightly closed lips, slapping her children wordlessly or ignoring them pointedly to show her displeasure. Helen had learned to discern her mother's moods and meanings by the tilt of a shoulder or the angle of a head. When Malka wanted her to set the table, she would catch her eye or poke her on the arm, and then, without a word, point to the table. Helen would nod and get the dishes.

She know that her mother had favorites and that she, Helen, was not among the favored. With fierce determination she set out to make herself, if not loved, then at least needed by that cold, peculiar woman who, for reasons Helen never understood, attracted and fascinated her so intensely. For a flicker of recognition, Helen washed clothes, scrubbed floors, prepared meals, ironed. She ran herself ragged for the smile she never received. Only once did she remember her mother touching her for something other than a demand. And it was over so quickly that Helen wondered if it had really happened at all.

"Helen!"

Startled, Helen jumped, dropping the handful of cherry tomatoes she had been washing. She watched two of them disappear down the garbage disposal. She rescued the remaining tomatoes and turned around to see her mother-in-law behind her holding out a cucumber and a bunch of scallions.

"You scared me," she said quietly, taking the vegetables.

"What were you dreaming?" asked Yuspeh.

"I was thinking about my mother."

"Twice I had to call you. What were you thinking?"

Helen carefully cut each small tomato in half and dropped them, skin side up, atop the lettuce in the salad bowl. She began to peel the cucumber.

"So, tell me." Yuspeh, who had never met Malka but had through the years heard much about her, waited impatiently. "That woman never even came to your wedding," she said. "That woman, may she rest in peace, was a crazy woman."

Helen smiled. "I was just thinking about that," she said.

"What," asked Yuspeh, "that she was crazy?"

"No, I was thinking about a wedding."

"Whose wedding?"

"You don't know her."

"Tell me."

"Ruthie Diller."

"Who is Ruthie Diller?"

"She lived in the next house from us on Hendrix Street. I must have been about twelve or thirteen when she got married."

"So?"

Helen leaned against the sink. The memory was so etched in her mind that she could almost feel the sharp, hard grains of Uncle Ben's rice that she had held tightly clutched in both perspiring palms.

"I was standing with my friends by her stoop, waiting for

Ruthie to come out. Mr. Diller's Plymouth was parked at the curb all washed and clean, with shoes tied to the back bumper. Ruthie's brother, Heshy, was sitting on a rocking chair on the porch in a blue suit, rocking. The whole neighborhood was there, waiting for Ruthie to come out in her gown." Helen paused and smiled at her mother-in-law.

"That's the story?" asked Yuspeh.

"You really want to hear all this, Ma?"

"What else I got to do?" said Yuspeh, exasperated. "Finish already."

"Where was I?"

"Waiting by the stoop."

Helen nodded, her fists clenched as though she were still holding the rice. "Well, all of a sudden, the door opens and Ruthie's mother and father come out. Mrs. Diller has on a lace dress, beige, with a hat to match. She tells Heshy to stop rocking and stand with her by the door. Mr. Diller goes down the steps and opens the back door of the car. On the way he smiles at everybody and shakes hands. I say hello to him, we all say hello. My brother Ben says, 'Mazel tov, Mr. Diller,' and then everybody says 'mazel tov.' "

"Natural," agreed Yuspeh. "That's what you say for a wedding."

"And then Ruthie comes out in her gown. I still remember it—the sleeves were long and tight with seed pearls on the pointed cuffs and on the skirt. It was fitted at the waist and gathered in a flounce in back."

"A flounce," whispered Yuspeh.

"On her head she wore a headpiece like a crown with white iridescent sequins and pearls. The veil hung down behind her like a cloud."

"She had a bouquet?" asked Yuspeh.

"She had a bouquet. It was roses and ferns and babies'-breath with white satin ribbons coming down. I thought she was so beautiful. She didn't look like Ruthie Diller; she looked like a queen."

Helen paused and sighed. Both women stood quietly, eyes unfocused, caught up in Helen's memory. "She wasn't wearing her glasses," Helen said softly. "She took them off special for the occasion. My friend Pessie passed around the box of rice, and we all took more. When Ruthie got to the steps, Mrs. Diller gave Heshy her handbag and bent down and picked up Ruthie's train and veil."

"It shouldn't get dirty on the steps," said Yuspeh.

Helen nodded. "Yes," she said. "Then Ruthie came down the steps with her mother behind her, holding up the dress, and we all threw the rice. Ruthie laughed and bowed her head, so the rice shouldn't get in her eyes. I reached over to Pessie for another handful of rice, and I saw my mother, standing behind me, to the side. She was looking at Ruthie. She had her hands folded across her chest, and was staring at Ruthie. Then, why I don't know because it wasn't like her, she reached into Pessie's box of rice, took a handful and threw it in Ruthie's hair, in the front where the veil wasn't covering it."

Helen stopped talking and stood very still. She closed her eyes and, picking up the dishcloth, began to twist it. Yuspeh waited, her breathing audible in the quiet kitchen. "And then," Helen whispered, "she put her hand on my head. I couldn't move. Her hand was so heavy and so light. It must have also been wet because there were grains of rice sticking to it, and some of the rice got on my hair. Mr. and Mrs. Diller put Ruthie in the back seat and Mrs. Diller got in next to her. Mr. Diller and Heshy sat in front. Ruthie's father started the car and they left, the shoes scraping and bouncing down the street. We all watched until the car turned the corner, and then everybody started talking and laughing and the crowd broke up. But my mother and I stood where we were. I was afraid to move because her hand was still on my head. I was afraid that if I moved, she would take her hand away. 'What is she marrying?' my mother asked me. I told her a pharmacist. Then my mother said, 'Luck is like money. Some people have a lot, some a little, some none at all.' I couldn't move. Then she said,

'You will have luck, Celia,' and she took away her hand, turned around and walked back to our house. She . . . my mother thought I was Celia."

Unable to continue, Helen stopped and with the dishcloth wiped away the tears that had begun to roll slowly down her face. She opened her eyes and looked at Yuspeh, who laid her hand gently on her daughter-in-law's wet cheek. "Even so," she said, her voice shaking, "even so, I walked around for the rest of that day with the rice from my mother's hand still in my hair." Helen fumbled for a tissue in her apron pocket and blew her nose. Then she turned around, washed her hands and picked up the half-pared cucumber. "Where did I put that peeler," she cried, distraught. "Where is it?"

Yuspeh, overcome with pity, stared at her daughter-in-law's back. "Come, Helen," she said quietly. She took the cucumber from her limp hand and placed it on the counter. "We have plenty of time yet for the salad." Putting her thin, veined arm around Helen's waist, she led her, unresisting, to the table. "Come, my darling, my birdie," she crooned and sat her down. She placed the still-warm cup of tea into Helen's hands and as Helen lifted wet empty eyes to look at her face, she tenderly murmured, "Drink, drink, my little love, before it gets too cold."

Chapter 7

IRA PUSHED ASIDE A STACK OF CONTRACTS, removed his glasses and rubbed his eyes. He sometimes felt that he would have made a very convincing and adequate actor. Through the years, marriage to a person who couldn't stand him had made it necessary for him to portray the part of a contented husband— not only for his own sake, but for that of his children, his wife's family and his clients, who, although many of them led turbulent personal lives themselves, felt that the life of the man to whom they entrusted their money had to be stable and unafflicted, so as not to affect his efficient handling of their affairs. It was very hard, and Ira yearned for contentment. Very often the idea of divorcing Marilyn would shine before his eyes, only to be dimmed and dismissed by the spectre of loss. It wasn't Marilyn he feared losing, it was the loss of her parents, now his, that he couldn't bear. He had already lost one set of parents and refused to go through another bereavement.

It was also his children's certain pain at the loss of *their* family unit that made it impossible for Ira to leave. Ira found himself incapable of inflicting an agony like the one he had suffered on his boys. So he sacrificed his personal happiness to retain and maintain his family. More often than not, he felt it was worth it. But it was very hard, and bargains had to be made. Since Marilyn, despite her constant threats, also seemed incapable of leaving him, compromises were arrived at. For the sake of Ira's career, the pretext of normalcy was maintained.

Ira and Marilyn and the children had dinner together every evening. They entertained clients at home and went as a couple to all social affairs connected with Ira's business. They slept in the same room so that there would be no questions raised by their boys, guests or maid. Somehow, perhaps because both knew it was a pretext, or because both hid behind the roles they were portraying, they managed to carry it off with people they weren't very close to. The children, aged six and a half and four, seemed fine, albeit somewhat nervous, and annoyed and embarrassed the family by sucking their thumbs and picking their noses, sometimes simultaneously, and often in public. It relieved Ira to know that much of their care was given over to Ophelia, the housekeeper, and to Natalie, who, unlike her sister, adored them.

Because being despised was unsettling for Ira, he spent most of his time at the office. He left the house after breakfasting with his sons, returned for dinner, and then went back to the office. By the time he got home again, Marilyn was asleep. Occasionally, after a party or during a period of truce or because they got suddenly horny, Ira and Marilyn would have sex. When this happened, they would have a kissless, silent fuck and lapse into depression. Also occasionally, Ira would, instead of returning to his office after dinner, go to Marina Del Rey and fuck Brenda Mortenson, who was a secretary for an agent in an office down the hall from his. Brenda had red pubic hair and sometimes did commercials. At times the sight of a box of detergent or a packet of drink mix would send Ira scooting down the San Diego Freeway to Brenda's apartment, where he would lay down his attaché case and then lay down Brenda. She was a clean and agreeable girl who enjoyed sex and didn't mind if he came in her mouth. He hoped that it was understood by Brenda that their affair was a temporary and pleasant arrangement with no opportunity for advancement.

Often Ira would lend her money which she wouldn't return, and sometimes he would get her house seats for a show that one of his clients was involved with. Ira was pleased with Brenda because she didn't seem to be in love with him; would eventually quit her office job and leave—and never winked knowingly at him in front of other people. He found her very attractive and surprisingly intelligent. Despite the fact that she swallowed, he never thought her cheap.

The one event in the week that Ira most looked forward to was Friday night dinner at Marilyn's parents' house. There he felt appreciated and loved. He considered Helen and Lenny his family, Natalie and Phyllis his sisters. He even liked Yuspeh, whom he secretly considered to be somewhat aggressive for an old lady. Phyllis's husband, Neil, occasionally irritated him because of his uninhibited remarks, which Ira thought were out of place at a dinner table. Ira was not fond of angry, liberal young men who used street language and made obscene references to bodily functions when food was served.

Last Friday night, after Marilyn had made her usual snide insinuations about the state of their union and Ira had smiled helplessly at Helen and Lenny, Neil launched into one of his angry denunciations. Neil and Phyllis owned and operated a health-food store and restaurant in Venice. Usually, after Marilyn's introductory threats about divorce, Phyllis and Neil would deliver their threat of becoming vegetarians. But this time Neil drew his brows together and furiously informed them of all his problems with certain customers who patronized his place of business.

"Society is breaking down," he announced, shoving a forkful of chopped liver into his mouth. "Not only is this earth overpopulated, it's overpopulated with primitives, animals. Do you know what happened on Wednesday?"

"Listen to this. Just listen to this," said Phyllis.

"This last Wednesday," Neil went on, "this woman, a regular, came in with her two brats and their friend. They all sit down at the salad bar and she orders a Yogananda special for herself and vegeburgers on sprouted seven-grain for the kids."

"*Gevalt,*" muttered Yuspeh, smelling the liver.

"After they eat, she tells the kids to go to the bathroom. They go, and after about ten minutes I hear them laughing and carrying on. I go back there to see what's doing, and I almost drop dead."

"Just listen to this," said Phyllis.

"Do you know what those animals were doing back there?" demanded Neil, angrily.

"Just listen to this," said Phyllis through pursed lips.

"Those animals were peeing on the doorknobs!" After waiting for a second to let this sink in, Neil went on. "First, they opened the door, it opens in, and peed on the outside knob, then those bastards held the door by the frame and peed on the inside knob. The object of all this, of course, was to make the next customer, who had to go, get his hands all full of piss when he went to turn the knob to open the door." Neil banged his fist down on the table, making the silverware jump, and looked around at all of them, outraged.

"Is that the worst? The pits?" he demanded. "And these are the offspring of supposedly highly evolved souls, who are aware enough to eat health food!" Savagely he jabbed his fork into a cherry tomato, spattering juicy red-green seeds on the white cloth.

Lenny, who had just dipped his spoon into the chicken soup, looked at it for a moment and then put his spoon down. "This is a dinner table, Neil," said Ira in quiet disgust.

"The only reason I didn't beat the shit out of those little pricks is because of all the meditation I do. Fortunately for them I was on a plateau of forbearance."

"I wish *I* were," said Ira.

"That was a terrible thing, Neil," soothed Helen. "I know you like to keep the store spick-and-span."

"Yeah," said Neil, shaking his head. "I bust my ass sanitizing the place, and they act like The Cosmic Cucumber was a goddamn McDonald's or something."

"Who wants more soup?" asked Helen, and Neil nodded, pushing out his plate.

"So, Ira," said Lenny. "What's new with Trans-America?"

"Not much, Dad," smiled Ira.

Natalie stood up and began to stack the empty soup plates. "Are you finished, Ira?" she asked, reaching for his plate. Ira nodded. "Let me help you," he said, pushing his chair back. "Give me these." He took the plates and began to walk toward the kitchen. Natalie followed him, carrying the rest of the bowls.

"I'll bring in the brisket, Ma," she said. She found Ira stacking the soup bowls in the dishwasher. "Leave them, Ira. I'll do that later." Ira straightened up. "How's it going, Natalie?" he asked. "The same," she replied. "Did you have a good week?"

"The same."

"Is Marilyn still bugging you?"

"Is Billy Carter still drinking beer?"

"Poor Ira."

Ira leaned over and kissed her on the cheek. "The guy who gets you is going to be a lucky man, Sis," he said.

"Well," laughed Natalie, taking the brisket from the oven, "he better hurry up. Tempus is fugiting."

Ira held open the swinging door of the kitchen and Natalie walked into the dining room carrying the brisket platter. As she passed Neil, he looked into the platter. "Red meat," he said, disapprovingly. "No good for you."

"There's chicken, Neil," Helen said. "Would you like some chicken?"

"Yeah," answered Neil. "We never serve red meat at The Cosmic Cucumber."

Marilyn looked over at him, annoyed. "You know what you can do with your Cosmic Cucumber, Neil? You can shove it up your cosmic ass."

"Marilyn!" cried Helen.

"Feh, such a language," scolded Yuspeh.

"Shut up, Marilyn," said Phyllis. "You've got your nerve."

Ira smiled. It wasn't often that he and Marilyn agreed. "Now, now," he said mildly.

"Don't open your fat mouth to *my* husband," yelled Phyllis. "Ira *has* to take your crap, but Neil doesn't and neither do I."

Lenny stood up and glared at his youngest daughter. "You be quiet," he said, pointing to Phyllis. "You too, Dolly. Ira and I want to eat in peace. Your mother worked hard to prepare this meal." He sat down again and rubbed his arm. "Arthritis," he said to Ira. He looked over at Marilyn and smiled: "How's my Dolly?"

"I'm fine, Papa."

"Good, good. Let's eat."

For Ira, the best part of Friday night was the talking with his in-laws. He rarely discussed his marriage with Lenny, not wishing to upset him. They would instead sit contentedly together, discussing business and investments, the economy and the Middle East. Helen or Natalie would bring them coffee, which they would sip slowly and with which they would split a Danish or a piece of home-baked lemon cake. Ira would push away his troubles with the wave of a spoon, unable even to acknowledge the possibility of a divorce separating him from these people whom he found so dear.

Helen would occasionally bring up the subject of marital difficulties and also express her fears over how a divorce might affect their—Ira's and the family's—relationship. "What can we do with her, Ira?" Helen would ask, her eyes dark. "How can we lose you?" She would lean back in her chair for a moment, lost in thought, and then sit up abruptly, her mind made up. "It's ridiculous, we can't lose you."

"It will never come to that, Ma," Ira would comfort. "Even if worst comes to worst, we won't lose each other. You're stuck with me."

"Ira, Ira," and then Helen would heave a huge sad sigh. "I know you mean that, but conditions alter. You'll remarry, have maybe a new family, drift away little by little, God forbid. Things happen, son. Even when we don't want them to."

This kind of talk made them all nervous and uncomfortable, and Lenny would try to whitewash their fear. "Marilyn's a good girl. She'd die before she'd hurt me. Of that I'm positive."

At their next dinner, Lenny's "good girl" called her husband a "piss ant." Phyllis giggled and told Marilyn, very sarcastically, that she "surely had the gift of gab." But Ira no longer reacted. For one thing, he really didn't much care, and for another, his indifference to her insults made Marilyn even more furious. It was Marilyn's family, but they were on Ira's side. His lack of angry response, his self-control, his dignified demeanor, contrasting so strongly with her bitchiness, only made him look better. Only made the family more partisan. Even to Lenny, at least in this situation, Marilyn was the bad guy. Ira tied them more firmly to him with good deeds. He did their taxes, gave them investment hints; he had even lent Neil money to open The Cosmic Cucumber. Marilyn saw all this and was powerless to counteract it. It was Ira's revenge.

But it was hollow and joyless. Ira, who, like everyone else, usually took great satisfaction in revenge, felt only sad. Because it was simply a matter of time. Marilyn couldn't sit on a tack forever. Ira knew very well that something or someone, somehow, would give her the impetus she needed, or whatever it was she needed, to propel her into action. She even had said so herself. Ironically, that conversation took place at Herb Lighter's wedding reception. Herb had remarried two years after a very messy divorce. Marilyn and Ira, who was Herb's business manager, were two of thirty invited guests. Just as Ira spotted Herb and his new bride, Blanca, walking happily toward them, Marilyn had turned to him and said, knowing how much he hated her using "dirty" language, "I don't know what it's going to take, Ira, but one of these days someone or something's going to shove a lit firecracker up my ass and blow me right the hell out of this fucking marriage."

Strangely enough, they had sex that night (Ira smiled to himself when he realized that even in his thoughts he couldn't call what they did "making love"), and when they were done,

Marilyn looked at him with tears in her despair-filled eyes and told him that what he shoved up her couldn't, in any way, shape or form, be compared to a firecracker. Even an unlit one. Ira knew then that he was, as Neil would have put it, "a highly evolved soul." Anybody else would have killed her. Ira just got out of bed and stood there, watching her cry. He was sorry for them both.

His intercom buzzed four times before Ira heard it. "Yes, Lisa?" he asked, pushing down the button.

"It's six-fifteen, Mr. Stillman."

"Thank you, Lisa. Dial my wife and then go home." He took his finger off the button and picked up the phone.

"Natalie, how nice," he said, surprised.

"I'm babysitting."

"Where's Marilyn?"

"She went to group."

"Where?"

"Group therapy," said Natalie. "Do you want the number?"

"No," said Ira. "Natalie, tell the boys I won't be home for dinner. Tell them I'll see them in the morning."

"Okay, Ira. Oh, Ira?"

"Hmm?"

"Is there any message for Marilyn?"

"Not for your ears, Sis."

Ira hung up. Group therapy. He stood up and began putting papers into his attaché case. "Firecrackers at forty-five bucks an hour," he said out loud. After he had finished packing his attaché case and closed it with a snap, he picked up the phone and dialed.

"Brenda? I'm coming over, okay? . . . Good. I'll bring some wine and we'll celebrate . . . Oh, I don't know . . . let's pretend it's the Fourth of July." He smiled ruefully to himself, hung up the phone and walked to the door. Before he left, he turned off the light and locked his office.

"Boom," he said, and rang for the elevator.

Chapter 8

Marilyn had graduated fourth in a law school class of three hundred and sixty, and almost immediately had been grabbed up by the law firm of Deiter, Sidaris, Ostern, Caputo and Wernick, her first choice. True to his word, Ira had dutifully recommended his wife to those of his clients who had need of an attorney—and because they trusted Ira, Marilyn eventually was inundated with contracts to be drawn up, complicated "deals" to be investigated and numerous, intricate divorce cases. It was upon the latter that her growing reputation as a legal miracle worker was based. Ira's clientele consisted largely of show-business personalities, whose fabulous and erratic careers and personal lives seesawed continually between glorious highs and appalling lows, which, like the stars themselves, seemed much larger than life.

Although Marilyn secretly felt that the *real* dramas took place in the modest and tacky tract houses of the Valley, it was obvious that the rest of the world did not share her opinion, and consequently it was her cases involving the glamorous and the celebrated that made the headlines. Her ability to cut to the core of a situation, her uncanny knack for getting warring parties to agree to logical compromise, the practical courses she convinced her clients to follow and thereby avoid nasty and public displays of their agony, began to be included in chic Hollywood party conversation.

It was at one of these gatherings, to which Marilyn herself was not yet important enough to be invited, but a client of hers was, that her name first came up.

The client in question was the wife of a motion-picture producer whose husband was screwing around in the mobile dressing room of the female star of his current film. Outraged, but refusing to be outdone, she propositioned the male lead of that same film, who happened to be tall, black and twelve years her junior.

On one memorable day the producer husband, intending to go over script changes with his star, walked, without knocking, into the trailer of the male lead. There, he discovered his wife going down on him with an enthusiasm she had never, ever displayed on those all-too-rare occasions when, after much pleading and head-pushing, she had finally and reluctantly agreed to perform a similar act on her legal spouse.

The producer sued for divorce, asking for legal custody of his three children, whose welfare, he claimed, would be damaged if they continued to live with a mother who was a promiscuous pervert. In one of the trade magazines the next day, an item appeared that said, "Which well-known producer is divorcing his socially prominent wife for doing what to whom on the set of his latest film, due to be released next fall?" In the other trade mag, a headline read, "Tall, very dark and handsome young actor excites talk about his performance in new film as well as in off-screen antics with wife of film's producer."

The producer was Ira's client and had already hired a famous Beverly Hills divorce attorney. Ira advised the wife to hire Marilyn, who, as a woman, might be more sympathetic to the case—and who as a fledgling attorney would try harder and charge a smaller fee.

With the retainer in hand, and aware that the publicity value of this case was high, Marilyn got busy and in a very short time knew more about the producer than his wife of eleven years.

"Am I correct in assuming that you wish to avoid a messy custody fight?" she asked her client.

"I don't want that cocksucker to get my kids," responded the socially prominent client.

Marilyn grinned. "Be careful, Lori," she cautioned, "he might very well, and probably has, said the same thing about you—and with greater accuracy, I might add."

Tearfully, Lori nodded. "What am I going to do?" she wept.

"Are you willing to take a risk?" asked Marilyn.

"What?"

"I know your husband. I know him better than he knows himself—and I'm willing to bet that if you don't contest the custody, not only will you keep it out of the papers, you will also, within two months, give or take a week, have not only the kids back, but also higher child-support payments than you ever dreamed of asking."

"But how can you be sure? That's a pretty big chance to take."

"I'm not sure. That's the risk. But based on what I know of your husband, as well as your kids, they'll all be so crazy after two or three weeks that he'll beg you to take them back."

"You said two months," corrected Lori, blowing her nose.

"I'm adding on the extra time to allow for spite, hate and revenge," said Marilyn. "You probably won't need it."

Marilyn was wrong about one thing. It didn't even take a week and a half.

"So if you ever need a good lawyer," the satisfied Lori advised her avidly listening friends at the party, "get Stillman. She's very smart, and she'll break her ass for you."

A passing waiter held a tray of hors d'oeuvres before the ladies, which they dubiously examined, carefully calculating the calorie content before making a selection.

"After everything was settled," continued Lori, taking a dainty bite of shrimp ball, "I called to thank her again. 'Why were you so eager for custody?' she asked me. Well, I was sort of surprised at the question, you know?"

Her friends nodded.

"What did you say?" asked one.

"I told her I wanted them because they were my kids!"

Her friends nodded again in agreement.

"And you know what she said to me?" asked Lori. "She said to me, 'So what?'"

The ladies were silent for a moment. Then one of them, wiping her fingers on a cocktail napkin, looked at Lori. "I agree with her," she said. "Why can't *I* be the one to take them to dinner occasionally and have them every other weekend? If I had it all to do over again, I'd give my ex the kids in a minute. Let him and his bitch of a second wife have those pains in the ass, and let *me* have the freedom."

"She's got a point there, Lori," laughed another of the ladies.

"Yeah, yeah—that's what she says, not what she does," retorted Lori, helping herself to a glass of champagne from the tray of yet another hovering waiter. "What kind of mother gives away her kids? I couldn't make ends meet without the child support."

"And if you don't have the kids," declared a tall brunette, "you don't really have sufficient grounds to include your house in the settlement—sometimes, if the bastard is guilty enough, you can do that, you know."

"Look—to each his own," said Lori impatiently, already growing bored with the conversation. "All I'm saying is, if you need a good lawyer, I recommend Stillman."

As her reputation grew, and consequently her caseload, the contrast between her satisfaction in her business life and the lack of it in her private life became even more marked. Instead of being elated by each professional victory, she merely became more aware of her personal failure. Divorce comprised eighty-five percent of her practice. Why was she so incapable of dealing with the actualization of her own? Her marriage was over—had been for years. Her conversations with Ira, when they spoke at all, dealt only with the clients they now had in common. To those who were unaware, she and Ira were an enviable couple, both successful, both attractive, and in their social life, which was a necessary adjunct to their careers, they were viewed as an entity. As a result of the affairs they attended, the party invitations they accepted, new clients were continually added to the roster. For Marilyn, this was especially important, for although former clients continued to get married and divorced, they didn't do so daily, and replenishment was essential. She and Ira continued to go out together in public and fight or ignore each other at home. To the world, she was a very together, successful attorney. To her own family, she was merely Marilyn, the source of their heartaches.

Chapter 9

MARILYN PULLED INTO A PARKING LOT wondering what she was going to say in her group-therapy session. She was feeling anxious and even a bit excited about going. She couldn't explain her unhappiness to her own family; how could she explain it to seven total strangers? Once, when an acquaintance she hadn't seen for a while asked her what Ira was like, Marilyn thought for a moment and said, "Ira was born wearing glasses and hating finger food. He is good in math, fair in baseball and lousy at charades. He's the type of man who gives his wife a blender on her birthday. His favorite things are useful, and he has never fucked a prostitute, not because it's common, but because it's chancy and illegal in some states. He loves children, I.Q. tests, neat drawers, Bobby Fischer, lentil soup, the color beige and being on time. He's a wonderful provider, a family man, adores my parents, and I'm very lucky to have him—except I don't realize it."

The acquaintance, a girl with whom she had gone to college, gave her a nervous smile. "Oh," she said. "Well, uh, is he over six feet?" Marilyn grinned. "I don't know him *that* well," she had said, and, waving goodbye, left. Maybe she would tell that to the group. What she would absolutely *not* tell them was her attitude toward her children, Ira's children. Not even her *father* knew that.

Bedford Drive, south of Little Santa Monica in Beverly Hills, is an interesting street lined with medical buildings, boutiques of all sorts, pharmacies, a bank or two and parking lots. Along with Roxbury Drive, one block over, it houses the offices of three-quarters of the city's medical doctors. Between these two blocks, all the ills and infirmities, both physical and emotional, that afflict the citizens of Beverly Hills are diagnosed and treated.

On every floor of every building, behind discreet doors on which are small plaques inscribed with room numbers, and larger plaques just below on which are inscribed the name of the doctor or doctors who practice within, are waiting rooms filled with nervous people. The couches and chairs are soft and expensive, the magazines are neatly aligned and current, the nurses are soft-spoken and efficient. The doctors are, for the most part, Jewish, bespectacled, short, and forty-three.

No matter for what time the appointment was made, the minimum time spent in the waiting room, seated on furniture upholstered in understated fabric patterns, is rarely less than twenty-two minutes. The doctors are always busy, the waiting rooms always full, the schedule always approximately twenty-two minutes behind time. No patient is ever interrupted in the middle of a fascinating article in *Esquire*, *Time*, *Newsweek*, *Better Homes and Gardens*, *Vogue*, *Harper's Bazaar*, *Today's Health* or *House Beautiful*. There is plenty of time to finish whatever you start—indeed the whole magazine. Orthopedists can keep you waiting outside for about a week, but generally the longest waits, sometimes between forty and sixty minutes, are in the offices of gynecologists and obstetricians. The shortest are in the offices of ear, nose and throat men.

The one place where there is no wait at all, unless you arrive early, is the waiting room of a psychiatrist. Psychiatrists' offices are laid out in such a way as to ensure that one patient never sees another. In all other offices, you leave through the same door that you entered from. Psychiatrists have two doors. The walls are soundproof. The magazines are all copies of *National Geographic*. The table decorations are boxes of tissues. There are no visible receptionists or nurses and the door leading from the waiting room to the inner office is locked and opens only from the inside. One sits there all alone and wonders about whether or not one is being watched by unseen eyes taking notes.

At her introductory session alone with Dr. Leventhal, all Marilyn could seem to start off with was that she was very unhappy for reasons that no one could see, and that she herself found difficult to verbalize.

"Go on," the doctor told her.

She wanted to go on. She wanted to explain about her marriage and the inertia that gripped her around the ankles and kept her from freeing herself. She looked up at Dr. Leventhal. "I know your wife, Bobbi," she said. Dr. Leventhal nodded and waited.

"Uh, she's very nice. Tall. Nice and tall."

The doctor nodded again.

"So are you," said Marilyn.

He smiled. Marilyn sat and twisted the strap of her handbag. She opened it and took out a cigarette.

"Marilyn," said Dr. Leventhal. He pointed to an elegantly lettered sign beneath his diploma. It said, "For the sake of your health and the convenience of other patients, kindly refrain from smoking." Marilyn looked pointedly at the pipe Dr. Leventhal held clamped between his teeth.

"How come you don't refrain?" she asked.

"Tell me about your anger," answered Dr. Leventhal.

"What anger? I'm not angry. I just think that if *you* can smoke, you should extend the same privilege to your clients, I mean patients," said Marilyn, putting away the cigarettes. "But I'm not angry, I mean it's your office and if you don't want anyone *else* to smoke, that's up to you. It's your office, and you can do what you want. Personally, I don't think it's fair, but you're the boss here and, uh, you can do what you want. I just think I would find it easier to talk with a cigarette, that's all. I'm certainly not angry."

Dr. Leventhal leaned back and put the tips of his fingers together. "Go on," he said.

"If I'm angry at all, it's at my own ridiculous inability to divorce my husband, whom I've been wanting to divorce ever since we've been married. It's been eight years already, and I don't know, for some reason I just can't seem to do it. I'm very unhappy with him, and very worried about myself, because I can't get myself to do what I think will help myself. I don't know why, and it's making me nuts. What's wrong with me? The whole world's getting divorced, why can't I?"

Marilyn reached for a tissue on the table next to her. She didn't want to cry and was annoyed with her eyes for filling without permission. "Anyway," she went on, dabbing carefully at the corners, "that's why I'm here."

The doctor sat up, and placing a tissue flat on his desk, began to remove the burned tobacco from the bowl of his pipe with a small silver tool.

"That can be dangerous," said Marilyn.

"Do you feel you're in danger?" asked the doctor.

"Only if some of that tobacco is still burning," she answered.

"Are you afraid of fire?"

"Not particularly. My father once burned a whole building down."

"Tell me about your father," said Dr. Leventhal.

"He loves Ira, my husband," she said after a moment. "My whole *family* loves Ira. I'm the one who's supposed to love him, but they're the ones who *do*."

"How do you feel about that?"

Marilyn shrugged. The doctor waited. "Sometimes," she said softly, "I think the only reason I married him was because my father was so fond of him. He was so happy about it."

"Go on."

Marilyn frowned in annoyance. "There's nothing else to say. Ira is a perfect son-in-law, and my father loves him. That's all."

"Does that bother you?"

"I don't know. Maybe."

"Do you think your father loves Ira more than he loves you?"

Marilyn sat up and laughed. She wadded up the tissue and tossed it into the wastebasket under the table. "Are you kidding?" she asked, looking directly at Dr. Leventhal. "My father? Uh, uh, doctor, there's *nothing* my father loves better than me."

Dr. Leventhal cleared his throat and then glanced at his watch. "Our time is up," he said. "I am putting you into the Wednesday group. We meet from four to six each week here in my office." He stood up and walked Marilyn to the door and shook her hand. "I think we can help you," he said.

"Thank you, doctor. I surely hope so." She took out a cigarette and a red plastic disposable lighter from her purse, waiting at the door until the cigarette was lit. She turned and blew a cloud of smoke into the room. " 'Bye, Doc," she said, grinning. "I'll see you next week."

Dr. Leventhal had told Marilyn to come a bit early so that she could be seated on the chair to his right when the rest of the group trooped in. He told her that Arnold usually sat in that seat, but he wanted her there now because first-time patients in group therapy feel more secure being within reaching distance of the doctor. When she entered the room she saw that the chairs were arranged in a circle facing the armchair in which Dr. Leventhal reclined, his feet on a hassock. There were footstools in front of all the other chairs, too.

The wall behind the doctor was lined with shelves filled with books. On the wall opposite Marilyn were two windows with slightly open, thin, silver-blue blinds. One window was equipped with an air conditioner. The draperies were heavy, bluish and undrawn. There were two paintings behind Marilyn, both copies of Van Goghs. Next to Marilyn's chair was a small side table with the omnipresent box of tissues and the doctor's pipe, tobacco pouch, tools and a large pewter-colored ashtray with a raised wooden indentation for pipe banging. A "No Smoking" sign identical to the one in his consulting room was affixed to the wall between the two Van Goghs. There were softly shaded lamps in the corners and more small tables bearing large tissue boxes scattered around the room between the other chairs. The carpeting was gray-blue, thick, and semi-expensive.

Dr. Leventhal greeted Marilyn with a smile and directed her to her seat. He told her that the group would begin arriving in about five minutes.

"How was your week?" he asked her.

"So-so," she told him. "Does the group know about me?"

"I believe I informed them that you were joining us last Wednesday."

"Oh." Marilyn felt uncomfortable. "I really wish I could smoke," she said after a minute.

"Yes, I know that," said Dr. Leventhal.

"Uh, how's your wife?"

"Very well, thank you. Try to relax."

Marilyn stood her purse on her lap. He was very cool, this Dr. Leventhal. A soft chime announced the opening of the outer door, and a moment later a tall, middle-aged man entered the room. He smiled at and greeted the doctor gravely and looked at Marilyn.

"Fred," said Dr. Leventhal, "I'd like you to meet Marilyn. She's joining the group."

"Hello, Fred."

Fred nodded and walked to his chair, hitched up his pants and sat down. The chimes sounded again, one after another, and two more people walked in, a man and a woman.

"Bitsy, Joel, this is Marilyn."

"Hi."

"Welcome to the group, Marilyn," said Bitsy. Joel waved a hand, and both sat down after saying hello to Fred.

"She's sitting in Arnold's chair," said Joel.

"Yes, I know," answered the doctor. "Arnold will have to sit somewhere else today."

The chimes chimed, and a shortish, heavy-set man with a large curly brown head of hair and an equally large curly brown beard walked in, smiling broadly at the doctor.

"Hi, Doc," he said heartily and then, spying Marilyn, stopped dead in his tracks and stared at her.

"Who's this?" he demanded.

"Arnold, I'd like you to meet Marilyn."

"Hi, Arnold," said Marilyn guiltily. She wondered if she should offer him his chair back. Arnold was now frowning angrily at the doctor.

"Where am *I* supposed to sit?" he asked belligerently.

"Wherever you like," replied the doctor.

Arnold looked around, turning his head quickly from side to side and then sat down directly opposite Marilyn and glared at her.

"That's Judy's seat, Arnold," said Bitsy.

"Fuck Judy," answered Arnold.

The chimes sounded again, three times in a row, and Marilyn was introduced to Judy, Hank and Roberta. The three of them all headed for two chairs across the room. Hank and Roberta beat Judy out and she, looking depressed, reluctantly sank into the chair next to Marilyn.

Marilyn looked curiously around her. She was, she knew, sitting in a room with seven admittedly unhappy people. Seven neurotic people. Seven *other* unhappy neurotics. How could seven malfunctioning people, who were self-involved enough to realize that something was wrong with them and their lives, ever be able to help her?

Hank shifted slightly in his chair. "I think eight people is too many for group," he blurted. "I mean, there were sessions with just the seven of us where I never even got a chance to talk."

"I agree with Hank," said Bitsy.

Fred cleared his throat and said nothing.

"Fred," asked Dr. Leventhal, "did you want to say something?"

"No."

"Are you sure?"

"Well," he said softly, "I'm not sure that Marilyn will fit into this group."

"Why is that, Fred?" asked the doctor.

"Well, I'm not sure."

Marilyn glanced at the chair beside her. Judy was staring at the floor, swinging her foot.

"I think we should hear what Marilyn has to say. Why are you here, Marilyn?" asked Joel.

Marilyn looked over at Joel. He was a pleasant-looking fellow, about thirty-eight or thirty-nine, Marilyn thought. He was chewing gum and had his arms folded across his chest. He looked at her as though he had just challenged her to an arm wrestle.

"I'm here because the doctor thinks that this group can help me with my problems. I'm beginning to doubt that. You all seem very hostile and unwelcoming. Well, that's tough. It's Doctor Leventhal's party, and he can invite whomever he wants!" She couldn't stop talking. "If you don't like it, well, now you've all got one more problem. I don't even *care* if you like my being here or not. I'm here." It felt good, she thought, not having to worry about being polite.

Joel sighed and looked around knowingly, an old hand at group. "You didn't answer my question," he said, "and besides you're pretty hostile yourself."

"I'm only reacting to you people," retorted Marilyn.

Arnold, who hadn't taken his eyes off her, began to speak. "I think," he said pompously, "that Marilyn is a good talker, but not a very good listener. I agree with Fred, I don't think she'll fit in with this group."

Judy looked up. "Well, I say we should give her a chance, Arnold," she said softly. "You're not being very nice."

"Shut up, Judy," Arnold replied. "You're only angry because I'm in your chair."

"Well, isn't that why *you're* angry?" asked Marilyn. "Because I'm in yours?" She leaned back in satisfaction and smiled around the room.

Bitsy put her hands on the arms of her chair and leaned forward. *"You* are *very* hostile, and *very* aggressive. We are not interested in what you think. In group therapy we are only interested in what you *feel."*

"How do you feel about what Arnold said?" asked Roberta.

"About *what?"*

"About you being a good talker but a lousy listener."

Marilyn thought for a minute. "I don't think *any*thing about it. He's entitled to his opinion."

"Hah," said Roberta, "she's intellectualizing."

"Yes, you didn't say how you *felt,"* said Judy.

Bitsy leaned back in her chair. "I know that I would have been *crushed* if anyone said that to me."

Fred nodded in agreement.

"I can't stand pushy people," said Arnold to Marilyn, "and you are very aggressive and controlling."

Hank looked over at her. "And dishonest," he added, "emotionally dishonest. If you weren't, you would admit that Arnold's remark upset you."

"I don't give a shit about Arnold's remark," said Marilyn, "because I don't give a shit about Arnold. He doesn't know me. He started off this session by not liking me, you *all* started off by not liking me. So why should I care about what you say?" Marilyn was enjoying herself immensely. "You know what's wrong with you?" she went on. "You're all angry because I wasn't crushed. You wanted me to feel bad, and I don't and you hate that I don't. Shame on you." She smiled broadly at the group and turned to Dr. Leventhal. "I didn't realize how healthy I was until I came *here,"* she said.

"She's very defensive," Joel remarked to the group.

"Must we spend all our time on *her?"* whined Hank, looking at his watch. "She's not being open, and I've had a really rotten week that I want to deal with."

"I'd still like to know why Marilyn's here," said Bitsy.

Dr. Leventhal shifted his pipe to the other side of his mouth and nodded reassuringly to Marilyn. "Before we can help you," he said, "we've got to know with what."

Marilyn turned back to the group. "Well, in a nutshell, and because I don't want to waste the time of all you good people, my problem is my total inability to extricate myself from a marriage I never should have entered into and in which I've been miserable for eight years."

The group looked at her with interest.

"How long are you married?" asked Joel.

"Eight years."

"What is it that is making you so unhappy?"

Marilyn looked at Judy, who had stopped swinging her foot and was regarding her with interest.

"I think," she said slowly, "that I married Ira to please my father. He's . . . it's like he . . . I'm very close to my father, and Ira took care of me like my father does . . . sort of. I don't know." Marilyn looked down and began playing with the strap of her handbag. Her eyes had begun to fill, and she didn't want to gratify the group by crying. "I think," she continued, "that I want that kind of caring from my father and I thought I wanted it from Ira, but I don't. I don't need it from a husband. I need it from my father, and I've got it from my father, and Ira is a fingernail scraping on a blackboard to me. Everything about him irritates me. There's nothing really terrible about him . . . but I don't want to live with him and after eight years of not wanting to live with him, I'm still living with him." She blinked back the tears and looked up. "It's very difficult to explain," she said quietly. "I never should have married him." She wanted to add that she never should have had children, but caught herself in time. "And now even our careers are intertwined."

"Do you blame your father for your marriage?" asked Bitsy.

"No. I blame myself. My father only wanted the best for me, and he thought Ira was the best . . . and for any other girl he *would* be best, but not for me."

"So your father was *wrong*," persisted Bitsy.

"No, *I* was."

"But you did what your father wanted," she said.

"My whole family wanted it," said Marilyn, "I thought *I* wanted it, too."

"Don't you have a mind of your own?" asked Arnold.

"I guess not," said Marilyn, winding the strap of her handbag around her fingers. "I thought I loved him, too."

Fred looked up and cleared his throat. "I've been married for twenty-six years and have been unhappy for twenty-five."

"Well, I don't want that to happen to me," Marilyn said. "That's why I'm here." She looked up at Fred. "How long have you been in group?" she asked him.

"Three and a half years."

Marilyn stared at him. "Three and a half years?" she asked disbelievingly. Fred nodded. "Oh, shit," said Marilyn, and reached for a tissue.

Chapter 10

FOR SOME FEMALES the entry into womanhood is marked by their first menstrual period or first brassière purchase, whichever comes first. For Natalie Ritter, who got her period at ten and a half and her brassière a week later, those momentous milestones, of course, couldn't count. In no way can a ten-and-a-half-year-old be considered a woman, not even one with tits like Natalie's. How sad that the very same events that make most girls blush with exciting prospects made Natalie hunch over in dismay and hide her perky and precocious assets under voluminous white, Peter Pan–collared overblouses. Those very same endowments that were to give Dolly Parton her passport to superstardom gave Natalie round shoulders and a lifelong tendency toward self-consciousness, self-effacement and timid, low-eyed retreat to dark corners and solitary occupations.

While other little girls played jump rope, Natalie was forced into coloring, jacks, knitting, embroidery, and other similar activities that didn't cause her tits to bounce and her peers to giggle. Not having a character strong enough to turn this un-timely developmental tragedy into a glorious, blossoming, envy-evoking triumph, she subsided into shy regression and silent invisibility.

By the time it became desirable to have a frontage as formidable as Natalie's, the habit of slouching and hiding away and sitting in corners with arms folded across her chest, or sitting in corners knitting, was so ingrained and Natalie so far out of the world of her peers, that it no longer made a difference. She had become an echo, a person with no opinions or originality, a big-busted, myopic hooker of rugs and watcher of children's cartoons. She had returned to the time when she was flat and happy and could run and hop without the neighborhood kids hooting and pointing. Natalie wanted to be a third-grade teacher, so that she could spend time with children her own age. But unfortunately, because of an inability to master high school math or to pass physical education (due entirely to the trauma incurred at the thought of donning a supportless tank-type bathing suit in a required-for-graduation swim class), Natalie was not even accepted into junior college, much less an educational facility that offered a teaching credential. What she *had* managed to do was reach the age of eighteen without once getting felt up—no mean feat in 1968.

Helen was beside herself. Forced to gaze with horrified eyes at the unmistakable stain on the crotch of her ten-and-a-half-year-old daughter's underpants, Helen heaved a grim sigh and, because it was customary, smacked Natalie first across one cheek and then across the other. They then fell weeping into one another's arms. Helen kissed the reddened cheeks of her hysterical child-woman and tried to explain her action.

"No, no," she soothed. "You aren't bad. I didn't hit you because you're bad. I hit you to make the blood rush to your cheeks. It's the custom, darling, when a girl becomes a woman. You'll do it to your own daughter too, someday."

"No, I won't," hiccoughed Natalie.

Helen taught her how to deal with sanitary pads and belts and told her not to let anyone touch her and not to hug her uncles or boy cousins or people of the male persuasion.

"Can I hug Daddy?"

"Of course, Daddy," said Helen, "but no one else."

To her regret, Natalie obeyed only too well. She went to her sophomore dance with her cousin Matthew; her junior hop with her cousin Theo; and her senior prom with a blind date arranged by Marilyn—and neither hugged nor was hugged by any of them. The blind date later vented his rage upon Marilyn and asked what he had ever done to her to deserve being fixed up with her sister, Quasimodo.

After graduation, Natalie spent a week in fruitless job-hunting. She filled out applications and dutifully made the rounds of employment agencies. The only call back she received was from an agency specializing in domestic placements. She was offered a position as governess in a motherless home. "Light housekeeping, must drive. Uniforms supplied. European preferred. Beverly Hills home." Fortunately, it was Helen who took the call and politely refused the job. She angrily informed Natalie that she had brought down an embarrassment upon the family. "Have you gone out of your mind?" she demanded. "What do you mean taking a job as a maid?"

"I said 'governess,' " muttered Natalie sullenly.

Marilyn, who was working on a campaign poster, looked up from Robert F. Kennedy's smiling face and stared at her sister. "You applied for a job as a *maid?*" she asked disbelievingly.

"It said 'governess,' " repeated Natalie, almost in tears.

"If you would read something besides stupid gothic romances, you'd realize that in Beverly Hills in 1968 'governess' *means* maid."

Marilyn looked at her sister curiously. "Where's your head at?" she asked gently. "Where's your head at, you silly throwback? Come here, do you want to work with me on the campaign?"

Natalie shook her head.

"Why not?" asked Marilyn. "It's certainly better than light housekeeping. We *need* volunteers."

Natalie, who was the type of person who would apologize to

a total stranger for being so clumsy as to drop her glasses right under where he wanted to put his foot, was very brave in the bosom of her own family.

"Get lost," she screamed and ran upstairs.

Marilyn shrugged and went back to her poster. Helen pressed her lips together and called her husband at his office.

"Lenny, you have to do something about a job for Natalie. That child isn't ready for the world yet."

"What kind of a job?"

"A nice job."

"Helen, I'm very busy. Natalie types, yes or no?"

"Yes."

"Okay."

"So it's done?"

"So it's done."

Natalie sat upstairs in her room listening to the Beatles and dreaming of miracles. The fantasy was always the same. In it she was always blonde and blue-eyed, beautiful, brilliant, irresistible. In the fantasy, her name was Brooke. She had been unwillingly married off at the age of eighteen to Sean, who was as perfect in every way as Brooke, except smarter; but only a little. They were both told by their millionaire guardian, who had arranged the wedding, that they must remain married for a year and that the marriage must be consummated. If these conditions were met, Brooke and Sean would receive at the end of that year a million dollars apiece. Naturally, if so desired, they could remain together forever. Naturally, they both desired. The fantasy varied only in the details of Brooke's defloration, which occurred just before the year was up because, despite extraordinary willpower and mutual resentment over the forced marriage, both were enormously, extraordinarily attracted to each other. Their frenzied, long-awaited mating was, of course, ecstatic. The sex was perfect, and after the first time, neither could keep hands off the other. In time, Brooke and Sean had three sets of twins. All the girls were identical to the mother, all the boys to the father.

This fantasy gave Natalie great pleasure. She used it during times of turmoil (like now) and to get to sleep at night. She used it when she felt "sexy," which was very often. Natalie, although sexually inexperienced, was no stranger to desire. She was, as Marilyn often told her, to her vague irritation and Helen's extreme annoyance, "of normal intelligence, but limited. What it is, Natalie, is you have no frame of reference." But what Marilyn overlooked and Helen knew for a fact was that Natalie was a very basic and primitive organism. Although not particularly sensitive emotionally, she reacted physically and functioned perfectly. She ate when she was hungry and never when she wasn't. She slept when she was tired. Her bowels were regular and so were her periods. She did not have a sweet tooth and maintained a constant weight. Whenever illness had struck the Ritter household, Natalie was merely tapped and, without exception, always had the mildest case of whatever bug was flying around.

Her desire for sex was strong, and during the week or so in her cycle when conception was possible, her urge was strongest of all. It was as if she went into heat, like a cat. She had no man, but she had a fantasy. Since that's the way it was, Natalie made the best of it. Since she was healthy and had little imagination, Natalie made the best of everything, including what many another eighteen-year-old standing in her shoes might consider a valid reason for suicide. Once Marilyn, who was very curious about the internal workings of her sister because she had never been able to understand her, asked Natalie if she were happy and if so, how come? To the first question, Natalie answered yes. To the second, she answered "Why not?"

"Don't you ever get depressed?"

"Not much."

"You mean you can control whether or not you get depressed?" Marilyn asked, intensely curious.

Natalie, unused to internal examination, became impatient. "I don't know," she snapped. "What's the use in getting depressed? What difference would it make?"

"Logic has no effect on depression," said Marilyn.

Natalie was now cross. "Can I help it if I don't get depressed?" she retorted. "What do you want from me?"

"But how do you feel when you've had a disappointment, or a rejection, or a loss?" persisted Marilyn. "You've got to feel *some*thing."

Natalie shrugged her shoulders. "I say to myself, 'If that's the way it is, then that's the way it is.'" She took out a half-finished sweater and began to knit.

Marilyn stared at her sister, bent low over her knitting. She looked at her silently for about two minutes until Natalie lifted her eyes in annoyance. "What's with you?" she asked. Marilyn shook her head and walked away. Why, she wondered, if Natalie was so basic, so elementary, so *simple*, why then was she, Marilyn, so very intrigued and absolutely incapable of empathetic identification?

It wasn't until years later that she realized that Natalie was also very powerful. No one ever really challenged Natalie. So intent was the family on not hurting Natalie's feelings or upsetting her that they all seemed to tiptoe around her and make very few demands. Her achievements were minor, yet a great fuss was made over the slightest of them. When she cooked a meal or planted azaleas or finished a pullover, the reaction was spectacular. Helen all but threw a party if Natalie so much as bought a pair of shoes. She was never asked to do anything that might make her "nervous."

By the time Natalie was twenty-five, most of her friends were married. Her social life consisted of going to dinner with her parents and an occasional cousin's club meeting. She absolutely refused to attend singles dances or go away for weekends, since she had never been successful at any of those activities. Occasionally, she was "fixed up" by one of her sisters, or other family members and friends. The one desire of which she was aware was to get married and have children. That was all she really wanted. Sometimes she would awaken at night, terrified that it would never happen. She would lie in bed, rigid with fear, and when she was finally able to move, would run, panicked, to her mother's room. Together, she and her mother would go quietly into the kitchen, where over a cup of tea Natalie would sob out her dread. She would put her head in Helen's lap, and Helen would hold her and rock her and reassure her. After a while, comforted, she would return to bed, awaken her fantasy and fall asleep.

Her mother had assured her that all would be well, and Natalie believed her mother. Helen, not so lucky, would remain sleepless and anguished, appalled at the injustice that would give Marilyn and Phyllis whatever pleased them and Natalie, who wanted so little, nothing at all. She had even been happy for her sisters. When Marilyn married Ira, Natalie spent hours arranging her trousseau and packing her bags for her honeymoon. For Phyllis, who was married in a cornfield and wrote her own vows, Natalie labored lovingly with patterns and pins, staying up to all hours to make her wedding dress.

Helen would have sold her eyes for Natalie's dreams. She had tried almost everything else. What was inconceivable to her was the callousness of Phyllis and Marilyn toward their own sister, who would do anything at all for them, and already had.

"Phyllis," Helen begged over the phone, don't you know *any*body for Natalie? Doesn't Neil? Natalie worked for *two weeks* making your wedding dress."

"Mother," Phyllis replied, "haven't you considered the possibility that this is Natalie's karma? If she is meant to marry, she will, and if she isn't, she won't, and there's nothing anybody can do about it."

"What is this karma?"

"Well, I guess you can say it's destiny. It was decided by her former life."

"Are you crazy?" demanded Helen.

"That's relative," replied Phyllis, and Helen hung up on her in disgust.

Even Marilyn had been appealed to and had refused. "I've tried to help her, God knows," she had said. "I've gotten her dates. I've given her information on singles clubs; I sent away for the Club Méditerranée brochure; I bought her some decent clothes, which she never even *wore*; I told her to take some courses and go square dancing. I've done everything I know to do with the exception of putting an ad in the paper—and if I thought it would move her, I'd even have done *that*. She hasn't made the slightest effort to do one thing on her own. Well, I've had it. I refuse to lift a finger for any girl, even Natalie, who refuses to lift a finger for herself. I'm bored and disgusted with her. She's like one of your damn plants. All she does is react to stimuli. She leaves no footprints. If you ask me, she needs a good shrink."

"All I'm asking is for you to fix her up," said Helen.

"Sorry, I have had it with her."

In desperation, Helen called Celia, who arranged a date for Natalie with the son of one of Jack's longtime patients. His name was Howard. He was thirty-two years old, with dandruff and an acne-scarred face. Howard was a Ford salesman in Van Nuys, and on their first date he took Natalie to Bob's Big Boy for dinner and then to a free concert in the park. Natalie was home at 11:45 and told Helen that she had a nice time. On their second date, Howard took her for dinner at Ah Fong's and then back to his apartment, which was over his parents' garage. After a short discussion about monosodium glutamate and Ford Torinos versus Ford Country Squires, Howard pulled her onto the couch and forced his tongue into her mouth. Natalie let him because she thought if she didn't he wouldn't ask her out again, and also because the message in her fortune cookie had said, "Friendship flourishes in a climate of appreciation." After about four minutes of re-living shrimp in lobster sauce, Natalie gently pushed Howard away.

"What's the matter?" Howard asked, breathless.

"Oh, nothing," said Natalie, gulping air. "I have to get up early for work tomorrow."

"You work for your father," Howard panted, pulling her back into his arms. "He won't mind if you're a few minutes late."

With no ready argument to counter his logic, Natalie leaned into his lips. Encouraged, Howard put his hand on her right breast and, delighted by what he found under his palm, whispered, "You're a terrific girl, Natalie." As he kneaded her breast, Natalie began to have a good time. She sneaked a peek at Howard's lap and grew almost faint with excitement at the sight of his lumpy crotch. "Touch it," Howard gasped, frantically unzipping his fly. Impatiently he pushed her hand toward his now-exposed penis and, as her fingers closed around him, he shuddered uncontrollably and came all over her hand.

"Ah, shit," Howard muttered.

Still holding him, Natalie stared down at her hand. Stickily, she released him and then slowly rose and walked to the bathroom. When she emerged, Howard was cleaned, zipped and standing at the door with his hands in his pockets, whistling silently.

"Well," he said, "you're a terrific girl, Natalie."

"Thank you, Howard," she replied and on the way home told him that if he wanted, she would knit him a cardigan.

"What do I need a cardigan for?" he asked.

When they reached her house, Natalie invited him in for a cup of coffee.

"Nah," said Howard. "Coffee keeps me up. You want to go out on Friday?"

"I'd love to," Natalie said, primly.

"Okay," said Howard, pecking her on the lips. "I'll call you Thursday night. You're some terrific girl, Natalie—wow— what happened to me tonight never happens, you know? Far out."

That night Natalie fell into a deep sleep, happy and hopeful. On Thursday night, Howard didn't call, and Natalie never saw him again. On Friday, instead of sex with Howard, Natalie had dinner with her parents, her grandmother, Marilyn and Ira, Phyllis and Neil, just as she had done every Friday night for years. During dessert Ira remarked that she seemed a bit more subdued than usual and asked her what was wrong. Natalie was silent for a moment, and then looked over at Ira and smiled. "Oh, it's nothing," she said. "I suppose I'm a bit blue because I just broke off with my boyfriend."

Chapter

11

AMONG MARILYN'S MORE EXCITING CASES was this new
one she was handling, that of Beryl Sinclair, superstar, the only
female entertainer included in the list of international box-
office greats, along with Charles Bronson, Clint Eastwood,
Robert Redford, Paul Newman and the late John Wayne, to
name a few. What made it interesting was that Beryl was not
petitioning for a dissolution of her marriage—she had never
been married to Chuck Dennis. But she *had* been living with
him for over five years, and since the Marvin case, the break-up
of a live-in arrangement had become more complicated than
an ordinary, run-of-the-mill, legal divorcement. Especially when
millions of dollars in community property was involved. Beryl
had already been through six attorneys by the time she got to
Marilyn, and Marilyn was very grateful to Beryl Sinclair for
providing her with a work situation in which she could immerse
herself, a place to put her head and bury her personal unhappiness.

Chuck Dennis was a fashion designer, who had started by, of
all things, doing custom paint jobs on automobiles. From there,
with absolutely no formal instruction whatsoever, he graduated
into fashion design, and Beryl met him on the set of a film in

which she was starring and he was doing the costumes. He created a wardrobe for her which ingeniously disguised her many physical imperfections and gave her a body where once there was none. Within six months they were living together.

During the more than five years of their togetherness, Beryl the star gleamed as brightly as ever, if not more so, and Chuck, like the moon, glowed in her reflected light and eventually even picked up some starshine of his own. An obviously ambitious man, he sniffed out opportunity and pounced on it, the way a cat, claws extended and eyes glued in total concentration, leaps in a twinkling on a teasing ball of twine. He now had expanded his business and gone commercial with a fashion boutique on Rodeo Drive in Beverly Hills, which sold his designs and custom-created outfits for ladies who yearned to be original and could afford to pay for it. Occasionally he would even custom-paint a car for many of the new friends he had suddenly acquired since his association with Beryl. The two of them had a stable of cars, and their paisley-painted Rolls-Royce was a familiar sight on the highways and byways of Beverly Hills, Bel Air and Malibu. Because he visualized himself as an artistic genius with an infallible instinct in every area of creativity, and because Beryl just happened to have the same opinion of herself, they collaborated on several films together—he believing that the films grossed millions because of the innate class and brilliance of Chuck Dennis; she absolutely positive that the reason for the enormous grosses was due to the fact that in all of them Beryl Sinclair was the star. From just such arrogance do empires collapse, and had there been a Richter scale to measure such things, the magnitude of their disaster would have sent the needle right off the page. The gleeful whisperings began.

"Of course it couldn't last. I always said that the reason they lived in such big houses was because they needed three floors for their egos alone."

"It was only a matter of time. I mean, what the hell was he? Just some asshole painter. Some glorified Earl Scheib."

"Once he made it big, he was able to relax and take a good

look at her, and my dear, it's very obvious that she didn't get where she is on her looks."

"He paid heavily for his success, though. He had to fuck her, and what fun could *that* have been?"

"She was always too good for that slimy, ass-kissing, parasitic bastard. I'm surprised she kept him for as long as she did."

"You'd think she could get *any*body. If Beryl can't pick and choose, then who can? Why would a talent like that end up with such a nothing creep?"

And yet, when Marilyn saw her for the first time, she didn't even recognize her, so different was the person from the image. Beryl's secretary had called, asking if Marilyn would come out to the Broad Beach Compound so that Ms. Sinclair could speak with her and determine if Ms. Stillman was the right attorney to represent her.

"Sorry," said Marilyn indignantly, "I don't audition."

"Oh, of course not. Please don't misunderstand, but surely you're aware of the difficulties involved for a celebrity like Ms. Sinclair to leave her home, especially at this time," explained the secretary.

"Certainly I do. But the fact remains that although I may confer with Ms. Sinclair in her home *after* I have agreed to accept her as my client, *this* is where I do my business."

"Ms. Stillman, her doctor is a very busy man, yet he is considerate enough to treat Ms. Sinclair at home."

Marilyn sighed, annoyed. "Look," she said, "I don't make house calls. If you wish to make an appointment, I'll reconnect you with my secretary."

She pressed a button on her phone and as soon as she heard Ginger's voice, hung up. Marilyn sat for a moment and stared at the phone. "I have enough misery," she said to herself. "I don't need any more." Then she picked up a client's will and estate plan and began to read. She worked steadily for two hours, then pushed her chair back, stretched and glanced at her watch. "Ginger," she said into her telephone, "get me my father."

Natalie answered, they chatted for several minutes and then

Natalie informed Marilyn that their father was on the phone with a supplier who was six weeks late in his deliveries.

"Did they have a contract? A signed agreement of some sort specifying the dates of delivery?"

"I don't know."

"Natalie, you're Papa's secretary," said Marilyn impatiently. "If there was some sort of document, you must have typed it."

Natalie was silent for a moment and Marilyn could almost hear her thinking. "I don't remember," she said at last and apologized.

Marilyn put down the receiver and looked up as the door opened and Ginger walked into the room.

"She's here," gasped Ginger, so excited that her voice squeaked.

"Who's here? Beryl Sinclair?"

"Yes!" yelped Ginger.

"You didn't knock," admonished Marilyn.

"Oh—sorry."

"Very understandable, under the circumstances. What does she look like? Never mind. I'll see for myself. Give me a couple of minutes, Ginger."

Quickly Marilyn stood up and hurried into the bathroom. She ran a comb through her hair and applied fresh lipstick. Putting her face close to the mirror, she peered at herself, then straightened up, smoothed her clothes and returned to the office. No one could fault her on her wardrobe, not even Beryl Sinclair. Marilyn spent a fortune on clothes, and even the ratty stuff she threw on at home all had designer labels. Maybe even a few Chuck Dennis labels. Her intercom buzzed.

"Okay?" whispered Ginger.

"Okay," Marilyn replied and remained standing behind her desk as Ginger opened the office door and ushered Beryl Sinclair in. Again she forgot to knock, thought Marilyn, amused.

She walked toward her prospective new client and shook her hand. Then, motioning Beryl to a chair, she walked back behind her desk to her own.

"So you're the lady lawyer," observed Beryl. "Wanna know how I got to you?"

"As a matter of fact I would," replied Marilyn, leaning back and smiling. She already liked Beryl Sinclair, who, almost engulfed in the coffee-colored leather armchair, looked for all the world like Kermit the Frog—thin, small and boneless. Her eyes were almost yellow, large and gleaming, and the sense of energy she exuded seemed to crackle around the room. This must be what is known as "star quality," thought Marilyn. That this tiny, electric thing could also sing, dance and act seemed rather beside the point compared to the impact she made on a room.

"Lori Westfield told me about you."

"Oh, yes. It was good of her to recommend me."

"Yeah, well, I saw several lawyers before I got to you." Beryl looked around the room, her darting eyes missing nothing. "You got any diet soda?" she asked. Before Marilyn could reply, Beryl was out of her chair and already poking her head into the small refrigerator behind the bar in the corner of Marilyn's office.

"Not that I need to diet," she said, popping the lid and returning to her chair. "I just like it. What time is it? Three-thirty? At four we'll have a *real* drink." Then she put the can to her lips, tilted her head back and took a long swallow.

"Anyway," continued Beryl, "those other lawyers must have seen me coming. They jacked up their fees so high they needed oxygen just to tell me. Outrageous." She took another pull on her can of soda and looked at Marilyn over the rim.

"What do *you* charge?" she asked warily.

"Fifty dollars more per hour than anyone else," replied Marilyn, and both of them burst out laughing.

"Look—I'll pay you what you want if you ask a fair price," said Beryl, suddenly serious. "Just keep in mind the publicity value of this case. The hype alone that you get out of it will keep you in"—and here she eyed Marilyn's dress—"Missonis forever."

"Fair enough," grinned Marilyn. "Now—what can I do for you?"

"Get Chuck Dennis out of my life without my having to give him any more than he's already gotten—and that's considerable, believe me. I never should have become involved with him in the first place."

"Why did you?" asked Marilyn curiously.

"The truth?"

Marilyn nodded.

"Of all the men who came around after my second divorce, Chuck was the only one who could humble me."

Marilyn regarded her for a moment. "And now?" she asked.

"Now he's stepped over the line. He stopped treating me like a person and started treating me like dirt. He forgot that I'm not merely his roommate, I'm also Beryl Sinclair."

"I see," murmured Marilyn.

"I warned him—I warned him many times." Beryl looked up from her perusal of the can of Tab. "A terminal case of getting too big for his britches," she said quietly. "I may have been born Bernice Schnitzer, but I'm not Bernice Schnitzer anymore. I'm Beryl Sinclair: I've worked too hard and flown too high to be treated like a dishtowel by some guy who came to me with a can of spray paint in one hand and a spool of thread in the other."

"I'll need a financial record," said Marilyn, "and your income-tax returns for the past, oh, eight years—for starters anyway. Who's your business manager and does Chuck have an attorney?"

"Stanley Greenspan and Alan Jaffe, respectively."

"If you ever want to dump Greenspan, call me," said Marilyn with a thin smile. "I'm an expert on business managers." She began to make several notes on a yellow legal pad on her desk. "Have we got all the personal information? Addresses, phone numbers, etcetera?"

"Yes. Your secretary is very efficient."

"Now, Beryl, your job is to call Greenspan, tell him that I'm representing you and inform him that he is to supply me with whatever records and information I require. Because they won't expect it, I think we should get a set one interrogatory to Chuck right away, and we'll try to take his deposition as quickly as possible. We will, of course, have to have an in-depth conversation first, Beryl. How's your schedule?"

"I leave for Guaymas day after tomorrow," said Beryl. "I'm filming."

Marilyn shook her head. "For how long?"

"Ten weeks, with luck; then a much-deserved vacation."

"But—"

"Look, Ms. Stillman—Marilyn—I need this finished by the time I get back. So let's have our in-depth conversation tomorrow at my house here in town. I'm giving myself a small farewell-to-everything party and I want you to come. Party is at seven-thirty—dinner, drinks, don't overdress. You be at my house at five with your law stuff. Does that give us enough time?"

"But—" sputtered Marilyn, half standing.

"Good, it's a wrap. *À demain*, Marilyn, I'll see you tomorrow, your secretary has my address, *ciao, mi hija*."

And before Marilyn could recover, she was gone. Marilyn sank back into her chair feeling as if she'd just come off a roller coaster. No wonder Bernice Schnitzer had made it. She straightened her desk, picked up her bag and looked around the room. It had always been a haven, but suddenly it seemed very empty and very silent.

Beryl's house was high in the hills above Benedict Canyon and could not be seen from the road. All that was visible, and that hardly, was a narrow, winding path with a mailbox off to the side. But tonight, thought Marilyn, sitting entranced before a closed-circuit television monitor, even Helen Keller would have known that something was going on. Beryl had an elaborate security system—cameras hidden in trees, placed discreetly in the entrance hall and corridors throughout the huge, sprawling Tudor house. With the flick of a switch, one could observe the doings both inside the mansion and outside as well.

Marilyn, her attaché case bulging with the copious notes she had been taking for the past two hours, now sat relaxing, her eyes glued to one of the several television screens before her, watching the guests arrive. Down below, the valet service stopped the incoming cars and the beautiful people emerged, to be escorted into a waiting Cadillac limousine. When the limo was filled, a valet with a walkie-talkie called upstairs to his similarly equipped counterpart to ensure clear passage and check that no other limo was on its return trip down the one-lane road. When the all-clear was given, the valet signaled to the limo driver and the Cadillac started its slow ascent to the house. The guests' own cars would be parked by one of the small army of uniformed valets and then the next Mercedes, or Ferrari, or Rolls or Caddy would pull up. The cars kept arriving, the limos traveling up and down the road kept filling and disgorging happy party-goers, and Marilyn, recalling that Beryl had told her this was a *small* party, wondered in awe what one of Beryl's *large* parties must be like.

The huge patio was tented, and the twenty or more round tables, which seated ten, waited beclothed and beflowered for their occupants. A string quartet with piano played gaily in the main living room, waiters walked through the crush of guests carrying trays laden with goodies. There was a bar in each of the four party rooms, with the exception of the buffet area, where a large table was being set up, decorated with plates at one end, followed by endless chafing dishes, salvers and hot plates, mounds of fruits, salads, pâtés, breads, cheeses and sauces. Behind each large silver chafing dish stood a uniformed member of the catering crew—erect, earnest, eager to serve any guest wishing to partake of the poached salmon, Polynesian chicken, teriyaki beef, crisp Chinese vegetables, rice, shrimp curry—and, for those on the Scarsdale diet, platters of white-meat turkey, raw cut-up vegetables, grapefruit sections.

Next to this table and slightly to the side was another table, equally large, groaning under every variety of sweet and pastry imaginable: *pots de crème,* hot and cold mousses, powdered-sugared custard and fruit-filled crepes, chocolate-covered straw-berries the size of plums. Bowls of whipped cream, ice-cream toppings, petit fours and after-dinner mints. The wine, coffee, espresso and tea would be served at the dinner tables. Flowers were everywhere—on the piano, in the powder rooms, on the stairs, lining the paths and around the enormous swimming pool, in which floated gardenias on lily pads, a small, lit candle blinking in the center of each pad.

Marilyn, who was not exactly a stranger to Hollywood parties, had never seen anything like it, not even in the movies. Stroll-ing violinists strolled among the laughing, talking, drinking, chewing guests, taking requests and often having great diffi-culty in finding space enough to draw the bow over the strings of their instruments without poking someone in the eye.

Marilyn spied Beryl, seeming to be everywhere at once, kiss-ing, hugging, saying a few words to the arriving guests, walking among them, sliding into this cluster of people and that, bestow-ing a pat, a smile, a wave as she danced among them. Beryl must be, thought Marilyn, the most charming person in the world. And bright, and disciplined, and talented. She was, mused Marilyn enviously, very together, very much in control of her life. Thank God she wasn't beautiful.

As she walked downstairs, Marilyn knew *she* was beautiful—glamorous, faultlessly dressed and groomed. She had had her hair done by Sassoon, gotten a facial at Aida Thibiant's and a manicure and pedicure at Jessica's nail clinic. Her dress was one of Bob Mackie's more subdued creations, stunning, cling-ing, black and beautifully cut. Her shoes, from the Right Bank Shoe Company, were designed by Maud Frizon and cost two hundred dollars. She felt free, excited, happy to be unescorted by Ira, who weighed her down and stuck to her side at every party they attended together, clinging like a little piece of toilet tissue to the heel of a shoe, annoying, embarrassing, impossible to get rid of.

"Marilyn," cried Beryl, "stay right where you are."

Marilyn paused, her left foot on one step, her right foot on the step below. She looked inquiringly down at Beryl.

"Everybody," continued Beryl, "this is my new lawyer, the Abraham Lincoln of my life who will emancipate me, set me free. Say hello to Marilyn Stillman."

Blushing and somewhat uncomfortable, Marilyn nodded, a strained smile on her face, accepting as graciously as she could the "hellos" and the short burst of applause that followed Beryl's introduction.

"I just made you a career," Beryl whispered as Marilyn reached the bottom of the staircase. "Don't forget that when you add up my bill."

Marilyn noticed that Beryl was quite serious, not a smile in her eyes or on her lips. "I'm going to save you three million dollars," she whispered back, "remember that when you sign my check."

The string quartet and piano had now been joined by a clarinet, sax, trumpet, and bongo drummer, and the dancing began. In the den, down two stone steps from the musicians, activity of another sort was in progress. Joints, propped like ordinary cigarettes, stood in small Baccarat crystal glasses or lay in inlaid, enameled boxes, there for the taking, to be smoked down to the eighth of an inch, held in solid gold, often gem-encrusted roach-holders, which were whipped out of handbags and pockets. Small containers and pillboxes filled with coke, either the personal possession of a guest or provided by the thoughtful hostess, were also in evidence. Tiny silver spoons, almost small enough to be swallowed, were dipped into the precious powder and held beneath first one nostril, then the other and inhaled. The smokers and the sniffers, as well as those doing both, filled the den, sitting on the floor when no other place was available. Marilyn had to step over them when she walked into the room.

"Marilyn," called a familiar voice.

Marilyn looked around, then down, into the smiling face of Lori Westfield. "Care for a snort?"

"Later," said Marilyn, "right now I want a drink." She carefully made her way to the bar and ordered a vodka and tonic.

"He's here," said a voice behind her, and Beryl slid onto a stool.

"Who's here?" asked Marilyn.

"Chuck," she answered morosely, "and he's brought a hooker, at least I think she is."

Marilyn, looking in the direction indicated, saw a thin, attractive man in his middle thirties, of medium height and sporting a lush, Groucho Marx mustache. Beside him, smoking what appeared to Marilyn to be a pink cigarette, stood a striking redhead dressed completely in silver. She looked as though she were covered in skin-tight tinsel. Her body, fully outlined, was magnificent. It was obvious that she wore no underwear. Even in this milieu of extraordinary-looking people dressed in extravagant costumes, the redhead stood out. Marilyn stared, and when she looked back, Beryl was gone—off again.

With an appraising eye, Marilyn scanned the room, estimating that there were millions of dollars' worth of talent here. Aside from writers, producers, directors and network executives, all the performers in town had turned out. Famous faces were all over the place, Barbra Streisand, Sammy Davis, Carol Burnett, Burt Reynolds, Sally Field, Cher, Shirley MacLaine, Mel Brooks and Anne Bancroft, Ann-Margret, George Burns, even Johnny Carson, who never went anywhere, was here. Marilyn figured that if a bomb were dropped on Beryl Sinclair's house, the entire film, television and music industries would grind to a shuddering halt and be sucked into oblivion.

Several of Ira's clients had approached her, spoken a few words and drifted away. She sipped her drink feeling, even in the midst of this vast and glittering group, somehow isolated and apart. But that was okay. Marilyn was content merely to observe. She had just finished her drink and was about to light a cigarette when Lori Westfield walked over.

"They're serving the food," she announced. "Come and eat with us."

"I will, thank you," said Marilyn. She stood up and followed the crowd to the end of the food line. Lori informed Marilyn that she had already gotten her meal and would meet her at the table.

"Fine," said Marilyn. "Save me a seat."

"Isn't that the name of a book?" asked Lori.

"Yes," replied Marilyn, "read it. You'll love it. It's a wonderful book."

The line moved quickly, and Marilyn gingerly carried her plate, filled to overflowing, onto the patio.

By midnight, many of the guests had departed. Beverly Hills is an early town. Marilyn wandered through the emptying rooms admiring the art works and opulent furnishings. She made her way back to the now-deserted patio and sat down at a table to finish her brandy and smoke a last cigarette. The sound of laughter and soft-voiced conversation startled her, and she turned toward the source of it in surprise. There in the corner, half-hidden by the overhanging branches of a magnolia tree, was a table with four people sitting around it.

Marilyn recognized Chuck Dennis, the girl in silver and two other people who looked familiar, but whom she couldn't place. As she watched, Chuck suddenly leaned over and vomited onto the flagstone-paved patio. The man beside him frantically pulled his legs away and cursed angrily as Chuck obliged with an encore. Chuck lifted his head weakly, only to double up again immediately with a third attack of nausea, but this time from his rear end came a barrage of flatulence so ferocious that Marilyn, all the way across the patio, actually jumped. The two people next to Chuck and the silver lady sat like statues, stunned and immobilized. The redhead smiled, and Marilyn, over the sound of Chuck's unhappy plumbing, heard her say clearly, "The drums are beating out a message of love." Despite herself, Marilyn smiled. Galvanized, the man leaped from his chair, yanked up his flabbergasted wife, stepped carefully around the mess on the floor and stalked off in furious disgust.

The redhead and Chuck, now recovered, sat quietly, he wiping the perspiration from his face and she smiling in amusement and smoking a pink cigarette.

Marilyn looked in wonder at the lights of Los Angeles winking below. She looked at the huge house, the lush surroundings. Then she looked back at the table and the mess on the floor. "Even here," she mused, "there's no difference at all. That kind of human and primitive thing is not supposed to happen to people who live like this."

Suddenly weary, Marilyn drained her glass. She ached to get away from here and back to her own unhappy and ordinary, but somehow less soiled life. She was just about to leave when Chuck and his date rose from their seats.

"I'm absolutely humiliated," she heard him say. "How can I face anyone? This will be all over town by tomorrow."

"Come on, Chuck," the redhead replied. "It really coulda been worse."

"How could it have been worse?" protested Chuck. "I farted all *over* the place!"

And as they passed her table, Marilyn heard the redhead say with a grin, "Well, for one, Chuckles, you could of shit."

"The prosecution rests," whispered Marilyn, and she picked up her handbag, got her attaché case, wished Beryl good luck on her new film, told her to stay in touch and left.

Chapter 12

BY THE FOURTH SESSION of group, Marilyn felt she was becoming one of them. They accepted her now, and although she was still "intellectualizing," they seemed to like her better. One time after Marilyn told Judy that she was "perpetuating her own loneliness," Joel told Marilyn that she had shown "good insight." When by her seventh session, she finally cried while doing a monologue on her mother, Hank leaned over, handed her a tissue and said, "Thank you for sharing with us, Marilyn." She was, she discovered, "getting in touch with her anger, feeling the rhythm of her pain instead of analyzing it" (whatever that meant) and saying things like, "I feel that I understand where you're coming from." She was invited to go along with them for after-session coffee, and Bitsy had taken to calling her at home.

The group, however, wasn't helping her to divorce Ira. On the contrary, when Arnold commented that in his opinion, "People usually do what they *really want* to do and don't do what they *really don't want* to do," all the group agreed.

"In my opinion," said Arnold, "if you *really* wanted to divorce Ira, you would. The fact that you haven't indicates to me that you really *don't* want to divorce him at all."

The group suggested that perhaps she and Ira had much more in common than she realized, even their careers were connected. Perhaps the bonds that kept them together were stronger and more deeply embedded than she had heretofore believed. Perhaps Arnold was right, and the reason Marilyn had for eight years been unable to end their marriage was because in her heart of hearts she really needed and wanted their relationship to remain intact. "Perhaps," they suggested, "it's merely another rebellion calculated to inflict pain on your unspeakable mother."

"Maybe," said Judy, "you should work harder on getting in touch with your core."

"I feel," said Roberta, "that you should re-evaluate your true intent and rework your definitions."

"But I don't want to be married to Ira," protested Marilyn.

"We think you do," said the group.

That evening Marilyn declined the coffee invitation and went straight home. Ira wasn't in, and Natalie and the boys, through with dinner, were playing bingo. Marilyn marveled at her sister, who enjoyed engaging in all the activities that Marilyn loathed.

Natalie seemed to have infinite patience with Todd and Jeremy and could sit for hours playing "Go Fish" and "Candyland" and watching TV with them. She made their Halloween costumes, took them to the park for pony rides and sat in sandboxes with them, making castles and pies.

Naturally, Ira, feeling that a good father involved himself with his children and shared their interests, was also an avid participant in all these things that gave Todd and Jeremy happy faces. Marilyn on the other hand took great pleasure in having Ophelia dress her sons and packing them off to Marineland, Magic Mountain, Disneyland or picnics with Ira or Natalie. The only thing that Marilyn hated worse than picnics was cleaning toilets, and picnics seemed to run in her family. Even as a little girl she couldn't abide sitting on scratchy blankets with nothing to lean back on and eating soggy mashed sandwiches with bees buzzing and ants crawling and flies circling and other people's dogs sniffing around. She hated the sun beating down on her head and on the food, heating the once-cold drinks and softening the fruit.

Helen, perhaps aware of Marilyn's extreme dislike, used to arrange family picnics every Sunday. Marilyn went on only two of them and ever after refused to accompany her parents and sisters on any other such excursion. Even sitting home with her grandmother was preferable. By the third picnic, her father, feeling that the family wasn't really a family without Marilyn, earned Helen's undying enmity by also refusing to go.

After a long and angry discussion, her mother took Natalie, Phyllis and the picnic basket and marched furiously off to picnic in the park, leaving Marilyn and Lenny behind. They stood at the window watching them go, and as soon as they were out of sight flew to the car and drove to a Chinese restaurant. There they sat happily in a dim, cool booth, chewing on spareribs and smiling at each other. Eating Chinese food with her father was one of the delights of Marilyn's life. Even now, he could lift her out of a depression by calling up and saying, "Hey, Dolly, what do you say to a little dinner at Hap Lo's, just you and me, huh?" They spoke to each other every day. Lenny would call her from work just to talk, and she would call him before bedtime just to say goodnight. When she was particularly upset and couldn't sleep, Marilyn would call him at any hour of the night or early morning. He would always comfort her, chat with her and often drive over, even at three A.M., for a cup of something and a soothing conversation.

Helen, lying in bed, sensing the change in temperature or atmosphere, would stretch out a leg, explore the queen-size mattress, find it empty, and knowing he'd gone to Marilyn's, pound her pillow in fury. She seethed at Marilyn's lack of consideration and at Lenny's incredibly stupid acceptance of his daughter's selfish demands. "What's the matter with you? Are you crazy, getting up from your sleep and driving over there at two in the morning? Don't you know that only encourages her?"

"So what?" Lenny would reply. "What's so crazy about a father helping his daughter?"

"At *two* in the morning?" Helen would scream.

"At any time," Lenny would thunder.

"She has a *husband*."

"A husband is not a father!"

"She has a *fool* for a father!"

"Helen," Lenny would say, quieting down. "If it doesn't bother me, why should it bother you?"

"Because my husband belongs with *me*, not with *her*. You belong with *me*!"

"Helen, Helen, she needs me."

Helen would glare at him, her face contorted. "And my needs, Lenny? Don't *I* have needs?"

"Different, Helen."

"And if I can't sleep in the night, Lenny? Who takes care of me?"

Lenny would sit quietly, unable to explain, and Helen would sit hopelessly, unable to understand. Then she would stand up and look bleakly at Lenny. "I was wrong. Marilyn has *two* husbands, hers and mine."

And Lenny would shrug, sorry for causing his wife pain, yet unable, as he called it, to "abandon" his daughter.

Once Helen said bitterly, "Maybe I should call up Ira at three in the morning and tell him I'm depressed."

"Ira wouldn't mind," replied Lenny.

"Neither would Marilyn . . . that's why I don't do it," said Helen.

"Natalie," Marilyn called, "where are you?"

"I'm putting the boys to bed."

Marilyn walked into the kitchen and began to make coffee. She thought about her group session. Could they be right? Was she still married to Ira because she still *wanted* to be married to Ira? Impossible. She measured out the coffee and spooned it into the pot. She took out two mugs, two spoons, and a cake plate. She went to the refrigerator and got a box of donuts which she emptied onto the plate. Then she sat down and reached for the phone.

"Hello, Mother."

"How are Ira and the children?"

"Fine, we're all fine . . . yes, Natalie's still here . . . I will . . . after we have a coffee. Is Papa there?"

"Yes."

"Well, can I talk to him?"

"No."

Marilyn took a donut and broke it in half. "What do you mean, no?"

"He's here but you can't talk to him. He's lying down with a headache, maybe because he was on the phone at three in the morning."

"Is he asleep?"

"I hope so."

Marilyn picked up a donut half, nibbled off a piece of chocolate and put it back on the plate.

"Well, will you please *look?*"

"I don't want to disturb him."

Marilyn clenched her fist.

"I'll tell him you called."

"No, you won't."

Marilyn hung up and checked the coffee. She hollered up the stairs and told Natalie to hurry. Then she poured two cups of coffee. She needed to talk to her father.

"All tucked in," Natalie said, walking into the kitchen and sitting down. "How was group?"

"Interesting. Natalie, did Ira say when he'd be home?"

"Nope." Natalie went to the refrigerator and got a container of milk.

"I wouldn't be surprised if he had a *girl* somewhere," mused Marilyn.

Natalie stared at her in astonishment. "Oh, I would," she said.

"Yes, *you* would." Marilyn poured some milk into her coffee and began to stir it. "The group wants me to try to make it work with Ira." She stirred her coffee and watched little brown whirlpools form and disappear. She wanted to talk it over with her father, who she knew would encourage her to follow the suggestions of the group. "I've got to make a decision about my life," she said to Natalie. "Wouldn't *you* like to do something else with your life?"

Natalie nodded. "Yes, I would."

"What?"

Natalie took a donut and examined it, turning it over and over until the chocolate stained her fingers. "I want to get married," she said. "I want a husband and children."

"What about a career?"

Natalie put the donut down on the edge of her napkin and licked her fingers clean. She looked at her sister, who was living her, Natalie's, dream and hating it. Natalie suddenly felt angry. She had been given the wrong life. Somehow there had been a mix-up and Marilyn had gotten her life and no wonder she was dissatisfied. How can someone be happy leading another person's life? Natalie wondered whose life *she* was living.

"The only career I want is marriage," she said.

"Be realistic, Natalie," scolded Marilyn, "and liberate yourself. Get the hell out of Papa's office."

Natalie lifted her mug of coffee with suddenly shaking hands. The mug tilted, spilling some of the liquid on the table. She wiped it with her napkin and steadied her hands. She felt like crying. "I'm not like you, Marilyn," she said, her voice quivering. "I'm not smart like you. I could work from now to forever and from then to next Tuesday and I'd never get to be a liberated woman." She put her mug down and looked at her sister. "Now you, you could work yourself up to something, a big lawyer, a really important person." She leaned forward and took Marilyn's hand. "You're smarter than me, Marilyn," she said rapidly, "you made Arista . . . I could work and work and never come in late and do everything right . . . and it would never amount to anything. I would start out as a secretary or something, and in ten years you know what I'd have worked myself up to? A secretary or something."

The kitchen was very quiet. Natalie dropped Marilyn's hand and put both her hands around the warm mug of coffee, holding it tightly, feeling the smooth heat of it. "I need a man," she said quietly. "I want that around me. Liberation wouldn't work for me . . . we're different, Marilyn. You're a star—you shine and people notice you. You're quick . . . but I'm not. I'm just not," she whispered.

The sisters sat silently. Natalie's fingers were white against the blue mug. "I'm an average girl, nobody special and I never will be." She spoke so softly that Marilyn had to strain to hear her. "I know what I am," she murmured. "I know I need a man to love me and support me, not just with money," she said, raising her eyes, "not just with that, Marilyn, but someone who really loves me and would take care of me and be nice to me and hold me up . . ." Her voice broke and she stared down into her coffee. Marilyn reached across the table and patted her sister's arm. "I wish I were Santa Claus," she said huskily, "so I could give you Christmas."

Natalie smiled. "So do I." She stood up and took the coffee pot off the stove. "More coffee?" Marilyn nodded and Natalie refilled their cups. "Be a big lawyer," said Natalie, "but first make it good with your husband." She paused. "Do you know what's wrong with you?" she asked.

"If I knew that, would I be helping Doctor Leventhal pay off his mortgage?"

"You weren't single long enough."

"Oh?" said Marilyn, looking questioningly at her sister.

Natalie put the pot back on the stove and sat down. "You weren't single long enough for the fear to set in . . . so that when you married Ira there was no . . . there was no *gratitude*—and not enough miserable experiences behind you to make marriage look like the Garden of Eden." Natalie took a sip of her coffee, made a face and added more milk. "You never felt that Ira had done you a favor by marrying you . . . and that you owed him a favor in return."

"Bullshit!" exploded Marilyn.

"You don't realize," said Natalie softly, "what it's like out there, what it's like to be alone. You don't realize how good marriage looks to someone who's single. It's too bad," she added, "because Ira's a nice guy . . . Do you know something?"

"What?"

"If I were married, if I met a guy who liked me so much that he was willing to support me, and love me, and step on a wine-glass in public for me, and worry about me, and tell me to drive carefully because he doesn't want me hurt, because he needs me, a guy who feels happy to see my car in the driveway when he gets home and brings me tea when I'm sick and kisses me just because he wants to kiss me, and takes me out on my birthday and New Year's Eve . . ." She picked up her soggy napkin and began shredding it. "If I were that lucky, you know what I would do?"

Marilyn shook her head, her eyes riveted on her sister. "I would thank him every day of my life. I would hold him and thank him, you bet your liberated ass I would." Natalie was breathing hard and speaking so quickly that her words rattled like pebbles in a wooden box. "And I would be liberated my-self then—liberated from being single and lonely and scared in the night." She lifted up her coffee mug. "And if this were champagne instead of coffee, I'd drink a toast to my liberator, whoever, wherever he is . . ." She paused and looked at Marilyn. "You know something?" she smiled. "Your whole life would have been different, Marilyn, if only you'd met Ira when you were twenty-nine and shaky . . . like me."

When Ira came home, Marilyn was already asleep. She awakened at two-thirty A.M. and looked for a long, long time at the man sleeping beside her. Then she picked up the phone, called her father and told him, to his great joy, that she was going to try to fix her marriage.

For three months she and Ira did their best. They tried to laugh together, to have fun. By the end of March she knew finally that the group had been wrong, that her father was wrong, that she had been stupid even to attempt to put this Humpty-Dumpty marriage back together again, that she, of all people, should have known better, that it was impossible. Everything was the same, she was as unhappy as ever, more so in fact, because now she was also two months pregnant. She called Dr. Leventhal and told him to shove his group, along with his pipe, right up his ass. When she hung up the phone, she put her hand on her stomach and began to cry.

After about fifteen minutes, she wiped her eyes, called Dr. Lighter and told him she wanted an abortion. He said he would examine her and arrange hospitalization for the following week. Then she called her mother and asked Helen if she'd take the kids for a few days next week.

"Why?" asked Helen. "Are you going somewhere?"

"No," Marilyn replied, "Ira and I just want to be alone for a few days."

"How are you feeling?" asked Helen. "When I was pregnant with you I was sick for nine months."

Marilyn found it difficult to engage in mother-daughter talk with Helen, who was overjoyed by the pregnancy. Talking with Helen made her uncomfortable and tied up her tongue.

"I'm sick, too," she said.

"Maybe it's a girl, then," laughed Helen.

Marilyn was silent. "I have to go, Ma," she said after a pause.

Then she called her Aunt Celia and arranged to stay with her until she recovered from surgery. She also vowed her to secrecy.

"Are you sure about this, Marilyn?" asked Celia.

"I don't want anyone to know, Aunt Celia."

"This will be the end, you know that," said her aunt.

"I know that."

"You bleed on my Wamsuttas, Marilyn, and I'll disown you."

Marilyn laughed. "Maybe I need to bleed," she said. "It's not only this baby that I'll be aborting."

"I know, dear heart. Well, at least you've found the means to end your marriage. I'm only sorry that you didn't find a less messy and painful means. You always did everything the hard way."

Marilyn shifted the receiver to her other ear. "I'm going to need a good lawyer," she said.

"Isn't it fortunate that you're in such a superb position to get yourself one," answered Celia.

Marilyn hung up the phone and lay down on her bed. She felt light, like a bird or a ballerina. She would be rid of Ira. She would lie on the operating table in a brightly lit room, her legs wrapped in sterile sheets and placed in stirrups. They would put her to sleep, and while she slept Dr. Lighter would scrape away the cells and tissues of an unwanted child. Marilyn knew that when she awoke her womb and her spirit would be scraped clean. The fetus and the marriage would be in pieces, dead and gone, and she would be packed and bleeding and free.

She reached for her cigarettes and saw that her hand was trembling. Her mother, on a strange close day, had first told her the story of how her grandmother Malka had once given birth to a dead and six-fingered baby and how the one before that was a mongoloid idiot. She told Marilyn that she was named for a woman who had watched that baby die, who had, in fact, killed it. Her own child.

Marilyn lit her cigarette and inhaled deeply. What was the saying? As the twig is bent, so grows the tree—or something like that. How interesting. She had been named for a woman who had killed her own child, and now she, her namesake, was also about to kill her own child. No. Not to kill. To sacrifice. Was it genetic? Was she Malka? Marilyn lay on her bed and smoked. A sacrifice.

Her mother had told Marilyn that Malka was called a murderess. Marilyn took a last puff and put out her cigarette.

She sat on the edge of her bed and wondered uneasily if, since she wasn't Abraham, she would be punished. She wondered, If you destroy a life, even an unborn one, then what happens to you? Malka had been punished and banished and branded. A murderess. She had died young.

Marilyn lit another cigarette and lay down again. She lay her hand gently on her stomach and felt it pulsing and quivering. She knew that somewhere under her hand a heart was beating, and she felt an aching, gnawing emptiness. It was her little baby in there, and Marilyn had loved them all—until they were born.

She put her cigarette in the ashtray and laid her other hand on her stomach, covering it, protecting it. She held the child she would never hold, and when at last she removed her hands, she knew that she had offered it up and consecrated it. She knew that she had sacrificed that new and blameless and innocent life for her own. On Sunday, she dropped the boys at her mother's, and on Monday she had the abortion. From Celia's house she called Joe Wernick, an attorney at her firm, and asked him to file for her divorce. She would be out for a few days. By Friday the bleeding had almost stopped, and she was up and around and able to go to dinner at her parents'.

Chapter

13

WHEN NATALIE WAS TWENTY-FOUR YEARS OLD she read
a book in which the heroine was a young and beautiful heiress
who, along with all her other wonderful attributes, was also an
accomplished equestrienne. One day while the heiress was out
riding, she leaned into the saddle in such a way as to cause, no
doubt by her posture and the movement of the horse, a strange
and pleasant sensation in certain areas of her body. Indeed the
feeling was so delicious that the heroine decided to ride into the
woods, dismount in a secret copse known only to herself and
attempt to reproduce the sensation on her own—since she was of
strong and independent character and it was beneath her to depend on a horse. By judicious application of her soft but firm small
white hand, she managed to re-create that lovely sensation, nay,
to intensify it, so that it surpassed by far any other feeling she
had heretofore felt.

While she was thusly engaged, the young and handsome heir
to the neighboring estate wandered in, and, seeing that the
heroine was preoccupied, cleared his throat and offered to show
her a better way. The heroine thanked him prettily, said, "Please
do," and being chivalrous, he did.

Natalie put the book down and thought. Then she took her
own hand and, after some experimentation, proceeded to experi-

ence the very same throbbing ecstasy as had the heroine of her book. So impressed was Natalie with the benefits of reading, that she applied her newly acquired knowledge again and again with ever-increasing skill, every chance she got. She regretted, of course, that there was no one around to show her the better way, but all in all she was satisfied. Now, after five years of active and frequent self-manipulation, Natalie, with a smile, referred to herself as an old hand. When, in *Annie Hall*, Woody Allen defined masturbation as "having sex with someone you love," Natalie burst into delighted adult laughter.

After work, she would sit at home knitting her sweaters or making ribbon pillows and dream of being a Rosemary Rogers heroine, of sweet suffering à la Barbara Cartland. She enjoyed the time with her nephews, and whenever they were out together she pretended they were hers. She called them "my boys." She yearned for marriage and a home of her own so achingly that it was almost a physical torment. Because her own life was as empty and unfurnished as an abandoned old building, she adopted the lives of others. She, as Marilyn's stand-in, went to the PTA meetings and baked the cakes. She went with the Stillmans to open-school week; when she could, she delighted in driving carpools. All the chores that modern housewives loathed and deplored, Natalie held out eager arms for. She was thrilled at the news of Marilyn's pregnancy and bought soft pastel-colored wool and angora. She began to knit tiny hats and bootees and look with measuring eyes at pottie seats, baby toters and nursery lamps. She ached to bathe and hold a tiny infant.

During the few days that Todd and Jeremy were at her house, she tightened the buttons on their sweaters, took them for haircuts and read them bedtime stories. With a happy smile she informed them that when they were with her, she was their mother.

The first spark of suspicion was ignited when Ira came over to see the boys and join the Ritters for dinner. He seemed relaxed and content, talked about how much he wanted a baby girl and seemed to see nothing ominous in the fact that Marilyn was staying at Celia's for a few days. When Helen and Natalie evinced a mild concern, he told them that he'd lived long enough with Marilyn to know that she was unpredictable. He said they were trying hard, and he was taking one day at a time. But he drummed his fingers on the table during dinner and kept rubbing the side of his nose. Yuspeh sat looking at them all, shaking her head and clicking her dentures. She was old and knew that people were more often fools than not and could drink all the milk yet never once think of the cow. After dinner, Lenny, smiling, broadly announced that he had a surprise. For his vacation this year he was taking himself and his wife on a trip to Europe. He stood up and from his pocket pulled a travel agent's brochure. Helen stared at him in astonishment.

"Europe," she whispered. "Now?"

"Of course now," he said. "It's spring. If you're ever going to love Paris, now is the time."

"But . . ."

"No buts, Mama," said Natalie. "How can you even hesitate? You're going."

"Absolutely," Ira said, walking over to Helen and putting his arm around her. "You both deserve a vacation. Have you got your passports?"

"We can't go now," she said. "You're dreaming, Lenny." Helen leaned against Ira. She felt very tired. She looked at Lenny and the sight of his fading smile grieved her.

"Look, sweetheart. It's wonderful what you did. I love you for it, but how can we go? Who will take care of Mama while we're walking around London? Who will check on the children when Marilyn is throwing up and we're off singing with Italians in Rome?"

Lenny carefully folded the travel pamphlets and replaced them in his jacket pocket. He sat back in his chair and picked up his newspaper. "What about Paris, Helen?" he asked. "You left out Paris. Maybe the business will go bankrupt while we're climbing the Eiffel Tower, maybe a nuclear war; who knows?" He frowned disgustedly at Helen and, without another word, buried his head in the business section.

Yuspeh stirred and glanced over at her son and then at Helen, leaning against Ira and looking upset.

"I was born in Czechoslovakia," she said, "so I been already in Europe. Nobody got to watch me. I can die whether you're here or not here and watching won't make a difference. So don't stay home for me." She paused for a minute and took a loud sip of her tea. "And what do you got to watch Marilyn for? She can't vomit with no one watching? Natalie is home, Ira is home, I'm home. We can all watch her vomit, and also the children who she don't take care of, anyway. Go. Lenny is tired. He wants to go to Europe, let him go to Europe. Me, I couldn't wait to get out from there." She put down her teacup with a bang and a snort and folded her arms across her chest. Lenny looked up at his wife hopefully. "What do you say, Helen?"

Ira squeezed Helen's shoulders. "Go ahead, Ma," he said. "You'll love it."

Helen smiled and patted his cheek. "We'll see, darling," she said, and walked to Lenny, staring down over the wall of newsprint at the top of his bent head. With a start she realized that his hair was almost all gray. She could see the pink of his scalp through the fine strands. He looked weary—and old. With her forefinger she gently pulled the paper away from him, and as he looked up, she smiled. "Let me think on it, sweetheart," she said. "Give me a chance to digest. It's not a closed issue, and maybe we can both use a second honeymoon."

"Well," Lenny muttered, somewhat mollified, "I got to know soon. It's the season over there, you know."

Natalie sat at the edge of her chair, her elbows on her knees, her cheeks cupped in both hands. Paris, London, Rome. The cities sang in her head, and she wondered if she'd ever in her lifetime get the opportunity to sing in those cities. She doubted it. Her friends, the few she had, were married and out of touch. She absolutely couldn't go alone. Maybe a tour. But then she'd be with strangers, and knowing herself, she realized that unless *they* approached *her*, they would remain strangers. Marilyn had once told her that she was a phenomenon. That if she were a stone thrown into a pond, she'd cause no ripples. As much as Natalie resented that remark, she admitted its truth. Did this inability to get up and go, to change direction, to make ripples, run in her family? For eight years Marilyn had been unable to alter her situation. And she, Natalie, like a large and weightless stone, stayed in her spot, too, moving only when someone moved her. On her own, she had accomplished nothing. She loved the theater but would only go if someone else invited her, bought the tickets and drove. She enjoyed being with interesting people, yet made no effort to seek them out or discover their haunts. She affected nothing, and nothing was altered because she existed. And that was all she did: existed. And the only evidence of that was innumerable sweaters, pillows and needlepoints. She took off her glasses and rubbed her eyes. Maybe she'd get lucky and get stuck in an elevator for ten hours with the man of her dreams. It would probably be the only way she'd ever come across someone who would spend that much time with her. And with her luck, instead of getting stuck with Burt Reynolds, she'd get stuck with an elevator repairman.

She opened her eyes to find Ira examining her latest knitting project. "What's this going to be?" he asked with a smile. "Bootees for the baby? You're really something."

Helen looked over at Ira and Natalie and was convinced anew that there was no justice. It wasn't a trip to Europe that she wanted. It was for Natalie to find and marry a man like Ira. She sat down with a sigh. What was Marilyn doing staying with Celia? What was she up to? Helen made a note to call Celia in the morning and find out what was going on. Marilyn didn't deserve a man like Ira. But *Natalie* deserved a man like Ira, because Ira deserved the best. She sighed again. Some people have no luck. Her mother used to say that. Because Malka spoke so seldom, Helen remembered practically every word she uttered. Helen remembered also the silences that reduced all of them to furtive whispering, as though speaking aloud were a punishable offense. Their apartment had windows on three sides, yet the pall of silence hung so heavy and so low that the rooms seemed dark and the street noises muffled and far away. As a child she had always been startled by normal tones. While her father was living with them, Malka's muteness had not been as noticeable, but when he moved out, her silence blared and proclaimed her strangeness. On the rare occasions when she uttered audible words and spoke her thoughts aloud, they hung in the air like spider webs on windless days. And it was always about luck—generally the lack of it—pushed through thick teeth and out of tight lips to fall at last with a clatter on the ears of her children. Helen had never, not once, been told by her mother that she loved her. She had mentioned that one day to Marilyn.

"Why not?" Marilyn had asked.

"Because she didn't."

"Well," Marilyn had replied, "at least she was honest."

For some reason Helen rarely mentioned Malka to Natalie or Phyllis. Only to Marilyn. But she had never wondered why, and neither had Marilyn. What she did wonder was why she had been chosen to have a peculiar mother and a peculiar daughter as well. What determined these things? For a third time, Helen sighed. She looked over at Natalie, who smiled back.

"I love Paris in the springtime," Natalie sang.

"I was born in Europe," said Helen. "Fortunately I had a peculiar mother and we had to leave. I should thank her because we left just in time. They restricted immigration after that. And then of course . . . Hitler. I came over on the *Aquitania*."

"Maybe you'll fly back on TWA," grinned Ira.

Helen smiled. "Maybe. The first black person I ever saw in my life I saw on that ship. I was so frightened I ran screaming to my father."

"Aunt Natalie, Grandma," came an outraged yell from the stairs. "Todd wiped his booger on me."

"He kept switching channels, that's why," hollered Todd indignantly.

"Why aren't you boys in bed?" called Ira.

They heard a scramble and the soft closing of a door.

"Works all the time," said Ira.

Natalie picked up her knitting. "When I finish these, I'll make you a cardigan," she told him.

"You're a sweetheart," said Ira. "You're a beautiful person."

Natalie looked up with a start. No one had ever told her that before. "Oh, sure," she said, embarrassed. She began to knit furiously. There were many women in the world who were swamped with compliments. For a moment Natalie wished she knew what it was like to be given a compliment and be capable of accepting it—secure in the knowledge that it was truly meant and well deserved. She wondered what it felt like to be beautiful. To look every day into the mirror and smile at yourself, pleased. To look like Cinderella. To go to a party and know you'll be asked to dance. To be assured that you'll look good no matter what you put on. She wondered if beauty gave one an extra edge over lesser-endowed people. If it banished myopia or squared off round shoulders or whitened teeth or cured insomnia or provided energy. What must it be like to go to sleep every night and wake up every morning with high cheekbones and long eyelashes? To be pretty or even cute or even good-looking or even attractive or even not bad. She wished she knew.

Once Phyllis had told her that she'd be more than passable if she made up properly and got rid of her glasses. Her grandmother kept saying that she could be "maybe not a beauty, but not a homely either" if she'd only improve her posture. Her mother said that she had inner beauty and that's where it counted. Marilyn had been present when she said it. Marilyn had looked surprised and laughed out loud. "That's bullshit," she had said, still laughing.

High cheekbones, high arches, high color, high breasts, high head, high fashion, high-powered, high-handed, high-hatted, high and mighty. To be beautiful was a constant high, thought Natalie. To be plain, on the other hand, was troublesome and embarrassing, because if you were plain everyone knew your heart's desire. Everyone knew what your birthday wish was going to be. Everyone knew that when you squeezed your eyes shut, crossed your fingers, took a deep breath and blew out your candles, you had just wished, very desperately, to be beautiful. And when everyone knows your wish, of course it never comes true. Everyone knows that.

Natalie held up her needles and looked critically at her handiwork. She couldn't wait to hold in her hand the tiny foot that would wear this soft, white bootee. When she was in high school, a girl in her English class named Ivy was forced to end her school career abruptly due to pregnancy. The entire junior class rose up giggling and clucking, armed with every intimate detail, including the name of the probable father—a fact of which not even Ivy was positive. The girls in the class generally agreed that Ivy had been stupid to get caught and that now her life and rep were ruined. But not Natalie. Natalie had thought she was lucky.

"A penny, Sis," said Ira, breaking into her thoughts.

Natalie sat up and resumed her knitting. "Just daydreaming," she explained, flustered. "Not even worth a penny."

Ira smiled and sat down beside her. "You look like I feel when one of my clients is getting audited. Is anything wrong?"

"What could be wrong?" she murmured.

"Daddy." Ira looked up to see his son Todd standing halfway down the stairs. "Kiss us goodnight, Daddy."

"Get into bed. I'll be right up."

Yuspeh stood up with him. "You got nice children," she said.

"Why not?" grinned Ira. "They take after me."

Yuspeh shuffled toward the stairs. "Don't be a smart aleck," she said. "I'm also going to bed." Ira walked over to her and took her arm. "Come on, Grandma, I'll tuck you in."

Yuspeh's shoulders shook in silent laughter. "And then you'll also maybe kiss me goodnight?"

"Would you like me to?" Ira grinned.

The old woman turned and looked him right in the eye. "That's your trouble, Mr. Smart Aleck. You ask instead of doing. A sick person you ask—for a well person, you do." She began climbing the stairs, then stopped and looked at Ira over her shoulder. "Asking is like sleeping, a waste of time."

She continued up the stairs, followed by Ira. "I'm going to kiss you goodnight," he said.

"Too late now," snapped Yuspeh.

The ringing of the telephone brought Lenny to his feet. "Maybe that's Marilyn," he said. He was so eager to get to the phone that he wobbled and almost tripped over the coffee table.

"Lenny," Helen called sharply, "watch where you're going. Marilyn can wait a minute. That man," she sighed when he had gone. "Why are you slumping?" she asked, looking at her daughter.

Natalie straightened up. "Mama," she whispered.

Helen went to her and gently took the knitting from her hands. "Don't worry," she said softly. "I know. I know, Momeleh, and I'll take care. You'll see." She leaned over and kissed her daughter's cheek. Then she walked back to her chair. "You'll see," she said again. "I'll fix it so you'll be happy—you'll see." For a fleeting moment her eyes, hard with pain and resolution, looked like the eyes of her mother, Malka.

Chapter

14

MARILYN SAT AT THE TABLE and pushed her peas and carrots from one side of the plate to the other. She talked angrily to them in her head every now and then, mashing a stubborn pea that eluded her fork and tried to get away. Oh, no, you don't splat. You do what I tell you to. She made a path through the mashed potatoes and pushed the peas and carrots along competently, methodically, not one was permitted to escape. This must have been how they marched the Jews to the gas chambers, Marilyn thought. No wonder they got them all—like her peas and carrots, the Jews also had had no chance.

Sometimes, while stuffing watermelon rinds down into the churning garbage disposal, she saw Jews stuffed into ovens, every last one, like garbage, annoying and smelly, one after the other, in you go, goodbye. They weren't people, they were eggshells and chicken bones, they were coffee grounds and watermelon rinds, so what did it matter? All of history, she thought, boiled down to people and nations and boundaries getting pushed around, incinerated, crushed, ground up and engulfed, to emerge in the end altered but unchanged. Same ingredients, different form: water to ice, bone to ash, solid to molten. You couldn't ever destroy matter, everyone knew that, so what did it matter. No one who marches and shoves peas and carrots down a path carved through mashed potatoes should ever be surprised.

She lifted a forkful of vegetables to her mouth and chewed thoroughly. Her family was discussing her parents' forthcoming trip to Europe, a place where hideous crimes had been committed. A place of gruesome history and beautiful, blood-watered scenery. In Europe, unspeakable events had occurred, and for thousands of years the blood of millions had seeped in and been absorbed, nourishing and contaminating the ground. How could anyone eat carrots and peas grown in the soil of Europe? People said Europe was quaint, and Marilyn wondered why, when tainted was indeed the better word. She herself, along with every other American of European ancestry, was tainted with the plasma and perhaps even the genetic attitude of human beings who were fed from that land and breathed that air. No wonder we're all doomed, thought Marilyn, the history major—we're all full of ghastly shit.

She laid her fork and knife carefully on her plate. "I filed for divorce," she said quietly. "Ira will be served with the papers very shortly." She looked up and found them all staring at her, motionless, like the characters on Keats's Grecian urn, or in the Sleeping Beauty fairy tale—immobilized with forks halfway to open mouths, knives poised to slice, teeth frozen in mid-chew. Ira began to cough and reached for his glass of water.

"Congratulations," said Phyllis, sarcastically.

Ira took a sip of his water, put down his glass, and very deliberately speared a piece of meat and began to eat it.

"Come on," said Neil, "she's only talking."

Marilyn looked over at her father, who was sitting straight up, holding on to the edge of the table with both hands. His face was pale and his eyes filmed with shock. He knew that this time she wasn't only talking. "I'm sorry, Papa," she whispered. "I just couldn't any more."

Lenny closed his eyes and leaned his head on the back of his chair. He picked up one hand and rubbed the side of his face.

"I'm sorry, too," he said in a thick voice. "I'm sorry, too." He sighed heavily and looked down at his half-filled, gravy-smeared plate. "Did you hear that, Helen?" he asked the plate.

"Yes, I heard," said Helen, "having a fool for a daughter doesn't make a person hard of hearing."

What it does, she thought, what Marilyn has always done, is far worse than cause a physical malfunction. It seemed to Helen that Marilyn had reversed the proper order of things, had confused and upended the lives she touched. Like riders sitting backwards on a horse, all their perceptions were distorted. Years ago, Helen and Lenny went to the movies and saw a film called *The Bad Seed.* What horrified Helen was not the fearsomeness of evil clothed in innocence; what horrified Helen was her immediate association between the bad seed and her daughter Marilyn.

She now glared at her, this daughter who from conception had rankled like a boil in her armpit, threatening her very being with insidious infection. Marilyn, like a sly pickpocket, had filched even her mother's husband, unfairly dividing and appropriating Lenny's husbandly devotion, that concern and caring that should have been hers, Helen's, exclusively. Marilyn was not content with merely her own personal allotment—she greedily gobbled up Helen's and Natalie's and Phyllis's portions as well. She had taken the mother love that Helen had eagerly extended, and deflected it. Helen admitted at last that she—no, she still couldn't say "hated"—that for many reasons, those she was aware of and those she wasn't, she had no love for her daughter Marilyn, and never really had had.

Marilyn's eyes were fixed on her father's bent head. "It was a mistake, Papa," she pleaded, "the whole thing was a mistake." Lenny looked up, and the pain she saw in his eyes tore into her. "A mistake?" he asked, wearily. "No, Dolly, a mistake is not a reason . . . a mistake is something you make in arithmetic."

"And isn't your timing a bit off?" asked Phyllis, who appeared to be enjoying the whole scene. "I mean it's your space and your options, but your timing—it's rather lousy."

Irritated, Marilyn looked away from her father and glared at her sister. "What the hell are you talking about?"

Phyllis put down her knife and fork and pushed her chair slightly away from the table. "What I'm trying to say," she answered, crossing one leg over the other, "is that a divorce is not something you get *after* eight years, *after* two children, or *after* you become pregnant with the third."

Neil smiled approvingly at his wife and patted her raised knee. "Right *on*," he said and turned and grinned at Marilyn. "You want to dump Ira, you can't hack it together, that's cool. I'm all for free will. But I agree with Phyllis here, if you want a divorce you should get it *before* the wedding." Pleased with himself, he looked around the table. When no one applauded, he shrugged and helped himself to another spoonful of peas and carrots.

Natalie, who had been sitting motionless, stunned by Marilyn's announcement, now opened her mouth to speak. Her voice was dry and muffled. "They're right," she gasped, "you can't."

"On the contrary," replied Marilyn. "I can and I have."

"But what about the baby? You're pregnant," Natalie whispered, almost in tears.

Marilyn took a deep breath. "Not any more I'm not," she said quietly.

Like string-pulled marionettes, every head snapped up and turned. Only Yuspeh reached for a slice of egg bread and with it began mopping up the gravy on her plate. She stuffed a hunk of bread into her mouth, barely waiting to chew before cramming yet another gravy-browned piece down her throat. She ate steadily, pausing every now and then to glance at Marilyn, shake her head knowingly and return to her meal. From the corner of her eye, she saw Ira slump in his chair and begin to rub the side of his nose. Later he would recall that the room was so quiet that the sound of Yuspeh swishing the bread around her plate was clearly audible.

He could even hear her swallowing.

After a few moments, Helen shifted in her chair. She stared

across the table at Lenny, who was sitting motionless, his face so white that Helen became frightened. "Lenny," she cried sharply, and when he lifted his dazed eyes to hers, she placed both hands palms down on the table and pushed herself up. She leaned toward him, her arms stiff. "This is your reward," she breathed. "This is how your Dolly thanks you . . . by having an abortion." Then she turned and stared at Marilyn with eyes so full of loathing that Marilyn actually recoiled.

"So that's why you went to Aunt Celia's," said Phyllis, nodding her head.

"Bravo," said Marilyn, and looking at her brother-in-law, Neil, added, "and don't tell me that the best time for an abortion is before conception."

Yuspeh took her napkin and wiped her mouth and chin. "We never before in our family had an abortion," she said, matter-of-factly, dipping the napkin into her glass of water. "Miscarriages we had plenty, but no abortions." She began rubbing her cheeks with the wet napkin, droplets of water sprinkling her neck and chest.

"Well, now we've got one, Grandma," said Neil. "A famous first."

Ira slowly rose to his feet. His lips were white. "I think I'll go home now," he said softly, "and see to the two babies we have left . . . the ones she didn't get around to aborting." He stared unseeingly at the lit candles on the table. "I intend to sue for custody," said Ira, watching the candles flicker. A drop of liquid wax began to roll down the stem of the candlestick, and Ira watched it fall and harden, a waxen icicle.

"You don't have to sue," said Marilyn expressionlessly. "You can have them—they'll be better off with you, anyway." She took her napkin from her lap and laid it on her plate. "All I want is out, a civil business relationship with you, and my half of the house."

Ira nodded and sat down again. He looked at Natalie, who had started to cry into her hands. Helen straightened up.

"Natalie," she snapped, "stop that and go into the kitchen and get dessert. While you're there, turn on the flame under the coffee. Phyllis, you start clearing the table. Me," she went on sarcastically, "I'm going to stay right here and listen to the soap opera." Her eyes, opaque and unblinking, bored into Marilyn like a dental drill. "Don't stop now," she told her daughter, "we already have divorce, abortion, and child abandonment. What are you giving us next, big lawyer? An axe murder?"

Helen felt an unnerving mixture of fear and fury—the way she had felt as a child watching her mother, Malka, lumber into the kitchen early in the morning with her hair undone, looking wild and disheveled. By the time she was twelve, Helen was convinced that Malka was unbalanced, that the darkness had taken over, that if Malka were X-rayed, there would be discovered within her a vast, black swamp, seething and boiling and astir with awful and terrifying demons.

Malka had always fascinated her. The suspense, the constant unpredictability, the repulsive yet beckoning promise of peril, the absolute precariousness of the atmosphere that Malka created, lured Helen, and like quicksand, sucked her down. Even at twelve she had sought protection, building her shelter, weaving her camouflage, yet knowing all the while that Malka could undo her efforts and rip the fragile coverings with one vicious slash. Just like Marilyn. But where Malka was blindly and randomly destructive, Marilyn seemed to her wanton and spiteful. Malka had stolen her childhood, but Marilyn had stolen her husband, her grandchildren, her son-in-law and the laboriously constructed peace of mind that housed her life and held it together.

Helen looked at her daughter. "You poison everything you touch," she said. "And what kind of a woman destroys and gives away her children? I don't understand, I just don't understand how, with all your education, you never learned the difference between right and wrong."

Phyllis stood up and began to clear the table. She scraped the food off the plates and began to stack them. "Look, Ma," she said, "Marilyn has the right to do what she wants with her own body and her own life."

"Destruction is no one's right." Helen frowned at Phyllis and turned to her husband. "So, Lenny?" she asked, "what do you say to your darling Dolly now?"

"What can I say?" he answered wearily. "The whole thing is giving me a headache." He sat back and began to massage his temples. "Phyllis, get me an Excedrin."

"No," said Neil, making a face. "That stuff just pollutes your body and throws off your biorhythms. What you should do," he went on, "is meditate away your pain."

Yuspeh stared at him in amazement. "I'm sorry for your mother," she said.

"Meditate away your pain, Dad," Neil repeated.

"Shut up, Neil," snapped Marilyn. "My father prefers to medicate not meditate. Here, Papa." She reached into her pocket and extracted two Excedrin from a small gold pillbox. Lenny smiled his thanks and washed the pills down with a sip of water.

Neil shrugged. "It's your body," he said. "You want to clog it up with shit, that's your prerogative."

Ira sighed. "Must you continually assault our ears with profanity?" he demanded, "especially at the dinner table."

"Look, man," Neil retorted, "you got enough to worry about. Back off."

Natalie entered, carrying two cake platters, which she placed on the half-cleared table. She put two silver cake servers beside the platters and sat down. "I forgot the dessert plates." She jumped up again, knocking her water glass to the floor, where it shattered. Her hand flew to her mouth like a child's, and she looked at her mother with frightened eyes. "Oh," she whispered. "I'm sorry."

Helen laughed bitterly. "That's the difference," she told the family. "Natalie breaks a glass and says she's sorry. This one"— she pointed to Marilyn—"breaks everyone's heart and says, 'So what?'" Still pointing an accusing finger, she turned on Marilyn. "Who do you think you are? How dare you change right to wrong and leave your children like you left your dirty bloomers—lying around for other people to clean up? How dare you wreck this family?" Helen strained toward her daughter, the veins in her neck and the side of her head standing out and throbbing. Then her voice dropped to a hoarse whisper. "Well, you won't get away with it," she hissed. "I'll make you pay for this. If it kills me, I'll make you pay. I'll make you rue the day you were born—just like I do."

Slowly Marilyn rose from her chair, her eyes locked with her mother's. Lenny threw his hand out in horrified protest, and for a moment she faltered, then straightened again. Her voice was low and deadly. "I hope it does," she said, enunciating every word. "I hope it *does* kill you." Abruptly she sat down again, so hard that she almost bounced. Lenny half-stood, his face green with shock, his lips moving wordlessly. Before he could collect himself, Ira shot out of his chair so swiftly that it fell to the floor with a clatter. He ran around the table, grabbed Marilyn by the arm and violently yanked her up. He spun her around and, still holding her with one hand, began to shake her, and then he threw her back onto the chair. She gasped and stared at him, eyes wide, mouth open in amazement. Ira stood staring down at her, breathing heavily, his fists clenched. Then, without a word, he turned and walked out of the room.

Carefully, Phyllis put down the plates she was holding and expelled the breath she was also holding. She picked up a server and began to section the cake. "Anyone for dessert?" she asked, looking around the table. Six pairs of eyes stared back at her. After what seemed like hours of silence, Yuspeh held out her plate.

Chapter 15

THE FROZEN SILENCE of the room had so upset Phyllis that when they returned home she confessed to Neil that "my heart was in my toes."

"You mean in your mouth," he corrected. She narrowed her eyes and regarded her husband. "It's *my* heart, Neil," she said sharply, "and I know where it was. Don't you ever dare tell me again what I mean."

"Hey," said Neil, surprised.

"Because when you do that, it makes *me* feel silly and it makes *you* look like a pompous asshole."

Neil nodded and pulled her toward him. "I shouldn't have invaded your space," he told her, stroking her hair. "I'm sorry, baby, and I'm proud of you for sharing your feelings." He ran his finger along the side of her face. "I got the best banana in the bunch," he told her fondly. "How did you ever manage to come out of that family intact?"

Phyllis grinned. "By shunning sugar?"

"Could be," Neil said thoughtfully. He put his finger under her chin, tilted it up and kissed the tip of her nose. "Do you know what *keeps* you so intact?"

"Shunning sugar?"

"Nope."

"What then?"

"Being my old lady."

Phyllis pursed her lips and thought for a minute. "Could be," she smiled.

They walked into the kitchen and Neil began to brew some valerian herb tea. "I wonder what she's got up her sleeve," he mused.

"Who?"

"Your mother."

Phyllis lifted her eyebrows. "What can she do? Marilyn has the right to do whatever she wants to with her own life."

"I agree."

"It's her marriage and her kids."

Neil took two cups from the cupboard and poured the tea. He carried them to the table and set one before Phyllis. In the four years of their marriage, the tea-drinking before bedtime had become a ritual. Neil and Phyllis lifted their cups and clicked them together. "To us," Neil toasted, "and to poor Ira and Marilyn."

"Poor Ira, yes," said Phyllis. "But poor Marilyn? Why poor Marilyn?"

"Because she's got your mother for an enemy."

"My mother can't keep her from divorcing Ira."

"I'm hip," said Neil, "but she can keep her from enjoying it. She'll take it away."

"How?"

"Beats me," shrugged Neil, sipping his tea. "But," he said, peering at her over his cup, "take my advice and stay on your mama's sunny side."

"Come on," laughed Phyllis, "my mama's a buttercup."

"And I'm the Incredible Hulk!"

"Oh, yeah?" grinned Phyllis, draining her cup and climbing into his lap. "Go on and prove it then."

By twelve-thirty she was not yet asleep, but lay in bed thinking about what had transpired at dinner. All her life she'd been fascinated by the currents that ran through her family. She had watched with interest how they were generated, how they built up and ebbed, pulling them all like little toy boats into deep and frequently treacherous waters. She supposed she took after her Grandma Yuspeh in that respect. Both of them were avid instigators and sardonic observers. Her father was the honey-spreader, the ineffectual but persevering peacemaker who ran confused and despairing back and forth between Helen and Marilyn, the enemies. Ira, prized by one, despised by the other, stood in the eye of the hurricane, while the winds swirled about him. Natalie, loved and pitied by all, the weeper and beseecher, sat wringing her hands in confusion, too weak to affect any of the major players or events. And dear Neil, untouched and disdainful, was too strong and too far away to be drawn into the whirlpool of her family's existence.

How would it end? Marilyn had just shot the first arrow. It was now up to Helen to retaliate. Phyllis, lying awake, wiggled her toes in anticipation. Neil insisted that Helen was the more formidable of the two, that she possessed, like the iceberg that sank the *Titanic*, unseen but deadly capabilities. Maybe he was right. Marilyn had always *appeared* the stronger, if only by dint of her seeming lack of conscience in regard to the effect her actions had on others. She was very self-centered, Marilyn was, going her merry way, heedless of the havoc she left behind, concerned solely with her own satisfactions. And yet she was easily swayed. She loved only her father and herself. Phyllis, turning over her pillow, figured that that meager output was possibly very strengthening. Helen, on the other hand, loved more people than Marilyn did. And she loved her plants. Could her powers therefore be sapped—diffused and dispersed by the caring? Phyllis sat up, careful not to disturb the sleeping Neil, and propped her pillow behind her. She reached under the mattress and pulled out a crushed, half-empty pack of cigarettes with a book of matches stuck in the cellophane. Glancing again at Neil, she satisfied herself that it would take an atomic war to awaken him, and lit up. She inhaled with great pleasure, savoring the risk as well as the smoke. Giving up smoking was the second thing Neil made her do after their wedding. The first was going down on him in the shower. The third was asking her family for a loan so that they could open up The Cosmic Cucumber. She had reacted negatively to all three demands, resisting strenuously until she realized she liked the first and could sneak the second. The third she agreed to do if Neil would agree to attend the Friday night dinners. And so contentment reigned. Phyllis discovered that the secret of a happy marriage was as easy as one, two, three.

And everyone thought *Marilyn* was so smart. Hah! Was it smart to be miserable? Was it smart to turn even your own mother against you? Once, at some Friday night dinner, Marilyn had started in with Grandma. They had been reminiscing about the old neighborhood and some girl they all knew named Blanchie Ackerman, who lived on the block. Blanchie had broken her mother's heart by marrying a Polish plumber. Her mother, who wrote to Helen announcing the nuptials, had included a P.S. pouring out her sorrow: "My Blanchie is marrying a Polish boy, a plumber by the first name of Walter. I'm heartsick since he is not our religion, but thank God, at least he belongs to the Union."

Phyllis had scarcely any recollection of Blanchie Ackerman. "Was she the blonde one whose father was a glazier?"

"No. That was Floris Blatt," answered Helen. "Blanchie was the one who lived next door to Sammy with the one arm."

"I thought that was Silverman," protested Yuspeh.

"Silverman lived on the *other* side."

"I wonder what made me think of Blanchie Ackerman," mused Marilyn. "We could hardly be called friends. She wasn't in my MGM classes."

"What's this MGM? You went to movie school?" asked Yuspeh.

"Mentally Gifted Minors."

"Hah!"

"What do you mean 'hah'?" frowned Lenny. "Dolly was a brilliant student."

"So how come she's so stupid now?" asked Yuspeh.

Marilyn looked at her grandmother and marveled at the life-prolonging properties of malice. "Oh, shut up," she said.

"You sharrup, you!" cried Yuspeh, offended. "That Blanchie Silverman . . ."

"Ackerman," corrected Helen.

"That Blanchie Ackerman," continued Yuspeh, "dumb in school, no college, a husband a Polish plumber, that Blanchie with *nothing* is happier than this Marilyn, with her MGM, her B.A., her M.A., and her C.P.A. That's why you thought about her and that's why you're a dumbbell!"

Yuspeh hated to be told to shut up. She gazed at Marilyn with angry, expectant eyes.

"You are old, Grandma," said Marilyn quietly.

Yuspeh shrugged. "I said you were stupid, not blind," she retorted.

"And you're nasty," Marilyn went on, "and ridiculous."

Yuspeh drew herself up. "I'm smarter than you *because* I'm old."

"Bullshit," said Marilyn, "older doesn't make smarter."

"Oh, yes."

Marilyn regarded her adversary curiously. She wasn't fond of Grandma, but the old lady interested her. "If older means smarter, you would be an Einstein by now."

Yuspeh shrugged and looked disdainful. Marilyn waited for the rebuttal, and when none came glanced over at Yuspeh in surprise.

"Why does older make smarter?" she asked grudgingly after a moment.

Triumphantly, knowing she had hooked her fish, Yuspeh delivered her *coup de grâce*. "Older makes smarter because . . ." she paused for effect, ". . . some things, mine darling, just take longer to figure them out . . . *that's* why." She clicked her dentures and sat back, pleased.

Neil laughed out loud. "Right on," he said, clapping his hands. "I dig where you're coming from, Grandma."

Yuspeh threw him a withering glance. "You don't know nothing," she said. "You're even dumber than her." And she pointed a supercilious finger at Marilyn, who smiled despite herself.

"You left out my J.D., Grandma," and as the old woman looked at her blankly, Marilyn added, "Doctor of Jurisprudence."

Phyllis smiled at the recollection. She hoped she would end up as secure and as sure and as *brave* as her grandmother. She took another long pull on her cigarette, fanning away the smoke as Neil stirred. She loved him. She loved his inflated pronouncements and sudden enthusiasms. The way he leaped into things feet first, so positive that he was absolutely right about whatever he was saying or doing. He delighted her with his pompous, cocksure innocence and contradictory orientations. Neil was a true and pure Gemini, Leo rising. She had loved him instantly. When they met, he had put down what he called her "middle-class rebel mentality" and laughed at her efforts to impress him with her "pseudo antiestablishmentarianism." He informed her that pill popping, pot smoking, coke sniffing, was all the rage in Ohio and Nebraska and hardly an indication of sophisticated, offbeat nonconformism. It was his opinion that being straight was far out. "I'm a pendulum sitter," he told her. "I swing with the times, I'm the man of the hour, any hour." And perhaps he was right, because within an hour of meeting they were making it in his van—she, rather surprised; he, rather pleased and somewhat disapproving. Only her obvious inexperience saved her from his scorn.

"You're pretty new at this," he told her. "Spontaneous screwing isn't your style, don't try to deny it. Why are you here?"

"I don't know. Am I a silly fool?" She opened her eyes very wide. Neil lifted his head and regarded her suspiciously. She kept her face quite still and trembled just a bit. He looked at her face for a while, then bent and kissed her breasts. "Your instincts are terrific," he murmured. "You need a guy like me."

She gently pressed his head, lifting her breasts to his lips. "Do you really think so?" she whispered.

"Uh-huh," he sighed, his mouth busy. Phyllis lay back, relaxed and slightly smiling. "You're very wise," she breathed. "I trust you, Neil."

Later they went to dinner, and when he took her home, he told her that he'd see her around. "I hope so," she had said earnestly. "You're the only guy I've ever been able to have an orgasm with." Four months later they were married.

Phyllis reached over and put out the cigarette in the glass of water she kept on her bed table. She wrapped the butt in a piece of Kleenex, aimed for the wastebasket across the room, and tossed it in. "Two points," she said out loud, and sprayed her mouth with Binaca. Then she tucked the cigarette pack back under the mattress, flattened her pillow and lay down. She wished her grandmother would quit being so snotty to Neil. Of course, things like that never bothered Neil. He always assumed that hostility was the problem of the donor rather than that of the recipient—especially when he was the one on the receiving end. Phyllis greatly admired his self-confidence and was therefore pleasant to her in-laws, grateful to them for instilling such positive thinking in their son. Neil had been a premature baby, born when his mother was over forty. Because his survival remained in doubt for many months, his parents truly believed that even the fact that he breathed was an earth-shattering achievement. As he grew up, they maintained this attitude and applauded his every act. Whatever their Neil did or didn't do, got or didn't get, they considered terrific as long as he didn't die. To them, the fact that their son was alive was so marvelous that all they ever demanded was for him to continue to remain that way. That he did so signified to them a heartwarming indication of filial thoughtfulness, consideration and love.

They told Phyllis often that she was a lucky girl and Phyllis agreed wholeheartedly. Neil grew up believing that there was a good chance he was the Messiah. Opening up a health-food store and restaurant was just one of his many methods of helping humanity, of making the world a better place and bestowing upon its more aware citizenry a headstart health plan for eternal spiritual and physical salvation.

He educated Phyllis in the preparation of beneficial food combinations and taught her to worship brewers' yeast, blackstrap molasses and folic acid. He dressed her in tight orange T-shirts with "It's Natural" written in block print over her firm, bouncy, braless boobs. He introduced a line of cosmetics made from natural ingredients and gave them cute names, like Phacials from Phyllis, and Phyllis's Phantastic Phoundation Base—we give phree samples.

The Cosmic Cucumber prospered, and Neil figured that if Lenny and Ira were to hint around about repayment of their loans, he could swing it easily and have enough left to open another store, perhaps in Beverly Hills, perhaps with a line of clothing made from natural fibers which perhaps he'd call Phashions by Phyllis—let The Cosmic Cucumber show you how to eat your way to a more phabulous phigure. Neil knew he possessed a special grace, that God had a personal interest in his well-being. He didn't doubt for a minute that everything he touched would turn to gold, a natural element. There was no end to the possibilities—exercise classes, spas, hair and nail clinics, organic cooking and gardening instruction, and on and on. He was a blessed man who loved his life, loved his wife, and loved himself.

Phyllis moved onto her side and fitted herself to her husband's body, spoonlike. Neil stirred. "What's the matter?" he mumbled. "I can't sleep."

Instantly awake, he turned over and took her in his arms. He bent one knee and put it high between her legs, stroking her body with his hand. "I know a great way to relax you," murmured the ever-wise, ever-loving, ever-erect Neil Cooper to his lucky, smiling wife.

Chapter

16

CELIA CUTLER WAS THE SORT of woman who told the truth as though it were a lie. This gained her the reputation of being interesting, probably because it confused people and made them unsure. She was forced into this mode of communication by her husband Jack, who after twenty-seven years of marriage decided to give up fidelity. He relinquished it with a passion Celia hadn't known he possessed, and with equal ardor embraced and was embraced by an army of women, most of them younger and seemingly more appreciative of his sexual skills than his wife was. Because Celia hated feeling like the fool she felt Jack's escapades made her appear, and because she was outraged to tears over his actions, which to her indicated an undeserved lack of true consideration and thoughtfulness, and because she wasn't about to become a divorcee entitled only to half the amount of communal property, which although considerable, still paled beside the whole, and because she was frightened, forty-nine and very angry, Celia resolved to hang in, hold on and make every effort to hand out to Jack as much misery as he was handing her.

She was also quite intelligent, and realized that denying the situation would make her look even more ridiculous than Jack did. So she, unlike her husband's conquests, became an honest woman. Her friends, sniffing her sorrow, rallied around and pried. Where previously the conversation leaned toward tennis scores, designer clothes and mastectomies, it now descended to husbands, marriages and who was fucking whom—subjects that had already been exhausted many years ago when the threat was less personal and the poor betrayed wife was some other lady.

Generally, Vivian would begin by detailing with relish what happened to a friend of hers when she discovered her husband was screwing his secretary, and ended with "What would you do if you discovered that your husband was cheating?" Naturally it was to Celia's answer that the greatest interest and attention was given.

"Well," persisted Vivian, "what *would* you do, Celia?"

"Nothing," she said, lighting a cigarette and wrapping Vivian in a cloud of smoke. "Jack fucks everything that walks anyway —he'd even fuck you, Viv, if he were in a charitable mood."

"Are you serious?"

"Walk by him and see."

The ladies looked at each other.

"Well," asked Kaye, "how do you feel about that?"

"How do I feel?—why, terrible, of course," grinned Celia broadly. "Where's my Bloody Mary?" She kept them guessing all right. But she was humiliated.

She protested often to Jack, wept, and even hit him a few times. His standard reply was that it was a tribute to her that he had been faithful for as long as he had and if it were any comfort, he didn't intend to divorce her—but neither did he intend to refrain from or curtail his philandering ways. "I'm fifty-three years old," he explained. "I only go around once."

"I hope you get so dizzy that you fall off your fucking merry-go-round right on your fucking face," she cried.

Jack tried to comfort her. Celia laughed bitterly and told him it was small comfort at best, but thanks for the reassurance.

Because she was afraid, she never delivered an ultimatum. Because she was proud, she refused to buy black lace nightgowns in an effort to lure him back. She *did* toy with the idea of taking a lover herself since Jack's outside activities drained him, so to speak, and their sex life had all but petered out. What stopped her from doing so was not based on morality or ethical principles. "The reason I don't fuck around," she told Vivian, "is not because I'm nervous about breaking a commandment. It's because of my thighs."

"What's wrong with your thighs?"

"They have an independent life. They jiggle to a different drummer."

Bewildered, Vivian laughed. That Celia was always kidding around. "Maybe you should try an exercise class," she suggested.

Celia sighed. "Look, Viv. You know me for eighteen years. Don't try to sell exercise class to a person who gets exhausted cleaning an ashtray. After I bend down to tie my tennis shoes, I need a rest. I make the goddamn bed and I have to lie back down on it." Celia grinned and patted her friend's knee.

"But you play tennis," protested Vivian.

"That's because it's a requirement for living in Beverly Hills," laughed Celia. "It's in my lease."

Vivian looked at her friend. Celia was beautiful and looked very young. She was crazy. "You're crazy, Celia."

"Thank you, dear heart."

After two years or so, during which time Jack exhibited no signs of remorse or of returning to the ranks of monogamy, Celia still had not accepted her situation. She remained depressed, scared and furious. She still felt smirked at. She and Jack had had a peaceful, secure marriage. She was comfortable with him, and until he developed this aggravating new life style, she had often stated that if she had it all to do over again, she'd do it all over again. Now she felt unsteady, like the perilous ground of California, shaken by a nerve-wracking upheaval. She had been stunned by an earthquake, numbed by the after-shocks, the whole ordeal made even more terrible because she had never realized she was standing on a fault.

There was nowhere to go. Her only recourse was to wait it out and pray for endurance. She cried often, aware that even when it stopped, if it stopped, the chances of another quake were excellent. She was living in unstable country and would never again feel safe. How could Vivian imagine that an exercise class could repair her insides? Celia never considered herself naïve. She knew her situation wasn't unique. Jack, like many others, wanted his moment. Unfortunately, fulfillment for him wasn't being picked B'nai B'rith Man of the Year. It was screwing assorted females up, down and sideways. He didn't do it in front of her. He didn't do it in their bed or on the front lawn. She wondered if he expected her to be grateful for his attempts at discretion.

"I don't want to hurt you," he told her.

"Really!" she cried, astounded. "Are you telling me that this is your way of making nice? How on earth could your behavior *not* hurt me?" Celia stared at him, wondering at the peculiar denseness of men who knowingly gouged your heart out and believed it to be a painless procedure.

"If you had deliberately set out to devastate me you couldn't have found a better way." She paused. "I'll make it simple. You're hurting me, Jack . . . a lot."

Jack gazed sadly at his wife. "Well, I don't mean to, Celia, and I'm sorry."

"Thanks," she replied wryly. "I feel better now."

Jack took both of her hands in his. "Maybe it's the times, Celia. I've never felt free. I've been hemmed in by consequences all my life. I can't do this because *that* might happen; I can't do that because *this* might happen. I'm not proud of my method for finding the fountain of youth, but I'd like to live out *one* fantasy before I die." He bent and kissed her hands, which she allowed him to do before pulling them away. He straightened up and took a deep breath. "I'm trying to find myself, Celia."

"Up someone's twat?" she screamed.

Jack looked at her reproachfully and said nothing. Celia tried to control herself, to understand this man she had been married to for almost thirty years and thought she knew inside and out.

"So you need to find yourself?" she asked, her voice shaking in an effort at steadiness.

"I'm looking for Jack Cutler," he said quietly, "wherever he may be."

Celia stood up and tried to appear helpful. "Why don't you look in the toilet?" she asked pleasantly, and then, almost in tears, slammed out of the room.

She couldn't divorce him. Damaged as she was, she knew it would destroy her to be alone. She marveled at Marilyn's decision and wondered if one's ability to be alone depended upon bravery or the lack of it. Whereas her great need was to keep her husband, Marilyn's was to divest herself of hers. Which one of them was the coward, which the heroine? Celia knew now that marriage was risky, that loving could be treacherous. It had taken her a long time to find this out. Was it craven or heroic to exert every effort to preserve them? Celia remembered how alone her mother had always been. When she heard of her death, she had cried a little, not because she was grieved, but because she wasn't. "She died lonely," Celia recalled saying to Jack. "No, she didn't," he replied. "She died alone—there's a difference."

"Not to me," said Celia.

A car started up in the driveway, and Celia ran to the window in time to see Jack drive off. Even after all he'd done to her, she didn't want to be without him. Celia realized how very different she and Marilyn were, despite the fact that they looked enough alike to be mother and daughter. One of them had opted to hold on, the other to let go. Being alone held no terror for Marilyn, while Celia felt that next to "cancerous," "loneliness" was the most awful word of all. To Celia Cutler both words meant death. She adored Marilyn, and wished her the very best of everything. She hoped her decision to divorce Ira was a wise one, and Helen wouldn't crucify her for it. As for Celia, she would sit and cry and wait until Jack's pecker pooped out and he came on home.

She stood at the window and watched the pink sky deepen and grow dark. The palm trees, black against the dusk, looked like the butterfly-wing pendants tourists buy in Florida. Celia now felt like a tourist stranded in a strange town, regretting, with every missed connection, her wanderlust. "Worse," she whispered, "I'm stuck in the cold because of *Jack's* wanderlust . . . worse—Jack's lust."

The telephone rang, and Celia jumped. She ran to answer it, eager to submerge her sorrows in light conversation. Her friends called every night now, curious, ravenous for information. But Celia had never discussed her pain or its cause with any of them. She bandaged her wounds in banter, and the frustration of her friends soothed her like a salve. She teased them all. It was her only pleasure. But it was Helen on the phone, and Helen was no fun at all because she neither knew nor suspected anything. All she ever did was inquire about everyone's health and complain about Natalie's singleness and Marilyn's wickedness. Celia always felt weary after a conversation with Helen, and tonight was no exception. Helen did a good twenty minutes on how Marilyn was destroying everyone's life, "But don't worry, I'll fix her."

"All right, I won't worry."

"Why do you always take her side, Celia?"

"I love her, Helen."

"Can't anyone you love do wrong?"

Celia smiled ruefully and nodded as if Helen could see her. "Yes," she whispered, "they sure as hell can."

"What's the matter?"

"What could be the matter?"

"I don't know—you sound funny."

"I *am* funny."

"Listen, Celia, I need to talk to Jack."

"What about?"

"Lenny had a little accident—nothing serious. He came home tonight and drove into the garage."

Celia waited, concerned. When Helen said no more, she pressed her. "What about the accident?"

"That was it."

"*What* was it?"

"He drove into the garage."

"I know that," said Celia impatiently, "and then what?"

"Then nothing. I heard a bang and ran out."

"Do you mean he drove into the garage, or *into* the garage?"

"He drove *into* the garage."

"Is he hurt?"

"A little shook up, a couple of bruises. He thought he was driving into the garage and instead he drove right through it. The whole front of the car is bashed in and so is the garage. I think he needs new glasses."

"Call Doctor Milkis tomorrow. Jack isn't home."

"Celia."

"What?"

"Why did he drive into the garage, Celia?"

"I don't know. Did you tell Marilyn?"

"I'm not talking to Marilyn. This whole thing is from the upset she caused."

"Stop that, Helen. I'll tell Jack when he comes home."

"Ask him why Lenny did that."

"I will. Stop worrying; Lenny is fine."

Unfortunately, Celia was wrong. She had thought it would take an act of Congress to reform Jack Cutler. She was wrong there, too. Lenny did it with an act of God.

During the three weeks Helen and Lenny vacationed in Europe, most of their time was spent writing postcards and shopping for presents to bring home. Of course, they also dutifully visited museums and cathedrals as well, and Helen broke a heel on a cobblestoned street in Paris and had her purse stolen in a restaurant in Rome. They saw the crown jewels and the changing of the guard in London, the city Helen liked best because she understood the language and the natives were polite and seemed to know their place. They spent their last three days in Monaco, and that was nice, too, except for the rocky beach where Lenny hurt his toe and the casino where he "threw away" eight hundred francs. Helen, in a postcard to Natalie, wrote of seeing the yacht that belonged to "Niarchos, a rich Greek," and went into ecstasies over the color of the Mediterranean—"such a blueness mixed with aqua like I've never seen before. I would love to have a dress that color—and clean, not like the Pacific that we have in Los Angeles."

They bought French bread and Brie at an open-air market, saw the palace wherein dwelt the Grimaldis and once caught a glimpse of a man they suspected was Ringo Starr. Helen felt that the fruit was "fresher and tastier in California," but that the "service was better and the atmosphere very European, abroad." Nothing bad happened to them in Monaco except that once they got locked out on their balcony. "Fortunately," Helen wrote, "our room overlooked the hotel entrance and parking lot. so we yoo-hooed in English, and they sent up a bellboy to open the door. It was an embarrassing adventure that wouldn't happen in the States because the doors back home don't jam like that."

They sunbathed on chaises at the rooftop pool at Loews Monte Carlo, watched disapprovingly while one woman removed her bikini top, and eavesdropped on conversations in French, German, Italian and one language they couldn't identify. Helen would have enjoyed herself if she hadn't had so much on her mind. She worried about Natalie, about Yuspeh, and about Ira and the children. The divorce and its possible ramifications kept her up nights. She even worried about her beloved plants. But it was Lenny who worried her most of all.

He didn't complain, but Helen knew her husband. She saw him swallow Excedrin when he thought she wasn't watching. She saw him rubbing his arm and bumping into furniture. He had received a series of painful cortisone shots for his arm and complained that they hurt more than they helped. Dr. Milkis had recommended that Lenny see a neurologist when they returned from their trip, and that word "neurologist" sent a great tearing fear through Helen. Neurologists were big business already, and even though Jack said it was standard procedure when there was a loss of peripheral vision, still Helen was not comforted.

Lenny's own concern, masked though it was, added to hers. He claimed to be upset at the thought of Marilyn living all alone at the beach. Only occasionally did he make a reference to his physical distress and wonder uneasily at its cause. But Helen heard the strain in his voice and knew that Lenny was also afraid. They talked in bed for hours, about inconsequential things, the children, old memories and shared experiences. They exchanged philosophies and reaffirmed their devotion, sometimes till the early hours of the morning, hoping that with caring and conversation they could push away the dread possibilities that gather strength in the night.

After Lenny fell asleep, Helen would torture herself with horrible diagnoses. Lenny was going blind, Lenny had cancer, Lenny was dying. All the medical terminology she had learned from the newspapers and TV kept popping out of her memory and danced, leering, on her face. Aneurysm, subdural hematoma, mitral stenosis, cerebral hypoxia—words of whose ominous definitions she was totally ignorant yet whose very sound filled her with such terror that her heart would pound, her hands would sweat and her eyes dilate with fearsome visions. She prayed and talked to herself, tried to convince herself that there was a treatable solution to Lenny's ailment. Sometimes she could even ease herself into sleep, only to dream of Lenny dying in agony, and on the last night in Monaco, she awakened both of them with her screams.

She always felt better in the morning. The sunlight somehow banished the horrors and lighted up the dark corners in which they flourished and sprung at her in the blackness. The light brought rationality and reason, and shamefaced but relieved self-disgust at her groundless pessimism flooding back. Lenny had a frozen shoulder and needed new glasses. What was the matter with her?

They both enjoyed the lovely ride through Cannes to the airport, the short flight to Paris and eating *glaces* under the plexiglassed labyrinths of Charles de Gaulle Airport in Paris while they waited for their Air France connection to Los Angeles. Helen had a whole handbag full of packets of Boursin cheese and little bottles of cognac she had collected from her various flights. They passed uneventfully and unusually quickly through customs. Lenny laughingly supposed that they looked too harmless to be dope smugglers or international spies.

Natalie, Ira and the children met them at the airport, and the sight of those people she loved so much shoved out the fears. Helen, embracing them all, wept, feeling for the moment that all her agonized imaginings had been left behind in Europe, along with the red thongs and shower cap she had forgotten to pack.

A few days later, when they recovered from the jet lag, they called the neurologist Dr. Milkis had recommended, a very busy man who couldn't see them for three more weeks. Almost immediately after the appointment was made, Lenny seemed better. His arm improved, his headaches abated and he drove like his old self. "See," he smiled, "I'm so healthy I don't even have to see a doctor, all I have to do is call him and I recover."

Helen, much relieved, could now return to her brooding over Ira and what she called "the hell Marilyn created for us all." She spoke to him daily, asked him to dinner every night, would have moved him and the boys into her house if she could.

One day Yuspeh cornered her. "What's the matter with you, you crazy?" Yuspeh asked. "Why you don't leave that boy alone?"

"Isn't it better he should be with the family instead of rattling around that house by himself?" Helen retorted.

"No."

"What do you mean, no?"

"No is no. You don't know what 'no' is?"

"Why are you saying this?"

Yuspeh, who was sewing an apron for the late Golda Meir, stuck her needle into the fabric and scowled at her daughter-in-law.

"I know you got a reason," she said, "and I don't like the reason." She pulled out the needle and resumed her backstitch. This was her fifth apron for Golda, whose death had stunned Yuspeh but not deterred her from the completion of her project.

The first one, Sunday's apron, made some time ago, had been given to Natalie to press and then wrap in tissue paper, place in a box saved from some department store or other and take to the post office to mail off to Israel. She had included a little note informing Golda of her admiration, along with the hope that she would wear the apron in good health. She cautioned her not to worry if she got grease on it because another apron was in the works and would soon be on its way. Each apron had three pockets, one in the bodice and one on each side of the skirt. The bodice pocket had the letters G. M. embroidered on it; on the right-hand skirt pocket was embroidered the day of the week. Each apron tied in the back, and the edges of both the bodice and the skirt were ruffled.

She had received one letter of thanks from the now-departed Mrs. Meir, which she treasured and kept hidden in her stocking drawer, under the newspaper that lined it. Much encouraged by that letter, Yuspeh planned an even grander surprise for Golda. She would complete two more aprons, so that the ex-prime minister could change every day of the week—and, as soon as the seventh apron was on the plane, she would commence work on a really monumental project, a housedress for Golda, so "she shouldn't be ashamed when somebody important—a Dayan or someone big like that—dropped in." Because this one would be a large package, and understanding the need for security precautions, she planned to write THIS IS NOT A BOMB, IT'S A DRESS on the wrapping, so Golda wouldn't be afraid to open it.

Yuspeh was already up to Thursday when Golda died. On the day of the funeral, Yuspeh put away her sewing box, not to take it out again for months.

"Do you need a reason to invite your son-in-law and your grandchildren to dinner?" Helen demanded angrily.

Yuspeh lay Thursday's apron in her lap and looked up at Helen. "If he's over here every night, he can't be somewhere else, somewhere else with *somebody* else," declared Yuspeh, proud of her analysis. "You don't want him to meet a girl and maybe marry her." She once again picked up her sewing.

Irritated, Helen stood up. "I have enough on my mind without listening to your nonsense," she said and walked to the window. She peered out, looking and listening for Lenny's car. She had lately begun watching for him each evening.

"You watch the pot and it never boils," came Yuspeh's voice from the other side of the room. Helen was still shocked at Yuspeh's lack of reaction to the possibility of her son's illness. Yuspeh had even joked about it once. "What's the worst that can happen?" she had asked. Helen stared at her, her mouth open. "The worst is he'll die," said Yuspeh, answering herself. "And then," she continued, "you'll have to marry his brother—it says that in the Bible." She threw back her head and cackled loudly. "But Lenny don't got no brother," she roared, slapping her thigh in mirth, her eyes shining, while Helen stared back in wordless amazement. What could you expect from an old lady who made aprons for dead people? Yuspeh's laughter dwindled and at last stopped. She wiped her eyes and looked back at her daughter-in-law. "If a mother's tears could save her child," she said softly, "there wouldn't be so many dead children."

A week later they went to the neurologist, Dr. Hoff. After a short wait, during which time they filled out various forms, a nurse ushered Lenny into the examining room. Helen sat outside, trying to read a magazine but unable to concentrate. Finally, she gave up and just sat there, still as a stone, staring at nothing, the magazine lying in her lap under her restless hands, one of which was busy picking the cuticles of the other.

She carried on a free-form prayer monologue in her head, pleading over and over, "Please God, let him find nothing wrong, oh dear God, please let it be nothing. What am I carrying on for, of course it's nothing. Please, dear God, let Lenny be all right."

At last the door opened and the nurse summoned Helen into the doctor's office. Lenny was already seated and gave Helen a dazed smile as she entered. His face terrified her, and she stopped abruptly in the middle of the room, reaching out for something to hold on to. Gently the nurse took her arm, and as though Helen were blind, led her to the couch and sat her down next to Lenny, who clasped her hand tightly and touched his shoulder to hers. They sat there, joined like Siamese twins, waiting for Dr. Hoff.

The nurse left, closing the door with a soft click, and Helen turned to her husband. "Tell me," she whispered hoarsely. "What did he say?" And even as she spoke, her fear at his answer seemed to knot in her stomach with an actual pain. Lenny shook his head. His eyelids were red with the effort to hold back the gathering tears. "Lenny . . ." Helen began, but stopped when the door opened and Dr. Hoff entered the room.

He nodded to them and walked around the desk and seated himself. He pressed a button on his phone. "No calls, please," he told the nurse. Then he cleared his throat and looked over at the couch. His eyes found a space on the wall between their heads, and he addressed that space. Seeing this, Helen's grip on Lenny's hand tightened and her other hand flew up to her chest. She began to breathe rapidly and her eyes, unable to meet the doctor's, stared at his mouth.

"My examination of Mr. Stillman indicates to me that his various symptoms are being caused by a cerebral abnormality. I cannot determine the nature of this abnormality here in my office, and I have therefore instructed my nurse to arrange for his admittance to UCLA hospital for further testing."

The doctor said all this in an emotionless, almost hypnotic monotone, and only after he delivered his pronouncement did he meet Helen's horrified gaze. He reached into his pocket and pulled out a pack of Parliament cigarettes. He lit one and inhaled deeply, holding the smoke for several seconds before expelling it. Helen, mesmerized by his voice and the smoke, watched it curl and glide in the air. She remembered hearing somewhere that neurologists smoke heavily and take time off every few weeks because their specialty is such an emotionally debilitating one and the information they impart is, ninety percent of the time, so shattering. It occurred to her that neurology was probably a very dangerous field back in the days when they killed the bearers of ill tidings.

Lenny cleared his throat. "Is it a . . . tumor?" he asked, almost gagging on the word.

Dr. Hoff took another long drag on his cigarette, and his words and the smoke emerged together. "That possibility exists," he said quietly. "We will know more definitively when we receive the results of the tests."

Lenny slumped, his chin on his chest. He closed his eyes and rested his lowered head on the palm of his hand. Helen stared at the doctor. "Dear God," she gasped.

Dr. Hoff straightened in his chair and for the millionth time wondered silently why he hadn't specialized in obstetrics, where most of the patients left smiling, or, better yet, pathology, where one saw no patients at all. He pulled his chair back and rose. "See my nurse on the way out," he said, "and she'll give you the necessary information." He looked down at the two Ritters, sitting shrunken on the couch. He was used to that pinched look of absolute terror that sat in their eyes, sunk the cheeks and slackened the lips. He had seen people change and shrivel right before him on more occasions than he cared to remember. It seemed to Bernard Hoff that he had handed down a death sentence more often than any judge on any bench anywhere. By now he was sufficiently detached so that he could return home after work, kiss his wife and eat dinner without feeling queasy. But there had been a time when the first thing he used to do was rush into the bathroom and scrub his hands, unwilling to look into the mirror, afraid he would see reflected there a grotesque death's-head, a skeleton face, cloaked and hooded in black, a scythe gripped in the white and bony hands.

"Try not to jump to conclusions," he said gently. "Let's see what the tests tell us." He walked quickly to the door and left. In the hallway, he shook his head and sighed heavily. It would be even more difficult, he knew, when their worst fears and dread suspicions were corroborated. Thank goodness it was the neurosurgeon who would have to deal with that.

Helen and Lenny remained on the couch, unmoving. Finally, they struggled to their feet, got the instructions from the nurse and somehow made it home.

Chapter 17

THAT HER FATHER MIGHT have a malignant brain tumor was so unthinkable to Marilyn that she blocked out the implications entirely. She spoke to him and visited him in the hospital every chance she got, even passing new cases on to other attorneys so that she would have more free time. She held his hand, walked him through the hospital corridors, played gin rummy with him in the lounge. Lenny seemed cheerful, eager for his testing to be over so that he could come home and get into regular clothes instead of the pajamas and bathrobe which were his costume at the hospital.

Marilyn told him that she loved living at the beach, was finding her work very satisfying, had many friends and that she wouldn't take no for an answer, he must promise to stay with her for a few days when he got out. Lenny promised. He told her how proud he was of his accomplished daughter. He tried very hard to keep up his optimism. He assured himself that they would find nothing—that if they *did* find something, it would be benign; if it proved to be malignant, it would be operable; if it weren't operable, the chemotherapy would kill it. That was as far as he went, being incapable of going beyond hope. He would talk to Marilyn about the other patients—"the poor guy in 853 who had a tumor on his optic nerve and was going blind; the fellow across the hall who was burned by the radiation"— and would shake his head in sympathy for the suffering of his fellow patients. He, Leonard Ritter, was going to be one of the lucky ones. But sometimes he would get a look in his eyes that turned Marilyn's stomach to jelly and made her ears ring.

Sometimes, on the beach, she would notice a solitary stroller stop in his tracks and turn toward the ocean, staring at the gray horizon as though he could see beyond the meeting of water and sky. That was the look Lenny had, except that her father's eyes were bleak, not awed like those of the stroller. It was as though he had succeeded in piercing the horizon, of peeping through the double barrier, and instead of sighting Hawaii or Japan or glory, he saw, stretching before him, nothingness . . . limitless limbo. At those times, Marilyn would stare at his head, aching to have X-ray vision like Superman and glimpse through the hair and the bone the action within. How could a head, so ordinary-appearing from the outside, so normal-looking, house death? She began to take a Valium before each visit so that she wouldn't cry in front of her father and make him cry too. Marilyn knew that crying was a giveaway, a strangler of hope, an admission of doom.

The whole family would gather in the lounge, all hostilities buried, perhaps even forgotten, in an effort to entertain Lenny, to cheer him up and take his mind off things. They would laugh and make jokes—a party. All the angers seemed to evaporate and Celia and Jack would hold hands, Marilyn and Helen would nod civilly. Now that the divorce was final, Ira and Marilyn were able to be friendly. Yuspeh, in one of her many annoyingly philosophical moods, had once said, "Death is a big giant. In front of him, everything else is a shrimp." Of all of them, Yuspeh was the most calm. Her life would be little affected if Lenny died. She had lost her husband years ago, and her daughter, Florence, had died of peritonitis at the age of fifteen. She couldn't do anything about them, and she wouldn't be able to do anything about Lenny either—except weep. When you're old, everything dries up, everything but the tears.

The brain scan showed that Lenny had a malignant tumor. When the results came in, the neurosurgeon, Dr. Zeigler, had taken Jack aside, informed him of the findings, asked him to tell the family and all but run off—relieved at unloading an odious task.

Chemotherapy was begun immediately because surgery had been ruled out. The tumor could not be excised without turning Lenny into a vegetable. "They've done wonders with chemotherapy," Jack assured them, his face white. Helen nodded and turned to Ira. "Who's with the children, Ira?" she asked.

"Ophelia."

"That's good," said Helen, and lapsed into silence.

Marilyn, in a panic, demanded to speak to Dr. Zeigler, and ran down the corridor in search of him.

"Dr. Zeigler," she called, "I must speak with you."

The neurosurgeon took her into his office and offered her a cup of coffee, which she declined. His office was behind the nurse's station, a cheerless room lined with filing cabinets and one wooden table surrounded by eight chairs. In the corner was a metal cart on wheels that held a thirty-cup electric coffee maker, a stack of Styrofoam cups, a batch of Sweet-'n-Low packets and several thin red-and-white plastic stirrers.

They sat down at the wooden table, which was piled with books and ledgers. Marilyn saw her father's name on one of the ledgers.

"Didn't your uncle explain?" asked Dr. Zeigler.

Marilyn nodded. "Doctor," she said, "tell me about my father, and don't give me any shit. I want the truth."

He picked out the ledger bearing Lenny's name and opened it. Dr. Zeigler was used to these scenes. They all said they wanted the truth, but he knew better. What they really wanted was for him to deny it.

"What exactly do you want to know?" he asked.

"What kind of tumor does my father have? What is it called?"

"Your father has a malignant tumor of the brain, a glioblastoma." He looked up from the ledger. "I'm going to have a cup of coffee. Are you sure you won't change your mind?"

"Okay. I'll have one. What's a glioblastoma?"

The doctor placed a cup before her, and Marilyn watched the steam rise.

"A glioblastoma is a very malignant, very fast-growing tumor."

"How do you know he has that?" she asked, taking a cautious sip of the hot coffee.

"It has a specific configuration."

"Why can't you operate?"

"It is too widespread. Surgery would necessitate removing too much of the brain tissue."

She nodded, lit a cigarette and dropped the match into her practically untouched cup of coffee. "Doctor," she said, staring at the table, "has anyone in my father's condition ever recovered?"

"The chemotherapy has enabled some people to live for quite a few years."

Marilyn shoved back her chair and stood up. "How long?" she asked, her voice breaking.

"I don't know," said the doctor wearily. "It varies from patient to patient. The longest has been about two, two and a half years."

Marilyn gasped and willed herself not to break down. "And my father?"

"Probably less . . . that's all I can tell you . . . I'm truly sorry."

She fell back into the chair and laid her forehead on the table. Dr. Zeigler looked at her bent head for several seconds and rose. "I'm sorry," he said again, and without another word walked to the door, opened it and left. A minute later a nurse came in and asked Marilyn if there was anything she could do for her. Marilyn sat up, and oblivious to the floating match, took a sip of coffee.

"Is Doctor Zeigler a good neurosurgeon?" she asked.

"The best," said the nurse and left.

After three weeks of chemotherapy, which destroyed his immunities and left him open to attack by even the most innocuous of bacteria, Lenny developed pneumonia. A tracheotomy was performed to enable him to breathe. No one was permitted to enter his room without first donning a sterile robe, mask, cap and shoe covers. The family was informed that his chances for recovery from the pneumonia were slight, only about twenty percent. The tumor seemed to lose importance as they all focused in on the pneumonia.

Seeing her father in intensive care with tubes in his arms and up his nose, a hose taped to the bloody hole in his throat and attached to a respirator that pumped air into his pus-filled lungs, crazed Marilyn and drove her wild. She lunged at Dr. Zeigler, who was leading a pack of young residents making rounds, and grabbed his arm. Startled, he spun around, and recognizing Marilyn, shook off her hand and asked her how she was. "Not too pleased with the results of your treatment," she replied loudly. "How is it," she cried, her voice shrill in the suddenly silent corridor, "that a man with terminal cancer is dying from pneumonia?"

The young residents looked knowingly at one another and then turned and stared contemptuously at this unhinged woman who had the audacity to question the great god Zeigler.

"What is he doing with pneumonia?" Marilyn screamed. "When he came in here all he had was *cancer!*" She stood glaring at the doctor, her chest heaving.

Nurses, hearing the commotion, stopped in mid-ministration and peered out of rooms and stations, thermometers in hand, to stare in amazement at this unheard-of event—a layman actually castigating a doctor, and even worse, Dr. Zeigler, the foremost neurosurgeon of UCLA hospital, possessor of a worldwide reputation for excellence in his field.

Dr. Zeigler drew his brows together in a great frown of fury.

"How dare you criticize my method of treatment?" He pulled his head back as though he were recoiling from a person with onion breath and looked at her distastefully. "I have never been so insulted," he said.

Marilyn actually shook. She stared at Dr. Zeigler and ached to smash his face, to rip out his eyes. "Insulted?" she shrieked. "You're *insulted?* My father is dying of pneumonia because of you, and *you're* insulted? What the hell do you think *I* am? . . . you son of a bitch, you're the one who has insulted *me!*"

Dr. Zeigler turned and, nodding to his disciples, began to walk away. "I'll be glad to answer all your questions when you have calmed down." He halted a few feet away from her and looked back; the residents piling up behind him almost collided with him and one another. "Your reaction is quite understandable under the circumstances," he said, and walked on like a Pied Piper, turned left and disappeared with his band into the next intensive-care ward. Not ten minutes ago the mother of one of his patients had kissed his hands—just reached out, grabbed his hands and kissed them.

After a moment, the nurses returned to their nursing, the hall returned to normal and Marilyn was left standing alone. Drained, she turned and re-entered her father's room. She pulled over a chair, sat down beside his bed, laid her hot forehead against the bed bars and began to cry softly.

The next day Neil brought in a faith healer and no one objected. The healer remained in Lenny's room for thirty minutes and would accept no payment for his services, explaining that he would lose his special powers if he were to do so. Lenny recovered from the pneumonia, and Neil took most of the credit.

By now they knew all of the families of the various patients on the floor. Relatives would gather in the lounge and exchange news of their husbands', or mothers', or wives' or fathers' conditions. Helen became friendly with a woman whose identical twin had the same affliction as Lenny. They often sat together, and Helen got upset when Marilyn told the healthy twin that perhaps it would be a good idea for her to have a check-up herself, being identical and all. Helen felt that Marilyn was cruel, and told her so.

"What else is new?" Marilyn retorted.

A close camaraderie developed among the lounge regulars. All rejoiced when an operation was successful, when someone went home. All were grieved at setbacks. Phone numbers were exchanged, and the social workers on the floor, there to offer both emotional and practical aid to the families of the patients, became personal friends. They were well-trained in crisis intervention and could refer a tormented family member to the appropriate agency.

Lenny was well enough to be wheeled into the lounge, and they would sit him in a sunny spot near the window, ask him if he wanted a 7Up or a magazine and make enormous attempts not to cry at his appearance. Marilyn had to take two Valiums now before she could compose herself sufficiently to visit him. One morning she awoke and couldn't open her eyes. She groped her way to the bathroom and washed them with warm water until they unstuck. Her eyelids were blood-red and the whites of her eyes were crisscrossed with a bright-red network of thin lines. She stared at herself in the mirror and then went back to her bedroom and changed the stained pillow case. She called her office and told Ginger to cancel her appointments, then she dressed, put on dark glasses and went to the hospital. When she arrived, she was refused permission to visit her father because of her eye infection. She went instead to the ophthalmology department, was examined and had eye drops prescribed.

Nothing helped. She awoke every morning with eyes glued shut and cheeks blotched with yellow crust. Only when Lenny completed his current chemotherapy series and was permitted to return home until the next series commenced did her eye condition clear up.

"I reacted physically," she explained to Celia. "It was as though I couldn't bear to look at him, to see him this way, so my body, my eyes, made sure I wouldn't."

Lenny arrived home much improved. The chemotherapy and

radiation had shrunk the tumor and alleviated the pressure on his brain. Helen, Yuspeh and Natalie hovered over him. Max and Murray came to the house and discussed business. Helen cooked his favorite foods and sat watching him while he ate, her heart like a boulder in her chest. Lenny held her hand and tried to talk to her about the future, but Helen couldn't. Lenny persisted, and Helen, seeing it comforted him, at last agreed. Quietly they conversed about insurance, his will, investments, taxes and so forth. He told her not to worry, Max and Murray, Ira and their lawyer would deal with everything. "And Marilyn is a lawyer, too, don't forget." "No one will deal with anything," Helen cried. "You're going to get better."

"I know that," Lenny answered, "but just in case."

Helen nodded. "Okay," she said, "eat your chocolate pudding. Natalie made it special for you."

Phyllis and Neil visited every third evening, bringing organic herbs and sure-fire cures. Patiently Lenny listened to Neil recite the wondrous properties of his wares. Lenny even tried some of them, while Neil and Phyllis approvingly looked on. "You'll feel like a new man," Neil told him heartily, and, to make him feel better, Lenny told Neil that he already did.

He instructed Ira privately to take care of his family, to help Helen, to forgive Marilyn. When Ira broke down, Lenny held him while Ira wept on his chest, angry enough at having lost one father, enraged at the possibility of losing two. Natalie knit for him, and mufflers, foot-warmers, afghans leaped from her needles to pile on her father's bed, warm symbols of her love, damp with tears.

Yuspeh watched her son settling his affairs and putting his house in order. He was informing them with his papers, his advice and his instructions that he was going to die. Even though she knew that Lenny wasn't really consciously aware of the signals he was sending, on some level his mind was, and it kept him busy and the busyness coated the suspected but still incompletely acknowledged awareness of his inescapable destiny.

Yuspeh had seen too much of death to mistake the look of it. Lenny hadn't really accepted it yet, but Yuspeh had. She sorrowed for him and agonized over the terror that would slice into his heart when the blinders of hope dropped off and the horrible shock of comprehension waltzed in. Her poor, poor son. Yuspeh wished she could tell him that dying was far less brutal than much of the living that preceded it. She wanted to talk to him, to explain things the way she had when he was a child, but she knew he could no more listen today than he could then.

Every night now before she got into bed, she would take from her stocking drawer the picture of her husband, Morris, which lay next to the letter from Golda Meir. The picture showed Morris standing in his bathing suit on the beach at Coney Island. His hands were on his hips; he was showing his muscles and smiling broadly. Behind him was the ocean, with a huge wave just cresting, curled and foam-tipped, preserved forever in its most impressive posture, as was Morris. Seconds later, both were gone, the mighty wave nothing but a trickle and Morris dead of a heart attack, face down in the sand. She talked to him. She told him that his son was dying and asked him if it was at all possible to please intercede for Lenny. "Ah, Morris," she sighed, "there is nothing but pain with a child. It hurts to bear them, and it hurts to raise them. But to bury them, Morris, that is the worst pain of all . . . and I will have done it twice . . . Do you ever see Florence?"

Then Yuspeh would kiss the picture and replace it in her drawer. Like a prophet, she knew what lay ahead. By the time death came to Lenny, he would welcome it. It would be for him like butter for a burn, and he would reach for it, eager for easement. And at his funeral, none of them would understand how a mother could lose her child and never shed a tear. The fools would shake their heads and go, "Tsk, tsk, what can you expect from someone that old." Only Marilyn would never recover. Helen was steel, she was granite, a diamond of hardness. She had to be to have survived the inferno that was Malka, and she would survive now, as well. Phyllis and Neil were young; only if they lost each other would they truly grieve. Natalie had her mother. But Marilyn's loss would be total; she had no mother. Yuspeh slept. A week later Lenny re-entered the hospital.

Chapter

18

ALTHOUGH IRA STILLMAN was not her only "friend," he was her only presently vulnerable one. Brenda, not a girl to let opportunities slip by, began to consider giving up her career. It was time to settle down. Lenny Ritter's illness had seriously affected her business by curtailing the visits of two of her most generous clients. She hardly ever saw Jack and Ira nowadays. Ira was home with his kids, and Jack was home with his wife. Even though she was used to seeing her friends come and go, as it were, Brenda was not a carefree forgoer—especially when there was a single, well-to-do, emotionally weakened possibility on the scene. She called Ira at his office and offered, along with her sympathies, various suggestions as to how she could, using special techniques known only to her, take the edge off his pain. She would even, understanding his devotion to his children, make a house call.

She arrived with a package from Jurgensons, Shrinky Dinks for the kids, and no underwear beneath her green jersey Halston. Todd and Jeremy were pleased, Ira was embarrassed, and Helen, who had dropped in unexpectedly, was, to say the least, extremely put out. Here, disguised in the ample form of Brenda Mortenson, was personified her second most dire threat. The divorce papers were barely dry, and the vultures had already begun to zero in on her vulnerable, much beloved ex–son-in-law. Helen pounded the steering wheel on the way home, distraught over Lenny, beside herself over Ira and stunned over the enormous anguish that God was giving her. She still believed that prayer and good deeds would help cure Lenny and placate God. But only immediate action would salvage Ira.

Preoccupied with the severity of her ordeal and bewildered as to its causes, Helen vented her rage and despair on anyone available. She broke down over the slightest mishap, lapsing into near hysteria over forgetting to buy paper towels or adding too much detergent to the wash. She practically lived in the hospital with Lenny, her pain multiplied at the sight of Marilyn, who also seemed, despite her caseload, to be permanently there, intruding herself between her and her husband. They had so little time left, and Helen wanted total possession of whatever time remained. So did Marilyn, and Lenny was fought over as he always had been.

At night, lying alone in her bed, unable to sleep, gripped with unbearable terror at her impending loss, Helen would sob out her anguish, curse her misfortune, plead for mercy and miracles. She was unable to fall asleep without pills, and even Valium and Seconal couldn't keep her oblivious for more than a few hours. Only caring for her plants and feeling concern over Ira's situation seemed to take her mind off her grief, however slightly. In a desperate attempt to relieve her unbearable despair over Lenny, she would force herself to concentrate on a solution to the problem with Ira. She had to. How much could one human being lose?

And Marilyn. Marilyn, too, would be destroyed. When she realized how much satisfaction that gave her, Helen, horrified at finding a source of gratification in her husband's dying, literally gouged pieces of skin from her arms, and at feeling the sting was reminded that Marilyn had always been able to make her bleed. Helen lost weight and her eyes, dark from weeping and lack of sleep, seemed to burrow into her head. When she wasn't with Lenny, she spent time with her plants, devoting hours to planting and replanting, potting and repotting. They were her only comfort. Since she was almost constantly at the hospital Natalie would leave work early to help in the running of her own house as well as the management of Ira's. Because Ira was away all day and Ophelia didn't drive, Natalie became a surrogate mother to the boys—and so doing, found a measure of contentment, despite her pain over her father.

Yuspeh sewed her aprons and drank her tea. She would occasionally accompany Helen and Natalie to the hospital and sit beside her son's bed, staring at him, smoothing his sheets, shaking her head over the food that lay untouched on his tray. After a while she stopped going. Half the time Lenny didn't know she was there anyway. He couldn't walk now, and when he was able to sit up, his head tilted to the side. He spoke with difficulty, rarely completing a sentence, forgetting his thought after the second word. Mostly he would lie in bed staring un-blinking at his visitors, memorizing them and unnerving them all with the vacant intensity of his gaze. He had by this time completed his radiation and chemotherapy series. He was totally helpless, unable even to scratch his nose.

To Marilyn, sitting in the hospital and watching her father disintegrate before her eyes like a film dissolving and fading from one frame to the next, the enormity of this helplessness was staggering. He seemed to be approaching death by re-living all the stages of development—descending the evolutionary ladder and traveling backwards in time like some reversed rerun gone haywire. He was a baby again. Soon even his physical state would alter. He would drop from animal down to vegetable down to thing. This kind of dying, this most awful method of dying, even this immeasurably incomprehensibly fiendish form of dying seemed to follow a pre-set and orderly course. It was enough to make you believe in God.

Marilyn buried herself in law books. Because every time she closed her own eyes she saw her father's, she slept little, spend-ing night after night with torts, contracts, divorce laws, working on cases she neglected during the day. She made insane deals with God or Satan or whoever was the boss of the miracle department. Maybe it was lack of sleep; maybe her anguish; whatever it was, Marilyn believed that if she successfully handled Beryl's case the tumor would shrink—if she was invited to write an article in the *Harvard Law Review*, it would disappear entirely. By the end of the year she had and it hadn't.

One evening she walked into her father's room and found the whole family, including Ira, surrounding the bed. Upset because she wanted to be alone with Lenny, she went to the lounge to smoke and wait them out. She greeted the familiar faces and sat down at one of the round, white tables that sported an ashtray. She lit a cigarette and stared out the window at the lights and rooftops of Los Angeles. It was a relatively clear night and she could make out the planes landing and taking off at LAX. The hospital quieted down at night. The nurses seemed to walk more softly and chatter less. There were fewer carts and lifesaving machines rolling quickly and noisily down the halls. The undecipherable demands of the PA system were muted, its voice less strident. Marilyn put her feet up on a chair and closed her eyes. For some reason she felt close to herself, almost cozy in this oasis of a lounge. Outside it was dark and full of strangers. Here, in the quiet corner occupied by whispering, never-tranquil faces, she was surrounded by people who, in a sense, were related to her, who shared with her the common bond of misery. She almost smiled at the realization that mutual suffering made a most effective icebreaker. She felt more at home in the lounge than she had at any party any time, where icebreakers were planned in advance and guaranteed to thaw even the chilliest of attitudes.

She looked up and put her feet back on the floor as a very attractive, very well-put-together young woman pulled out a chair and sat down at the table across from her. She looked familiar, but Marilyn could not recall where she had seen her.

"You're Marilyn Stillman, aren't you?" she asked, smiling. "I once saw a picture of you in Ira's office, and I saw you once at a party at Beryl's, and I recognized you right off." She stopped smiling and looked sympathetically at Marilyn. "I'm really sorry about your father," she added.

The silver lady, toned down, remembered Marilyn. Phooey. Somewhat annoyed at the intrusion, she said abruptly, "Thank you."

"I'm Brenda Mortenson," continued her new table-mate. "I'm a friend of Ira's. We were on our way to dinner, and Ira decided to stop off and see your dad."

Interested, Marilyn looked her over. She was surprised. She wouldn't have thought Brenda was Ira's type. "How good a friend?" she asked.

"We're very close."

"Meaning what?"

"Meaning we fuck."

For the first time in months, Marilyn laughed out loud. "You just gave me your sympathies," she said, still smiling. "Now you've got mine."

Brenda rooted around in her handbag and pulled out a Gucci cigarette case. From it she extracted a pink cigarette and lit it with a lighter that even from across the table Marilyn could tell was solid gold.

"Oh, I don't know," said Brenda, inhaling deeply, "I've had plenty worse." She leaned back and thought for a moment. "He's what I call a number seven."

Again Marilyn smiled. "He's what *I* call a fucking bore—or a boring fuck. Take your pick."

Brenda grinned and flicked her cigarette ash on the floor. "He's always spoken highly of you," she said. "Want a pink cigarette?"

Marilyn took one and examined it curiously. "What kind of cigarette is this?"

Brenda shrugged. "I have them made," she explained. "Go on, light up, it's only tobacco." She flicked the top of her lighter and held it out to Marilyn. The cigarette was nice. It had a sweet, pleasant taste.

"Are you and Ira serious?" asked Marilyn.

Brenda sighed and rolled the glowing tip of her cigarette along the rim of the ashtray. "I am, he's not—not yet, anyway."

"Well . . . hang in there."

The two of them sat quietly smoking, feeling easy with each other. Then Brenda put out her cigarette and stood up. She began to replace her lighter and case in her bag, then took the case out again. "Want one for later?" she asked.

"No, thanks. Where are you going?" Marilyn was surprised at her reluctance to see Brenda leave.

"I'm going to wait in the car. I don't want to be here when they come out . . . you know, it'll just upset your mother, who, by the way, is not too crazy about me, and that will upset Ira, and that will make it lousy for me . . . and it's lousy enough." Brenda picked up her bag and put her jacket over her arm. She looked at Marilyn. "I guess it's just a lousy time for everybody," she said quietly. Unable to speak, Marilyn just nodded.

"Well," said Brenda, "you take care now," and as she passed Marilyn's chair, she patted her shoulder.

Marilyn wiped her eyes and felt sorry that she hadn't accepted Brenda's offer of another sweet, pink cigarette. Her shoulder was still warm from Brenda's touch, and Marilyn realized with a start that she hadn't had a friendly hand, or indeed any hand, on her person for a long, long time. She was all alone, really all alone. Well, thought Marilyn, maybe it's better. The closer you get, the easier a target you make. She reached for her own pack, lit up and glanced at her watch. Just as she was wishing that her mother and Ira and the rest would get the hell out of her father's room, she sensed a subtle change in the atmosphere of the floor. Others in the lounge, like Marilyn—blood kin to the living dead lying in dark humming rooms all over the section who, as she, were also attuned to the slightest change even in the nuance of a breath—sensed it too, and lifted their heads, instantly alert, bodies tensed, eyes darting, sniffing like cornered deer at the smell of death. The hall suddenly was filled with the ominous sound of hurrying, soft-soled shoes. From the room of some patient still well enough to retain his intuition and human need to know what was going on, came a panicked yell of curiosity.

"Nurse, what's happening?"

Marilyn leaped to her feet, heart pounding, and clutched the back of her chair. Another patient had awakened, and from his half-open door she could hear him muttering, moaning over and over again, "Jesus, help me, sweet Jesus, help me, help me, God, oh, God, oh, Jesus, help me."

The elevator door suddenly opened and three people, their faces contorted in dread, flew out. Marilyn recognized them immediately. It was the identical twin, her husband and her brother-in-law. Involuntarily Marilyn moved toward them. "Frances," she cried, but none of them heard her as they raced down the hall. She stood staring after them and remembered that once, on a sunny afternoon, while sitting in this lounge, she and Frances had had a conversation.

"It's weird," Frances kept repeating, "it's weird, it's like I'm in the Twilight Zone. I look at my sister lying in bed, and it's *my* face on the pillow, it's *my* body under the covers. I look at her, and it's *me* who's lying there. When we were little, no one could tell us apart. Sometimes I have a nightmare and when I wake up I don't know who's the sick one, me or Frieda. I swear to Christ, Marilyn, the nurse gives her a needle and I feel the sting in *my* arm, God strike me dead if I'm lying."

Marilyn watched the three of them disappear into Frieda's room, two nurses close behind. Then she turned and walked back to her chair. The people in the lounge looked silently at one another and began to relax and whisper. Some poor tormented soul had died, or was dying, but it wasn't any of theirs.

From down the hall, Marilyn heard Frances begin to scream. "I'm dead," she shrieked. "God help me, I'm dead."

Chapter

19

MAYBE SCIENTISTS KNOW why there are more births and more deaths at night. Helen wasn't concerned with the mathematics of it, she just felt that when there are big doings, privacy is important. Neither one's entrance into the world nor one's exit from it are pretty things, and are therefore more appropriate to engage in under cover and in the dark. Propriety had always been important to Helen. Even though she didn't approve of dying from cancer, she did feel that Frances's twin, Frieda, had shown good taste in choosing to depart at night when the nurses were less busy and most of the patients asleep. Daytime dying lacked dignity. Everybody knew about it; it frightened and depressed the patients, it inconvenienced the medical staff and unnerved the visitors. The whole business of sneaking the body out of the room, calming the loudly grieving relatives, removing the roommate of the deceased to more cheery surroundings, disinfecting and remaking the bed, packing the personal effects of the former occupant—all those necessary procedures somehow seemed ludicrous when performed while the jovial, warming rays of the sun poured in and gaily flooded the scene. It was the contrast, thought Helen, that made it all so unseemly.

At Frances's scream, Helen had rushed into the hall, saddened for Frances, yet glad that Lenny seemed to be asleep and oblivious to the commotion outside. Seeing that her husband was there and that Frieda's husband seemed in control, Helen remained in the doorway, leaving the comforting of the wailing, near-hysterical Frances to her menfolk. She watched for a while, then sighed and softly closed the door. She walked back to the bed.

"What happened?" asked Natalie.

"The twin, Frieda, just passed away."

"Poor Frances," Natalie whispered, "poor Frances."

"A sister is closer in blood than a mother," said Yuspeh, who had surprised them all by her decision to visit Lenny. "Sisters got the same blood, that's why it says in the Bible for a widow to marry her husband's brother—brothers also got the same blood."

"Stop that," cried Helen, angry at Yuspeh's nonsense. "How many times are you going to say that?"

Ira took his jacket off the back of a chair and put his arm around Helen. "Try to stay calm," he said, kissing her cheek. "I'll see you tomorrow." Helen nodded. She knew where Ira was going, and with whom. "Be careful," she told him. When Marilyn had married Ira, Helen was so pleased that for a moment she entertained the notion that there might be some hope of patching things up between them. She felt that Marilyn had given her a present, whether she knew it or not, and was grateful for it. She remembered saying to Yuspeh that this was the only decent thing Marilyn had ever done for her.

"It wasn't for you," Yuspeh replied. "It wasn't for her either; it was for Lenny." But Helen hadn't cared. She was happy, and even if Yuspeh were right, it still was the only happiness she had ever received because of Marilyn. Well, she should have known better. Marilyn had been kicking her in the heart even while she was carrying her. Even in the womb she had given her grief.

By two A.M., and despite the Valium, Helen had not fallen asleep. Her eyes felt raw, and she went into the bathroom to wash her face. She was so weary, so drained. She stared at herself in the bathroom mirror and for a moment couldn't recognize the woman staring back. Her face was frightening, ravaged, as though a war had been fought on it. She put on her robe and tip-toed down the stairs to the kitchen. Neil had brought her some valerian herb tea. Maybe it would help. She filled the kettle and set it on the stove. "Lenny," she whispered, as the steam began to rise. "Lenny."

She poured boiling water into the cup, watching the tea bag rise with it to the rim. She took a spoon and pushed the bag down, then carried the cup to the table and lowered her body onto a chair. She waited until the water darkened—Neil said herb tea has to steep—then took a spoonful and blew on it several times before cautiously putting it into her mouth. It tasted awful. How Neil and Phyllis could drink this vile stuff, it even smelled awful, was beyond her. But everything was beyond her now. "Lenny," she whispered again and pushed away the tea-cup. Folding her arms on the table, she laid down her head. She felt swollen with grief, a huge balloon. "Help me, Lenny."

It was ironic, she thought, that of all the people in the world, probably the only one who would understand, who would share her ocean of sorrow, was Marilyn. But Marilyn had never shared. Helen sat up and reached again for the cup. She took a long sip and gasped as it burned its way to her stomach. It didn't seem so bad now, maybe she was getting used to it. It occurred to Helen that life was the same way. Life was so awful, it even smelled bad. The only way to get through was by getting used to it until you reached the point where it didn't seem so bad any more. Well, she had tried. She had gotten used to it. So now look.

"Time, Helen," Celia had once said, in an attempt to comfort her. "Time. In time, you'll adjust, you'll get used to it. It won't be good, but it will be better." Helen shook her head. Baloney. The asylums were full of people who hadn't been helped by time or anything else. Maybe, thought Helen, those aren't really crazy people. Maybe they're only people who couldn't, even with time, get used to it. Her mother, Malka, never had. The bitter and the sweet didn't exist for Malka. Only the bitter. She had tried to help her mother by doing things the other girls did that pleased *their* mothers. So she won spelling bees and got a certificate for never once forgetting to come to school with a clean handkerchief pinned to the front of her dress. But Malka wasn't like the other mothers. When news of the Nazi genocide made the front pages, Malka washed the kitchen floor and covered it with the newspaper to protect it from the dirty shoes of Celia and Helen, the only children left at home. Celia pointed in horror at the floor. "Mama," she wept, "they're killing Jews." "They're always killing Jews," said Malka.

"They're burning them in ovens; they're gassing them."

"There are many ways to murder," said Malka.

"Six million Jews, Mama."

"Better than seven million," said Malka.

Celia was stunned. "Don't you even care?" she gasped.

"No."

"But you're a Jew."

"I am nothing."

Celia was silent. "Maybe it's better to be a Christian," she said at last.

"It's better to be a Jew," said Malka.

Celia looked at her in confusion. "But all the Jews were victims," she protested.

"All the murderers were Christians," said Malka.

The other day on television, Helen had heard Elie Wiesel say the same thing, and Elie Wiesel was a brilliant man, a writer. Imagine that. She was a strange woman, Malka. Why was it, if she also possessed brilliance, that only the strangeness showed. No, Malka wasn't like other mothers. She wasn't like anything. And neither was Marilyn. When the girls were little, she and Lenny had taken the three of them to see *Peter Pan*. The children were entranced, and when Tinker Bell was in trouble and the audience was requested to applaud to save her life, the theater exploded with the frenzied clapping of the children. Every single one of them applauded. Except Marilyn. She sat in her seat, eating peanuts. Natalie and Phyllis banged their hands together until their palms were red. Noticing Marilyn's lack of response, Helen nudged Lenny, who turned to Marilyn in surprise. "Clap for Tinker Bell," he urged her. "No," said Marilyn. "Why?" asked Lenny. "She'll die if you don't clap." "Let her die," answered Marilyn. "She was mean to Wendy." Of course, Lenny thought that was cute, but for Helen it was a reaffirmation of her oldest daughter's lack of compassion. To Helen this was just another indication of Marilyn's selfish, cold, rotten character.

Helen picked up the half-empty teacup, walked to the sink and poured the remaining tea down the drain. Her life was so bleak, so joyless. Her husband was dying. Her son-in-law and her only grandchildren would soon be lost to her as well. Phyllis and Neil had very little need of her any more. And Natalie . . . every time she looked at Natalie, a piece of her heart broke off. Helen felt that her life was over. That when Lenny died, she would be as good as dead herself. She went to the stove and turned on the burner under the kettle. She took a bag of Swee-Touch-Nee tea and put it in the cup. Then she added two teaspoons of sugar. If her life lacked sweetness, at least her tea wouldn't. She poured in the boiling water and returned to the table. A dead person drinking tea. She looked up in surprise when the door opened and Yuspeh shuffled into the kitchen. "I also couldn't sleep," said Yuspeh, and pouring herself a cup of tea, she joined Helen at the table.

"I can't forget Frances's face," said Helen. "Soon my face will look like that."

Yuspeh, who was stirring her tea, put down the spoon and sat very still. Both women were silent, hunched over the table.

"My mother didn't believe in God," said Helen at last. "I used to think that was terrible . . . I don't any more . . . she was right."

Yuspeh frowned and, picking up her spoon, began stirring again.

"She was not right, she was crazy," said Yuspeh.

"Not crazy. Different."

"Crazy," repeated Yuspeh.

"Concentration camps and cancer . . . and she's the crazy one? Hah!"

"You only see death, Helen," said Yuspeh sadly.

"Because it's all around me," cried Helen.

"So is life."

"Some life," said Helen bitterly. She looked up and gazed angrily at her mother-in-law. "I don't understand you. Your son is in a hospital dying of cancer."

Yuspeh picked up her cup and dipped her forefinger into the tea. Then she licked it off and took a sip.

"I'm talking to you," snapped Helen.

"I'm thinking."

Again they sat silently. After a few moments, Yuspeh got up and went to the refrigerator. She opened the door and stood for a while scanning the shelves. Then she took out some rye bread, farmer cheese, butter and honey, and carried it back to the table. As Helen stared in amazement, Yuspeh got two plates, two knives, two napkins and the salt shaker. These she also placed on the table and then sat down. Still without a word, she buttered a slice of bread, cut off a chunk of farmer cheese and salted it. Then she began to eat. A bite of bread, a bite of cheese. She opened the jar of honey, dipped in her spoon and sucked it off. Feeling Helen's eyes upon her, she looked up and met the astounded gaze of her daughter-in-law.

"Have something," she said.

Helen remained speechless. Yuspeh pushed the bread, butter and cheese in front of her. "Go on," she urged, "eat." She buttered a slice of bread and put it on Helen's plate. "I had a friend, Dutchy, who ate always like a horse until she looked like a horse. So I said to her, 'Dutchy, how come you have such an ambition to get fat?' So Dutchy says to me, 'I feel better when I eat.' 'Well,' I told Dutchy, 'from how your behind is looking like a mountain, it seems to me, you're feeling wonderful.'"

Helen picked up her bread. "What is that supposed to mean?"

"It means eat your bread, maybe you'll also feel better."

Helen looked at her bread and obediently took a bite. "What am I going to do, Ma?" she whispered.

"Have with it some cheese," answered Yuspeh.

"About Lenny."

"Can you cure my son, Helen? Are you a genius doctor?"

"I wish I were."

"But you're not."

"So I should eat cheese?" Helen asked incredulously.

Yuspeh shrugged. "You got something better to do?"

"No," said Helen softly. "I got nothing better to do." She cut off a slab of farmer cheese.

"A person who can eat is a living person," Yuspeh said. She thought for a minute. "Marilyn is too thin."

"Marilyn."

"She has nothing—no husband, no children, no mother, no father . . . no appetite . . . nothing."

"It's her own fault."

Yuspeh shook her head. "No," she said. "Natalie's life is her own fault. Marilyn's life is not."

"I don't want to talk about Marilyn."

Helen began to gather the food. She took it and replaced it in the refrigerator. With her napkin, she wiped the crumbs from the table.

"Marilyn is Lenny's daughter, not mine."

"And she is also losing what she loves."

Irritated, Helen crumpled the napkin and threw it on her plate.

"She didn't have to be left with nothing," cried Helen. "She had a husband, a wonderful husband and wonderful children, and she threw them away! And because of her I'm losing them, too. I'm losing everything."

"You're a fool." Yuspeh stood up and leaned over the table. She put her face close to Helen's and glared angrily into her eyes. "What's in the heart you can never lose," she said loudly. "Even when my son dies, you will have people around you who love you. Marilyn won't."

Helen took Yuspeh's napkin and wiped her face, which Yuspeh had peppered with spittle. "It serves her right."

Yuspeh sat down abruptly. "You're a hard woman," she said, "like your mother."

"Ma, go back to sleep," Helen told her wearily. "I'm tired of your opinions, your sayings from the Bible. You sound like Dear Abby."

"So I should make her money," grumbled Yuspeh and stood up and walked out of the kitchen. Helen finished clearing the table. As she rinsed off the dishes, she composed letters to Dear Abby. "Dear Abby," she whispered, "my husband is dying. How do I go on living? Signed Grief-stricken in Encino." She took the dishtowel and began to dry. "Dear Abby, I have two single daughters. One can't find a husband, and the other threw hers away. Signed Heartsick in Encino."

Suddenly Helen stood stock-still, her eyes wide open and staring. Her heart began to pound, and she grabbed the sink for support. After a long time, she finished drying the silverware and replaced it in the drawer. For the first time since his illness, Helen was not thinking about Lenny. She was thinking about Dear Abby. She walked slowly to the door and shut off the light. As she climbed the stairs, she composed her third letter. "Dear Abby. Thank you for everything. Signed Grateful in Encino." She took a Valium, and got into bed. Within minutes, she was asleep. When she awoke at nine-thirty the next morning, the first thing she did was call Ira at the office. She told him how troubled Natalie was, having to work at Blaze Lighting, where she was constantly reminded of her father. She told Ira that Natalie needed a change of scene to take her mind off her grief. She asked Ira to give her a job in his office. Then she hung up, got dressed and went to the hospital. She didn't feel happy, the enormity of her tragedy left no room for that. But she felt better.

Chapter 20

CELIA KNEW THAT JACK, only two years younger than Lenny, had been badly shaken by the illness of his brother-in-law. In his specialty Jack rarely encountered medical accidents that could be termed acts of God. He was a plastic surgeon, and he spent his days mainly correcting the acts of man and modifying the accidents of birth. His practice consisted, for the most part, of cosmetic surgery, and he and Celia could have lived wonderfully well off the breasts, behinds and noses of Beverly Hills. No one close to Jack had been struck down the way Lenny had, and the spectre of his own impossible-to-protect and fragile mortality began to beset him. "There but for the grace of God . . ." became a habitual part of his speech. Like a second-year medical student, he started to assign ominous meanings to even the slightest twinge, and an innocent headache would throw him into a panic.

Guilty to begin with, Jack began to fear retribution. He came home to Celia. Because he felt that if Celia punished him, perhaps the Almighty wouldn't, he meekly submitted to her rightful and constantly chastising behavior. Now that she had him where she wanted him, Celia really let him have it, and Jack gratefully took it.

All this Marilyn learned from Brenda Mortenson, who had

decided to become Marilyn's friend. She was, although stunned by the revelation of Celia's past situation, even more surprised over the eagerness with which she welcomed Brenda's interest. Now that she was finishing up with Beryl Sinclair, Marilyn often found herself idle and directionless. With nothing to put her mind to, she was totally occupied with brooding and constantly assailed with depression and terror. She spent hours at the hospital, made uncomfortable by the proximity of her mother and devastated by the condition of her father. She even visited Todd and Jeremy, took them to lunch and bought them Junior Scrabble games which they couldn't play and didn't want. The children were sullen all through her visit, nervous and uneasy with her. When Todd knocked over his milk, he instinctively threw up his arms in protection at what he felt would be his mother's enraged reaction, while Jeremy cowered wide-eyed in a corner of the booth like Chicken Little, waiting for the sky to fall. This, more than the overturned glass of milk, infuriated and embarrassed Marilyn. It took all her willpower, and the fact that they were in a public place, to restrain herself from giving them exactly what they so obviously expected.

After lunch she shoved them into the car, took them home and drove off as soon as they stepped onto the sidewalk. She went to the hospital and found her mother there, holding a straw to her father's lips so that he could drink from a can of 7Up. She stayed for a while, holding Lenny's hand, trying to smile at him until she could bear it no longer. Then she went home and paced her empty apartment. She finally stopped when she caught sight of herself in a mirror and realized that in movies that took place in mental hospitals, the mad woman in the film paced as she did, going nowhere, around and around in constant random movement, with identical desperate eyes.

She called Natalie but was told by Yuspeh that her sister was where Marilyn ought to have been—with her children. She called Celia, but was told by the housekeeper that the Mister and Missus were out. After failing in an attempt to lose herself in a book, she turned on the television set, switching from channel to channel and discovering, much to her disgust, that the only programs that held her were the evening game shows. She had no idea why. What would she do when they were over? She wanted to call her father. "Help me, Papa," she said out loud. "Help me, I'm all alone."

At seven-thirty, since there were no more game shows, she turned off the set. She reached for her cigarettes, and finding she had only two left and would have to go for more, was grateful to have something to do. She would walk over to the market and get cigarettes. Quickly she put on her coat, grabbed her bag and almost ran to the door. When the telephone rang, she stopped abruptly, unused to the sound, suddenly frightened beyond reason that it might be the hospital. Who else would be calling? Terrified, she picked up the phone and without saying a word strained to hear the background noises.

"Hello? Hello? Have I got anyone?"

Marilyn relaxed. It wasn't the hospital.

"Yes, who is this?" she asked and sank into a chair, so relieved that her legs almost buckled.

"This is Brenda Mortenson, do you remember me? I met you in the hospital and gave you a pink cigarette."

"Hi, Brenda."

"You doing anything?"

"No."

"Neither am I. I was supposed to see your ex tonight, but, thanks to your mother, he's home playing fucking Scrabble with your sister and the kids—and I'm sitting here, high and dry on a Saturday night."

"Horrors," smiled Marilyn.

"Anyway, if you're in a similar condition . . ."

"What did you have in mind?"

"Close Encounters."

"The movie?"

"No. The singles bar."

"I've never been to a singles bar."

"Well," said Brenda, "you can't stay a virgin forever. I'm coming over," and she hung up.

A moment later the phone rang again. "3246 Seascape, apartment 8C . . . and bring cigarettes," Marilyn said.

Within half an hour Brenda arrived. She looked over the apartment with a critical eye and informed Marilyn that it was an armpit compared to hers. "Move to Marina Del Rey," she advised. "This neighborhood sucks." While Brenda was examining the apartment, Marilyn was examining her. Her costume was startling. She was braless, and her formfitting flesh-colored Danskin leotard, into which she had somehow oozed herself, emphasized the fact that Brenda Mortenson was not one of the world's shy and self-conscious citizens. Around her neck were at least fifteen gold chains, some plain and others with lapis butterflies, ivory elephants and opal hearts dangling from them. The most impressive was a large, linked, Florentine chain sporting an enormous gold cross, complete with a pain-wracked Jesus, who, Marilyn hoped, derived a measure of solace at being nestled between Brenda's full, perfect, completely outlined breasts.

Beneath the leotard she wore sheer pantyhose, and over those, a pair of tight, transparent jeans that appeared to be made of Saran Wrap. On her feet were very high, open-toed pumps with sling-back heels, also transparent, decorated with rhinestones. She looked wonderfully naked. Next to her, Marilyn, in white, lightweight, French wool slacks and a navy-blue silk shirt, all but disappeared. Unable to disguise her fascination, Marilyn stared. Delighted, Brenda stretched and preened, twirled herself around to give Marilyn a complete perspective. "Like it?" she asked.

"It's spectacular," gasped Marilyn. "When I turn queer, you're going to be number one on my list."

Brenda walked over and began unbuttoning Marilyn's blouse. "Hold it," said an alarmed Marilyn, pushing Brenda's hands away. "I said, 'When I turn queer'—I'm not there yet."

"Relax, dummy, neither am I," replied Brenda. "You got that

blouse buttoned up to your eyeballs, and it looks like you're trying to hide the treasure of Sierra Madre. Nobody buttons a blouse that high. Even my aunt, Sister Mary Angelica, knows better than that." Again, she began to unbutton Marilyn's blouse, opening it to her cleavage. Then she stepped back and checked it out appraisingly. "Take off your bra," she ordered. "Tits look super under silk. You got any chains?"

"No to both," said Marilyn. With a withering look, Brenda removed three of her own and fastened them around Marilyn's neck.

"Not great, but better," decided Brenda. "And those are not gifts, kiddo. I give my friends advice and support, but my gold I keep. Here's some cigarettes. I also give cigarettes." Smiling, she tossed two packs of Salems to Marilyn, who caught one, dropped the other and felt inordinately touched that Brenda had remembered her brand.

"I don't even know you," Marilyn said softly.

"So what? Am I asking you to marry me? All you got to know is I like you and I'm not after anything you've got . . . I'm after what you *used* to have, but you can't help me with that. So stop the crap, move your ass, and let's get the fuck over to Close Encounters before all the good stuff gets grabbed up—and take your own car."

"Why can't we go together?"

"It's not the going, dummy, it's the leaving once we've got there." Brenda shook her head in wonder at Marilyn's ignorance of the protocol. "Look, if I meet some guy, I do not want to have to take you home. And vice-versa, of course. You're not bad, you've got as good a shot, better even, than most of the motley crew you'll find there."

"Oh," said Marilyn.

"Look—you want to be my friend? Then remember one thing. We are not joined at the hip. I like big, grown-up girls—and no smart remarks," she added, seeing Marilyn about to speak. "You know what I mean?"

"If I don't, be sure and tell me," said Marilyn, dryly.

Brenda looked at her curiously. "Where you been?" she asked. "You've been divorced a good couple of months already. How come you're so out of it that you go to a singles bar dressed like a delegate to a 'Women for Christ' convention?"

"I've been spending a lot of time in courts," replied Marilyn primly.

"Law or tennis?" asked Brenda.

"Sometimes it's hard to tell the difference."

Brenda stared at her. "What the hell are you," she asked, "a voyeur or something?"

"That's one way of putting it. Actually, I'm an attorney."

Brenda looked awed. "I'm impressed, really impressed. Good for you."

"Thank you. *Now* maybe I'll get a little respect here."

"You'll get it from me, I'll tell you," promised Brenda, and looking over Marilyn's shoulder, she asked an unseen audience, "Can I pick 'em or can I pick 'em?" She turned back to Marilyn and smiled at her in delight. "Well, come on, Counselor," she said, bowing, "get off your tort and let's split."

Close Encounters made every effort to deliver to its patrons exactly what its name promised. The lighting was subdued, with a preponderance of "baby pinks"—the lights that certain movie stars kill to stand in, since they flatter even the most imperfect of skins and facial formations. The center of the room was taken up by a huge circular bar, arranged specifically so that everyone sitting at it had an unobstructed view of everyone else sitting at it. On the bar, placed conveniently within reach of the patrons, were small copper bowls of meatballs, complete with decorative toothpicks; plates of cheese cut in bite-size pieces, with an assortment of crackers, and bowls of guacamole dip and corn chips. A small, rolled, complimentary packet containing two Certs was served with every drink.

Lining the walls were small tables with two to four chairs. In the center of each table was a drink list, an ashtray, salt and pepper, more Certs, and a pad and pencil. On the top of the pad was written: "I met." The center of the pad was blank—to be filled in, of course, with the name, address and home/office telephone number of the lucky meeter, and at the bottom of the pad was written, "At Close Encounters. Good drinks, good food, good people—our specialties." In the margins around all four sides were cute little pen drawings of people eating, drinking and tastefully mating. At Close Encounters it was not considered a successful evening unless one departed the premises with the pickup of one's choice, and at least four filled-in sheets of the pad, folded carefully in one's purse or pocket.

Each small table was situated next to a mirror. The standard procedure at Close Encounters was to closely encounter someone at the bar or in the cruising area between the bar and the tables, feel pleased enough to invite him or her to a table in order to become better acquainted, decide that you like the other sufficiently to spring for dinner and, after the meal, replete with food, drink, confidence and mellowness, to suggest making a night of it at your place or my place or the Close Encounters Motel, located exactly adjacent to the club. The mirrors were there to enable one surreptitiously to case the room in the event that the new friend across the table failed to live up to one's expectations, failed to agree to shack up after dinner or failed to look as good as the new piece of stuff that either just walked in or you missed hitting on the first time around.

The waiters and waitresses were all gay. It was the policy at Close Encounters to have something for everyone, no matter what turned you on. Decorating the walls were pictures of smiling couples who had encountered each other right here, and with a sincere desire to reassure the clientele that their time and money was well spent, had gone on to autograph and write on the lower right-hand side of the photograph a heartfelt expression of thanks to the management of Close Encounters, who made it all happen and who also generously paid for the photographer, the frame and the time of the lucky twosome.

There was a mandatory five-dollar cover charge, and drinks were extra and expensive. Uncivilized behavior—attempting to make a meal out of the hors d'oeuvres or nursing drinks—was discouraged, sometimes strenuously, and three enthusiastic supporters of acceptable deportment were on the premises to ensure the peace of mind of the management.

Marilyn and Brenda walked in, paid their five bucks each and had the backs of their hands stamped with the letters OK, which could be seen only under a special lamp. Evidently Brenda was well known by not only the regulars, but the help as well. With cheery welcomes, a place was made for them at the bar and a piña colada placed before Brenda without her having to order it.

"What's your pleasure, Sweet Lips?" the gay bartender asked, smiling at Marilyn.

"A glass of white wine, please." The bartender lifted his eyebrows and looked questioningly at Brenda.

"You give Clarence Darrow here anything she wants, Ellie—and the good stuff, not that moose piss that you hand out to the losers."

Ellie took a bottle from below the counter, uncorked it and poured it into an iced wineglass.

"Marilyn," said Brenda, "it's always a good idea to have a friend behind the bar—so I'm going to introduce you. If I go off, Ellie here will keep an eye on you. Right, Ellie?"

"Of course. Wasn't I a Saint Bernard in my former life?"

Marilyn smiled and took a sip of wine.

"Marilyn," said Brenda, "meet Ellie Vaytor. Ellie, this here is Marilyn."

Ellie picked up Marilyn's hand and kissed it.

"Ellie Vaytor?" asked Marilyn, curiously. "Why?"

"It's quite simple if you think about it," replied Ellie. "What does an elevator do?"

"It goes up and down."

"Well," grinned Ellie, "so do I," and he went off to serve another customer.

The place was beginning to fill up and most of the bar stools were occupied. Brenda, smiling and waving, seemed to be having a ball. Her eyes, Marilyn noticed, were constantly in motion, expertly scanning the room, despite the fact that at least six men were dancing around her, eyeing her breasts and vying for her attention. Already three piña colada glasses were standing empty before her, the straws, lipstick-tipped, leaning against them.

Marilyn was almost finished with her second glass of wine and wondering what the hell she was doing here. Even if her father were not dying in a hospital, even if her intestines were not in pieces over her grief, even then this wouldn't be her kind of place.

"I would offer to buy you a drink," said a voice next to her, "but I don't believe in any form of role-playing." Marilyn turned her head and looked into the appraising eyes of the man on the stool beside her. He was attractive, late thirties, shirt opened to his double-G Gucci belt. Over the shirt was a leather cowboy vest with fringes and beadwork. He wore a gold ring with the sign of Aquarius engraved upon it.

"Is that a mystical precept," asked Marilyn wryly, "such as astrology or alchemy?"

"Oh, nothing like that," he assured her. "I simply feel that the person who does the paying should not be determined on the basis of sex."

"Upon what basis do you think it should depend?" asked Marilyn.

"On none," replied the man. "If a person wants a drink, he or she should order and pay for it—most women feel that a man is obligated, even in this day and age, to pay for their food and drink. I happen not to agree."

"You don't like women assuming that you will bear financial responsibility."

"Or any man."

"Do you ever deviate from your stand?"

The man thought for a moment. "Not really."

"I see," said Marilyn. "What if you invite a girl to dinner in your home. Do you charge her for the meal?"

"Of course not," he answered, offended.

"Then why do you insist she pay when you invite her to dine outside your home? Isn't she still your guest?"

"I wasn't talking about that," he said coldly.

"Oh, it only applies to this type of situation?"

"No, I'm not a hypocrite. Ellie," he called to the bartender, "give me another." Then he turned to Marilyn. "You want more wine?"

"If I do, I'll ask for it."

He drew back in mock dismay and held up both hands. "Hey . . . fine . . . don't get so defensive."

"Ready for another one, Sweet Lips?" asked Ellie, placing the man's drink before him and eyeing Marilyn's practically empty glass.

"Yes, please."

"That's not on my bill," cautioned the man.

"I'm hip, sport. I've seen you here before," said Ellie, and giving him a disgusted sneer, moved off.

"My name is Lee Geller, and you are—?"

"Not interested." Marilyn took out a cigarette and before she had the chance to pick up her lighter, Lee had a flaming match to its tip.

"That's the trouble with you women," he complained, blowing out the match and tossing it into an ashtray, "you fight like the devil for equal rights and then get mad when you get them."

Just then Brenda glanced over and spotted Lee. "Uh-oh," she said, making no effort to lower her voice. "There's Lee Geller, the cheapest son-of-a-bitch this side of Boston Harbor. Hi, Lee." Then she nudged Marilyn. "Lose that sucker," she advised. Marilyn nodded and turned to Lee. "Get lost, sucker," she said.

"Get lost yourself," snarled Lee.

Brenda whirled around and, leaning across Marilyn, angrily regarded him. "Now look," she told him, poking him in the arm. "You're annoying my friend."

"Tough shit," said Lee, pushing her hand away. "I don't converse with hookers."

"Well, it's like this," Brenda went on. "If you don't get your ass the hell away from here, I'm gonna inform everyone that your thing is little and blue and Ellie here will back me up, right, Ellie?"

"Absolutely," lisped Ellie. "I could hardly find it."

Lee, embarrassed by the laughter, hurried away.

"You were a bit rough on him, don't you think?" asked Marilyn.

"He's got a rotten attitude," explained Brenda, "and there's nothing worse than a cheap hayshaker with a rotten attitude."

"What's a hayshaker?"

"A hick, a shit-kicker."

"Oh, I see."

"Good," said Brenda, and turned back to her admirers.

By now Close Encounters was so jammed that there was barely room to move around, yet the traffic was continuous. People kept changing locations, hoping to improve their luck. There was a steady stream to and from the bathrooms and so much noise that, even as closely packed as everyone was, it was almost impossible to hold a conversation. Beyond the bathrooms was a dance floor and, at eleven o'clock, Brenda informed Marilyn, music would be supplied by a live combo and the room would clear out a bit.

The small tables were as yet largely unoccupied, it being still too early for as important a commitment as dinner, and outside stretched a long line of singles waiting like anxious pilgrims to get into the promised land.

"Who do you have to fuck to get a drink around here?" yelled an angry voice above Marilyn. "Hey, bartender!" Marilyn looked up and saw a very tall, very annoyed man waving a five-dollar bill in a futile effort to attract Ellie's attention. Around his neck hung a huge and heavy medallion that threatened to hit Marilyn in the head each time he moved.

"Miss," he said, tapping her on the shoulder, "would you mind getting me a drink?" He handed her the five-dollar bill. "J & B and water—tell him heavy on the J & B, easy on the water, not the other way around."

"Will there be anything else?" asked Marilyn, sarcastically.

"Yeah—pass me a meatball."

"Is the word 'please' in your vocabulary? And get that lethal weapon that's hanging around your neck away from my head."

He picked up the medallion and put it in his shirt pocket. "That word doesn't seem to be in your vocabulary either. Maybe it's the atmosphere. I've heard it said that overcrowding breeds antisocial behavior."

Marilyn looked up in surprise.

"My drink?" he reminded her. "Please?"

"Ellie," she called.

"Name it, Sweet Lips."

"This gentleman," she said, indicating the man above and behind her, "is very thirsty. He is willing to pay well for a J & B and water. Can that be arranged?"

"I'll give it my all," said Ellie.

"I'd rather you gave it your speedy attention—and while you're doing that, give this kind lady a refill of whatever she's having—please."

Marilyn looked up and nodded. "Thank you," she said.

"You're welcome," answered the tall man. "Where's my meatball?"

"I draw the line at meatballs," she smiled.

"Now that I know that little idiosyncrasy, would I seem too pushy if I asked you to divulge your name or shall I have to make do with Sweet Lips?"

"That's four even," said Ellie, arriving with the drinks, and Marilyn handed him the five-dollar bill.

"You done good, Ellie," she said, "keep the change."

"I haven't even proposed yet," complained the tall man, "and already you're spending my money."

"Serves you right for talking to strangers."

"I'm hungry," he said.

"Thanks for confiding in me."

The man smiled. "What's your name, Sweet Lips?"

"Marilyn."

"Are you hungry, Marilyn?"

"Yes."

"Do you usually remedy that condition by eating?"

"Through the years I have found it to be the most effective way."

"We have a lot in common. Let's eat."

Marilyn nodded and slid off the bar stool. "Brenda," she said, tapping her on the shoulder.

"What?" asked Brenda, turning her head slightly.

"I have been invited to dine."

Brenda swiveled all the way around and looked with interest at the tall man with the medallion. "Who's your friend?" she asked.

"Come to think of it, I'm not quite sure." She looked up into his face. "My friend wants to know your name."

"Tell her it's Samuel Greenfield," he said, smiling down.

"Okay, I will. Brenda Mortenson, this tall person is Samuel Greenfield."

Brenda looked him up and down and around. At last, her inspection complete, she rendered her verdict. "Not bad," she said. "Except for one minor detail."

"What's that?" asked Marilyn.

"Nothing to pass up dinner for. I'll tell you later."

"It's settled then," said Sam. "I'll go get us a table. Would you and your friend care to join us?" he asked Brenda.

"Maybe so."

"Good," he said, "we could use a centerpiece."

"What are you, some kind of smart-mouth florist?"

"Don't you know a compliment when you hear one?"

Brenda narrowed her eyes. "I know it when I hear it, I know it even better when it's handed to me wrapped in a Tiffany's box, but I also know it when it's covered in crappola. What I just got from you was a candy-coated dig."

"It was sincerely meant."

"If you say so. Get a table, we'll join you in five."

Following Sam through the crowds seemed to Marilyn like walking through jungle underbrush. Sam, cutting and hacking a pathway, pressed on, carved out a trail, and they emerged at last into the clearing and sat down opposite each other. Marilyn felt tired and depressed. She hadn't accepted a social invitation in weeks. What was she doing here, making meaningless chatter, sparring with strangers, sitting in a place filled with noise and life, when she was filled with dread and fear? She felt ashamed and guilty for smiling. She felt she had offended herself and degraded the love, the enormous love, she had for her father, who was dying in a hospital while she was sitting across from a man she didn't know, at a table in a singles bar, waiting for a fag waiter to hand her a menu.

Marilyn realized it would have been more acceptable somehow if she had stayed home alone in her apartment and allowed the anguish to wash over her in scalding waves. How could she have permitted this betrayal? What the hell was she *doing* here?

"Is something wrong?" asked Sam.

"Yes."

"Can I help?"

"No."

Like a blind person, Marilyn groped for her cigarettes. Her hands had begun to shake so badly that Sam had to take the pack and get one for her. He put it between his lips, lit it, handed it back, and steadying Marilyn's hands, guided it to her mouth. She inhaled deeply, praying for self-control and forgiveness. As her trembling decreased, she knew she had somehow managed one of them. She doubted she would ever manage the other.

She looked up and saw Brenda coming toward them. The crowd seemed to fall away, giving her clearance, as though she were the Queen of England out for a stroll. Whistles and shouts of appreciation, as well as invitations and suggestions, followed in her wake as she made her way to the table. Behind her, all smiles, walked the lucky consort, almost blazing in pride at having copped the best-put-together piece in the place.

Sam, his eyes on Brenda, nodded appreciatively. "She does create a stir," he observed, and rose politely from his seat as Brenda approached.

"God," said Brenda, lowering herself into the chair next to Marilyn, "it's easier to get down Wilshire at rush hour than walk across this room. Marilyn, Sam, meet Anthony Santacroce, half Sicilian, half Polack, and all around odds beater."

The men shook hands and sat down. Brenda, immediately sensing Marilyn's distress, peered into her face. "Look, kid," she said, speaking softly for the first time that evening, "stop laying such a heavy trip on yourself. In the great cosmic picture it won't make a fucking bit of difference." She laid her hand over Marilyn's. "Look, if it'll make you feel better, you can suffer anywhere. You don't have to sit home to do it. Okay? Now knock it off before you louse up everybody's evening."

"Okay," murmured Marilyn. "I'll try."

"Marilyn," said Brenda in a normal tone, "say hello to old Anthony here."

"Hello, Anthony. Somehow I feel I already know you." Anthony smiled and nodded. "Why does Brenda call you an odds beater?"

"I think Anthony should be pleased he wasn't called worse," laughed Sam.

"I am," agreed Anthony. "This Brenda sure is one prejudiced woman."

"I am not," she said, looking offended. "I just call a spade a spade—except of course when I call him a nigger."

Anthony roared and slapped his palm down on the table. "Ain't she something, that woman?" he asked, wiping away tears of mirth.

"Brenda!" cried Marilyn, aghast.

"Just kidding. Don't get your liberal cholesterol up."

"Why do you call Anthony an odds beater?" Marilyn asked again.

"Because he is," said Brenda. "Lookit, this poor guy is half wop, half Polack, right, Anthony?"

"Right," chuckled Anthony.

"By all odds, he should be dumb, short, fat, dark, and have hair growing out of his ears. Instead he's smart, tall, and terrific-looking. By me that's beating the odds."

"I'll drink to that," said Sam, "as soon as I get a drink. Waiter," he called to a passing red jacket.

The waiter nodded and hurried over. "You rang?" Taking out his order pad and pencil, he put his hand on his hip in an exaggerated pose and inspected the table. Anthony stared back. The waiter was in full makeup.

Brenda nudged her date. "Quit staring," she hissed, "you look like a goddamn tourist."

"I am a tourist," said Anthony, tearing his eyes away.

"Do you want to give me your order?" asked the waiter, "or must I beg for it?"

They gave him the drink order, asked for the dinner menus, and Brenda told him that he had lipstick on his teeth.

"Wow," said Anthony, when the waiter went off.

"Where are you from, Anthony?" asked Sam.

"My home base is Phoenix, but I travel a lot."

"Tell them you got your own plane," said Brenda.

"I got my own plane," said Anthony.

"Can I pick 'em or can I pick 'em," crowed Brenda. "I caught myself a one hundred percent gen-u-wine capitalist." She leaned over and playfully punched Anthony in the arm with great satisfaction. Then she turned to Sam: "What do you do?" she asked.

"I build houses," he replied.

"You got a plane?" asked Anthony.

"No," said Sam regretfully. "I got a Pontiac."

"It's a start," comforted Brenda.

The waiter returned with the menus and the drinks. He named each drink as he placed it in front of them. He put the menus on the edge of the table. "Any of you good people in TV or cinema?" he asked. "It's not that I'm doing a survey," he explained, "but taking orders from people and waiting on them has somehow lost its joy for me."

"And you think it's time to move on?" asked Brenda.

"Yes, yes, yes!" cried the waiter eagerly.

"So what are you standing here for? Move, move, move!" she said, shoving him away. Again, Anthony laughed in appreciation. "I love a woman with a sense of humor," he said. "It's very important, a sense of humor. I even laugh at myself. Brenda here told me a joke at the bar that maybe if she told it to some other guy, he'd of broke her arm. But not me. I even laugh at myself."

"What was the joke?" asked Sam.

Brenda looked questioningly at Anthony, who smiled and nodded. "Did you ever hear the one about this half-Italian, half-Polack?" she asked.

"No," said Sam.

"He made himself an offer he couldn't remember."

Anthony shook with laughter.

"I think I'll go to the ladies' room," said Marilyn, standing up.

"I'll keep you company."

They elbowed their way through the crush to a small clearing with a bank of telephones on one wall and two doors on the opposite wall. The signs on the doors read "Foxes" and "Wolves." Marilyn flinched reading them, knowing in her bones that whoever had conceived those epithets considered each and every patron who passed through the portals of Close Encounters and similar establishments nothing but an animal. And Marilyn felt he had a point.

The ladies' room was crowded, but Brenda soon found space for them in front of the mirror. Marilyn sat down on a vanity bench and watched Brenda repairing her face and hair.

"Wanna fly to Vegas?" asked Brenda through newly glossed lips.

"I want to go home."

"He's a class guy, Sam. I like him. If he had real money, I'd make a play, but he doesn't."

Marilyn looked at her curiously. "What do you mean, 'make a play'?" she asked. "Sam's with me."

"So what?"

"What do you mean, 'so what?' "

"If I wanted him, I'd go after him, *that's* what I mean."

"But he's with *me*," said Marilyn unbelievingly.

Brenda put down her hairbrush and looked at Marilyn. "You know something? You could get a Ph.D. in lawyer and you'd still be dumb. Why would you even think that I'd sacrifice my desires for yours—or anybody's? Why should I?"

Flustered, Marilyn stared at her. "Well . . . because poaching is . . . dishonorable."

Brenda began to laugh. "You're really a phony," she grinned. "Dishonorable, my ass. Do you think your feelings are more important to me than mine? Do you really think I should give up what *I* want so you can have what *you* want?" She laughed again and picking up the brush, continued arranging her hair. "If you think that, you're a jerk. I'm not looking to get canonized, and I'm sure as hell not the fucking Red Cross. What I am is honest. I care more for me than I do for anyone else. If I put someone else's feelings before my own, just to live up to some ass-hole code of honor, I'd end up as phony as you." She paused for a moment, pursing her lips and tapping the brush against the palm of her hand.

"I imagine," she said thoughtfully, "that the only time I'd ever put myself second would be for my kids." She gave her hair one final brushing and replaced the brush in her handbag. "But I don't have any kids, so it's all academic."

Marilyn sat still, silently considering Brenda's philosophy. She felt neither angry nor threatened. Brenda took out her cigarette case and, opening it, held it out to Marilyn. "And whether you admit it to yourself or not, you're no different from me. I knew it the minute I laid eyes on you and that's why I called you. Have a cigarette."

They both lit up.

"By the way," said Brenda, blowing out a stream of smoke, "your friend is married, number one, and I don't want him, number two. You've got nothing to worry about as far as number two goes."

"I'm not worried a minute," replied Marilyn. "Sam's marital status concerns me not at all, number one, and any man who is interested in me will not be distracted by big tits and pink cigarettes, number two."

Brenda snapped her handbag closed and put out her cigarette. She gazed expressionlessly at Marilyn, who stared right back. "Well," said Brenda, giving herself a last inspection, "if I'm going to Vegas, I better get a move on." She straightened her pants and walked to the door. "If I think of it," she said, "I'll call you when I get back."

"Oh, you'll think of it all right."

"Why is that . . . dear?" asked Brenda, her hand on the door.

"Because I have three of your gold chains . . . dear."

They looked again at each other for a moment, then Brenda nodded, pushed open the door and left. Marilyn sat smoking her cigarette and feeling her depression return with even greater intensity. She didn't care about Brenda, she didn't care about Sam. She didn't even really care about the people she loved, or thought she loved. There were over four billion people in the world, and of all that incredibly vast ocean of souls she really loved and cared about only one. She became suddenly enormously frightened. She felt herself begin to tremble, the long ash on the pink cigarette broke off and fell unnoticed into her lap, leaving only a glowing tip in her shaking fingers. She stared unseeingly at the mirror, feeling empty, hollow, like an old, dead tree, and as the realization hit her that if her father died there would be not one living thing in all the world that would truly matter to her, the stub of the cigarette dropped from her numb fingers and fizzled out in a small pool of water on the mirrored counter top of the vanity. She looked at it, paralyzed, so nauseated that she began to gag and throw up. Dimly she heard voices asking if she was all right, and someone put a wet paper towel into her hand. She nodded, unable to speak, and waved them all away. She dragged herself to her feet and staggered into a toilet cubicle, locking the door behind her. Leaning against it, she tried to control her nausea, taking deep, ragged breaths. After a while it subsided and she sat down on the seat, drenched in perspiration.

She heard the restroom door opening and closing, and voices commenting in disgust at the mess she had made on the vanity top. Someone called the matron, who filled the air with furious curses directed at "those goddamn, fucking bastards who can't hold their drink and puke all over the whole fucking place—it's not enough I gotta clean shit and piss, now I got vomit." The room began to smell of ammonia, and after a while the attendant left. Marilyn got to her feet and wiped her hot face and neck with the paper towel. She threw it into the bowl and flushed it down.

There was a new shift of women in the bathroom now, and no one gave her a second glance as she emerged from the cubicle. She looked awful and felt exhausted. Without bothering to fix her hair and face, or even wash, she ran out of the bathroom and through a back door to the parking lot. She stood for a moment breathing in the ocean-scented air, feeling chilled as it cooled the perspiration that soaked her clothes and body. She found her car, unlocked it, got in and drove home.

She walked into the empty apartment and remained for several seconds in the doorway, disoriented, looking around her as though someone had come in in her absence and rearranged all the furniture. She felt she too had been rearranged, re-configured in some way, and was now unable to recall the original decor or how to undo the change. She looked at the telephone, remembering how it had connected her with her father whenever she needed to hear his voice. No more. And if there were no medical miracle, no remission, and she lost him, then out of over four billion hearts, not even one, not Celia's or her sister's, would have more than a mere jot of space for her.

What really broke her, what ripped the sobs from her throat and bent her with weeping, was the finally acknowledged, unalterable realization that when her father died, there would be no one, not one person left out of all those billions who really, truly *loved* Marilyn Stillman.

Chapter 21

AFTER THE LAST RADIATION and chemotherapy series was completed, the tumor became unstoppable. It grew like a vine in a rain forest, sending out strong, webbed tendrils that wound around and choked everything they encountered. It grew over, it grew under, it surrounded and clutched. It grew upward and downward, inward—spreading, invading. By the time it made its presence known, it was too late to exorcise or loosen the slimy, steely grip. It had begun to take over and conquer, a malicious, insidious, vicious parasite, stupidly devouring, poisoning, impairing, murdering its host, who now lay dying behind the closed door of the hospital room.

During his second hospitalization, Marilyn remembered the visit that had almost done her in. She had stood outside his door with her mother and sisters, waiting for the nurse to remove her father's penis from the beaker-shaped bottle into which it had been inserted so that he could urinate. Of all the indignities this illness had imposed upon the man she loved most in the world, this he considered the worst. He had confessed it to Marilyn after enduring in mortification and shocked horror the first time that impersonal female hands had handled his penis and put it into a bottle so that he could perform a function that even his wife, during thirty-six years of marriage, had never been permitted, even accidentally, to observe.

He was a modest man, private with his body, who did what he had to do behind closed doors, alone—until then. "Imagine," he had whispered, his eyes glued to an unseen picture on the wall behind his daughter, "imagine having to have this done to me . . . a man like me."

Marilyn couldn't look at him then, and swung her tear-filled eyes down her father's body, hidden beneath the starched white sheets. They stopped at the slight mound below his stomach and quickly fled back up to his chest.

"Papa," she said, unnecessarily pulling the sheet up higher, "before you know it, you'll be out of here and laughing about all this. We'll walk to town and get hot fudge sundaes. Right, Papa? With sprinkles, and double whipped cream."

"Right," he said, covering her hand with his, and they both stared at last into each other's lying eyes.

Now, again, they stood waiting.

The door opened and the nurse swished out, nodding to the family. They walked into the room and gathered around the hospital bed. Marilyn reached through the raised metal side bars and grasped the slack fingers of her dying father. "Papa," she whispered, knowing that if those eyes were to open for anybody, they would open for her. "Papa," she said again, "it's me, Marilyn. It's Dolly, Papa. Look at me. Please, Papa," she squeezed his fingers, "open your eyes. It's me, your Dolly."

"Marilyn, leave him alone," snapped her sister Phyllis, frowning at her from across the bed. "Stop pulling at him, you'll pull a tube out. Let him sleep."

"Shut up, Phyllis."

"Girls," said their mother, "please."

Marilyn looked at her mother and at Natalie standing at the foot of the bed. Her mother's right hand was resting on the blanket, palm up, her left hand held tightly in Natalie's. Her face was slack and expressionless, her eyes tortured. "Please," she repeated.

Marilyn wanted them all to leave. She wanted to be alone with what was left of Papa. He had always been her favorite thing, and she had been his. He was always there when she needed him to be. Except for now, during the most critical time in her life, when her *father* was *dying* and her need for him was more enormous than it had ever been. Now, when her fear was so overwhelming and the safety of his comforting arms so desperately craved, now of all times when she really, *really* needed him, he wasn't here to help his Dolly and make it all better.

"Get up, Papa, you bastard," she pleaded silently, looking at the still, pale face, the eyes closed, the skin loose, the mouth slightly open with white, dry spittle in the corners of the cracked lips. She saw every pore in his face, every groove, the stubble on his cheeks, each individual mark and mole and eyelash. This was her father lying here. Her Papa, and she knew that when this man was gone, she wouldn't be anybody's Dolly, not ever again.

"Come," said her mother, sighing heavily, "we'll have lunch."

Suddenly desperate, Marilyn turned to Helen. "Mama."

Helen looked at her in surprise.

"What?"

"I'm scared, Mama. I'm so scared."

"You're scared, Marilyn? So what are we? . . . Dancing?"

Her mother walked to the window sill and picked up her purse. "Come," she said. Natalie and Phyllis gathered their bags and coats and walked to the door.

"Come on, Marilyn," said Phyllis.

"I can't stand it. I can't breathe."

"You'll have some lunch, you'll feel better," said her mother.

"You think lunch will make me feel better?" Her voice rose incredulously. "Are you crazy?" She stared furiously at her mother.

"Marilyn," said Natalie, walking over and putting a hand on her arm, "don't make a scene, please."

"I'm not making a scene," she said, shaking off Natalie's hand, her eyes fixed on her mother's face. "Is a hot meal going to make *you* feel better, Ma? Is it?"

"Look, Marilyn, you don't want to eat, don't eat . . ."

"Nothing can make me feel better," she said heavily, looking down at her father's drawn and pale face. His head looked strange, the hair once so crisp and abundant now so sparse and dry. Reddened patches of skin, burned by radiation, dotted his scalp. He had lost much of his hair from the chemotherapy, and the chemotherapy, even more than the tumor, had destroyed him.

"I'll never ever feel better again. Never." She looked once more at her mother. "How can you even think of eating? He can die any minute. He can die while you're chewing a tuna fish sandwich."

Her mother frowned in annoyance. "Girls," she said to Natalie and Phyllis, "are you ready?"

"Come on, Marilyn," said Phyllis.

"No, I'm staying here."

"Stay," said her mother.

"Should we bring something back for you?" asked Natalie.

"No," said Marilyn. "I'm not hungry. My father is dying."

"So is Phyllis's father dying," cried her mother, suddenly furious, "so is Natalie's."

"Different," said Marilyn. "You wouldn't understand."

"Oh, wouldn't I? Girls," Helen turned to Natalie and Phyllis, "wait for me in the cafeteria—get a table." When the door closed behind them, she dropped her handbag onto a chair and moved quickly to her daughter. She grabbed Marilyn's shoulder and spun her around. She was breathing heavily, her nails digging into Marilyn's flesh, her lips parted in fury.

"I understand all right," she hissed through clenched teeth. She released Marilyn's shoulder and grabbed a handful of her hair, pulling her head back. "Do you think you're the only one who's suffering?" she cried, giving her hair a yank. "Do you think only you are scared?" She yanked again.

"My Papa is dying. I'm losing my Papa," sobbed Marilyn.

"Is that so?" Her mother released her hair and pushed her against the wall. "Look at that bed." She took Marilyn's chin in her hand and roughly turned her face toward the bed. "Do you know who is dying in that bed?"

"My Papa," wept Marilyn, her body shaking.

"No," said her mother, dropping her hands and straightening up. "That is my husband."

They stood absolutely still, eyes locked. "My husband," Helen repeated, and walked out of the room.

After her mother left, Marilyn fell into the orange vinyl chair near the window and stared at the still figure in the bed, numbed by her mother's almost triumphant cruelty. She shook her head. "Mine," she whispered. After a few minutes she got up and walked over to him. She put her two hands on his poor bristly head and, closing her eyes, began to concentrate. She concentrated very hard, picturing in her mind the awful thing that was growing in his head, growing and leaving less and less room for life, pushing that life out of his ears, his nose, his eyes. She concentrated on shrinking it, watching it get smaller and smaller, receding, easing the pressure. Her hands began to tingle. Through Neil, Marilyn had heard of healers who performed miracles that left doctors open-mouthed and disbelieving. She spread her fingers over her father's head and prayed for the power to change things.

When at last she opened her eyes and removed her hands, she half expected to see him stir and smile and sit up.

For her twelfth birthday she had received a red rain cape and matching umbrella from her Aunt Celia. Her birthday was in July, and it rarely rained in California in July. So she had prayed. She prayed to God and Moses and Abraham, Isaac and Jacob; she prayed to Jesus, Mary, Joseph, St. Jude. She prayed to Buddha and Mohammed and Aten. She prayed to every deity she had ever heard of. She prayed for days for a miracle. For it to rain in California in July. And, after a week, it rained. Joyous, and a bit awed by her power, Marilyn walked up and down the street in her red rain cape and matching umbrella, thinking, pleased and smug, that none of the surprised Californians, caught unprepared by the downpour, had the slightest idea who had caused this amazing deluge. "They didn't realize," she told an enraptured Natalie, "who brought on the rain. They had no idea that they were looking at the one who did it. Me."

Marilyn turned and walked back to the chair. She was thirty-four years old and knew now that she had wasted her one miracle on the weather. She was startled by a noise from the bed, a strangled snort fading to a gurgling moan. She flew to her father's bedside but found him unchanged, his face greenish-white, his mouth open. The respirator hummed, the tubing attaching it to her father's throat vibrated gently, his chest rising and falling in rhythm to the action of the machine, which was breathing for him. "Papa," she whispered, "Papa." She leaned over the raised railing of the hospital bed and touched his rubbery cheek, then took his hand and squeezed it gently, praying for an answering pressure, receiving nothing. She took his fingers and pressed them around her hand, holding them for a moment and then releasing them. She watched the slack fingers fall open again, slightly curled back onto the bed. She stared at the hands that had thrown her shrieking with delight high into the air and caught her again so surely, the hands into which she had trustfully placed her own when there was a dangerous street to cross, or when she begged to be twirled around and around, feet off the ground, flying.

"Papa," she whispered again, and her love generated a pain so enormous and a terror so overwhelming that her heart began to pound and her feet became numb. She breathed rapidly through her mouth and had to lean for support against the bed. She attempted to regulate her breathing to the pumping of the respirator, inhaling when it caused her father to inhale, exhaling when he did. She felt an awful, undirected anger, and suddenly realized that it was love and loving that had created her torment. Only when you love so much do you have so much to lose. She suddenly flashed on a memory, brought by the pain, the way a scent or a snatch of music can trigger a recollection. She was a little girl, sitting quietly, holding tightly to her father's hand, awed by the vastness, the strangeness, the bustling silence of the hospital waiting room. She gazed up into her father's face. It seemed to her that he was a shining person. His eyes gave light, the blueness of them blazing under the dull fluorescent tubes. His hair gleamed, clean and smooth, his forehead was high and bright and glowing. She lifted his hand to her lips and kissed it. He smiled down at her.

"When will the baby come, Papa?"

"Well," he answered, "babies come when they are ready to come. Not one minute sooner, not one minute later."

"Will it be a boy or another girl?"

"It will be what it is meant to be."

"We already have two girls, Papa. Me and Natalie."

The father looked down at the small ruddy head, two braids lying on her shoulders, tied with yellow ribbons.

"So, if this is a girl, we will have three little girls. That's okay by me. I love my girls."

"Will you love it if it's a brother?"

"Yes, I will love it, whatever it is."

"Papa?"

"Yes, Dolly?"

"Mama wants a boy."

"Maybe it will be a boy."

The little girl sat quietly. She played with her father's fingers, pushing them back and forth.

"Papa?"

"Yes, Dolly?"

"Will you love the baby better than me?"

"I will never love anything better than you." He gave the braids a gentle tug.

"Even if it's a boy?"

"Even if it's a boy."

"Do you love me better than Natalie?"

"This much better." He held his thumb and forefinger an inch apart.

The child leaned against her father's arm, content. She smelled the clean smell of his shirt and rubbed her cheek against the fabric. A wave of love washed over her so sharply that it became a physical pain. She put her free hand to her chest and felt a burning in her throat.

"I love you, Papa," she whispered.

"Good," he answered. "It's good to love."

"It hurts," said the child.

"What hurts?" he asked, taking her by the shoulders and looking into her eyes. "Tell Papa what hurts."

"Loving," she answered, pressing her hand harder against her chest and swallowing rapidly in an attempt to ease her throat.

The father smiled. "Come," he said, standing up and taking the hand from her chest. "We'll go get a Pepsi."

Marilyn closed her aching eyes. She walked over to the television set they had so optimistically ordered for her father and turned it on. She watched *The Price Is Right*, and correctly guessed the exact price of an Amana microwave oven. From the orange vinyl chair she won a car-packed showcase. During commercials she stood staring down at her father, touching him, returning to the chair when the show continued. She watched *Family Feud*, and wondered how her family would fare. She would go on the show with her mother, Phyllis, Natalie—not Grandma, she was too old, not Grandma's sixty-four-year-old son, he was dying.

When it was all over, the respirator shut off and the bed empty, Marilyn figured that at about the same time the Kaminsky family had won ten thousand dollars and were jumping and hugging one another, her father's heart had stopped beating and the pulse in his neck had grown still. While the music blared and the audience applauded wildly, his fingers had uncurled, his head had turned slightly to one side, and his lips had lifted over glinting, yellowed teeth in a grisly grin of congratulations for the victorious Kaminskys. Marilyn had been in the orange chair watching a game show, and not until the commercial, just before $20,000 *Pyramid,* did she realize, with a piercing, agonized shriek that brought two nurses and a doctor racing in, that her Papa had died—quietly, finally and all alone.

Chapter 22

WHEN SHE WAS ABLE TO, Helen packed all of Lenny's clothes and gave them to the Hadassah thrift shop. She wept over each shirt, each suit, each pair of pajamas. She pressed her face into his sweaters, breathing in the smell of him, finally putting on his favorite brown cardigan and hugging it to her body. She wore it every day, folding back the too-long sleeves and putting it over her nightgown instead of a robe. She wore it outside to garden in and threw it over her shoulders to ward off the chill in the frozen food section of the supermarket.

She kept for herself only that sweater and his pocket watch and chain, dividing the cuff links and the tie pins between her brothers and Ira. When she was done with the packing and saw the last bags and cartons picked up, she lay down on her bed, wrapped in her husband's sweater, and rested. The next day, while Natalie was at work, she went to her daughter's closets and drawers, examined all of Natalie's clothing, and sorted it. By the time Natalie returned home, three-quarters of her apparel was gone.

Yuspeh watched her daughter-in-law at work and wondered if Helen had lost her mind. "For what are you doing this?" she asked curiously.

"Natalie needs new clothes," Helen answered, shoving an armful of blouses into a shopping bag.

Yuspeh nodded. "Now, especially," she said.

Helen looked up, suspiciously, wondering what Yuspeh suspected. "What do you mean, 'now especially'?"

Yuspeh shrugged and looked from the empty closet to the pile of clothing and half-filled bags on the bed and floor.

"Especially now because you just threw everything out . . . you want her to go naked?" Yuspeh walked over to the bags and peered into them. "These are all good," she said, "not torn, nothing." She pushed aside a heap of clothing and sat down on the bed. Even before Lenny died, Yuspeh had known Helen was up to something—but what? She watched her daughter-in-law methodically sorting, folding, packing—dresses in one bag, skirts in another, pants suits in a third. She had a look to her that Yuspeh had seen before. It was the look of a zealot, a proselytizer. A plotting look, one that must many times have been on the faces of Machiavelli, Bismarck, Moses, Joseph's brothers, Richard Nixon. Helen had the look of a person with a mission, a Zionist maybe, or a fortune hunter.

"Why are you so all of a sudden worried about Natalie's clothes?" asked Yuspeh.

"She has to look nice."

"For what?"

"A lot of big people come to Ira's office. Producers, movie stars."

"Ah," nodded Yuspeh.

Helen loaded the last shopping bag, then closed the closet and drawers. "This weekend I'll take her shopping for a whole new wardrobe."

"What good is it if she don't stand up straight?"

"She will. With new clothes, she'll feel good about herself. She'll be a whole new image."

"You think a new dress can cure hunchback, Helen?"

"She doesn't have a hunchback," snapped Helen.

Yuspeh got up and walked to Natalie's dresser. She smoothed her hair in front of the mirror and stood for a moment gazing at herself. "Look," she said, pointing to her reflection. "Would you believe that this was once a beauty?"

Helen turned around and smiled. "Were you a beauty, Ma?"

"That's what everybody said. Why would everybody lie? My husband, Morris, may he rest in peace, once told me that I could have been Miss Atlantic City, maybe." She sighed, and turning away from the mirror, walked back to the bed. She smoothed the spread and arranged Natalie's handmade ribbon throw pillows into a neat row. "You want her to meet a big producer?" she asked.

"Why not? . . . Come, we'll take these bags downstairs." Helen picked up a bag in each hand and started for the door. At the door, she looked back and saw Yuspeh once again sitting on the bed. "Well—come on, they aren't heavy."

"Helen," said Yuspeh, "sit down a minute."

"What?" Helen was standing impatiently at the door, gripping the handles of the two shopping bags, which hung like balances to her ankles. "I want to get these things out of here."

"I feel like to talk to you."

"So talk."

"Sit down a minute."

Helen sighed in exasperation and released her grip on the handles. The bags dropped with a small thud beside her legs. She walked over to Natalie's desk, pulled out the chair and sat down. She stared for a minute at the poster of the Beatles that had hung for years on the wall opposite her. Next to the poster was a bumper sticker that urged, "Smile, you're driving behind a Cub Scout." Yuspeh, following her eyes, shook her head.

"Natalie is thirty-one years old," she said, "almost thirty-two."

"That's what you wanted to tell me?" demanded Helen.

"No."

"Then what?"

"I worry about you, Helen," sighed Yuspeh. "I don't want you should get a heartache."

Helen stared, surprised, at her mother-in-law. "What can hurt me more than I'm hurt already?" she whispered. "I'm three months a widow . . . for two years I lived in hell. What can hurt me?"

"You're not yourself yet," said Yuspeh earnestly.

"What are you talking about?"

"Your plans."

Helen stiffened. "What plans?" she asked sharply.

"About Natalie . . . that you think if you dress her up, she'll become suddenly a beauty and a big producer will want her."

Helen relaxed and leaned back in the chair. "Why not? It happens."

"Only in moving pictures," said Yuspeh. "In moving pictures the girl takes off from her the glasses, and all of a sudden she's a Marilyn Monroe."

Helen sat quietly and looked again at the poster-plastered wall. Gazing back at her from a small sailboat in the bowl of a huge toilet was a sad-eyed little man. "And you think *you* get dumped on?" he complained in large black script. Helen frowned and turned away from the poster.

"Maybe I'll take her to Doctor Milkis for contact lenses," she said.

"Helen, Helen," sighed Yuspeh, "I worry about you."

"That's a good idea," said Helen. "I'll call Doctor Milkis tomorrow and make an appointment." She looked over at Yuspeh. "Can we take the bags down now?" she asked. "Are you done talking?"

"They see beautiful girls every day. No producer will look at Natalie, I don't care what you put on her. Where's your sense? You'll only make her suffer if you put dumbbell ideas in her head . . . don't do it, Helen. Buy out the whole store, but don't put ideas in her head . . . and take them out from yours."

"Do you think I'd ever do anything to hurt Natalie?" asked Helen.

"No."

"So stop worrying."

"So stop dreaming crazy dreams."

Helen stood up. "Come," she said, "take a bag."

"Is she the receptionist there?" asked Yuspeh.

"No."

"What does she do there?"

Helen rolled her eyes and sat down again. "She writes checks, keeps accounts—I don't know. Whatever Ira tells her to do, she does."

"She doesn't sit in the front?"

"No," said Helen proudly, "she has her own little office in the back with one other girl."

"So who's going to see her? You're giving contact lenses she should impress this other girl? Who sees her?"

"A lot of people see her," retorted Helen, "she's not a prisoner."

"She's all day with one girl in an office. All who sees her is one girl and Ira."

"I don't want to talk any more. I want to clean up this room." Again Helen stood up.

"All who sees her is one girl and . . ." Yuspeh slowly raised her head and stared at Helen . . . "and Ira," she whispered.

Helen stood very still. Then she walked slowly to the door, bent down and picked up the shopping bags. "Are you coming or not?" she asked, still facing the door.

"Turn around, Helen," said Yuspeh.

Helen turned and faced her mother-in-law. Their eyes met, and after several seconds, Yuspeh began to smile. Her whole face seemed to dissolve into wrinkles and her eyes almost disappeared into her creased, crisscrossed cheeks. As Helen watched her, Yuspeh began to shake with silent laughter. At last she stopped and wiped the tears from her cheeks with the corner of her apron. She looked up at her stone-faced daughter-in-law with gleaming eyes made even brighter by her mirth. She nodded her head and clapped her hands together. Still smiling broadly, she rose from the bed and picked up a shopping bag, grinning at Helen all the while.

"Congratulations, Helen," she said softly. "Mazel tov. You have the head of a Kissinger."

Helen sank into the chair, the handles of the shopping bags clutched tightly in her hands. "He goes away for weekends," she whispered. "He goes skiing, he goes to Lake Tahoe. Do you think he is alone there?" She closed her eyes and lay her head on the wooden back of Natalie's desk chair. "I can't lose any more. I have lost enough." Yuspeh waited, her eyes on Helen's face. "If a widow should marry her husband's brother, can't a sister marry her sister's husband?" Helen opened her eyes and looked pleadingly at Yuspeh. "Can't she?"

"With Kissinger dealing, anything is possible," said Yuspeh, hugging her bag, "anything."

Helen lifted her head and straightened in her chair.

"But it's not easy," added the old woman.

Helen tightened her lips and looked into her lap. "Nothing is easy," she murmured.

Yuspeh walked over and laid her hand on Helen's shoulder. She patted it gently and then stroked her hair. "You got some head," she told her daughter-in-law. "You got a genius head."

"Natalie will be married . . . I will have Ira back, and the children," said Helen, looking up into Yuspeh's eyes.

"It's a genius idea," said Yuspeh. "I can't get over it." She shook her head in admiration. "But, however," she went on, "what if Ira don't want to marry Natalie?"

Helen nodded: "I know," she said. "He's the problem."

"What if Natalie don't want to marry Ira?" asked Yuspeh.

"She'll do what I tell her," said Helen.

Yuspeh's hand, lifted to stroke Helen's hair, dropped to her side. "Malka's daughter will find a way," she said, so quietly that Helen could barely hear her.

"What?" asked Helen, looking up.

"I said you will find a way. If there is a way, you will find it . . . you're Malka's daughter."

Helen sat absolutely still. "Hah," she said bitterly. "I was never her daughter. She despised me . . . worse, she never cared if I lived or died." Helen loosened her grip on the handles and looked down at the reddened lines grooving the palms of her hands. One of the bags fell over, spilling several blouses onto her shoes. "Marilyn," she breathed. "Marilyn is Malka's daughter . . . not me . . . I always wanted to be, but I never was." With the forefinger of one hand, she traced the grooves in the palm of the other.

"Marilyn is nothing compared to you," said Yuspeh. "Compared to you, Marilyn is oatmeal."

Helen bent down and pushed the blouses back into the bag. She stood the bag up, one hand poised to catch it if it toppled again. When it was stable, she straightened up. "I think my mother would have talked to Marilyn . . . the way she talked to Celia and Benny and Max. Marilyn is just like her."

"So are you," insisted Yuspeh. "Even more than Marilyn."

"Hah," snorted Helen. "That woman was made of ice over cast iron. Nothing moved her. She had a frozen heart, even to her own children, to her husband. I was never like that."

"What about to Marilyn?"

Helen's head snapped up and she looked angrily at Yuspeh, her movement causing the bag to topple again. "I tried with Marilyn," she cried. "Marilyn didn't want me either."

Yuspeh slowly stooped and picked up a fallen blouse. She examined it carefully, then put it into the bag, which she leaned against the foot of the chair. She wondered how Helen could have lived for fifty-odd years so ignorant about herself.

"Well?" demanded Helen.

"All I meant," sighed Yuspeh, "is that you are a strong woman."

"No, you didn't."

"I didn't?"

"No."

"So what did I do?"

Wearily Helen stood up and looked into Yuspeh's raised face. "You meant that I am to Marilyn like my mother was to me."

Yuspeh regarded her sadly. "Helen," she said, holding out her hand, "every woman is her mother's daughter—even you . . . and if that is so, then Marilyn is Malka's daughter, too. You know what I am saying?"

"I don't care what you're saying." Helen picked up her bags and, ignoring Yuspeh's outstretched hand, walked out of the room.

"I still say you're a genius," Yuspeh yelled after her.

"Hah!" exclaimed Helen from the hall. "You don't have to tell me what I am. I know what I am."

Natalie was only faintly annoyed at the sight of her practically empty closet and drawers. Her clothing was important to her in that it functioned as a cover-up rather than a decoration. She hid behind her clothes the way some people hide behind huge, dark-lensed glasses, and it seemed that the more she put on the less noticeable she became. Alone in her room, she would stand naked before her mirror and admire her unclothed body. She secretly felt that she was one of those women who looked ten times better undressed. Her breasts were large, her waist was small, her hips were curved. The first time she saw a nude by Rubens, she realized she had been born too late, that she was the possessor of an unfashionable form, an hourglass in a digital world. The loss of her shirtwaist dresses, tailored blouses, polyester pants suits, gathered, button-in-the-back shirts, bothered her far less than her mother's presumptive, unauthorized discarding. After all, they were her, Natalie's, garments, and her mother had some nerve throwing them out.

"We'll go to Bullock's and Magnin's and get you some new up-to-date clothes," Helen said.

"Wonderful," said Natalie. "They'll look just great on my old, out-of-date body."

"Nonsense, you have a very nice figure . . ."

"And if you stood up straight," interjected Yuspeh, "you would look not bad. Tell me, Natalie, why is it you have a picture of a toilet hanging on your wall?" Ignoring her completely, Natalie glared at her mother.

"Who gave you permission to go into my closet in the first place?" she demanded.

"Please, Natalie," said Helen sadly, "I thought it would give us both a lift . . . you know?"

Instantly contrite, Natalie took her mother's hand and dropped the subject. She looked disapprovingly at Yuspeh, and wondered why she was snickering into her tea.

On Saturday they went first to Dr. Milkis, who measured her eyes for soft lenses, and then to the shopping center, where Natalie, dizzy with trying on, bought everything her mother told her to. In three and a half hours they spent well over two thousand dollars, not counting boots and shoes.

On Monday, for the first time in her life, Natalie appeared in public not in a blouse, but in a short-sleeved yellow turtleneck cashmere sweater over not a pair of pants with an elasticized waist, but over a tight-fitting, properly proportioned pair of gray Cacharel slacks. She looked at herself and was appalled.

"I can't go to work like this," she howled. "You know I'm not comfortable in sweaters."

"So get comfortable. That outfit cost one hundred and twenty-six dollars."

"But I look . . ."

"You look fine, better than fine."

"You can see my *nipples* in this bra!"

"So take it off."

"The *bra*!?"

"Uh-huh."

"I can't go without a bra."

"So stop complaining—and stand up straight, you hear me? There's nothing worse than a round-shouldered girl in a yellow sweater with nipples. Well, what are you standing like a tree with its mouth open for? Go already, you'll be late . . . and, Natalie," Helen called after her, "don't forget to watch your posture."

"Will you please leave me alone?" cried Natalie from the

doorway. She stormed out of the house, slamming the door behind her.

Quickly Helen ran to the window. "Natalie," she called through the screen.

"What?"

"Leave off your glasses."

"I can't *see* without my glasses."

"The lenses will be ready soon. You have to get used to no glasses. They make marks on your nose." Before Natalie could reply, Helen shut the window and closed the blind. She heard the shriek of tires as Natalie shot out of the driveway. In over a year Helen hadn't truly smiled, but now she did, and was still smiling as she walked into the kitchen.

"She went?" asked Yuspeh, looking up at her from the table.

"She went," smiled Helen, and walked over to her plants. She pressed her face into the cool leaves and sniffed the clean, green smell of them.

"So," nodded Yuspeh, "now what?"

"Now a cup of tea and at ten o'clock you'll see what."

Yuspeh pushed her chair back and stood up. "You sit down," she commended, walking to the stove. "I'll get you a tea."

"I can't get my own tea?" asked Helen, seating herself.

"A woman with the head of a fox shouldn't get her own tea," Yuspeh said, placing a cup before her. "I even gave you a new tea bag."

"Thank you."

"You're welcome, I'm sure," said Yuspeh, and sat down.

"Where's the honey?" asked Helen, surveying the table.

"*Gevalt,*" sighed Yuspeh. She pushed back her chair again and stood up. "Give a finger, they take a foot." She shuffled to the refrigerator and brought back the honey.

"You want anything else before I sit down, tell me now."

Helen opened the jar of honey and frowned. "Why do you always put it in the refrigerator? Now it's all crusty and hard."

"I like it like that . . . sue me, kill me, cut off from me an arm."

Annoyed, Helen jabbed her spoon through the crust and added some honey to her tea. But today even Yuspeh couldn't aggravate her for long. Natalie looked wonderful. Maybe she wouldn't need to keep her appointment for the complete overhaul offered at Elizabeth Arden's.

"You heard from your sister, Celia?" asked Yuspeh, making conversation.

"A postcard."

"She's liking Hawaii?"

"What's not to like?"

"You heard from Phyllis?" asked Yuspeh, trying again.

"Yesterday."

"She's not pregnant yet?"

"Right."

"How come?"

"Ma," reproved Helen, "what's *with* you this morning?"

Yuspeh shrugged and looked at the clock. With an internal chuckle, Helen realized that her mother-in-law was not trying to pass the time so much as trying to make the time pass. Yuspeh was waiting for ten o'clock.

Helen finished her tea and again walked over to her plants. She emptied the tea bag into a newly repotted avocado tree and pressed the wet leaves into the soil.

"Tell me, Helen," called Yuspeh from the table, "how did it come to you such a genius idea?"

Helen walked to the sink and rinsed her hands. "Well," she said, drying them on a dish towel, "I began to realize that life is so short and love is so . . . what is that word?" Helen wrinkled her forehead and tapped it with her fingers.

"What word?"

". . . A word—like 'here today, gone tomorrow . . .' "

"Hmm," thought Yuspeh, "now you got it, now you don't?" she asked.

"Yes. And I realized that when Lenny died, I wouldn't be able to survive if I lost Ira and my only grandchildren as well."

"Natural," agreed Yuspeh.

"So I tried to figure what I could do to make sure that Ira didn't marry again and drift away from me."

"Smart like a whip," said Yuspeh, kissing her fingers.

"So then, it came to me that I had a single son-in-law and also a single daughter."

"What a head," murmured Yuspeh.

"And I figured that with one fell swoop I could marry off my daughter and keep Ira and the children, if I married *her* off to *him*."

"I'm telling you," sighed Yuspeh, awed.

"And so," smiled Helen, "I decided to do it."

"Just like that."

"Just like that," agreed Helen.

Yuspeh shook her head and began to click her dentures. "What a wonderful talent, Helen, to be able to take people and make them do what you want—like in a chess game—like a king, an emperor."

Helen swung round and looked sharply at her mother-in-law. They regarded one another in silence. "Why is it," asked Helen at last, "that every time you give a compliment, it sounds like an insult?"

"You think I'm insulting you?"

"Yes, I do," snapped Helen.

"Can I help what you think? Am I so powerful like that? Am I a dictator I can tell people what to think?"

"*Stop* that!" cried Helen.

"*Excuse* me," said Yuspeh, "*sue* me, cut off from me an *arm*." She stood up and began clearing the table. After placing the teacups and spoons on the counter, she picked up the honey and put it into the refrigerator. She closed the refrigerator door softly and glanced up at the clock.

"It's now ten o'clock, Helen," she prompted.

"Thank you, Big Ben," replied Helen angrily and glared, her arms folded across her chest, at her mother-in-law.

"Maybe I'll go make my bed," sighed Yuspeh, realizing that all was lost.

"You do that—there's no use you hanging around here."

Slowly Yuspeh walked out of the kitchen, feeling the heat of Helen's eyes on her back. When she reached the staircase and was out of Helen's sight, she quickly began to climb. She stood for a few moments at the head of the stairs and caught her breath. Then she hurried into her room, and locking the door behind her, moved to the bed and sat down. Her thin, veined, liver-spotted hand reached out and curved around the receiver of the telephone. Ever so slowly and gently she lifted it up and put it to her ear:

". . . since Lenny died. I really think, darling, it would be a therapy for her if you took her out to lunch—if you aren't busy, of course. Are you busy, Ira?"

"Well . . ."

"It would mean so much to me, darling."

Yuspeh removed the phone from her ear and carefully replaced it on its cradle. She sat on the edge of her bed studying the dial. Then she put her fingers close together, raised her right hand and laid it sideways, tilted over her eyebrow, like an awning.

"Helen," she whispered, "I salute you."

Chapter 23

WHEN BRENDA RETURNED to the table, Anthony was gone. "He told me to tell you he got called away on urgent business," said Sam, "and to take a raincheck on Vegas. He'll call you."

"Sure," said Brenda and stared glumly into the ashtray. She looked around the room, saw nothing that moved her and wondered if it was too late to call Ira. "Did he really say he'd call?" asked Brenda. "He really did," assured Sam. "Where's Marilyn?"

"Ladies' room." Abruptly she stood up. "I'm leaving, Sam. I gotta make a call."

She walked to the phones, but before using them, pushed open the door to the ladies' room and looked inside. She wrinkled her nose as an overpowering smell of ammonia made her eyes tear. Marilyn was nowhere in sight.

Brenda returned to the phones, put in a quarter, waited for the tone and called Ira. "Sure," he said, "come on over."

As she left Close Encounters she saw Sam still sitting alone at the table.

On the way to Ira's she calculated the odds on hearing from Anthony, thought about it and wrote him off. She was wrong. Three months later he called and told her to pack a bag for Vegas. Brenda was only too ready to go. Since his father-in-law died, Ira was a zombie and hardly any fun at all. By the time Anthony arrived, she was packed and ready.

Anthony Santacroce was well known in Vegas, at least in the casino of The Golden Cactus. They walked in and he was immediately greeted by smiling, tied-and-suited men. "Hey, Tony," they called to him, "how's it goin'?" "Goin' good," he answered with a wave. "Hey, Tone, you got good taste," they said, looking Brenda over appreciatively. "Why not," he answered, "costs the same as bad taste, don't it?"

Brenda looked quickly up at him, annoyed.

He bought one hundred silver dollars and steered Brenda over to the slots. "I'll be right back," he told her. "I got some business to discuss. You have a good time." And he handed her the money. As soon as he had gone, Brenda cashed in fifty of the dollars for a fifty-dollar bill, which she folded in half and put in a secret compartment in the back of her cigarette case. Then she returned to the slots and began to play. On her third try she lined up three pineapples and collected twenty-five dollars.

Anthony was at the bar, talking to two other men. She wondered if he was in the mob, in with the mob, in good with the mob, all three or none. It was hard to tell nowadays. Even the soldiers sometimes talked like college men, and she personally knew professors who sounded as if they were Brooklyn-born and raised. She inserted another dollar, hit a cherry and got back five bucks. She put two dollars into the machine next to hers and two into her own. Another cherry on hers and three oranges in the other. Okay, thought Brenda, dropping dollars into her cup, my moon's in money tonight—and none too soon, either. She had long ago quit her office job and was living off men and the residuals from her commercials. She knew the residuals would soon run out and hoped she had some time left before the men did. Brenda was thirty-two years old and well aware that she was nearing the shady side of perky. What she *needed* was an old, soft cock loaded with hard, cold cash. What she *wanted* was a forty-year-old millionaire who could still get it up.

What she *really* wanted was kids. She loved kids, even other people's. Ira, that prick, would have been perfect. Shit. You'd have thought it was his own father who kicked off, the way he carried on. He was committed up to his ears to in-laws, and that mother-in-law was murder. One weekend when they were in Tahoe the old bitch called four times on Saturday alone.

Brenda yanked the handle of her machine and three watermelons grinned back. Sixty-five bucks. Her handbag cost more than that, twice as much, come to think of it. She'd have to take it slow with Ira, but time and money were fast running out and he had yet to nibble. Her doctor had mentioned a couple of times already that if she intended to add to the population, she had better get a move on. She wished she could do it alone, that she had the money to provide her kids with the best there was. Then she could tell them all, all those peckers, wet lips and grabbing hands, to fuck off; then she could marry for love and stay home making chocolate-chip cookies, kissing her kids and carving pumpkins on Halloween. Brenda was not optimistic about her future with Ira. It was about as promising as a politician, and far less dependable. If Ira didn't come through soon, she'd have to cut her losses, pack it in and move on.

"How ya doin'?" asked Anthony, coming up behind her.

"Not bad," she said, showing him her dollar-filled cups. Anthony took her elbow and steered her away from the slots. "Come on," he said, "let's try blackjack."

"You got any kids, Anthony?" asked Brenda.

"One, a boy."

"Where's your wife?"

"Playin' the harp."

"*Dead?*"

Anthony nodded. "Four years already. God rest her soul."

"Jesus, she must have been young."

"Thirty-two."

Brenda felt her stomach jump. "How?" she gasped.

They reached the blackjack table, but Anthony, changing direction, led her to the bar area. They sat down at a table, ordered drinks and were served immediately. Brenda took a handful of peanuts and began eating them one at a time.

"What she die of, Anthony?" asked Brenda.

"Why?"

"She was so young."

"Yeah." He lifted his glass of Scotch over rocks and took a long swallow. "She was shot four times," he said. "Once in the stomach, twice in the chest, once in the head. It was the chest ones did it."

Brenda put a peanut in her mouth and chased it with a sip of piña colada. Her tongue was cold. "How old is your boy?" she asked after a moment.

"Seven."

Brenda nodded. "Poor little thing," she said. "Who's taking care of him?"

"My sister Theresa."

Brenda took another sip and twirled her ice with the straw. Then she put it again to her lips and sipped steadily until the glass was almost empty. She picked up the piece of pineapple on the rim and ate it. When it was gone, she wiped the corners of her mouth with the cocktail napkin, reapplied her lipstick and took out a pink cigarette, which Anthony, flicking a match with his thumbnail, lit.

"So, Anthony," said Brenda, through a puff of smoke, "tell me something. When you play blackjack, do you double down on nine when the dealer is showing a three?"

"Absolutely," smiled Anthony.

"Do you hit on sixteen?"

"Depends on what the dealer is showing. If he shows a six, three, four or even a five, I stay. If he shows a ten or a picture, I hit." He looked at her for a moment, and grinning from ear to ear, shook his head in admiration. "You are really something," he said. "I tell you my wife gets shot, and you are so cool, you don't even ask me who did it."

"Was it you who shot her, Anthony?"

"No," he said quietly.

"Was it because of you?"

"God, I hope not."

"But maybe?"

"Yeah," he said, heavily, "maybe."

Brenda ate another peanut. "Are you rich, Anthony?"

"I'm not Rockefeller, but close."

"Do you want more kids?" she asked.

"Sure. Why not?"

"Do you beat up on women?"

Anthony stared at her, offended. "I never hit a woman in my life."

"You want to marry me, Anthony?" asked Brenda.

"Sure. Why not?"

Brenda stubbed out her cigarette. "I'm not joking, Anthony," she said, raising her eyes to his. "I'm not joking one minute."

"Neither am I," he replied, staring levelly back. "I got a good sense of humor, but I don't joke about marriage."

"I'm a Catholic," said Brenda. "I don't like divorce, but it's better than getting shot."

"Absolutely," said Anthony.

"And I'm not greedy," she went on. "I'm expensive, but not greedy. If I split from a guy I would expect to leave with my kids and enough green to support them and me without having to count pennies or worry about the price of summer camp."

"Understandable," said Anthony.

"And I wouldn't fool around or cheat on my husband—and if he's smart, he won't fool around or cheat on me."

"What guy would want to cheat on you?" asked Anthony. "There ain't too many around who can compare to you, Brenda."

"My sentiments exactly."

"So what are we waiting for?"

"One more thing, Anthony."

"What's that?"

"You got to promise me one thing."

"What's that, baby?"

"Respect. You got to give me respect."

"Done."

"Even when you walk into the bathroom and catch me on the john, when you say hello, I got to hear respect."

"Brenda, you respect me, I respect you. You give it, you get it—you don't give it, you don't get it."

"Done," said Brenda. She looked at her hand, held tightly in Anthony's. His nails were manicured and his palms were warm but not sweaty. She put her free hand over his and they sat for a while, looking at each other, not smiling.

"What's your son's name?" she asked after a while.

"Anthony Junior."

"I love little boys," said Brenda. "My friend Marilyn, the one you met that night at Close Encounters, she has two boys, Todd and Jeremy. She's a lawyer."

"No kidding," said Anthony, looking impressed. "A person can always use a good lawyer. I know that for a fact. What's her husband do?"

"She's divorced . . . her father just died."

"Ahh."

"If you want to know the truth, I think she was married to her father, not her husband."

"That's sick," said Anthony, shocked.

"No, no," Brenda told him impatiently. "Not like that. She loved him, that's all."

"He was her father, of course she loved him."

"Yeah, but too much. He left no room for anyone else."

"Well, he's dead, ain't he? Now she's got plenty of room."

"No. Nothing grows there any more. You know what she does all day?" asked Brenda, earnestly. "She works and works and then goes home and works. You know what else she does when she comes home? Watches game shows on television."

"Sounds very sad," he said.

"It is."

Anthony pressed her hand and smiled. "Want another drink?"

"Nope," said Brenda, returning his smile. "I don't want to fall flat on my back at my own wedding."

"Right," grinned Anthony. "You'll be plenty flat on your back *after* the wedding."

"Well, I certainly hope so," she said and felt suddenly enormously happy. She had waited thirty-two years for a marriage that was decided upon in five minutes, to a guy she had seen only twice. Crazy.

"Why don't you call Marilyn?" suggested Anthony. "Ask her to come on down and stand up for you. Tell her I'll send the plane."

"She won't come," said Brenda. "She goes nowhere except to her office and once or twice a week to the market."

"She sounds nuts."

"She's in mourning," explained Brenda. "I call her every now and then—sometimes go up to see her. She's all right. Talks to her sisters, her aunt."

"Who's the first one you're gonna call after we get married? You got living parents?"

"Somewhere, I suppose. If they're dead by now I never got the news. I got a brother in Minnesota."

"Gonna call him?"

"Gonna call him a sumbitch, that's about all."

"I got a big family," said Anthony. "Three brothers, two sisters, one mother, one father, one son."

"And now one Brenda," she added.

"Right. One Brenda . . . one's enough, right?" he grinned.

"You better believe it," she said and laughed out loud. "You know something, Anthony?"

"Yeah?" he asked.

"I'm happy. I feel happy."

"Me too, baby. I feel happy, too." He leaned over the small table and kissed her gently on the lips, then flicking out his tongue, he licked her lips and the tip of her nose.

"Down, Fido," she grinned.

"Arf," said Anthony and looked over toward the bar. "I gotta get me a best man. Hey, Sal," he called. When the bartender looked up, Anthony pointed decisively at a man who was standing at the end of the bar, surveying the casino with eyes that seemed to be in constant motion. Sal whispered to him, and the man walked over.

"Steve," said Anthony, meet my fiancé, Brenda . . . uh . . ."

"Mortenson," she said quickly.

"What's the difference? Soon it'll be Santacroce. Brenda, meet an old friend, Steve Winograd."

Steve bowed from the waist, lifted Brenda's hand and kissed it. Then he clapped Anthony on the shoulder. "Congratulations," he said a bit uncertainly. "Is this on the level?"

Anthony frowned. "You ever know me to lie?" he asked in a low, lethal voice.

"Never, 'Tone." Steve turned quickly to Brenda. "I know Anthony Santacroce sixteen years and in all that time I never heard a lie out of his mouth." He spoke rapidly, his hands emphasizing every word. "Next to this guy," he said, "Abraham Lincoln looks like a Watergate conspirator . . . eh, Tone?"

"I got a good sense of humor," Anthony said, somewhat mollified, "but not about marriage. Nothing funny about marriage. It's a serious business."

"I couldn't agree more," said Steve, his head bobbing up and down. He put his hands together and beamed on both of them. "So when is the happy event?" he asked.

"Now," said Anthony. "Make the arrangements. I want a priest, two rings—fourteen-carat—flowers, champagne in my . . . our . . . suite, a bouquet for the bride here and so on. You been married three times, Winograd. You should know just what to do by now. And call Frank Lawicki and ask him and Betty to stand up for us. Get the license, and if there's any problem, Judge Brill will deal with it. You got a half hour, forty-five minutes at the most."

"See you at the chapel," said Steve Winograd, and hurried off.

Anthony turned back to Brenda. "You know what I like about this?"

"Yes."

"You do?" asked Anthony, surprised.

"Uh-huh."

"Okay, big shot. What?"

"The same thing *I* like about this," said Brenda.

"What?"

"That we've never slept together. We'll have a real old-fashioned wedding night." To Brenda's dismay, tears welled up in her eyes.

"Hey," said Anthony softly.

Brenda sniffed and gave a small, teary laugh. "Hey yourself," she said, and smiled as the tears rolled out of her eyes and strolled down her cheeks. She fumbled in her bag and pulled out a tissue. "The real reason I'm crying," she said, carefully blotting her eyes and cheeks, "is because my initials will go from B.M. to B.S. That's not a significant improvement, you know."

"Brenda."

She looked up into Anthony's eyes, her own still full of tears. His eyes were, even in the dim light of the lounge, the color of bittersweet chocolate.

"Brenda," he said again. "I got a feeling we're going to grow old together, you and me."

"Amen, Anthony," she whispered. "I'm going to send a thank-you note to the management of Close Encounters."

Anthony leaned back in his chair and began to laugh.

"What's so funny?" she asked.

"I'll hand-deliver the note," he chuckled, "and save you the price of a stamp."

"Oh, no, you won't. No more singles bars for you."

"Uh-huh, baby. I've been going to Close Encounters once a month since it opened. I don't intend to stop now."

Brenda's face paled and her mouth opened in shock. Speechless, she stared at him.

"Something bothering you?" he asked, laughing even harder.

Without a word, she picked up the cups of silver dollars and started to rise from her chair. Anthony's arm shot out and he grabbed her wrist, pulling her back down.

"I've got to hand it to you," she said, her eyes filling again, "you're some actor. You really had me going there for a while.

Goodbye, Anthony. Let go of my arm." She tried to shake him off, but he gripped her firmly.

"What's your hurry?" he asked, still laughing.

"I thought you were serious. I thought you didn't joke about marriage." Her voice rose, and she struggled to control it. "I thought . . ." She bent her head and her hair fell forward, over her cheeks. After a moment, she looked up, her face rigid. Anthony pulled her toward him and kissed her eyes. Then he loosened his grip on her wrist. "I meant every word I said," he whispered, suddenly serious, "every word."

"Sure you did."

"I did, Brenda." He glanced down at his watch. "In a half hour, you're going to be a married woman."

"Fuck you, you wop, Polack bastard."

"Jesus," he winced, "what a mouth you got."

"Let go of me."

"Oh, no," he said, "I never let go of a good thing."

Brenda stared at him, bewildered and angry. "Are we getting married, Anthony?" she choked.

"In a half hour."

"Are you going to go to singles bars after we're married, Anthony?"

He began to smile again and nodded. "Just Close Encounters, baby."

"How come, Anthony?"

"I got to, Brenda."

"How come, Anthony?"

"Because I own the fucking joint."

"All of it, Anthony?"

"All of it."

Brenda paused. "Know what I want for my wedding present, Anthony?" she asked softly.

His eyes widened and he gazed at her in stunned respect. "All of it?" he gasped.

"All of it, Anthony."

Slowly he nodded. "We'll see the lawyers on Wednesday," he whispered.

"On Monday, Anthony."

"On Monday," he agreed.

Brenda leaned back in her chair and opened her purse. "Close your eyes and open your hand, Anthony," she ordered. "I'm going to give you *your* wedding present right now."

Obediently he did so. Brenda took something out of her purse, put it on Anthony's palm and closed his fingers around it.

"I'm going to fix my face," she told him, standing up. "As soon as I'm gone, you can look at your present."

Anthony watched her until she disappeared into the ladies' room. After the door closed behind her, he looked down at his hand and slowly uncurled his fingers. He stared and burst out laughing. Lying in the palm of his hand was a round, flat, plastic packet of birth-control pills. He pulled out his handkerchief, shook it open and, wrapping the packet carefully, put it gently into his breast pocket.

He walked to the door of the ladies' room and waited. When Brenda emerged, he took her by the shoulders and enfolded her in his arms. They stood there, holding each other, oblivious to the hubbub in the casino, until Steve Winograd tapped Anthony on the shoulder and whispered that their limo was waiting.

They remained in each other's arms all the way to the chapel. The ceremony began at 12:01 A.M. and by 12:17 A.M. Brenda was Mrs. Anthony Santacroce. And at 3:30 A.M., so awash with happiness that she couldn't sleep, Brenda decided to share it, to do something nice for someone.

She got slowly out of bed, careful not to disturb her sleeping husband, and walked on tiptoe into the living room. She turned on the lamp, and picking up the phone, sat down and dialed. The phone rang six times before it was answered by a sleepy voice.

"Mrs. Helen Ritter?"

"Who is this?" Helen asked sharply, instantly awake.

"This is someone who, because she's happy, is going to make you happy too."

"I'm calling the police. Do you know what time it is?"

"This is Brenda, Mrs. Ritter. Ira's, ah, friend."

There was a short silence. "What do you want?" asked Helen. "How *dare* you call me at this hour?"

"I want to make you happy, Mrs. Ritter."

"The only way you can make me happy is by staying away from Ira," snapped Helen.

"Is that what you want?" asked Brenda.

"That is *exactly* what I want."

"Well, you fucking-A-exactly got it, Mrs. Ritter."

Brenda smiled and hung up the phone. She turned off the lamp and sat for a while, hugging herself and smiling. She picked up the phone again and called Marilyn. Then she tiptoed back to the bedroom. She slid into bed, wrapped her leg around her husband and fell asleep.

Chapter
24

MARILYN HAD NEVER RESPECTED SUICIDE. She understood it, but she couldn't imagine the depths of despair that could make a person actually go through with it and make it a public matter.

She did now. The only things in her life that had ever given her real happiness had been her father and her work. And they were both dead.

During Lenny's last hospitalization, all that had kept Marilyn sane was her ability to submerge herself in the only case she was still handling. Marilyn was aware that it was stupid as well as personally and professionally dangerous to refuse new cases, but as her father's decline became more pronounced and rapid, so did her knack for cushioning herself and sublimating her agony in work.

Two days before Beryl Sinclair's scheduled return, Marilyn received a telex from her client. "Have reconciled with Chuck. Have also wired Stanley Greenspan to reimburse you for all your efforts on my behalf. When you see the check you will realize that most people retire and live luxuriously for the rest of their lives on far less. Thank you for everything, be happy for me, and don't be mad—love, your client forever—Beryl."

Marilyn spent the day of her father's funeral walking on the beach. She walked for miles, plodding along, driven like some mindless, implacable machine, unable to stop or slow down.

That wasn't her father in the box, that was a greenish thing, a shriveled obscenity, planted like one of her mother's precious pits, bearing no resemblance at all to the ripe, fleshed and beautiful, sweet and nourishing entity from which it came.

Only the rocks at the end of the beach stopped her progress and Marilyn, like some blind tin soldier, bashed against them over and over until the key in her back wound down and finally stopped. She had no idea how she got home.

Celia called her the next day, Natalie called, Phyllis called. "What happened to you?" they asked her. "Why didn't you come? How are you?"

"Nothing. I couldn't. I don't know," she answered.

Her office called. "Take as much time as you need," they told her. "Come back when you feel ready."

"Yes, thank you."

Ira called. "If you need me, I'm here," he said. "Can I do anything for you?"

"I know," and, "Yes, you can kill me."

"I loved him, too," said Ira and began to cry. Marilyn listened for a while and then hung up.

She walked into the kitchen, opened the refrigerator and took a long drink of orange juice straight from the container. She carried it, along with a container of milk, back into the living room, where she turned on the television set. She sat down and placed the containers on the table next to the chair.

Days passed while Marilyn sat huddled in her big chair, staring unblinking at the television set which it was too much of an effort to turn off. Marilyn wasn't sure if she slept or not, but she must have, because when Brenda called, she somehow knew she had been unconscious until the persistent ringing made her react and reach for the phone.

"This is Mrs. Anthony Santacroce."

"You have the wrong number."

"It's Brenda, you stupe. Sadie, Sadie, married lady."

"Brenda."

"Even considering it's four in the morning, you sound lousy, Marilyn."

"Well, you see, my father . . ."

"Yeah, I know, but kiddo, it would break his heart if he's lookin' down on you from somewhere. You love your dad, don't break his heart."

"What day is this?" asked Marilyn.

"The day you get a grip on yourself. What's that noise?"

Bewildered, Marilyn looked around. "Oh," she said, "the TV."

"Well, turn it off, but hurry; I'm on long distance."

Painfully, Marilyn uncramped her legs, and pulled herself out of the chair. She stood for a moment, swaying. Then she dragged herself unsteadily across the room and pushed the button that shut off the set. The sudden silence seemed to paralyze her, and it was a minute or two before she could turn around, walk back to her chair and pick up the phone.

"It's about time," said Brenda. "Now, tell me something. You been eating?"

"No—maybe—I don't know."

"So. In that case, today is also the day you eat. I'll call you tomorrow. Have an egg or something. 'Bye."

Marilyn stayed in her chair for a long time. When she next opened her eyes, sunlight was pouring into the room. Her mouth felt very dry, and the two containers on the table next to her chair were empty. She felt very weak and her whole body ached. But she had to get up. Today was the day she was supposed to eat. She didn't want to break her father's heart.

Marilyn hobbled into the kitchen. She stood uncertainly for a moment, then opened the refrigerator and removed the carton of eggs. She placed it on the counter, and noticing a half-empty package of bread, picked it up. The bread was moldy. Almost trancelike, she prepared an egg, and as it fried and the aroma hit her nose, a pang of incredible hunger, so sharp as to be almost unbearable, doubled her up. She grabbed a packet of Melba toast, opened the cellophane with her teeth, carried it, the frying pan and a fork to the table, and trembling, not even pausing to seat herself, ate her first solid meal in about ten days. She was actually panting when she was done. Brenda called while Marilyn was cramming the last of eight slices of American cheese into her mouth.

"You sound better," observed Brenda.

"I can't stop eating."

"Don't worry, you will, but take it easy or you'll get cramps. What's that holiday you Jews have where you fast all day?"

"Yom Kippur?"

"Yeah, that's it. Sounds like you had yourself one helluva Yom Kippur."

"I think you saved my life, Brenda," said Marilyn, her voice breaking.

"Oh, yeah?" Brenda sounded pleased. "Good," she said. "Now you owe me one, and don't you start to bawl or I'll hang up."

Marilyn took a deep breath. "Okay," she whispered. "By the way, Brenda, congratulations."

"Thanks. I still can't believe it. I don't know how I got so lucky. I must have stepped in shit."

"What?"

"Stepping in it is supposed to be good luck."

"Oh . . . well, give my best to Anthony."

"I sure will. Marilyn, you take care of yourself now. I'll be in L.A. in a couple a weeks so I'll see you then."

"Brenda?"

"Hmm?"

"Thank you, Brenda."

"What's a friend for? I'll call you soon. 'Bye."

Marilyn hung up the phone, and then for the first time since the death of her father, she began to cry. She wept for days, and even when the downpour subsided and she lay dehydrated and completely exhausted, her eyes remained bloodshot and swollen. She stared for hours at the pictures of her father in the living room and bedroom and talked to them. She began taking long walks on the beach again, having heard somewhere that physical activity lessens depression. She called her aunt, needing desperately to hear a loving voice, and was told by the housekeeper that Dr. and Mrs. Cutler were in Hawaii. On one very bad day she even called Ira, but hung up after two rings.

Little by little she began to read again, ordering paperback novels along with her groceries. She would sit out on her balcony in the sun and read, munching apples or sunflower seeds until late afternoon, like the convalescent she was.

Natalie and Phyllis had visited her once but the sight of them so upset her, the tears that came whenever they looked at one another so unhinged her, that she asked them to please not come for a while, and they understood.

Marilyn knew she had survived when she experienced the first faint desire to return to work. Whatever the instinct is that causes a drowning swimmer to clutch frantically at the outstretched hand of a lifeguard, that forces even the frailest victim to thrash and arch his body in violent protest against the smothering pillow, that injects a small and diffident woman with the fierce, desperate, herculean strength to lift the end of a two-ton automobile from the legs of her wailing child—whatever it was, it still endured in Marilyn. She accepted that knowledge, as she accepted that everything else had died—and was gone as surely as her father. That place inside, which in Marilyn's case had never been sturdy, where pleasure breathes, where joy blooms, where contentment abides, existed no more. That's what happens when love walks in and takes you for a spin—and then walks out again, dragging your guts along behind it.

She returned to work as soon as she felt able and plunged in. The padded, impenetrable confines of discipline—the wills, litigations, copyrights, contracts, prenuptial agreements—provided a barrier between her and the constant pain and depression that launched its invasion as soon as she left the office. She began taking work home. It helped stave off the vicious assaults of irreconcilable loss. But not too often, and never successfully.

Sometimes, after taking two Valiums to assure a rapid descent into sleep, she would think about Ira and the children. She wondered what they were doing, how they would react if one day she were to pack her bags and move back in. The idea was strangely comforting. Her father would have approved—in fact, he would have encouraged her to do exactly that. And Ira would be patient and forgiving and kind—and boring.

"If it would bring you back, Papa, I'd move in with Ashley Wilkes, with Ebenezer Scrooge, the Boston Strangler, Howard Cosell—if it would bring you back, Papa, I'd even move in with —Helen Ritter."

One afternoon, as she was preparing to leave the office, Sam Greenfield called.

"Do you remember me?" he asked.

"I'm taking your call, aren't I?"

"What the hell is a Deiter, Sidaris, Ostern, Caputo and Wernick?"

Marilyn smiled. "It's a law firm," she replied.

"And your position there?"

"Let's see how smart you are—higher than a secretary, lower than a judge."

"Are you an attorney?"

"Bingo," said Marilyn.

"Well," said Sam after a moment, "aren't you something."

"What can I do for you, Sam?"

"The last and only time we were together, I was left sitting alone at the post after having put my evening on the line in the form of a dinner invitation. I mean, I've heard of eat and run, but you omitted the eat."

"Guilty as charged. Go on."

"Well, I'm hungry again, and I'd like to extend a second dinner invitation. Hopefully we'll get it right this time."

"I'm not very good company, Sam," said Marilyn.

He laughed. "You weren't last time either, as I recall, but— even the seasons change."

"Won't your wife mind?"

There was a short silence and Sam cleared his throat. "That's

260

tacky, Marilyn," he said, "and not your problem. Well? What do you say, yes or no?"

"Yes. Where?"

"Les Jardins. Seven-thirty."

"Fine. See you there."

Marilyn unpacked the work she had intended to do at home and spread it before her on the desk. She felt good now about having accepted Sam's invitation. It would be a pleasant, necessary diversion, certainly better than going home. She had not been out with a man socially since her divorce. With the exception of Ira, she had, in fact, not been out with a man for ten years. As for sex, Marilyn couldn't remember the last time. She hoped that sexual organs didn't atrophy from disuse, the way muscles did. Maybe she would find out. Sam was attractive, bright, married and clean. Altogether a very satisfactory possibility. Mildly excited, Marilyn began to work.

Les Jardins was a relatively new, very expensive and elegant eatery on Camden Drive in Beverly Hills. Diners had the choice of eating indoors or, weather permitting, on the open-air patio at umbrella-shaded tables. Open French doors connected the dining areas. Piano music accompanied dinner. The waiters were suited and tied, the busboys in black-and-white-striped aprons were quick and unobtrusive. The menu was continental, the food generally well prepared. A bud vase with a rosebud stood in the center of each white-clothed table, and almost everybody who was invited to dine there accepted, feeling that he or she must be well thought of to be taken to dinner at Les Jardins. People from the Valley also patronized the restaurant—but only on important occasions, like anniversaries or birthdays. One could celebrate there; it was that kind of place.

Sam was at the bar when Marilyn arrived. "You've lost weight," he observed.

"Oh dear, it must be around somewhere. Maybe in my other bag. Can you ever forgive me?"

"I'll let you know after dinner," he said as they were led to their table.

Sam ordered drinks and lit Marilyn's cigarette. "So," he asked, "what's been happening?"

"Do you remember Brenda and that guy Anthony?"

"Uh-huh."

"Well, they got married."

"A perfect pairing. And you?"

"I didn't."

"What *did* you do."

"I lost my father."

"Look in your other bag," said Sam, and then, seeing Marilyn's face, instantly apologized. "I'm terribly sorry, Marilyn. That was tasteless. Please accept my sympathies and my apology."

Marilyn nodded and pulled the ashtray closer to her plate. With her mixer, she squeezed the piece of lime floating in her drink. "That's why I told you I mightn't be good company," she said.

"I understand."

"Okay—and what have *you* been doing with yourself?"

"Working. I'm a builder and contractor. I did those condominiums over on Pecan Drive."

"I used to live on Palm."

"Who asked you?" smiled Sam, and Marilyn smiled back.

"Let's order," she said.

Dinner was good and the conversation easy. Over dessert, Sam told her that he kept a unit of the new condo for his own personal use.

"Who asked you?" she grinned. "Are you leading up to an invitation?"

"Yes," replied Sam.

"I'll let you know after I see how much you tip."

He smiled and took her hand. "What's a beautiful girl like you doing in an occupation like law?"

"I couldn't get into medical school."

"Why not?"

"I never applied—but enough small talk. Let's finish up here and go explore your condominium."

"No brandy?"

"After brandy and one more cigarette."

"Good. I like exploring new things." He leaned over, tilted her chin and kissed her lightly on the lips. "I'm going to love exploring you," he whispered.

"Don't jump to conclusions," murmured Marilyn.

"Do you believe in love at second sight?" he asked.

"I don't believe in love at all."

"Ah, but love makes everything better—even sex, which is plenty good on its own."

"Only before and after, or so I've heard tell. *During*, it makes no difference at all. Personally, I don't think that love and sex have anything whatsoever to do with each other."

Marilyn took a sip of brandy and shook a cigarette out of her pack. Sam lit it and looked at her thoughtfully. "That's a rather unfeminine attitude," he said.

"Ah, you men. Such emotional, sentimental creatures. Do you need to hear you're loved before someone can get you into bed? Afterwards, will you wonder if I'll still respect you?"

"Don't be sarcastic, Marilyn. It's unattractive."

He took a cigarette from his pack and put it between his lips. Marilyn reached for the matches, but Sam grabbed them from her hand and lit it himself.

"Having second thoughts?" asked Marilyn after a moment.

"Are you?"

Twenty minutes later they were in bed.

Afterwards, back in her own apartment, Marilyn tried to understand why she felt even more depressed than usual—enervated and terribly sad. It had been nice with Sam. He was easygoing; a sweet and graceful lover. A kisser and a soft-lipped nipper. His hands were smooth, his eyes appreciative. They lay for a while on their sides, the lengths of their bodies pasted together, and the feel of a warm body next to hers had given her such enormous pleasure that she pressed herself into him and put her feet between his. "Hold me, hold me hard," she repeated over and over, and he had. He told her she was beautiful; he held her breasts and gazed at them, kissed them with his eyes before he bent his head and kissed them with his lips. He kissed her everywhere, and when he lifted his head from between her legs, he whispered, "Honey, it's like honey; it's like dipping into honey." She had wanted him in her long before he was. She had wanted him in her so badly that when at last he was, she gasped against his shoulder and moaned into his neck, so very grateful for the delay. Twice. They had made love twice.

It was on her way home that Marilyn cried. The tears were as much in protest as in despair. On her way home she realized once again that not even passion could thaw her, not even a sweet lover's arms could melt her pain. At three in the morning, Marilyn sat alone and wept for her father.

Chapter 25

For a blind man, it is essential to live in an exact world. Rearrangement creates confusion, and the readjustment is often lengthy. Move a table one inch to the right in the room of a blind man, and his orientation crumbles. Ira, sighted though he was, had a blind need for symmetry and order. He was a certified public accountant, a successful business manager, and dealing daily in mathematical immutabilities steadied him and kept him secure and even. No matter what else happened in his life, no matter what the upheavals and disappointments, Ira maintained the unshakable certainty that if X netted, after taxes, one hundred thousand dollars, and he spent seventy-five of that on a small water craft that slept six, he was going to be left with twenty-five thousand, a nervous stomach and regrets. As long as one and one remained two, as long as there were six fives in thirty, Ira Stillman would survive. This basic need of his for precise harmony, for regularity, affected his every perception. If on some level he perceived that something was there that shouldn't be, that something was not there that should be, that something was unlike the way it was supposed to be, he would react with instant discomfort—and would remain discomfited until the error was discovered and the condition corrected. If, unfortunately, the change itself were to become the new status quo, he would, of course, being a reasonable man, eventually adapt. But in the meantime it was most uncomfortable, like an unscratchable itch in an unreachable area.

And there was something different about Natalie. After Helen's call, he buzzed her on the intercom. "Sis?"

"Yes, Ira?"

"You busy for lunch?"

Natalie looked over inquiringly at her office mate, Sheila, with whom she occasionally lunched.

"Go," whispered Sheila. "I have to return a bathrobe to May Company, anyway."

Natalie nodded and told him she wasn't busy.

"Can you be ready at, oh, say, twelve-thirty?"

"Okay, Ira." She released the intercom button and went back to work. She had a huge pile of canceled checks on her desk which had to be entered in the books. She worked diligently, pleased with her neatness and the rapid shrinking of the pile.

"You want coffee?" asked Sheila.

"No, thanks."

"Sure?"

Natalie looked up, smiled and shook her head.

"Stand up a minute," said Sheila, "I want to get a look at you in that outfit."

Embarrassed, Natalie stood.

"Look at me," ordered Sheila, "and for God's sakes stop slouching. You remind me of my daughter before she got her nose job, always looking at the ground."

Unused to disobeying anybody, especially her elders, Natalie straightened up while Sheila examined her. "Oh, come on, Sheila," she protested, "you're embarrassing me." Quickly she sat down again and reached for a check.

"You know something?" said Sheila in a surprised voice. "You really have a nice figure."

"Come on, Sheila," mumbled Natalie, blushing.

"I'm not saying you couldn't lose a few pounds, but all in all, it's not bad at all. I never noticed before because you dress like an old woman. I'm forty-eight years old and I dress younger than you. Look at these." Sheila lifted her denim skirt to mid-thigh and extended her leg. "Not bad for forty-eight-year-old legs, huh? That's because I exercise. Look at this." She turned around and lifted the skirt to her waist. "That ass is forty-eight years old, and it looks better than my daughter's. Come on, I tell her, exercise with me, but oh no, she knows better." Sheila dropped her skirt and perched on the edge of Natalie's desk. "I exercise every morning before work. You know Muscle Beach in Santa Monica? I went down there and asked the guys what kind of exercise do they do to get such terrific bodies, and they showed me. You ever been to Muscle Beach?"

"Come on, Sheila," groaned Natalie.

"You have a very nice bust, Natalie, but if you don't watch out, they're gonna sag to your kneecaps. I have an exercise for that. It strengthens the pectorals. I'm forty-eight years old, two kids, and look," Sheila stuck out her chest, "still nice and high. Where you see them is where they grow."

Natalie, in an agony of embarrassment, bent even lower over her books. "Please, Sheila," she begged. "I have to finish these."

"Are you sure you don't want coffee?"

"I'm positive, Sheila."

"Okay. Want me to Xerox a back exercise for you? It improves posture, and if you do it faithfully, you'll never get a widow's hump."

"Fine. Thank you."

"Stick out your bust, Natalie. Like I tell my own daughter, 'If you've got 'em, flaunt 'em.' "

Despite her awareness that Sheila's advice was kindly intended, it caused Natalie enormous confusion. She hunched even lower in her chair as if struggling to make her shoulders meet in front. By the time Ira buzzed her again to tell her to get ready, Natalie had decided to decline the lunch.

"No thanks, Ira. I've got work to finish."

"Come on, Sis, it will do you good."

"Really, Ira, I . . ."

"Look, who's the boss here?"

"You."

"Be ready in three minutes."

"But I'm not dressed right, Ira, I . . ."

"Three minutes, Sis," he told her and clicked off.

It was in the restaurant, sitting across from her, that Ira began to feel uncomfortable. He had been in Natalie's company many times; they had taken the children places together, she was often in his house, he was often in hers. This was not the first time they had broken bread together. He loved Natalie, he was grateful to her and appreciated her devotion to his children, he liked her company and thought highly of her. Natalie was sweet, kind, easy to be with, nonthreatening, generous, thoughtful and considerate. She was gentle, the best. Natalie was his sister. So why was he sitting like this and feeling so uncomfortable? She was easy to be with, conversation had always been unforced and natural. So why was he suddenly unable to think of anything to say to her?

The waiter walked over and asked if they wanted something to drink. Ira looked inquiringly at Natalie. "Like a drink, Sis?"

Natalie, hunched in her chair, her arms close together, her hands twisting in her lap, nodded. Perhaps a drink would serve to relax her and coat her nervous, self-conscious discomfort the way Pepto-Bismol coated queasy stomachs. It always seemed to work in the books she read and the movies she saw. She wished now that she was as sure as all the heroines in her books appeared to be. When she was eleven, she had found a copy of *Forever Amber* hidden behind *The Complete Works of William Shakespeare* on the bookshelf in the den. To this day it remained her favorite book, and she had reread it more times than she could remember. She wanted to be Amber St. Clair. She wanted to be irresistible to men, she wanted to be at ease with them and charming, especially charming.

"I'll have a double Bloody Mary," she blurted out and immediately blushed. Ira looked at her, startled, then turned and nodded at the waiter. "I'll have the same," he said.

When the drinks came, Natalie managed to finish hers in a few minutes. Ira, whose glass was still more than half-full, looked at her strangely and asked if she wanted another.

"Yup," said Natalie.

"Are you sure, Sis? That was a double vodka."

"Yup," said Natalie.

". . . and you're not used to drinking."

"Yup," said Natalie.

"Maybe you'd better just pass, okay?"

"Nope," said Natalie.

Despite his strong misgivings, Ira ordered her another drink. This one she drank more slowly. By now she was feeling much better. Carefree, in fact. Nice and loose. Her shoulders had unclamped, she felt relaxed and not bothered at all by the fact that she was wearing a yellow sweater over her double-D size nipple-revealing bra. She even sat up straight.

"Do you like the name Amber?" she asked Ira.

"For what?"

"For a name. Amber."

Again Ira looked at her. Natalie was not used to drinking. Ira had never seen her high before. And she was certainly high. Natalie was his sister. She wasn't supposed to be high. Ira squirmed a bit in his chair. "It's a very unusual name," Ira said.

"If I ever have a daughter, maybe I'll name her Amber," giggled Natalie, feeling wonderful. "I'd love to have a daughter," she continued, "I'd love to have anything, so long as it's a baby. I'd love to have a baby, because I love babies, children."

"I know that, Sis," said Ira, gently. "You'd be a wonderful mother. Todd and Jeremy adore you."

"And I adore them." She sat up and reached for a cracker.

The waiter returned and asked if they cared for another drink before lunch.

"Yup," said Natalie.

"No, thanks," said Ira. "We'll have some wine with our lunch."

The waiter reached for their glasses and Natalie smiled at

him. The waiter smiled back and glanced at her breasts. Ira, following his gaze, stared, startled, at her frontage. Immediately he pulled his eyes away and frowned at the waiter. "We'll have the menus, please," he told him coldly.

"Yes, *sir*," the waiter smiled. He looked at Ira and then deliberately winked at him, man to man. Outraged, Ira clamped his lips together. "Natalie," he said, and began to cough.

"Do like this," suggested Natalie, helpfully. And as Ira watched, she raised both arms high above her head. Her breasts lifted and thrust forward, the sweater tightened, her nipples nudged his horrified gaze and held it.

"Put your hands down," he choked, tearing his eyes way.

"Okey-dokey," sang Natalie.

Ira picked up his glass of water and drained it. A thin film of perspiration dotted his forehead and upper lip. Although he appreciated a pretty leg, a firm thigh, a high, rounded derrière, Ira was a dedicated breast man from way back. He knew this, and attributed his tit fixation to the fact that he lost his mother at an early age. He had been very attracted to Marilyn but had always regretted that her breasts, although more than adequate, were not as large as he would have preferred. Whenever he met a woman it was always the first thing he looked at. Brenda's were perfect, and during their affair he had spent much pleasant time there.

But Natalie was his sister. She wasn't supposed to have the kind of breasts that caused the unsettling, pants-tightening reaction he was now experiencing. With unsteady hands, Ira adjusted the napkin in his lap. He was disgusted with himself and felt dirty, slimy. Natalie was his sister. She was sweet, naïve, *guileless*. He rather pitied her and thought her somehow asexual. Naturally, he knew she had breasts; she was after all a female. But he had never really . . . her breasts had never . . . My God. She was his *sister*. Ira took out his handkerchief and wiped his forehead. He felt like a pervert.

"Are you all right, Ira?" asked Natalie, with a sunny smile.

"Yes," he answered hoarsely and cleared his throat. "I'm fine."

But he wasn't. He didn't know what to do—and with horror, he realized that he couldn't seem to control his eyes. They kept straying back to fasten themselves on his sister's frontage. Sister-in-*law*. *Ex*-sister-in-law.

The waiter returned with the menus. "Mademoiselle." He bowed, smiling, and handed one to Natalie. "Monsieur," he said, and as he gave one to Ira, the bastard winked again.

Somehow Ira managed to get through lunch. Natalie, at ease and chattering, appeared to notice nothing unusual, not even when, at her office door, she gave Ira a thank-you kiss on the cheek and he drew sharply away. Natalie walked, humming, to her desk. Sheila wasn't back yet and she had the office to herself. As she sat down and opened her account books, still humming, Natalie decided Bloody Marys were really very beneficial to shy people. She decided that if a guy ever asked her out, she'd order a double Bloody Mary because they made her feel so at ease, so unconstrained, so natural. They also made her feel a wee bit dizzy—so what, she'd gladly take dizzy, as long as she was guaranteed all the rest. Natalie looked up, smiling, as Sheila opened the door and breezed in.

"How are ya?" greeted Sheila.

"I'm charming," answered Natalie gaily. "How are you?"

In his private office, Ira sat dialing Brenda's number. He was informed that the number he had dialed was no longer in use and that no new number was listed. Ira hung up the phone and sat staring at his desk, depressed. He speculated over Brenda's whereabouts and realized suddenly that he had had neither her nor any other woman for several months. No wonder he had reacted to Natalie the way he did. He was horny, that was all, and when a man is horny even a picture of Phyllis Diller, even a chimpanzee giving suck to its young, could make it stand up.

Ira felt a bit relieved at this interpretation of his conduct and decided that it was imperative that he begin making some social contacts. Sexual contacts. His own sister, my God. Fortunately Natalie, being a bit stewed, had not noticed anything. The poor thing would have fainted. He wondered idly about her sex life, couldn't imagine her in any position other than upright, and immediately was ashamed of himself all over again. How the hell had this happened? What kind of sick person was he to have reacted sexually to his own sister? Well, sister-in-law, ex-sister-in-law. He better get out and start meeting someone. In the meantime it would probably be a good idea to avoid Natalie for a while—at least until he was back in the social swing. He pressed his intercom.

"Lisa, what's my schedule for the next few weekends? Any meetings?"

"This weekend is Sonya's opening in Reno, and next weekend is that Writers' Guild Disneyland thing."

"And after that?"

"Nothing so far."

"Thanks, Lisa."

"Your mother-in-law called. She said don't forget about dinner Friday night."

Ira smiled to himself. What a woman, he thought admiringly. He applauded her ability to go on, knowing that a lesser woman would have folded up and dissolved under the impact of the many blows that had been rained upon her. What a wonderful woman his mother-in-law was. Ira felt privileged to be her son, to bathe in her love. He would do anything for her. She had sustained and warmed him all through his miserable years with Marilyn, and even with Lenny so ill had bolstered and held him up during the divorce proceedings. He loved her—and why not? She was his mother.

Chapter
26

CELIA WAS WORRIED ABOUT MARILYN. Her niece had become a monotone. Like a can of soda left open in the refrigerator, she had lost all her fizz, all her life. She was flat and watereddown, no longer fun to drink. From what Celia could ascertain, Marilyn's existence seemed to center around her law practice and watching television. She had called her after returning from Hawaii, but Marilyn had been distant and distracted. No, she couldn't make it for lunch on Saturday; yes, she was glad they'd had a nice time; sure, she would definitely call tomorrow and arrange a date to say hello and pick up the muumuu Celia had bought for her.

Two weeks later, after no word from Marilyn, Celia drove over to her apartment and knocked at the door. Marilyn answered after a few moments, and at the sight of her Celia was so shocked that she almost dropped her packages. She was practically unrecognizable. Her eyes were dull, her hair uncombed. She was dressed in a dirty old terrycloth robe with the bottom two buttons missing, and the apartment was a filthy mess.

"My God, Marilyn," Celia gasped, as she walked into the littered living room, "what's happened to you?"

Marilyn gave a dry, mirthless laugh. "Haven't you heard, Celia?" she asked. "My father died."

Celia stared at her, appalled. "From the looks of things, dear heart, so have you," she said softly.

"Yes," Marilyn nodded. "So have I."

Wrinkling her nose, Celia pushed aside an empty Melba toast box and an opened, half-eaten tin of sardines, and laid her packages on the table. "It smells in here, Marilyn."

Celia took off her coat and looked for a clean place to put it. After a moment, she laid it over the back of a chair, then, pushing aside a pile of newspapers and several discarded pieces of clothing, sat down on the couch.

"Perhaps you should call Uncle Ben, or Doctor Leventhal," she suggested. "You need help, dear heart. You cannot live like this."

Again Marilyn shrugged and seated herself opposite Celia, in an armchair. She crossed her legs and leaned back. Celia noticed that she was still, at four in the afternoon, wearing her nightgown. On her feet were frayed, fluffy blue scuffs. The exposed heels of her feet were whitish-looking, dry, and callused. Her legs were unshaved.

"I brought you back some presents from Hawaii," Celia said at last, indicating the packages.

"Oh—thank you," replied Marilyn, not even glancing at the table. "That was sweet of you."

They lapsed into silence. From the bedroom, Celia heard the sound of the television set. She took her cigarettes from her handbag and offered one to Marilyn.

"Thank you," said Marilyn, and they both lit up. Celia looked around for an ashtray. Marilyn was using a glass half-filled with a disgusting brown liquid in which were floating the butts of other smoked-down cigarettes. Pieces of wet tobacco swam in the liquid and were stuck to the sides of the glass.

"I need an ashtray, dear heart," said Celia.

Marilyn leaned forward and looked around. She pointed to an overflowing ashtray on the floor near Celia's feet and leaned back again. Celia, following her finger, bent down and carefully picked up the ashtray. She held it away from her and dumped it into a page of the newspaper. The dust of old ashes rose in the air, and Celia coughed. She folded the newspaper over the contents of the ashtray and looked around for some place to discard it.

"Just leave it there," said Marilyn. "I'll throw it away later."

Celia sighed and pushed it toward the middle of the couch. They smoked in silence.

"Well," said Celia, when she had finished her cigarette, "besides your obvious descent into schizophrenia, what else is new?"

"I'm managing," answered Marilyn.

"That," replied her aunt, looking meaningfully around the room, "is a matter of opinion. I don't call this managing, dear heart. It's more like disintegration into self-pitying sloth, if you ask me."

"I'm not asking you, Celia."

"Be that as it may, Marilyn, unless you have acquired a garbage fixation, which is in itself rather sickening, it's quite obvious that you require taking in hand. I volunteer."

Marilyn shifted in her chair, annoyed. "I appreciate your concern, Aunt Celia. I'm sure it's lovingly meant. But what I require you cannot supply."

"Try me," insisted Celia.

Marilyn uncrossed her legs and, grasping the arms of her chair, leaned forward.

"I need my father back," she cried. "Can you do that for me, Aunt Celia?"

At the look in her eyes, Celia drew back. "Can living in filth bring your father back?" she asked, sternly.

"Leave me alone, Celia," whispered Marilyn. Her hands tightened on the arms of the chair. "From what I hear you have enough to do keeping your *own* house in order."

Celia composed her face and looked at her niece. "Do explain, dear heart," she said in a steady voice.

"I heard that Uncle Jack's been fucking around."

Celia drew her breath in sharply. "And where did you pick up that little tidbit?" she asked.

"From one of the fuckees," answered Marilyn, lifting an eyebrow, "who happens to be a friend of mine."

"I see." Celia groped for another cigarette, her heart beating rapidly, more over Marilyn's savage attack than over her knowledge of Jack's indiscretions. She lit the cigarette and inhaled deeply. "It seems you are traveling in a rather questionable social circle," said Celia. "Not only do you live in dirt, you also befriend it and spout it. But when you fling it and I am the target, then, dear heart, don't expect me not to protest—and I do, Marilyn, I protest vehemently. I thought you loved me." Celia's voice cracked slightly and she quickly looked down.

Marilyn put her head in her hands. "I do," she mumbled. "I do love you."

"You have an unusual way of showing it," said Celia. "You just stuck a knife in me, and yet you love me. What would you have done to someone you didn't love? I shudder to think. Twisted it, maybe." Celia glanced over at her niece. "Look at me, Marilyn," she ordered.

Marilyn raised her head and looked, dry-eyed, at her aunt. Her face was set and expressionless. Celia stared.

"You look like my mother," she whispered at last. "When she looked at Helen or Murray, or Ben after his accident, she had the same look you have now. Me, I was lucky. Max and I both were—and your uncle Ben before his accident—we were her favorites—her passports to immortality—and she needed us. She took good care of us—the way your mother tends her damn plants. God, the frustration. I never met frustration like my mother's. I hope I never do."

Celia brought the cigarette to her mouth and it bobbed between unsteady lips. "Poor soul," whispered Celia. "She was pitiful, Marilyn. And poor Helen . . . she tried so hard to get that woman to love her . . . and Malka never did. She couldn't. Helen was a weed, you see. Max and Ben and I—we were her flowers, but Murray and Helen—they were the weeds." Celia inhaled again and held the smoke a long time before expelling it. "You know," she said, "your mother refused to admit she hated her—but she *must* have. How could she not have? But Helen never admitted it, not even to herself."

Celia looked thoughtfully at her niece. "I often think," she said, "that the reason you two don't get along is because Helen transferred all that anger and hate to *you*. She's thrown it all on you, Marilyn, all that shit she couldn't throw at Malka."

Marilyn sat, her eyes riveted on her aunt. "She must have been a monster. My mother named me for a monster."

Celia put her hand up. "No, Marilyn. That poor woman was hardly a monster. She was a misfit, a sad misfit; born at the wrong time. Had she been your age today, she would have fit right in—there'd be no stopping her."

Celia tilted her head slightly and smiled at her niece. "In fact, I daresay she would have been a lot like you. An ambitious, liberated, successful woman; just like you." Her voice dropped, and when she spoke again it was husky, as if her thoughts were caught in her throat. "Your mother must, on some level, see this, dear heart, and that repressed shit we were talking about before—she heaps that on you. She couldn't on Malka, and still can't. Malka isn't here any more, but you are—Helen dumps it on the Malka in you."

Suddenly furious, Celia crushed out her cigarette viciously. Then she quickly stood up and glared down at her niece. "You're sitting neck-high in shit, Marilyn, and sinking rapidly. Look at you. Look at this place. My poor mother would have given her eyeteeth—" She stopped abruptly and then went on more calmly, "And you're a liar, Marilyn. You don't love me at all. You did once, I *think*, but I don't think so any more."

"Please, Aunt Celia . . ."

"Anyway," Celia continued, "let's hope it's only a temporary condition."

"Yes," cried Marilyn gratefully, "it's only been a little over three months. I'm not myself yet. I don't even love myself. And I'm sorry about . . . what I said. Please sit down."

Celia stood quite still for several seconds. Then she sighed and sat down again. "I'd like a cup of coffee, please," said Celia, "and I'd like it in a clean cup."

Marilyn got to her feet and walked into the kitchen. She felt tired, as if she'd just carried a grand piano up two flights of stairs. She regretted her attack on Celia because Celia was one of the few people left who still cared about her. But Marilyn, spooning instant coffee into two hastily rinsed out cups, admitted that it was true, she did not return the caring—she was drained of feeling and afraid . . . empty . . . pitiful . . . like Malka.

She turned the stove up to high and waited for the water to boil. For a moment, her sense of desolation was so keen that she caught her breath. She longed for her father and the total love and acceptance he had always wrapped around her. She missed him and that warm security blanket desperately. She needed to love someone—she needed to be loved by someone. Celia claimed to love her, but it was a single match compared to the furnace of her father's adoration. She would never have that again. She would never be warm again.

She poured the boiling water into the cups, and grabbing two paper towels—she was out of napkins—returned to the living room. Celia was sitting where she left her, smoking again. Marilyn handed her the cup and a paper towel and sat down in the armchair.

"I hate to see you like this," said Celia, "it's unhealthy."

Marilyn took a sip of coffee, burning her tongue and wincing. But at least she was feeling something. She smiled ruefully into her cup. She had always been able to feel pain.

"Give me time, Aunt Celia. I'm trying to work myself up."

Celia put her cup down on the small, dusty table next to the arm of the couch. She felt enormous pity for her niece and also, to her surprise, irritation. Why had she discarded Ira and her children? Why had she been so stupid, so reckless?

"It's my opinion," said Celia, "that if you had hung in with Ira and the kids, you'd be much better off than you are now. You wouldn't be sitting all alone in a filthy apartment. You'd *have* somebody." She reached for her coffee and took a sip. "That's why I never left Jack. I waited it out because I knew if I didn't I'd end up with nothing. My sons are grown and out. They have lives of their own. If I'd done with Jack what you did with Ira, I'd be sitting like you now. Alone. But I," she said, taking another drink, "at least would have shaved my legs."

Marilyn said nothing. She rubbed her tongue gingerly over her teeth and the roof of her mouth, grateful for the sting.

"Ira loved you," Celia went on. "You had a life with him. Your recovery would have been more rapid. Jack humiliated me, and I hated him for it. But I hung in and I have him."

"Was it worth it?"

"Yes, dear heart, it was worth it. Of course, I doubt that things will ever be the same. But I have him . . . and who knows, maybe it will even be better some day than it ever was."

"Maybe it won't."

Celia shrugged. "Maybe it won't," she agreed, "but I'm not alone. I have someone to eat dinner with. I have someone in my bed. I have someone to talk to. I have someone who owes me . . . What do *you* have?"

"I have hair on my legs," said Marilyn coldly.

"Wonderful," Celia replied angrily. "You can watch television together. There's nothing like the company of a hairy leg when you need an arm around you."

Marilyn put her cup on the floor and leaned forward. "What do you want from me, Celia? You want me to pat you on the back for keeping Jack? You want me to admit that you did the right thing and I did the wrong?"

"Well," said Celia, raising her eyebrows, "which one of us is better off?" She threw out her arm and indicated the apartment. "Look," she said softly, "wouldn't the loss of your father have been even a tiny bit easier to bear if you had Ira and the children around to comfort you and take the edge off?"

Marilyn straightened up. "You don't know me at all, do you?" she asked. "You don't know the first fucking thing about me!"

Celia frowned at her, disgusted. "I know a couple of things:

one, you're a mess. Two, you once mentioned to me that Ira
sometimes gave you the same feeling of total acceptance that
Lenny—that your father did. And three," she said, glancing at
her watch, "that I have to meet Jack for dinner soon." She lifted
her cup and drained it. Then she reached for another cigarette.

"You're smoking a lot," observed Marilyn. Celia tossed her the
pack, and they both lit up. "You and Phyllis," said Marilyn,
"you're both so happy and smug."

"Lucky us."

Marilyn puffed at her cigarette and looked over Celia's shoulder, her eyes unfocused. "But I did say that, didn't I?" she whispered, recalling her before-sleep fantasy.

"About Ira?"

Marilyn nodded.

"Yes, you did," replied Celia. "You said it several times as I
recall. You said, 'He smothers me in solicitude. I love it from
my father, I'm contemptuous of it from Ira.' "

Again Marilyn nodded. "I remember," she murmured.

"Well, maybe you wouldn't be so contemptuous now."

Marilyn felt her eyes begin to fill and bent quickly down to
retrieve her cup. She sat up, her hands shaking so badly that
some of the coffee sloshed over the rim and onto her robe. It
felt warm on her thigh.

"Why don't you call him?" suggested Celia softly. "Why don't
you, Marilyn?"

Marilyn looked wet-eyed at her aunt.

"Solicitude would feel very nice now, don't you think?"

Marilyn held her cup tightly in both hands.

"Call him," urged Celia. "You have nothing to lose."

"You think so?" she asked in a small, childlike voice.

"I do, dear heart. You need to be held; you need tender, loving care. Ira is an expert at that. Don't end up like Malka,
Marilyn."

Marilyn began to cry softly, and Celia rose and laid her hand
gently on her bowed shoulders. Marilyn reached up and put her
own hand over her aunt's, gripping it.

"Will you call him?"

Marilyn nodded, unable to speak. After a few moments, Celia extricated her hand and offered Marilyn her paper towel. "Blow, dear heart," she said quietly. "And now I too must blow. Do let me know how it went."

"I will," sniffed Marilyn. "Thank you, Aunt Celia."

She stood up and walked her aunt to the door. Celia kissed her goodbye and started to walk away. At the elevator, she turned. "Good luck, dear heart," she called, and disappeared into the waiting car. Marilyn stood there for a while, then closed the door. She took the boxes Celia had brought her off the table and carried them into her bedroom.

Tomorrow she would call Ira. Maybe now she would be capable of accepting what she had previously spurned. She was cold. She had no father. She had no feelings. Anything was better than that. Even Ira.

At nine-thirty that night, after returning from dinner with Jack, Celia hurried into her bedroom and phoned her sister, Helen. She was elated and excited by the news she intended to impart. Helen will be delirious, thought Celia with a smile. She dialed and waited impatiently for an answer.

"Hello?"

"Helen? It's Celia, and do I have news for you. Sit down, dear heart. I am going to bring joy to your weeping spirit."

"Okay, I could use some joy."

"Are you sitting?"

"I'm sitting. Talk."

"You know how upset you were over the divorce and the custody and losing Ira and all?"

"Of course I know," cried Helen impatiently. "How could I not know?"

"Well," said Celia smiling hugely, "I just fixed it."

"What did you fix?" asked Helen, alarmed.

"Wait a minute, I want to get a cigarette."

"Celia . . ."

"Okay," said Celia, lighting up. "I saw Marilyn today."

"Oh," replied Helen coldly.

"And I convinced her to call Ira."

"You *what*?"

"I convinced her to call Ira and give it another chance." Celia inhaled on her cigarette and waited, still smiling, for Helen's joyous reaction. Silence.

"Well? . . . Helen? . . . Are you still there?"

"I'm still here," said Helen faintly.

"So what do you think of *that*?" Celia asked triumphantly.

"Marilyn said she's calling Ira?"

"Yes, ma'am."

"When?"

"Soon."

"Dear God," gasped Helen.

"See? I told you you'd be happy . . . Hello? . . . Helen?"

"I'm here, I'm here," came Helen's faint reply.

"Is that all you have to say?" asked Celia, miffed.

"I'm just . . . I can't . . ."

"Well, aren't you thrilled?" insisted Celia. "Isn't this what you wanted? Helen, what's the *matter* with you?"

"She didn't say when she'd call?"

"No, she didn't," said Celia, annoyed. "I thought you'd be turning somersaults over this news."

"I'm just surprised, Celia . . . I'm just . . . shocked."

"Naturally," laughed Celia, appeased. "It's the answer to all your prayers. You'll have your precious Ira back . . . Helen?"

"Yes."

"Aren't you even going to *thank* me?"

"She said . . . Marilyn said, she was going to ask Ira for a reconciliation?"

"Uh-huh," mumbled Celia, taking a drag on her cigarette.

"What?"

"Yes."

"You're *sure*?"

"Of *course* I'm sure. I just left her a few hours ago."

"You think she called already?"

"I don't know, Helen. You're being very strange about this. I thought you'd be in seventh heaven."

"Oh, I am, I am."

"You certainly don't sound it."

"Well, I'm—breathless."

"Good, dear heart. When it's all settled, I'll expect you to take me to lunch at Chasen's."

"Oh, definitely," said Helen and almost choked. She hung up the phone with a trembling hand and slumped in her chair, too numb even to cry. She felt like strangling Celia, and her hostility toward Marilyn rose like bile in her throat. She clenched her fists in her lap and sat like a stone on the kitchen chair, thinking furiously. After about fifteen minutes she reached for the phone and called Ira.

"Hello, darling. Am I disturbing you?"

"No, Mom, I'm never too busy for you."

"So, what's new, Ira? Have you heard from anybody?"

"Noooo."

"That's good . . . I mean," said Helen, hastily, "are you still going this weekend to Disneyland with the children?"

"Yes, they can hardly wait."

"When do you leave?"

"Tomorrow morning, nine sharp. We stay over at the Disneyland Hotel, and we should be back about eight o'clock Sunday evening. Maybe even earlier because the kids have school."

"It sounds wonderful, darling. Are you driving there with anyone?"

"No. I have several clients going, but I'll see them at the Park."

"Oh."

"Why?" asked Ira teasingly. "Did you want to come along?"

"Do you have room for me?"

"Sure," laughed Ira, "I'll sleep in with the boys and you can have *my* room."

"That's wonderful, Ira. I'm getting all excited."

"Fine. You want me to pick you up?"

"Well, not me exactly."

"Then who exactly?" he asked, suddenly nervous.

"Natalie."

There was a long silence, and Helen's palms began to perspire. She switched the phone to her other hand. "Ira?"

"I don't know, Ma."

"She would enjoy it so, Ira. And she would take the children around so you could have time with your clients."

"I don't know, Ma," he repeated.

"But why, darling?"

Unable to reply, Ira was silent. Helen pressed the receiver to her ear, her hands sweaty. "Ira?"

"Yeah, Mom."

"Do it for me, Ira. I won't ever impose on you again."

"Mom," pleaded Ira, "it's no imposition, it's just . . ." His voice trailed off. How could he explain to her?

"Please, Ira." Helen waited, her heart beating so loudly in her ears that she held the phone slightly away from her, sure that somehow Ira would hear the pounding.

"For me, Ira," she begged, her voice breaking. She heard him sigh.

"Okay, Mom. Tell Natalie to be ready at a quarter of nine."

"Thank you, darling; thank you, Ira. She'll be a help to you, you'll see. Ira?"

"Yes?"

"Why did you hesitate? Is something the matter?"

"No, no," Ira assured her. "I . . . uh . . . just wanted some time alone with the kids," he said lamely.

"Oh, don't worry about that. Natalie is very understanding," said Helen, relieved. "I'll tell her to be ready—knowing her, she'll even be early."

"Okay, Mom."

"I love you, Ira."

"Ditto. See you tomorrow."

Helen hung up the phone and exhaled loudly. She wiped her wet hands on the sides of her dress and got her breath back. For a moment she wondered at Ira's reluctance to have Natalie accompany them, then put the thought aside. "Natalie," she called, walking to the steps.

"What?"

Helen began to climb. "Pack your small valise. You're going tomorrow with Ira to Disneyland."

"How come?" she asked, as Helen walked in and sat down on the bed.

"Because I said so," answered Helen, breathing rapidly from her climb.

Together they began packing Natalie's bag, with Helen selecting all the outfits. After a while Natalie went over to the mirror and began to practice inserting her contact lenses.

"There," said Helen, surveying the contents of the valise, "you're all packed, except for one thing. Wait a minute, I'll get it." She walked quickly out of the room, and Natalie heard her rummaging in her bureau drawers. When she returned, she was carrying something white and filmy over her arm. The scent of lavender sachet began to fill the room. "What's that?" asked Natalie. "It smells good."

"A nightgown," replied Helen and held it up.

The tissue paper around which it had been folded to avoid creasing floated to the floor. Curiously, Natalie walked over and looked at it. She ran her hand gently down its creamy, satiny length.

"It's beautiful," she breathed. "Where did you get it?"

"In Saks. I bought it for Phyllis to wear on her wedding night, but when I heard they decided to go backpacking for their honeymoon, with sleeping bags and tents, I decided not to give it to her."

"It's really beautiful," Natalie repeated. "Why are you packing it?" she asked, as Helen carefully refolded it and laid it in the valise.

"You'll wear it tomorrow night."

"Why?" cried Natalie.

"So it shouldn't go to waste," answered Helen calmly.

"But . . . why? It's too good."

"Better you should wear it than it should lay in the drawer."

"But . . ."

"No buts. Wear it and enjoy it. It will turn yellow in my dresser, and that would be a shame."

Helen closed the valise and clicked the latches shut. "And who knows," she teased, looking at Natalie and smiling, "maybe a Prince Charming will walk into your room in the Disneyland Hotel."

"Oh, sure," grinned Natalie.

"You never know," said Helen, walking to the door. "You never know what fate has in store." She turned and blew Natalie a kiss. "Don't forget to take a nice bath before you put it on, and Natalie . . ."

"Hmm?"

"Have a good time."

Chapter 27

QUICKLY IRA SHOWERED AND CHANGED HIS CLOTHES. He ran downstairs, knocked on Ophelia's door and told her he was going out for a while. Then he got into his car and drove to a singles bar he had often heard Brenda speak of, called Close Encounters. Ira felt the strong need for a close encounter. He wasn't really any longer concerned about Natalie's one-time fluke effect on him, but still it wouldn't hurt to have an insurance policy against its unlikely but possible recurrence. If he was anything, Ira was a careful man, and he pulled into the parking lot determined to get laid.

The bar was jammed, but despite the throng he spotted Brenda immediately. She was sitting at the bar smiling and holding court. She looked marvelous, and Iran felt himself stir from mere anticipation alone. He pushed and elbowed his way through the crowd, his eyes fixed on her. At last he made it to the bar and pulled his jacket, one side of which was still caught in the crush, back together and buttoned it. He smoothed his hair and approached her.

"Hello, Brenda."

She looked up, and the first thing she noticed about him was that of all the men in her immediate vicinity, only Ira was wearing a tie. "Good to see you, Ira."

"I tried to call you about two weeks ago. Have you moved?"

Brenda smiled and nodded. "Onward and upward, Ira, also southward. I now reside in Phoenix, Arizona."

He looked around for another stool, and finding none, leaned against the bar, his foot on the shiny brass rail.

"Why didn't you tell me?" he asked.

"It's a short story, Ira. I got married."

For a moment he stared at her, disappointment and surprise widening his eyes and parting his lips.

"Well—uh—congratulations," he stammered. "Anyone I know?"

"Not yet, but hold on a minute." She tapped the shoulder of the man next to her. He broke off the conversation he had been having with two other gentlemen and turned around.

"Anthony," smiled Brenda, "meet Ira Stillman. Ira, this is my husband, Anthony Santacroce."

"How ya doin' there, Ira?" grinned Anthony, extending a large, well-tended hand. "Any friend of the wife's is a friend of mine."

They shook hands, and Ira congratulated his new friend and wished him well. He felt uncomfortable, surprised at the sense of loss Brenda's marriage had engendered. "Let me buy you both a drink," Ira offered, forcing a grin of good cheer.

"That's real white of you, Ira," said Anthony and clapped him on the back.

"What'll you have?" asked Ira, moving slightly away.

"How about champagne?" suggested Brenda.

"Champagne it is," Ira said, "if I can get hold of the bartender."

"Hey, Ellie," bellowed Anthony, "how's about a little service here."

"Yes, *sir*," answered Ellie, hurrying over.

"Three glasses of champagne, please," Ira ordered. Ellie bent down and, after a few seconds, straightened up, a cold bottle of Dom Perignon clutched in his hand. He held out the bottle for inspection toward Anthony, who glanced at it and nodded ap-

provingly. Ira, annoyed that Ellie had not held it out toward
him, said, "That will be fine," just a shade too loudly. After the
wine was poured, Ira lifted his glass. "To many happy, fruitful,
and prosperous years together," he toasted. They all clinked
glasses and drank. Then Anthony turned back to the two waiting gentlemen and resumed his conversation. His hand, Ira noticed, was resting proprietarily on Brenda's thigh.

"I'm going to miss you, Brenda," he said in a low voice.

"You should have thought of that before," she answered
wryly.

"Yah . . . well . . ." said Ira lamely, "I guess so."

Brenda looked at him shrewdly. "Are you looking for action?"
she asked.

Startled, Ira stared at her. His eyes slid nervously in the direction of Anthony and then quickly back.

"Because if you are," she went on with an amused smile, "I
can arrange something."

"Oh, you can?"

"Can Beverly Sills carry a tune? When do you want it?"

"Tonight. I'm leaving for the weekend in the morning."

"Oh—alone?"

"No."

Brenda smiled. "I can get you warmed up for the big game,
lover boy—but it'll cost you."

"You mean a *prostitute?*" sputtered Ira.

"I mean Alma," answered Brenda, and pointed to a woman
seated on the other side of the bar.

Ira, looking in the direction indicated by Brenda's forefinger,
nodded and whistled softly. Alma was gorgeous. "And she's built
the way you like 'em, Ira."

He nodded again. "How much?"

Brenda thrust out her lower lip in thought. "Depends," she
said. "I would estimate about a hundred, maybe fifty if you don't
get hinky."

"I don't know," said Ira uncertainly.

"Well, when *you* know, let *me* know and I'll let *Alma* know, okay? But don't take forever about it, Ira. It's not the Camp David talks, you understand, and Alma's a busy lady."

"But a prostitute . . ."

Brenda's laugh was low and amused. "Ira, Ira," she chided him. "You're a hungry man. You want a steak, ya gotta pay the price. Sure you can get freebies in here, but who can vouch for the quality? Now with Alma I can guarantee you a prime good time with no worries healthwise. With the others . . ." Brenda lifted her hands, palms up, and shrugged. "Who knows?"

"It bothers me to have to pay for sex."

"Fine. Forget it. How are your little boys?"

But Ira's eyes were still on Alma. She was certainly steak. "Is she a prostitute or a call girl?" he asked.

"Six of one, half a dozen of the other," said Brenda, holding out her champagne glass for a refill. "Come on, Ira, drink up."

"She's really beautiful. Why does she . . . ?"

"Please," protested Brenda. "Don't ask me dumb questions."

Ira's eyes drifted over the female stool-sitters around the bar and paused at a blonde, large-breasted girl several stools away. "Do you know her?" he asked, pointing with his chin. Brenda looked over.

"Uh-huh."

"Is she a . . . ?"

"That's Charlene," she informed him, "and she's street stuff. My advice to you about Charlene is, when you go into that kind of weather, you better wear a raincoat."

Ira straightened up and drained his glass of champagne. "This is ridiculous," he said. "I've never paid for sex in my life."

Brenda laughed out loud. "Boy," she said through her laughter, "you sure got a lousy memory."

Ira reddened in embarrassment. "That was different. Those were *loans* I gave you."

"Sure they were," she chuckled, "except I never paid them back and you neither asked nor expected me to. Come on, Ira, call a spade a spade."

Ira looked at her, shocked. "Brenda," he whispered sternly,

glancing once again at Anthony, "you stop that. You never sold your body for money and you know it."

"Okay," she said, "if it makes you feel better, let's just say I rented it."

Ira sighed and nodded to the hovering Ellie, holding out his glass. When it was filled, he took a large swallow.

"You need a wife, kiddo," observed Brenda. "Nookie-hunting just isn't your sport."

Offended, Ira was about to reply when Brenda's husband suddenly ended his conference and turned, a gracious smile on his face.

"So, Ira there," he beamed. "How do you happen to know the missus?"

Ira began to cough, and before he could reply, Brenda cut in. "Remember Marilyn, Anthony?"

"Sure I do, baby, why?"

"Well, Ira here is Marilyn's ex."

"Oh, yeah?" asked Anthony.

Bewildered, but much relieved, Ira nodded. "Bartender," he called. "Give Mr. Santacroce . . ."

"Anthony."

". . . Anthony," continued Ira, "another drink."

Ellie emptied the bottle into Anthony's glass. "That's the last of it, Mr. Santacroce," said Ellie.

"Fine, fine," said Anthony. "Put it on my tab."

"No!" cried Ira loudly. "I mean," he explained, lowering his voice in embarrassment, "that was on me . . . in honor of your and Brenda's marriage." As Anthony opened his mouth to protest, Ira held up his hand. "Please," he said, "I insist . . . and I'd be honored to have you accept it."

"Hey," smiled Anthony, eyeing him with respect and clapping him on the back, "you're a good man, Ira. Thanks."

"My pleasure," declared Ira. He lifted his own glass and finished off the remaining champagne. He replaced the empty wineglass on the bar and glanced across at the luscious Alma. Anthony, following his gaze, leaned close to him.

"Ain't that something?" he murmured conspiratorially.

"Sure is," agreed Ira.

"If I wasn't so scared of my wife . . ." grinned Anthony, raising his voice and leering at Brenda, "I'd have a go at her myself."

Brenda lifted her eyebrows at her husband, and Ira saw Anthony lean over and lick the tip of her nose. Uncomfortable, he turned away and resumed his examination of Alma. She was black-haired and very slim. Her breasts, in contrast to what Ira could observe, seemed almost out of proportion to the rest of her body. Her skin was pale, and her eyes, large and dark above her high, delicate cheekbones, stared at nothing. Her arms and hands were graceful, the nails very long and polished. Ira moistened his suddenly dry lips.

"She came out to L.A. to break into pictures or TV," said Anthony, leaning toward him.

"Do you know her?" asked Ira.

"Not in the biblical sense," interjected Brenda, "but he knows her."

Anthony straightened up. "Wait a minute," he said to Ira and, getting to his feet, Anthony began to make his way around the bar. No sooner had he left than three guys made a beeline for the now-vacant stool and Brenda rapidly placed her purse on the seat. "This is taken," she informed the first one to reach it, "*ocupado*."

"Looks empty to me," said the man, and he lifted Brenda's purse from the seat, held it up and deliberately let it fall to the floor. Immediately, the two men who had been talking to Anthony rose and moved on either side of the claim-jumper. "You dropped something, sir," said one, "pick it up." As he said this, he grabbed the back of the man's neck and forced him down, holding him there until the purse was retrieved. "Now return it and apologize to the lady," he ordered, still in possession of the man's neck. The man hesitated, and Anthony's friend impatiently exerted some pressure.

"I said apologize," he repeated firmly.

The stool-stealer mumbled something and laid the purse on the bar in front of Brenda. Instantly his neck was released and his arms grabbed in its place. "As you were just leaving, allow me to escort you to the door," said Anthony's friend politely, and practically lifted the man from his seat. Anthony's other friend took a five-dollar bill and shoved it into the man's pocket. "Your cover charge has just been cheerfully refunded," he informed him. "Good night and be careful driving." He gave him a friendly wave as the man was rapidly propelled through the crowd and out the door. Ira stared, dumbfounded, following the man's progress until the door closed behind him. Then he turned to Brenda.

"What the hell was that all about?" he breathed.

"The management frowns on boorish behavior," explained Brenda, and placed her purse once again on Anthony's stool. "Only quality-type citizens are allowed to patronize the premises. That bum will never get in here again, I'll lay money on it."

Ira shook his head. "You don't even get three strikes in this ballpark," he whispered. "One strike, you're out." He looked up as Anthony approached, pulling Alma by the hand behind him. Anthony gave Brenda back her purse and, extending his hand, offered Alma the seat. When she was seated, he introduced her to Ira. She was even better close up. The skin was unblemished and flawless, the bone structure sharp and delineated. Her eyes, which Ira had thought dark brown, were not. They were navy blue, almost as black as her waist-length hair. She was the most beautiful girl Ira had ever seen. Alma bore his inspection patiently and placidly. Her hands lay still in her lap, her breasts rising and falling serenely with every inaudible breath. Ira couldn't take his eyes off her.

Brenda, laughing, raised and lowered her hand in front of his face. "Somebody goose this guy," she said. "He's either stunned or stoned."

Alma slowly turned her head and gazed at Ira. "Hiyah, sugar," she said softly, and suggestively ran her tongue over her lips. Ira blinked and cleared his throat. How could a beauty this pure veil a life so tarnished? How could anyone who looked that good, be that bad? "May I buy you a drink?" he asked hoarsely.

"You can do whatever you like, sugar," she purred.

Before he could reply, Brenda stood up. "Here, tiger, take my seat before your legs cave in."

Anthony offered his hand to Ira and as he clasped it, Anthony pulled him closer and whispered in his ear. "Happy birthday, pal." He jerked his head in Alma's direction. "Do it once for me."

"But . . ."

"No buts. You bought me champagne. I bought you a present in return. Anthony Santacroce don't like to owe."

As Ira stood transfixed, Brenda nudged him. "Say thank you, birthday boy," she prompted.

"Thank you," croaked Ira.

For a moment, Brenda and Anthony stood beaming upon him like proud parents, as if, thought Ira, he were a two-year-old who had just, on command, proved them to be expert toilet trainers and himself a good little boy. He felt so disconcerted that he almost squirmed, and when they at last were gone, he sank onto Brenda's seat.

Alma, it seemed, was not a particularly apt conversationalist, preferring instead to gaze at the air and at her long, perfectly shaped and gleaming nails. This didn't bother Ira. As far as he was concerned, anyone who looked the way Alma did was required, like a painting, merely to be there for the viewing pleasure of the lesser endowed. After about ten minutes of silent staring, he at her and she at whatever, they left Close Encounters and checked into the Close Encounters Motel. There she undressed, smiling like La Gioconda while Ira blinked at her, bemused.

"I don't understand," he whispered, "why the studios haven't grabbed you up."

"What do you mean?" asked Alma. "I made three pictures."

"You have?"

"Sure I have, sugar. *Fun with Dicks and Jane, The Mouth of the Mississippi* and *Ride 'em, Cowgirl.* Don't you keep up with fuck films?"

Ira stared at her, aghast. "You make pornographic films?" he squeaked.

"I got a new one coming out," she said proudly. *"In Love with Leather.* Try not to miss it. Personally I think it's the best thing I've ever done."

Ira abruptly sat down on the edge of the bed, and Alma, interpreting this as an indication of his readiness, knelt before him. But Alma, to her great surprise, was wrong. Ira, who since the age of twelve had been able to get it up at will, now sat shrunken like a newly washed and un-Sanforized cotton sock. And Alma, who had several times made senior citizens come in less than six minutes, sat bewildered and annoyed. "Sugar?" she asked softly, "you religious or something?"

Wordless, Ira shook his head, and after a moment, Alma bent to her task. It took half an hour of top-quality work to get Ira to the point, and then she ruined it by informing him that "even the hard-core fag I took on on a bet got it up faster than you, sugar."

Two hours and forty minutes later they checked out of the Close Encounters Motel, exhausted. Alma maintained that never had she labored so diligently for "two puny pokes and a push." "You sure are one stubborn man, sugar," she scolded.

Ira was devastated and wondered if perhaps he should make an appointment with an endocrinologist. It had taken him hours to make it once, and barely, with Alma. Something was wrong somewhere.

He drove home quickly, poured himself a shot glass of straight bourbon, tossed it down and collapsed, perturbed and dejected, into bed. He fell asleep and dreamed that he was driving to an important meeting of financial analysts, where he was to be the key speaker. En route he got a flat tire, and by the time he fixed it the meeting was over, his big chance gone.

Ira was not a psychologically oriented man, but he didn't need Freud to help with the interpretation of that one.

Chapter
28

MARILYN AWOKE EARLY on Saturday morning intending to clean up the apartment, shave her legs, call Ira and make an attempt to get her life together. She gazed at the picture of her father that stood on her dresser and read approval in his posed and smiling eyes. She spoke many times to the picture daily, pressed her cheek to it, kissed it. And, as in his lifetime, her father's reassurance and acceptance seemed to emanate from within the leather frame and flow out toward her in a big, warm "Okay Dolly, whatever you want is fine with me."

A month after her father had died, Marilyn had taken the works of Elisabeth Kübler-Ross from the library and read them avidly, deriving comfort from Kübler-Ross's theory that life was eternal and extended—that it was not ended by death, and that human matter, like all other matter, could never be destroyed but was merely transmuted into a different form of energy, into another state. Ross believed in life after death and said so on page after documented page, and Marilyn grabbed onto those concepts and clutched them close to her, aching with the need to believe. She tried to picture her father alive, living on some celestial body of higher consciousness, watching over her, taking care of her—altered, but still her Papa. And sometimes it worked.

Staring now at his picture, she felt he approved of her plans to call Ira, felt that it was his will that was urging her to do so and that Celia had merely been his intermediary. She got out of bed and walked barefoot into the kitchen. She put on the coffee and began desultorily clearing up the mess. But she felt cold in the cluttered, dirty kitchen, where there was no picture of her father. Her brief flurry of energy quickly dissipated. Feeling suddenly drained, Marilyn began stacking the unscraped dishes into the dishwasher and wiped the crumbs from the table onto the floor with a stained, used paper napkin.

The familiar heaviness and lethargy had returned. The depression that lay like a cannonball in her stomach now weighted her body, and she moved slowly, empty but for that enormous lump of agony and loss that never really left her. She dropped the napkin into an overflowing garbage bag, filled her cup with hot coffee, and carrying it carefully, returned to her bedroom. Placing the cup on her night table, she crawled back into bed and propped her pillow behind her. She drew up the covers and looked once again at her father. She would have given ten years of her life just to talk to him, to hear his voice even one more time. The yearning for his specific company, for the well-being that only he could give her, parched her mouth, and she began to lick her rough, dry lips. Lifting her cup, she took a long, hot swallow. Her father would want her to call Ira. He would want to tell her that Ira would be a substitute for him, a proxy cherisher, and if her father wished it, perhaps she would now be able to accept from Ira all she had previously rejected. She would again have someone to love her and hold her—even at her most disagreeable.

Marilyn took another swallow, put down her cup and lit a cigarette. She had tried a reconciliation once, and all it had resulted in was an abortion and divorce. But she had her father then and didn't need Ira. Now her father was dead. Marilyn inhaled deeply and reached for the phone. "Okay, Papa," she whispered and dialed Ira's number. She let the phone ring thirteen times before hanging up.

"I'll try again later," she promised the picture, "he's probably out somewhere with the boys." She reached again for the coffee, feeling a peculiar mixture of acute sadness, disappointment and relief. She sipped her coffee more slowly, her hand still on the phone, the room very quiet. The cigarette burned steadily in a butt-filled ashtray, and Marilyn idly watched the smoke swirl upward. She felt entombed in the smoky silence, where even the street noises seemed unable to filter through. Her heart began to thump, and it seemed to her suddenly that she was buried alive here in a messy, clothes-strewn bedroom, her coffin warm and sheeted, her only company a picture of a dead man and a half-filled cup of lukewarm coffee.

She smelled something burning and glanced at the ashtray. Her cigarette had ignited the filter of the stub on which it was resting, and she watched the filter blacken, curl, and send its own smoke and smell into the air. Even the realization that the over-flowing ashtray might burst into flame could not move her. "Some say the world will end in fire," she murmured softly. "Some say in ice." Deliberately, she lit another cigarette and laid it next to the first, almost-burned-down one. "From what I've tasted of desire,/I hold with those who favor fire." She could tell by the increased odor that another dead butt had caught and was burning. She noted with interest that the smoke was now darker, heavier, less blue and hazy. "But if it had to perish twice,/I think I know enough of hate/To say that for destruction ice/Is also great/and would suffice. By Robert Frost," she informed her father.

Marilyn sat almost trancelike watching the butts and crushed-out stubs of over two packs of cigarettes writhe and disintegrate in a round glass ashtray. Sniffing the unpleasant aroma of burn-ing ash and cottony filter, she assumed that if there was a hell, it would smell similarly. She took her hand off the phone and held it over the ashtray, catching smoke and heat in the cupped palm of her hand. A small burst of flame shot up as a red-tipped match buried somewhere in the ashtray suddenly ignited, and Marilyn yanked her hand back with a thin squeal of pain. She stared at a large blister on the pad below her thumb and shook

her hand rapidly up and down as if trying to shake off the pain
of the burn. She brought it to her nose and smelled it. Her hand
smelled like the chickens her grandmother used to singe over the
gas-lit flame of the stove. She shook her hand once more, blew
on it and then poured what remained of her coffee into the
smoldering ashtray. With a hiss and a fresh uprush of smoke, the
little fire died and the butts lay black and sodden in the pool of
coffee, some of which seeped through the indented cigarette rest
and dripped onto the night table.

She ran to the bathroom, turned on the faucet, and held her
hand under the cold water for several minutes. When the sting-
ing abated, she applied Unguentine to the burn and, holding her
hand gingerly, returned to the bedroom. She stood before the
picture of her father and extended her palm for him to see. "I
hold with those who favor ice, Papa," she told him, ruefully.
"Fire hurts, and it doesn't leave you looking too good." She remained there for a while, just studying him, missing him so
terribly that the smarting from her burn seemed to spread and
throb throughout her entire body. Lifting the picture, she kissed
the cold glass.

When the phone rang, piercing the silent room like a scream,
Marilyn was so startled she nearly dropped the picture. Steadying
herself, she replaced it carefully on her dresser and walked to the
bed. "Shit," she muttered as she lifted the receiver with her
Unguentined hand, and wiped the phone off on the sheet before
changing hands and putting it to her ear.

"Shit yourself," said an amused voice. "Has 'hello' gone out
of style?"

"Brenda?"

"None other. Can you meet me for lunch?"

"Well . . ."

"And bring along my chains."

"I've got to make a call . . . I don't know."

"That's more important than seeing a pal?"

"I have to call Ira."

"In that case I'll see you at oneish. I'm on a health kick, so meet me at a place called The Cosmic Cucumber on Mariner and Sixth in Venice. Ira's away for the weekend."

"Where—with whom?"

"What am I, the Secret Service? All I know is he's away for the weekend. See you at one."

"I . . ."

"And don't forget the chains." Brenda hung up.

Marilyn remained seated on the bed for a moment looking at the blister on her hand. Then she stood, picked up the coffee-filled ashtray, and carried it carefully to the bathroom where she dumped its contents into the toilet and flushed them away. She put the empty ashtray on the tile countertop and turned on the bathtub tap. She stood there, her hand on the faucet, watching the water pour into the tub. Ira, who had never been able to impress her with his importance, who had never really *interested* her, suddenly for some curious reason became more attractive to her at this moment than ever before. At last, at long last, he had become a challenge, and Marilyn, excited by challenges, found herself eager for the chase, sniffing like a hound after the fox. She wanted Ira back now, now that he had become so elusive, independent—and amazingly, surprisingly, desirable. Where had he gone? With whom?

She bathed and shaved quickly, wondering about her ex-husband's romantic status. Did he have someone? Was he in love? Had he become a singles prize package? And even if he proved to be the same old Ira, as Marilyn suspected he probably was, even that wouldn't matter because now she was seeing him with different eyes. She, Marilyn, tortured and mutilated by her father's death, was a changed Marilyn, for whom the same old Ira appeared to have acquired a luster she had never glimpsed before.

Sam had been lovely, but Sam had a life of his own and could never meet her inordinate demands. But he *had* been lovely.

Smiling, she rinsed off the razor and toweled herself dry. Ira. She began to understand that it wasn't really stupid to want something that didn't want or seem to want you. It was normal.

Nobody liked "no." The grass did indeed look greener. The more difficult the conquest, the more valuable appeared the prize. Even as a little girl she had demanded cornflakes only when the box was empty. Funny how she had never realized that about herself before.

Nude, Marilyn walked into the bedroom and glanced at the clock. Eleven-forty-five. She lit a cigarette and hunted around for a dry ashtray. Although she didn't doubt for a minute her ability to win Ira back, she hoped he wouldn't prove too easy. It was more fun the other way. She dressed and made up, tucking her unwashed hair under a turban, while the cigarette burned down unsmoked in the ashtray. Then she called her cleaning lady and asked if she would mind coming in today. She felt a surge of satisfaction at having taken some sort of action—even one so small as arranging to have her apartment cleaned. Perhaps this signified that she was beginning to dig out of the depression in which she had buried herself. Perhaps. But even as she thought this, Marilyn knew it wasn't true. She knew she would fall back many, many times before she emerged. If she ever did. She had put all the love she possessed into one person, and when he died he disproved the cliché that you can't take it with you.

Suddenly upset again, she lit another cigarette, squeezing it between her fingers and beginning to pace agitatedly back and forth. As she had once explained to Brenda, "I have a heart that's turned to sand—and nothing grows there any more." She tried desperately to hold on to her momentary feeling of optimism and purpose, squeezing the cigarette even harder until it flattened and would no longer draw. But the feeling was gone.

She stopped pacing, and evened out the flattened portion of the cigarette and inhaled deeply, holding the smoke. Slowly she walked to her bed and sank down, her eyes fastened on her father's face. She remembered how a long time ago, when she was no more than nine or ten, her Aunt Celia had given her a music box that played the theme of a film called Lili. Marilyn had loved it instantly, the pretty box as well as the music. "Play it as often as you like, dear heart," Celia had said, "but be very

careful never to overwind it because the spring will break."
Marilyn played it over and over again, terrified with each turn
of the little silver key that she had gone too far. After a while
her fear of breaking it overcame the pleasure it gave her, and at
last one day, enraged at the bittersweet conflict the music box
created, she viciously wound it and wound it until the spring
snapped and the key turned unresisting on the bottom of the box.
She held the dead toy in her lap and stared at it, dry-eyed, feeling
only intense relief. Even as a little girl she knew it was an
unusual reaction. Even then, the strain of loving and the price of
it had been too high.

Well, nothing had changed. The price was still too high, and
sitting on her bed staring at the picture of what once was
enormously loved and now lay dead, she acknowledged absolutely what she had been too horrified to admit before: she
wanted never to love anything or anyone again. And also, as
before, relief poured through her, and she felt unexpectedly
calm. She had sustained the greatest torment of all when what
she loved was ripped out of her life—but it could never happen
to her again. She wouldn't let it. All she wanted now was Ira . . .
not to love, there would be no more of that. But rather to love
her. Poor Ira, with his foolish, ever-fertile heart. The music-box
tune came back to her now, and she hummed it softly as she
looked at her father. "A song of love is a sad song . . . a song of
love is a song of woe." For the first time since the onset of her
father's illness, Marilyn felt serene. She accepted and understood
that by her rejection of love, by evicting it from her personal
premises, she had finally found peace.

She crushed out her cigarette, put Brenda's chains into her
purse and left the apartment, placing the doorkey under the mat
for the maid. It took her more than half an hour to walk to The
Cosmic Cucumber. Phyllis, delighted to see her, seated her near
the window, promising to join her as soon as she could. Neil,
every inch the gracious proprietor, grinned and waved from
behind the counter. Marilyn sat smiling and running her hand

over the delicate fern, grown from a carrot top, that decorated the center of her table. Sweet-potato vines trailed from large glass ceiling pots and curled around the windows, giving a filtered green glow to the room. The tables and filigree-backed chairs were white and spotless. Four ornate white cages, each with a wonderfully hued and chirping parakeet, hung amid rich, wavy grape ivy, swaying gently. It was a pretty place. Marilyn felt she was sitting in a cool, shadowy garden, and only the small signs meticulously advising that "Smoking is harmful to children, adults and all other living things" marred her pleasing reverie.

She was glad that Brenda had suggested The Cosmic Cucumber. She looked up as Phyllis, minus her frilly apron, walked over. "Free at last. Great God Almighty, free at last," sighed Phyllis, sitting down. "Well, what do you think?" she asked, waving her hand at the room. "Some difference since the last time you were here. We took over the shop next door and moved the merchandise and market section in there. Hopefully," she said, shifting around and pointing to the opposite wall, "we'll be able to take over the other side soon and enlarge the restaurant area." She turned back to Marilyn and smiled complacently. "I'm glad to see that you've returned to the world of the living."

"Don't let appearances fool you," replied Marilyn, "but I do feel rather better today."

"Good. It's really unhealthy to mourn forever and isolate yourself like some hermit, the way you've been doing."

"We all react individually, Phyllis. You mourn in your way, and I'll mourn in mine. Don't get judgmental on me."

"Okay, okay," said Phyllis quickly and, after an uncomfortable pause, asked her sister if there were any special reason for her dropping in.

"I'm meeting a friend for lunch," explained Marilyn.

"Anyone I know?"

"Brenda Mortenson."

"Oh," said Phyllis and began playing with a frond of the carrot fern.

"Do you know her?" asked Marilyn.

"I've heard her name. I think Mama once mentioned her." She moved the plant a fraction of an inch to the right and looked up at her sister. "Do you mind if I join you and Brenda for lunch?" she asked.

"Not at all. Be my guest."

They sat quietly for a moment, and Phyllis absently brushed a nonexistent speck off the table. "I feel as though I hardly know you," she said softly. "You're my sister, and we've lived under the same roof for much of our lives, and yet we've become so separated . . . I really regret that."

Marilyn nodded.

"I mean we're more closely related to each other by blood than to anyone else in the world. We're sisters. We should be close, the three of us. I mean, let's face it, when all is said and done, all we really have is each other, in the end, I mean. You never know what life . . ." Her voice trailed off and she wrinkled her forehead in frustrated word-searching. ". . . holds for us—you know?"

Again Marilyn nodded. She felt amused and almost tender at Phyllis's efforts to explain.

"At the end," Phyllis went on doggedly, "all we might have . . . I don't mean, like Neil, I mean of our own blood, our own family of origin. There'll be just the three of us left."

"I hear you," said Marilyn.

Phyllis sighed in relief. "We should not allow ourselves to drift apart and lose contact," she said earnestly. "We all should exert ourselves to avert that. It would really be a shame . . . you know?"

"Yes," said Marilyn. "I do."

"We should all see each other regularly . . ." She broke off as a shadow fell across the table, and both looked up at Brenda, who stood smiling down at them, dressed in yards of pink satin tunic over red satin harem pants, her auburn hair blazing. She looked like a valentine. Phyllis's mouth dropped open, and Marilyn, shaking her head in wonder, marveled at Brenda's ability to look right, even tasteful, in what on anyone else would be totally ridiculous and garish.

"Who are you?" asked Brenda, pulling out a chair and eyeing Phyllis curiously.

"Brenda, I'd like you to meet my baby sister, Phyllis. Phyllis and her husband, Neil," Marilyn inclined her head in the direction of the counter, "are the proprietors of this delightful eatery —as well as of the market next door."

"Oh, yeah?" And Brenda nodded to Phyllis.

"So happy to meet you," Phyllis said politely. "Welcome to The Cosmic Cucumber."

"Quite the little hostess, isn't she?" grinned Brenda to Marilyn. Then she turned back to Phyllis. "You've made a super spot out of this place, baby sister. I hope the food is as terrific as the surroundings."

"You'll soon find out," said Phyllis and waved over one of the three waitresses working the tables. "Rainbow," she ordered, "bring us some menus, please."

"*What's* her name?" asked Brenda. "*Rainbow?*"

"Yes, isn't it pretty?"

"Weird, I'll give you—I'm not sure about pretty," she said, and turned to Marilyn. "So—what's happening, how goes it? You any better?"

"I'm trying to cope."

"You succeeding?"

Marilyn sighed and looked beyond Brenda at a green-and-blue parakeet swinging on a wooden bar. "I don't know," she replied. "Sometimes."

"What's taking that Rainbow so long with the menus, baby sister?" asked Brenda. "Is she printing them?"

"Oh, she'll be along in a minute," said Phyllis. "We work easy in The Cosmic Cucumber. We like to think of ourselves as a refuge from the stressful hustle-bustle of the outside world."

"Hmm," said Brenda, eyeing her, "hustle-bustle, eh?"

"You get to sound more like Neil every day," said Marilyn, looking at her sister.

Rainbow arrived with the menus and handed one to each of them. The menus were shaped like a long, fat cucumber and made out of shiny, bumpy green plastic.

"Would you like a cocktail before lunch?" asked Rainbow in a soft, dazed voice.

Brenda looked surprised and turned to Phyllis. "You got a liquor license here?"

"Rainbow meant a cocktail from our juice bar."

"You mean like fruit juice?"

"Or vegetable juice—whatever you prefer."

"I think I prefer to pass on a cocktail," said Brenda, and buried her head in the menu.

"Marilyn?"

"I pass too."

Phyllis smiled brightly at Rainbow. "I'll have the 'energy explosion,' please," she said and turned back to Marilyn and Brenda. "It readies the intestines for digestion," she explained, "and aids in lubrication and a general feeling of well-being."

"I'll remember that," promised Brenda and closed the menu. "What do you recommend, baby sister? I'm not too familiar with health-food language."

"For starters, I recommend you stop calling me 'baby sister.' "

"And then?" asked Brenda.

"Then I suggest the eggplant parmigiana. It's wonderful." Brenda nodded and handed her menu to Rainbow.

"I'll have the steamed nut-and-vegetable medley supreme au gratin," said Marilyn.

Rainbow slowly wrote down their orders and faded away.

"What about you, Phyllis?" asked Brenda. "Aren't you eating —or do you know something?"

"I've already eaten. The 'energy explosion' is enough for me— and wait until you see the desserts. Not one grain of refined sugar."

"I've stopped eating dessert," said Brenda. "Since it goes right to my hips anyway, I might as well save myself the trouble of chewing and apply it directly." She reached down and patted the aforementioned area.

Phyllis regarded her with interest. So this was the woman who had struck terror into the heart of her mother. This was the wicked kidnapper of the precious Ira. And a friend of Marilyn's, yet. For a moment Phyllis wondered if Marilyn, hoping to give Helen an anxiety attack, had instigated the whole affair—had been the very one who sicked Brenda on Helen's favorite son. It was just exactly the sort of thing that her oldest sister would think up for a giggle. As far back as Phyllis could remember, Marilyn had delighted in aggravating her mother. It was a hobby of hers. Of course, Helen always made sure to avenge herself, and it drove everybody crazy. Except for Phyllis, and Grandma. The two of them used to make bets and give points to the weekly winner. As Phyllis recalled, the score ended up pretty even, with neither her sister nor her mother gaining a significant victory. Except for now. Marilyn with an abortion and a divorce and a relinquishment of custody was clearly ahead, and Phyllis pondered on what Helen could possibly come up with to parry Marilyn's thrust. Whatever it was, it was sure to be a stunner— and probably very imminent. Helen had never waited this long for retribution before, but of course Lenny's death had impeded things.

Phyllis made a mental note to call her grandmother and find out what was going on and what Helen was up to. Neil had very early on discerned the pattern of her mother's and Marilyn's method of warfare and had cautioned Phyllis to be on the look-out for Helen's counterattack even before her father had become ill. Phyllis glanced over at the counter and caught Neil's eye. He winked at her, and she smiled back and blew him a kiss. It seemed to her that they fit together like puzzle pieces, like meshed and matching gears, grooving and turning in concert, complementing one another. They were more committed now, more necessary to each other than they had been on their wedding day, and Phyllis felt herself blessed. Of the three Ritter girls, she was the most fortunate. She made a small fist and knocked on the underside of the white wooden table.

"I love you," Neil mouthed silently, and Phyllis floated in the cozy, secure arms of mutuality. Brenda, having observed the entire exchange, empathized instantly, sharing completely the kinship that exists between women who are loved. And Marilyn, alien and apart, pitied both her sister and her friend for their raw, unprotected vulnerability and their total, love-based dependence. Yet she felt uncomfortable and as out of place as a Southern Baptist at a bar mitzvah.

Phyllis, sensing Marilyn's discomfort and mistaking it for wistful envy, laid her hand over Marilyn's. "Don't worry," she soothed. "Some day when the right man comes along, it'll happen to you too."

"Amen," added Brenda fervently.

Marilyn withdrew her hand and smiled with the superior wisdom of those who have learned the hard way. "God forbid," she said, and leaned back slightly to enable the dreamy Rainbow to place a steaming, fragrant plate of food before her. Then Marilyn, in an effort to please her sister and assure her that they were indeed so closely blooded they could give each other a bone-marrow transplant, confided to her that she intended to call Ira and ask for a reconciliation. Brenda looked confused, but Phyllis clapped her hands and in a burst of congratulatory generosity—even at the risk of Neil's displeasure—informed Brenda and Marilyn that since her sister's news was cause for celebration, lunch—as well as Rainbow's tip—was on the house.

Chapter

29

At the honk of the horn, Helen stuffed a small wicker picnic basket into Natalie's hand and pushed her out the door. "Call me when you get to your room," she instructed, "so I can get in touch with you if I have to. Have a good time." She blew kisses to her grandsons and waved to Ira, who had gotten out of the car to put Natalie's valise into the trunk. Helen stood at the open door, one hand on the knob, looking after the car until it turned the corner and disappeared from view. Then she closed the door softly and returned to the kitchen, where she made herself a cup of tea and sat down to drink it, staring over the rim, seeing nothing and smiling faintly. It was almost done. Just a few more details to insure as far as was possible that all would come off satisfactorily. Those she would take care of later.

She sat, leaning forward on her elbows, holding the teacup between both hands. Ah, Lenny, she thought, if only you could be here to see how I'm fixing. You always said I was a pip, well, I'm about to prove it. You would be proud.

The whole business with Marilyn puzzled her, yet at the same time she understood. Marilyn was alone, she had lost the source of her strength and arrogance. She needed something, somebody to feed her ego the way Lenny had done and was therefore turning back to Ira. Well, that was just too bad. Marilyn had never deserved Ira, and she, Helen, had other plans for him. Marilyn had had her chance and spit on it. Now it was too late for her. She, Helen, would make sure of that. It was Natalie's turn for happiness, and she, Helen, would make sure of that, too. Now that Marilyn was helpless, Helen no longer hated her. She thought of her as a malignant tumor that had been excised. She even pitied her somewhat, the way she had pitied her mother, Malka, when she too had failed and been left alone—no longer a threat, no longer able to inspire fear.

Helen sat and sipped her tea, musing over the amazing mystery of heredity. How alike Malka and Marilyn were. How awesome were the genetic components and hand-me-downs. How strange it seemed to her that character traits could be transmitted, like eye color and hemophilia and the curve of a nose. Her mother, Malka, had been ferocious, intense—a raper of her own children, filled with frustration and torment at her inability to succeed and be recognized either on her own or through her offspring. All the children, even the favored, had taken after Joseph. But so strong was Malka, so fierce, that here she was, back again in the guise of her granddaughter Marilyn. The coldness, the desperation, the scorn, the intelligence, the single-mindedness, the oddness, the disrespect, the perversity, the madness had been handed down intact and unmistakable. Not one of Malka's children would ever stand up and call her blessed. Neither would Marilyn's. But hers, Helen's, would. Natalie and Phyllis and Ira and perhaps even Neil would. Marilyn . . . well, Marilyn was not her child. She was Malka's.

Helen was aware of no similarity between herself and Malka. Yet Yuspeh maintained they were alike. How ridiculous. How stupid. Yuspeh said that Helen treated Marilyn the way Malka had treated *her*. Nonsense. She had *begged* for her mother's love; Marilyn had turned her back on it. Yuspeh must be getting senile. Malka yearned to live *through* her children. She, Helen, lived *because* of her children. Yuspeh had really missed the boat on this one. She, Helen, was a loving woman, warm, normal.

She sacrificed herself for her husband and children; her mother, Malka, had sacrificed her husband and children for herself. In no way were they alike.

She wondered if Marilyn were trying to call Ira. Hah! Let her try. A lot of good it would do her. She was stronger than Marilyn. She had the strength of goodness, of unselfish intent— and because of that she would triumph. Marilyn was finished, defeated.

Yuspeh, standing at the kitchen door, shuddered at the look on Helen's face. She felt frozen in place, wishing to attract Helen's attention by neither her entrance nor her departure. So she just stood there, trying to breathe quietly. It seemed to her that Helen was like the wind, a sweet breeze when at peace, a vindictive tornado when aroused. For once, she didn't want to know what Helen was thinking.

Helen finished her tea and stood up, catching sight of her mother-in-law in the doorway. "Why are you standing there like a statue?" she asked. "Come in and have breakfast."

Yuspeh busied herself at the refrigerator while Helen fixed her a cup of tea. Then Yuspeh, still silent, sat down to eat.

"You're very quiet this morning," commented Helen. "What brought about *that* miracle?"

Yuspeh shrugged and continued eating, her spoon dipping, her head bobbing, her mouth moving, in methodical concentration. She jumped when the doorbell rang, and looked at Helen curiously. Helen ran to the window and peered out. "Oh," she said, surprised, "it's Celia," and walked into the hall to answer the door, while Yuspeh licked her teaspoon of honey.

"What brings you to the Valley?" she heard Helen ask, and looked up as both women entered the kitchen.

"You want tea?" asked Helen.

"Coffee," said Celia and sat down opposite Yuspeh. "How are you, Yuspeh?" she inquired pleasantly.

Yuspeh nodded, eying Celia's outfit.

"Sugar or Sweet 'n Low?" asked Helen.

"I'll have some of this honey," said Celia.

Yuspeh broke her silence and gazed disapprovingly at Celia. "Honey don't go with coffee," she stated.

"Why not?" asked Celia, smiling indulgently at the old woman.

"Because it goes with tea," said Yuspeh. "Sugar goes with coffee."

"Where is *that* written?" asked Helen, bringing Celia her coffee and pushing the honey jar over to her. "Anything can go with coffee, except salt."

Yuspeh shrugged again.

"To answer your original question, dear heart," said Celia, spooning honey into her cup, "I'm in the Valley to have my car tuned up. Jack dropped me off here and will pick me up later."

"He's not working today?"

"He is—at Encino hospital. The garage will call me here when the tune-up is finished, and I'll call him at the hospital. Really, we have it all worked out."

"You want some toast?"

"No, thank you, dear heart, just milk."

Helen leaned over and pushed the container of milk closer to Celia.

"Where's Natalie, sleeping?"

"No, no," said Helen. "She went out early today," and looked warningly at Yuspeh, who had paused, a spoonful of farmer cheese halfway to her suddenly smiling lips.

"Tell me, Celia," Yuspeh asked, "how is Marilyn?"

"Much better. Didn't Helen tell you?"

"Helen don't tell me nothing," she said, the farmer cheese forgotten, her eyes beginning to gleam. "What didn't Helen tell me?"

"Marilyn is going to call Ira for a reconciliation," replied Celia, with great satisfaction. "I talked her into it."

Yuspeh stared at her, then slowly laid her cheese-filled spoon on the edge of her saucer. With her thumb and forefinger she nipped a morsel of cheese and put it into her mouth.

"Isn't that wonderful?" asked Celia.

"No."

"Mama," said Helen quietly, warningly.

"What do you mean 'no'?" asked Celia, astonished

"It's too late," replied Yuspeh, licking her fingers.

"Mama," repeated Helen.

"Nonsense, dear heart," retorted Celia. "It's never too late." She stirred her honeyed coffee, removed the spoon and took a sip. "You were right, Yuspeh," said Celia, making a face, "honey does not go well with coffee."

"I told you," Yuspeh said.

"It's all right, I'll finish it," Celia told Helen, who had stretched out her hand to remove Celia's cup. "Why didn't you inform Yuspeh of such a major miraculous development?"

"I did. She just forgot."

"Hah!" sniffed Yuspeh.

Celia, confused, gazed from one to the other. "May I have an ashtray, dear heart?" she asked, and Helen rose reluctantly to get one for her.

"How could you forget such a thing, Yuspeh?" asked Celia, lighting a cigarette.

Helen handed her sister an ashtray and sat down again. "I don't like smoking in front of my plants," she said. "The smoke is bad for them."

Celia ignored her. "That's pretty big news to forget," she said to the old woman.

Yuspeh shrugged her shoulders and picked up her spoon. "Old people forget things," she said, filling her mouth with farmer cheese, and watching Helen relax and lean back in her chair. "Even sometimes big news like that."

Celia and Helen glanced at each other. "Well, it's true. She promised to call him today. I wouldn't be at all surprised to hear about a wedding in this family in the very near future."

Yuspeh began to cackle, spewing farmer cheese over the table and down the front of her bathrobe. "Oh, yes, you will, you'll . . ." choked Yuspeh, roaring with laughter and beginning to cough.

"Take a sip of tea," urged Celia, alarmed that the old woman might inhale the farmer cheese.

Helen began to hit Yuspeh on the back. "Hold up your hands," she ordered.

In a few minutes, the coughing subsided, and Yuspeh, still chuckling, took a napkin and began wiping the cheese off her robe and from the table. She collected the white bits in her palm and deposited them into her saucer. Then she took a sip of tea and cleared her throat.

"Why will I be surprised?" Celia asked curiously. "Don't you think we'll soon be dancing at a wedding?"

"Don't make her talk," snapped Helen. "She'll start to choke again."

"I'm all right," gasped Yuspeh. "Stop banging on my back." Then she turned to Celia. "I think, number one, there will be a wedding and I think, number two, you will be so surprised you'll faint from it."

Again Celia glanced at Helen. Their eyes met, and Helen nodded meaningfully, shrugging her shoulders at Yuspeh's obviously age-inspired confusion. Celia nodded in understanding and took a puff of her cigarette. Annoyed, Yuspeh picked up her cup, took another sip of tea and slammed the cup back onto the saucer.

"We'll see who's crazy," she said, pursing her lips. "I once had a friend, Elka Pinchuk, who had a son, Eli. For three years Eli is going with a girl, Rosalie. Elka knows the family from the Temple—she and Sol go to their house—they go to Elka and Sol's house—from everybody's opinion it's settled, Rosalie and Eli are getting married." Yuspeh paused in her recital and took a slurp of tea. "Then," she said, re-dipping her tea bag, "the families are making plans, they make a date, Rosalie's mother gives a deposit. Everybody calls the relatives and tells them a wedding is coming. Two weeks later Eli married a girl named Charlotte, from Passaic, New Jersey. Hoo-ha, was everyone surprised." Yuspeh stopped talking and shook her head up and down in emphasis, clicking her dentures. Helen and Celia stared back, speechless, Celia's cigarette nothing but a long, filter-tipped ash.

"So what do you say to that?" demanded Yuspeh loudly.

Celia jumped and the enormous ash broke off and fell intact to the table, where it disintegrated and spread over the white Formica surface. "I don't think I truly understand," Celia said feebly, wiping the fallout into the ashtray with her napkin.

"It's not important," Helen said irritably.

"But what's the point?" Celia asked her, completely at a loss.

"The point is that my mother-in-law talks like a parrot and often makes about as much sense."

Yuspeh turned her head and stared levelly at Helen. Her face was very set and very quiet. Gone was the laughter, leaving only a dangerous glint in her bright, sunken eyes. "You better be careful, Helen," she said in a low and threatening voice. "You watch yourself." Then she looked at Celia and explained in a more normal tone, "What the point is is this. Elka didn't say a lie to her relatives. Eli got married, there *was* a wedding. But everybody was surprised because it was a different wedding. Not the expected." Yuspeh gazed at her hopefully, and Celia stared back, bewildered.

"I'm sorry," Celia said at last, "I still don't understand."

"Don't worry about it," said Yuspeh.

"I imagine Rosalie was a bit surprised," observed Celia, taking a sip of coffee and making a face.

"Oh, absolutely," said Yuspeh. "She made some tantrum, and her mother was also crazy because she lost the deposit from the caterer."

"What happened to her?"

"She told the caterer, you don't give me back the deposit, I'll sue you, I'll tell all mine friends with daughters . . ."

"No, no," interrupted Celia, "I meant what ever happened to poor, jilted Rosalie?"

"Rosalie? Rosalie married an optometrist. A nice boy with a little bit a limp. Nothing serious."

Celia began to laugh and, reaching over, took one of Yuspeh's hands and patted it gently. "You are one in a million, Yuspeh," she said fondly.

Yuspeh patted Celia's hand in return. "I know," she replied. "My husband, Morris, may he rest in peace, once told me I could maybe have been Miss Atlantic City."

"You'd get *my* vote, dear heart." Celia pushed away her coffee and lit another cigarette.

Helen stood up, took Celia's cup to the sink, emptied it and rinsed it out. Walking to the stove, she spooned in some instant coffee and poured boiling water into the cup. "Sugar or Sweet 'n Low?" she asked without turning around.

"Sweet 'n Low."

"I told you honey don't go with coffee," sniffed Yuspeh. "So, Celia, how is it with your sons?"

"Just fine, dear heart."

"They're getting married soon?"

"Not yet."

"Don't worry. They're doctors. All doctors get married."

The three of them sat and chatted companionably until, after about an hour of conversation, during which time Marilyn's name was not mentioned again, the garage called to inform Celia that her car was ready. At eleven-thirty Jack picked her up, and Celia, feeling vaguely disoriented, left.

All during the ride back to Beverly Hills, she pondered over the morning's conversation, recounting it to Jack and asking his opinion as to what had actually transpired. "I felt like a swimmer caught in a riptide," she told him. "Never have I been so tossed about in undecipherable undercurrents—with the exception, of course," she added, giving him a sidelong glance, "of the wringer *you* put me through."

Jack squirmed in the leather bucket seat and pressed a bit harder on the accelerator, knowing that Celia would continue to gouge and nip at him whenever an opportunity arose. He sighed and stroked her knee. He deserved it. He had been a bad boy. Celia pushed away the stroking hand, holding it for a moment, before replacing it on the steering wheel. "Ah, Jack," she said regretfully, "wouldn't it be wonderful if events could be undone, like straightening out a knotted shoelace."

Jack maneuvered a sharp curve and answered her. "Maybe that's what the old lady meant with her Eli story."

"What?"

"That events *can't* be undone. That when he married that girl from Passaic, it was all over for Rosalie, it couldn't ever be undone."

"And you think that applies to Marilyn?" mused Celia. "Do you think Yuspeh meant that Marilyn's divorce can't ever be undone?"

"I can't say that with certainty," replied Jack, "but yes, I think so."

"Then why did she say I'll be surprised? Why did she imply that there would be a wedding, but not the one I expect?"

Jack shrugged. "Maybe Ira has a girl friend."

Slowly Celia nodded her head. "I bet you're right," she said. "I bet that's it. No wonder Helen didn't tell her . . . But why on earth," she asked, puzzled, "didn't Helen tell *me*?"

"She didn't want to upset you."

Celia shook her head. "No," she said, and the two of them sat without speaking until they reached home, where Jack parked Celia's car and exchanged it for his own. They spoke then about dinner plans, and Jack kissed her and went to his office.

Celia walked into her house, and lost in thought, wandered about watering her plants, glancing through the mail, straightening her collection of crystal. She toyed with the idea of calling Marilyn for lunch, of calling Ira, of calling Phyllis, but suddenly realized she didn't actually know what to ask them.

Months later, she would frequently wonder what would have happened—or not happened—had she made the proper connections and correctly interpreted all the implied signals. She might have altered the entire course of events—or not. Most probably, even by that morning in Helen's kitchen, or even much, much earlier, it was already too late. Perhaps long before Einstein designated "time" as being the fourth dimension, the wheels had been relentlessly put into motion, the ribbon was unwinding, the mills of God were revolving in their inexorable grind. The destiny of Helen's children was already laid out, and like some great Greek drama, the outcome, the finale, was preordained and inevitable. Perhaps.

Chapter
30

By the time they got to the ramp of the Santa Ana
Freeway, the four of them were on their second go-around of
"One Hundred Bottles of Beer on the Wall." Natalie, convinced
that this was an educational song, sang lustily, sitting half-turned
in her seat, nodding approvingly at the children each time they
correctly subtracted a bottle of beer.

Ira, being a disciplined man, had successfully managed to put
aside the trauma of the previous night, and feeling subdued but
calm, harmonized badly but gamely. This loudly singing lady in
the seat next to him was the Natalie he knew, doing what she
was supposed to do. The sun was shining, the freeway was un-
crowded and his two sons, diverted by song, were not yet car-
sick. He was looking forward to a relaxed weekend, where everyone would have a wholesome good time and Natalie would take
over the children if he happened on an interesting lady or business cropped up and it became necessary to repair to the hotel bar
for private, serious discussion. Helen, bless her, had been absolutely right. Taking Natalie along had indeed turned out to be a
decision beneficial to all.

At exactly 10:01 they pulled into the already rapidly filling
parking lot outside the Disneyland gates, and Ira, discount tickets
in hand, arranged for the luggage and led them all inside.

Disneyland was truly a wonder, and one of Natalie's favorite places. She had been taken there often as a child and was as enchanted now as she had been then. She would love to have lived in Disneyland, waking up every morning in that young-ster's dream come true, had she ever been given a choice. Still so childlike, Natalie passed through the gates of this manmade fairy tale and was instantly pierced with delight. Also being chil-dren, Todd and Jeremy shared her pleasure, absorbing blissfully the jolly airs, the wondrous smells, the capering, prancing, liv-ing cartoons that cavorted in this lovely land of Disney. Before them stretched the streets of the town, lined with pretty, quaint shops, a firehouse complete with engines, arcades and souvenir booths. In the distance soared the pennanted towers and turrets of the Fantasy Land Castle, awaiting them at the end of one of five joy-capped cul-de-sacs.

They decided to take the train ride that wound around and through the park, giving its passengers a brief glimpse of each and every fun-packed section. They were permitted to detrain at any station they wished for further, more intensive exploration. Ira and his happy party elected the round trip and when they returned to the starting point, began leisurely walking through the village, stopping wherever they fancied, going on any ride that beckoned to them. Ira was touched by tenderness at Natalie's obvious, innocent enjoyment. She went on every ride with the boys, waving at him from the Carousel, giving him a shriek-filled smile from Space Mountain.

The four of them took their time, savoring each attraction. There was no need to rush, tomorrow awaited them with more of the same. At noon, they lunched in "New Orleans," and at two-thirty boarded the monorail for the Disneyland Hotel. The boys were getting tired and needed a nap.

Ira checked them all in while Natalie took the boys to their room, undressed them and tucked them into bed. Her room adjoined theirs through a locked double door, and as soon as the children were settled, she unlocked the door on their side, in-tending to unpack and rest her feet. She fiddled with the turn latch only to be met by the blank face of the door which opened from *her* room. She glanced at the boys lying, heavy-lidded, on their rollaway cots, and tiptoed out of the room and into the one next door, locking the door behind her and opening the one that adjoined the boys' room, so that she could hear them if they called. She quickly unpacked, hanging carefully the two dresses, as yet unworn, that she had brought along at Helen's suggestion, "just in case you go to a fancy place." Her sweaters, slacks, underwear and Phyllis's wedding-night nightgown she placed neatly in the drawers. Her shoes, one pair to go with the dresses, another with the pants, she lined up precisely on the closet floor. She put her knitting bag on the night table, along with a soft-cover romantic novel, her place held by a bookmark. It was called *Sweet Savage Love* by Rosemary Rogers, one of her favorite authors, and Natalie wouldn't dream of dog-earing the pages.

Opening the plastic bag that contained her toiletries and makeup, she began to lay them on the counter next to the bathroom sink. The bag was rather heavy, containing as it did every bit of her makeup, moisturizer, bubble bath, and so on, and one unfamiliar item that her mother must have included, because Natalie had never seen it before. It was a bottle of perfume, sealed and new. The name of it was "Climax." Natalie uncapped it and brought the stopper to her nose, sniffing it appreciatively and dabbing it behind her ears. She felt suddenly glamorous, sophisticated—a contact-lensed, sweet-smelling woman of the world. She thought of her ever-thoughtful mother with love and immediately remembered that she had to call her. Quickly she folded the plastic bag, put it into a drawer, and closing the double doors halfway so as not to disturb her nephews, dialed her home number.

"Are you having fun?" asked Helen. "Oh, how you used to love Disneyland."

"I still do, Ma."

"Good. Where's Ira?"

"Downstairs."

"Why is he downstairs and you upstairs?"

"The boys got tired. I put them to bed."

"Are they asleep?"

"I think so."

"So go downstairs also and find Ira."

"I can't leave the boys alone."

"Why not?"

"What if they wake up?"

"They won't wake up. Go."

"Are you sure?"

"Of course, I'm sure. Go downstairs and enjoy yourself. Wash your face."

"Okay. Ma: thanks for the perfume."

"You're welcome, darling. You like it?"

"I love it."

"Then I'm happy. Kiss Ira for me and I'll call you later. What's your room number, and what's Ira's?"

Natalie supplied her with the requested information, exchanged goodbyes, and reopened the double doors. The boys were sound asleep. She fixed her makeup, dabbed on some more perfume and ran a comb through her hair. She stared at herself in the mirror, wishing she had some tops other than sweaters. Sweaters made her self-conscious no matter how strong an effort she exerted to be confident, cool and charming. Already she was beginning to feel anxious about going downstairs alone and parading through the lobby in her search for Ira. It wouldn't have been so bad if Todd and Jeremy were along. They seemed somehow to provide the camouflage she needed to hide behind. She peeked again at the boys. Fast asleep. Natalie stood in the doorway between the rooms, immobilized with indecision. What finally pushed her out of the room was the sound of her mother's voice and the look on her mother's face if she were to give in to her cowardice. Not for a moment did it enter Natalie's mind to remain in her room and lie to her mother. Not for even half a moment.

She hurried into a waiting elevator, where she huddled in a

corner, staring at her shoes. The lobby was crowded and noisy, filled with conventioneers on an away-from-home high, families grimly determined to have a good time and various other assorted guests and visitors. Natalie stood timidly, and she hoped inconspicuously, against the wall, her eyes desperately searching the bustling, milling throng for the face of Ira Stillman. She remained there for more than ten minutes, scanning the room again and again. But she couldn't see him anywhere and felt that unless she bestirred herself people might mistake her for a lonely lady making herself available for a pickup. Already the same man had passed her twice and that—the idea that a man might want to pick her up—inspired her with the confidence she needed to move.

With her eyes lowered, Natalie hesitantly made her way across the lobby, her shoulders curled almost around her neck in an effort to avoid physical contact with the shifting, jostling crowds. She arrived at the cocktail lounge and peered inside. In a few moments her eyes adjusted to the dimly lit room and she spied Ira almost immediately. He was sitting at a table on the side of the room, drinking and talking with a man and a woman. Blinking with relief, Natalie diffidently approached the group. Ira noticed her about two feet from the table, and breaking off his conversation, rose with a smile. The man and woman turned and smiled as well.

"Natalie Ritter, meet Bo Baker and Sue Feldman." Ira pulled out a chair for her, and she gratefully sank into it.

"Hi, Natalie," said Bo, "what are you drinking?"

"I'll have a double Bloody Mary," Natalie replied promptly, noting that Bo seemed to need even more fortification than she. In front of him, lined up like soldiers, were four shot glasses of whiskey. As Bo gave Natalie's order, the smile slowly faded from Ira's face and was replaced by consternation.

"Natalie is my sister-in-law," he informed his friends.

They resumed their conversation, and Natalie sat silently, listening and impatiently awaiting her drink. Evidently Bo and

Sue were writing partners, working on a pilot for a possible TV series. Both were clients of Ira's. After about fifteen minutes, during which time she hadn't opened her mouth, Natalie ventured a surreptitious look around, searching for the waiter. Sue, noticing, waved imperiously.

"Where's that drink we ordered?" she called loudly. "Let's get some service around here." She nodded reassuringly to Natalie and turned her attention back to the discussion.

Within two minutes, Natalie's drink arrived. She gave it a quick stir, removed the mixer, and took a long, thankful swallow. Three swallows later, but for the ice, a piece of lime, and a stick of celery, the glass was drained. Natalie lifted a relaxed hand, plucked out the celery and began to chew. She leaned back and smiled lazily, all the stiffness and tension gone. She felt free, loose, exactly the way one should feel on vacation. Someone must have said something funny, because suddenly Bo, Sue and Ira began to laugh. So Natalie laughed too. Bo summoned a waiter and ordered another round. "And we'd like fast service," Natalie said to the waiter. Ira gave her a wary glance, shifted nervously in his chair, picked up a pretzel and popped it whole into his mouth.

"Where are the children?" he asked.

"In sweet dreamland," replied Natalie.

"You mean you left them all alone?" demanded Ira, outraged fatherhood and irritation over Natalie's drink-inspired metamorphosis crimping his mouth.

"Come on, Ira," interjected Bo, before Natalie could speak. "What can happen to them?"

Natalie looked over at Ira, a hint of concern beginning to intrude into her mellow sense of well-being.

"Do you think I should go up to them?" she asked. "Because I will if you want me to."

"I don't think they should be alone," said Ira sternly, feeling a surge of guilt.

"Okay, okay."

But just as she began to rise, the waiter approached with the drinks.

"You finish your drink, Natalie," said Sue, placing a restraining hand on her arm. "A few more minutes won't hurt. They're probably out like lights anyway."

"They're really out like lights, Ira," pleaded Natalie. "Can't I finish my drink?"

She looked at him so wistfully that Ira relented. He admitted to himself that the problem was his, not Natalie's. It wasn't fair to punish her for his discomfort. Besides, his previous physical reaction to Natalie wasn't her problem—and surely it was under firm control. But suddenly, violently, almost as though his eyes had a will of their own, Ira's glance dove to her chest, driven there, he reasoned later, by some spiteful and negative force.

"Please, Ira?" begged Natalie, and put her hand on his arm. He ripped his eyes from Natalie's front and looked at the hand lying on the sleeve of his jacket. It was a little hand, like a child's, the nails bitten, the cuticles gnawed. For the second time that day a wave of tenderness broke over him.

"Sure, Sis," he said gently.

"So, Natalie," said Sue pleasantly, "how do you justify your existence?"

"How do I what?" asked Natalie, perplexed.

"Justify your existence," repeated Sue.

Natalie ran her lip over the rim of her glass. She had no idea what Sue was talking about. She took another drink and, putting her glass down, looked around the table at the three friendly, waiting faces looking back.

"To tell you the truth," she confided, "I don't think I justify my existence."

"Why not?" persisted Sue.

"I don't know how."

There was a short moment of silence, and then Sue began to laugh and Bo to nod his head in appreciation.

"You know, Ira, she's absolutely delicious," Sue exclaimed.

Ira smiled, pleased. Natalie, who had never before been so described, blushed with pleasure. "Thank you," she murmured.

"What kind of work do you do, Natalie?" asked Bo, downing the contents of the second shot glass of bourbon lined up on the table before him.

"I work for Ira."

"How come we've never seen you at the office?"

"Ira keeps me in the back, with the files," giggled Natalie. "But it's okay, I like it there."

"Why is that?" asked Bo, lifting his third glass of bourbon.

"I don't really know," said Natalie, bemused. "I suppose I can't justify that either. Sometimes I sit back there feeling like a file myself, like a Manila folder, hiding under my neatly typed title, and unless some curious person opens me up, I'll be a secret forever, like an unexplored attic." Amazed by her eloquence, she lapsed into silence.

"Thas really beautiful," Bo said after a moment. "She's really beautiful, Ira."

"I know," said Ira, and he leaned over and kissed Natalie's cheek. A faint, spicy scent wafted up his nose and Ira retreated, surprised. Somehow he expected that if Natalie were to wear perfume (and if she did, he had never previously noticed it), she would choose a floral scent, like lavender or vanilla or something. Suddenly Bo, by now totally sloshed, hiccoughed loudly.

"Are you married, Natalie?" asked Sue quickly, attempting to cover her partner's lapse in taste.

"Nope," said Natalie, waving her ringless fingers.

"Engaged?"

"Nope," said Natalie sadly.

"Anybody open your folder yet?" Bo asked, a lewd grin decorating his flushed face. Sue frowned at him and smacked his hand, and Bo hiccoughed again. She stood up and pulled her partner to his feet, where he swayed over the table like a feather in the wind.

"See ya," said Sue abruptly, and dragging a stumbling Bo behind her, strode rapidly out of the lounge.

Natalie gazed after them regretfully. She had been having such a good time.

"We better leave also, Sis," said Ira, calling for the check.

Natalie hurriedly gulped her double Bloody Mary. "Is Bo an alcoholic?" she asked. "I've heard lots of writers are."

Ira nodded. "If he's not, he's certainly on the way. I've never been with him when he's managed to end the evening upright. He's wrecking their career, and Sue is going up the wall."

"Maybe you should talk to him."

"I have. Everyone has, but Bo is a very self-destructive man."

Natalie nodded wisely, pleased to be engaged in adult conversation.

"I don't understand people who are their own worst enemies," said Ira.

"Neither do I."

"I feel that everyone must cultivate self-discipline, especially in a world that offers such a variety of dangerous, self-indulgent temptations."

"So do I."

Ira crossed his arms on the table and leaned forward. Natalie was very easy to talk to, and unlike the last time, she seemed unaffected by her drinks. And he, happily, was unaffected by her. In fact he was enjoying himself.

"How have you been, Natalie? Has it been very hard?"

"It's been hard, Ira," she said quietly, "but that's life."

"I think you have an intelligent attitude."

Encouraged, Natalie went on. "I have a philosophy," she confided. "I feel that if that's the way it is, then that's the way it is. People die and crying won't bring them back. I don't mean I never cry," she added hastily, "because I cry a lot, but even when I'm crying I know it won't make a difference." She sat back and regarded Ira seriously. "Can I tell you something, Ira?"

"Of course," he said warmly.

"It's a compliment."

"In that case, I insist you tell me."

Natalie leaned close to him and lowered her voice. He smelled her perfume, and it reminded him of his mother's handkerchief drawer. When he was a little boy, he used to open it, delighted by the fragrance, and bury his nose in the clean, wonderfully aromatic squares, breathing deeply, hypnotized by the mysterious quality of a woman's smell. Natalie's vodka-tinged breath was warm on his cheek.

"I'm not self-conscious when I talk to you," she whispered. "I am with most people, but not with you. That's why I order a double Bloody Mary. It takes away my nervousness."

"You have nothing to be self-conscious about," said Ira gently. "You're a wonderful person, and when you realize that, you won't need this." He pointed to her almost-empty glass. "That's artificial courage," he said.

"I know." She moved back and sighed heavily, saddened by all she lacked. She looked trustfully at Ira. "What should I do?"

"Just be yourself," he advised. "I like you just the way you are."

Natalie sat straight up with pleasure, her lips curving into a huge, happy smile. She raised her hand and laid it on her heart in gratitude for Ira's words. Ira looked at the small hand and then at what lay beneath it. Immediately, and to his horror, he felt himself harden.

"I'm so glad you're my brother," beamed Natalie.

Ira, sitting beside her with an unbrotherly erection, abruptly pushed his chair back. "Where on earth is that darn check?" he muttered. "Waiter!"

Natalie stared at him, her hand still on her chest, bewildered by his sudden shift in mood.

Ira glared at her. "Are you planning to pledge allegiance?" he asked sarcastically.

Natalie's mouth opened in dismay and she hastily dropped her hand in her lap, banging the bone of her wrist on the edge of the table.

The waiter arrived with the check, and Ira practically grabbed it off the tray. He scrawled his name and room number on the bottom, flung it back at the waiter and began to stand up. Half-crouched over the table he quickly buttoned his jacket. "Let's go," he said, carefully rising. "The boys are all alone."

Natalie stared up at him, massaging her wrist, so stunned she could barely move. Then unsteadily she rose to her feet and followed Ira out of the lounge, through the lobby and into the elevator, like an old-fashioned Japanese wife. He stood far away from her in the elevator, his hands clasped over his bulge, staring straight ahead. When the doors opened, he strode out and sped down the hall; Natalie, almost running, followed.

Without a word he unlocked the door of his room, walked in and let it slam behind him. Wearily Natalie entered her room just in time to see Ira pulling her double door shut. She stood staring at it and heard the lock on his side turn and click. She sank down on the bed and removed her contact lenses. She placed them carefully and correctly in their case and put it on the night table next to an ashtray. There was a blue bruise on her wrist, and it hurt. She cried a little, then pressing her face into her spread-covered pillows, fell asleep.

The ringing of the telephone awakened her. She groped for her phone in the dark room, straining to read the time on the luminous dial of her watch. She found the phone and put the receiver to her ear, knocking the ashtray off the table and hearing a thud as it landed on the carpeted floor.

"Natalie?"

"Hello, Ira."

"I want to apologize. I was unpardonably rude."

"That's all right."

"No, Natalie, it isn't. It was inexcusable of me to take out my foul humor on you. I'm sorry."

"That's all right, Ira."

"We're getting ready for dinner. Uh, are you hungry?"

Natalie turned over on her back. "What time is it?"

"Six-thirty."

"Oh."

"We thought we'd grab a bite in the coffee shop. The boys want hamburgers."

"Okay."

"Then we were going to take the monorail back to Disneyland for the Electric Light Parade."

"Okay."

"Can you be ready by seven?"

"Yes."

"Wear a jacket, it might be chilly."

Her eyes were now accustomed to the dark. She hung up the phone, and straining to reach the lamp, turned it on. She lay back for a moment, blinking, then rolled over on her side to the edge of her bed and scanned the floor for the ashtray. Her wrist was black-and-blue. She replaced the ashtray on the night table and swung her legs to the floor, her face contorted in a huge yawn. She rubbed her eyes, stretched and shuffled barefoot into the bathroom. The shower revived her, and she was combed, dressed and made up by the time Ira and the boys knocked on the door.

Ira was subdued and polite all through dinner. He avoided looking at Natalie, concentrating instead on his sons. Todd and Jeremy fiddled with their food, eager to be on their way back to Disneyland and the parade. They were quiet, well-behaved children and obeyed promptly when informed by their father they would go nowhere unless they cleaned their plates. Natalie ate her bacon, lettuce and tomato sandwich neatly, pleased that when she bit into it, nothing dripped or dropped from the bottom. She told the boys about the time she was a little girl and Grandma Helen and Grandpa Lenny had taken her to the Electric Light Parade for her birthday. Occasionally she would glance at Ira and smile hesitantly, distressed at his formality and attempting to convey to him that as far as she was concerned, bygones were bygones and please don't feel bad. She hadn't the slightest idea as to the cause of his abrupt descent from amicability to irritation but accepted the fact that people are only human and subject to mood swings. She assumed that Bo's inebriated condition was what had upset Ira so terribly. And Ira marveled at Natalie's ability to forgive and forget.

They decided to have dessert in Disneyland. Ira paid for dinner, and the four of them left the hotel and boarded the monorail. Natalie looked forward to the parade, and when they arrived at the Park, she walked between her nephews holding a little hand in each of hers. She was sure that all the people she passed assumed that she was the mother of these lovely children and that they were all a family. She looked quickly at Ira and blushed.

The parade was beautiful, the brilliantly colored, marching lights holding the spectators spellbound in enchantment and admiration. At midnight the last light flickered farewell and the parade was over. Todd and Jeremy, despite their naps, were nodding and yawning. They had had an exciting day and didn't protest when Ira told them it was time to leave.

"Goodnight," Ira said at the door to her room. "I'm going to put the boys to bed and then turn in myself."

"Okay," said Natalie. "Goodnight, Ira." She bent down, hugged and kissed her nephews, waved to Ira and walked into her room. As soon as the door closed behind her, the phone began to ring.

"Hello?"

"Natalie? Where were you?"

"We went to dinner and the Electric Light Parade."

"Remember Daddy and I used to take you?"

"Of course. I told the boys."

"You ate in a nice place?"

"The coffee shop."

"Oh. So you didn't wear the green dress?"

"No."

"Where's Ira?"

"Putting the boys to bed."

"They had a good time?"

"Yes."

"He's going to bed also or going out?"

"He said he's going to turn in."

"So you go to sleep, too."

"I'm not tired. I think I'll read a little."

"First take a nice bubble bath and brush your teeth."

"I took a shower before dinner."

"That was hours ago. You take a bath, Natalie. I know what I'm talking about."

"Okay."

"Then put on the new perfume and Phyllis's nightgown. It'll make you feel wonderful."

"Okay."

"Did you lock the door?"

"Yes."

"Good. Aunt Celia and Uncle Jack once got robbed at the Hilton in their sleep. They forgot to put on the chain, and the crooks just walked in on them in the middle of the night. Did you put on the chain?"

"Yes."

"Did Ira put on his chain?"

"How should I know?"

"You have connecting doors?"

"Yes."

"Lock that one too."

"Why?"

"You don't want the boys to walk in on you, do you?"

"All right. I'll lock it."

"Do it now. I'll hold on."

Natalie put the receiver on the bed, walked to the connecting door and turned the lock. Then she went back to her bed, sat down and picked up the receiver. "I locked it."

"Now get undressed and take a nice bubble bath."

"What is it with you with baths?"

"You don't put on a nightgown like that on an unwashed body."

"Okay, Ma, I'll take a bath."

"And put on perfume."

"I'll put on perfume."

"Good. I love you. Sweet dreams."

"You too, Ma."

"I'll call you tomorrow. I know you'll have a lot to tell me."

"Like what?"

"You'll see. Life is full of surprises. You never know."

"Okay, Ma. I love you."

"You're a good girl, Natalie. Of all my girls, you gave me the least trouble. You were never fresh. You were always a comfort to me. You still are."

"Thank you, Ma."

"Now I have something to tell you. Never let an opportunity slip by. You never know when an opportunity can walk into your room. If an opportunity walks into your room tonight, Natalie, and you let it walk out, don't bother to come home. I mean it, Natalie. Don't bother to come home. You understand?"

"What are you talking about? Don't say that."

"Never mind. Just you remember what I said. Do you remember?"

"I remember, I remember."

"Good. Don't forget. I love you. Have a good time."

After she hung up, Natalie sat on the edge of her bed completely mystified. She kicked off her shoes and pushed them under the night table with her foot. Her mother was a sensible, intelligent woman, but sometimes she came up with things that made no sense at all. Not three minutes ago she had just locked all the doors. How could anything, even opportunity, get inside? Still, her mother's surprising threat gave her a bit of a chill.

She shrugged and took off her sweater. Then she went into the bathroom, washed out the tub, and began to run her bath. She poured a capful of bath-oil bubble beads into the water and inhaled as the scented grains burst into oily bubbles, guaranteed sweetly to smooth, soften and lubricate her skin, giving it, as was promised on the label, a satiny sheen. She finished undressing and stepped into the tub, gently lowering herself through the cool bubbles into the warm water below. With a sigh of pleasure she leaned back against the tub, closed her eyes and smiled. She loved bubble baths. Through the wall she heard the faint ring of Ira's telephone. After one ring it stopped. Ira must have rushed to answer it, not wishing the jangle to awaken the boys. She heard the soft, low murmur of his voice. When the bubbles began to disappear, she washed quickly, turned the knob that lifted the metal plug and stood up, bubbles still clinging to her soft, shining, satiny skin.

Wrapping herself in a towel she stepped out of the tub. Ira was still on the phone. Natalie didn't wonder who had called him. The hotel was full of clients and people he knew. Ira was a successful business manager for successful upper-bracketeers. Of that fact she was absolutely sure, if the checks she made out and entered in her books were any indication.

She walked to the sink and brushed her teeth, rinsing with Scope. Then she removed the towel, hung it neatly over the rack and looked at herself in the large mirror extending from wall to wall above the sink. She tossed her head back in a conglomerate of all her envied heroines and threw herself a "knowing look from beneath lowered lashes." Slowly and sensuously she began running her hands over her voluptuously curved, sweet-smelling, satin-sheened body . . . Abruptly Natalie lowered her hands and straightened up. She had managed to arouse herself. She took a deep breath and reached for the bottle of Climax. She applied it behind her ears, knees and elbows. She dabbed it between her breasts and inner thighs. She looked at herself once more before shutting off the light and leaving the bathroom.

From the dresser drawer, she removed the white, shimmering nightgown and slipped it over her head. It floated around her and settled over her body, soft, cool, unbelievably smooth. It was a very lowcut, Empire-styled affair, lightly wired below the breasts, emphasizing their size and pushing them up and practically out of the bodice. The full skirt cascaded in soft natural folds from the center of the underwire and clung like silvery skin to her body. Wide-eyed, Natalie stared into the mirror, dazzled by the sight of herself. Her nipples hardened and pushed against the thin, opaque fabric. She stood there motionless, mesmerized, breathing shallow, rapid breaths, until after a while the reflection of the lamps on the night table began to distract her, and she tore herself away from the dresser mirror to turn the three-way lamp down to its dimmest illumination, so that only a faint, rosy glow lit the room.

Dreamily she brushed her fingers across the high round arch of her upthrust breasts and against her taut, protruding nipples, wishing achingly that they were someone else's fingers. Her body, so primitive, so basic, so perfectly tuned to react to stimuli, functioned in every respect like clockwork, but her sexual response had never been tested—except by herself.

Her fingers wandered down her ribcage to her stomach and below, and she began to tremble with excitement. So engrossed was Natalie that she did not hear the soft knock on the door until it was repeated several times. And even when the sound of it entered her consciousness, she couldn't for a moment identify it. The knocking grew sharper, and Natalie leaped from her daze with a small, startled squeak and whirled around. The rapping sounded again, and Natalie's head swung toward the door.

"Who . . ." she whispered hoarsely and cleared her throat. "Who is it?"

"It's Ira. Are you asleep?"

Her eyes flew to the connecting doors, and her heart began to jump. "N-no," she stammered. "Just a minute."

Natalie looked wildly around for her bathrobe, but her mother had forgotten to pack it. Perhaps Helen hadn't thought she'd need her bathrobe. Ira knocked again, and her feet slowly began to move toward the door.

"Natalie, are you all right?"

"Yes . . . I'm coming."

She turned the lock and opened the door. Ira was waiting behind it, wearing blue pajamas and a belted navy robe piped in white.

"Mom just called and asked me to . . . Jesus," he whimpered and turned to stone—all but his eyes, which wrapped themselves around her body, rampaging over it, to fasten at last on her heaving, lush, overflowing bosom—and all but his penis, which immediately sprang to its zenith and seemed to vibrate like a tuning fork.

"Oh, my God," moaned Ira in a high, thin voice, and falteringly he began to back away. Natalie, almost swooning, swayed in panic against the door and then, suddenly, stiffened and caught her breath. The voice of opportunity, sounding suspiciously like her mother's, began to scream and clamor in her ears. Almost languidly, she raised her arm, reached out and curled her hand around the knot of Ira's loosely belted robe. He gasped, and his eyes glazed and his heart jerked and flopped like some hooked and hapless gill-pierced fish.

Slowly but ever so firmly, Natalie reeled him in.

Chapter

31

THERE IS NO DIFFERENCE between night and day in hotel
rooms whose windows are covered with double-lined, snugly
drawn draperies. One awakens in the same atmosphere in which
one fell asleep, and if the doors are thick and sturdy enough to
muffle the sound of the housekeeper's rolling cart, and if one
has hung the "Do Not Disturb" sign on the doorknob, it is difficult, upon awakening, to ascertain how many days or hours or
moments have passed. But when Natalie's eyes opened, she was
instantly aware of a difference, an altered ambience pervading
the room. The lamp was still dim. Her shoes were still under the
night table. But on the floor, crumpled and stippled with blood,
lay the nightgown, flung there by frenzied hands. And beside
her, his head on her shoulder, his hand cupped around one
breast, his cheek resting on the other, lay opportunity, which, as
per her mother's instructions, Natalie had seized by the belt and
made the most of.

She looked down at him, this magical man who had waved
his wand and changed her life, this Santa Claus who had given
her the wondrous gift for which she had waited and yearned for
such a very long time—this Ira. Because of him, she had discovered and uncovered her one enormous talent, a genius, in fact,
that she had never known she possessed. Natalie, even by the

most generous of praisers, had never been called brilliant. Well, that was no longer true. Natalie was brilliant at making love. She made love as though she had a doctorate in it. As though she were a Phi Beta Kappa who had studied it and researched it and practiced it all of her life.

She looked down at Ira and kissed his hair, her entire being flooded with warmth and gratitude and almost unbearable joy. She was Christmas, she was Thanksgiving, she was Arbor Day. Ira stirred and slowly opened his eyes. He lay quietly, gazing at the view. From his present position, all he could see were breasts —under his hand, over his face, next to his mouth. He was surrounded. For a moment Ira wondered if he had died and gone to heaven. Without lifting his head, he raised his eyes to her face and saw Natalie smiling down at him. "Good morning," she whispered, "or good afternoon. Whatever it is, it's good."

"Natalie," said Ira. His voice sounded muffled. "Natalie," he repeated, and she chuckled, making Ira's head bounce up and down.

"Wasn't it grand?" she asked.

But grand wasn't the word for it, thought Ira. Even spectacular was an understatement and wouldn't do justice to what had transpired between them. Phenomenal, perhaps. Inspired. Or transcendent. Ira had, in his day, made love to a respectable number of women. Most of them were fine. With Marilyn it had been erratic, with Alma a fiasco, with Brenda fabulous. But Natalie . . . Natalie was magnificent, and she had made him magnificent too. They had made love five times in a row. And each time had been better than the one before. The future loomed pleasantly ahead, filled with ascending delights.

Ira lifted her hand, frowned with concern at a bruise on her wrist and kissed it tenderly. Now that he had finally found a woman with whom he could have peace, ease, comfort, companionship and the best sex imaginable, Ira wanted to guard and protect her as fiercely, as conscientiously, as he would an investment or a million-dollar merger. How could he ever have wasted so much time and been so stupidly blind as not to have recog-

nized the treasure that was Natalie? Even Sue Feldman, even Bo
Baker in his drunken confusion, had liked her and found her
unique. Why, she would even be an asset to him in business.
And she had been a virgin. He, Ira, was her first man, and he
had always, although he never advertised it, wanted to marry a
virgin. Ira was aware that this attitude was very old-fashioned
as well as highly unrealistic. Still, it was the way he felt.

Ira had always hidden this feeling of the rightness, the reason-
ableness, the rationality of the double standard beneath a liberal
and accepting exterior. And all this time, right under his nose,
had been Natalie—probably the only thirty-one-year-old virgin
left in America. Out of an enormous haystack, Ira had plucked
the needle. Out of eight years of Marilyn and misery, he had
emerged to a miracle. He would have a pure, obedient, devoted
wife, his children would have a loving mother, his tax forms
would have a joint return. Ira sighed in absolute bliss and hugged
Natalie tightly and possessively in his arms.

"I want you to marry me," he whispered.

"Okay," said Natalie. She started to sit up, then fell back on
the pillow with a surprised gasp of pain.

"What is it?" cried Ira.

Natalie blushed and lowered her eyes. "It's nothing," she murmured. "I'm just a little sore . . . down there."

Ira patted her arm in commiseration and then smiled so
proudly that Natalie thought his face would break.

While Natalie lay in a hot, soothing bath, Ira took the boys
on part two of their Disneyland tour. All that marred her pure
joy was her regret over the ruined nightgown and her soreness
over too much ardor too often. Absolutely thrilled by the wonder
of the extraordinary turn her life had taken, by the miracle of
her dreams coming true, Natalie could think of nothing else in
all the world that she desired—except perhaps for her soreness
to go away so she could do again the only thing she had ever
done well.

The phone rang in her room beyond the closed bathroom door.
Natalie didn't even stir. She floated in the hot water like a fetus

in the womb, trying to decide whether or not when she married Ira, to buy new draperies for the living room. After a few minutes, the ringing stopped. Natalie was sure it had been her mother, and her toes curled with pleased excitement over the amazing events she would impart to her. She savored the forthcoming telling of it with relish and intended to delay her announcement so that she could see her mother's face when she heard the good news. How surprised she would be. How thrilled. It was much too important to do over the phone. And truly, she had her mother to thank for all of it. If her mother hadn't called Ira and insisted that he check on her well-being, all this would never have happened. It was her mother who was calling when she heard Ira's phone ring last night, not a client as she had supposed.

"She was worried about you," Ira had told her during a short breather the previous night. "She said ever since your father died you have trouble falling asleep, and when you do, you have nightmares. She absolutely insisted that I go to your room and look in on you." Then he began kissing her breasts again. "And I'm so glad I did . . ." Well, so was Natalie—although her mother's concern rather puzzled her. She had never had trouble falling asleep in her life. She had never, to her recollection, had a nightmare. Natalie wrinkled her forehead and pondered her mother's mistaken assumptions. She hadn't the slightest idea why her mother should have thought that, or who had put that notion into her head. Well, what difference did it make? Natalie smiled. "Thank you, Mama," she whispered.

She stood up cautiously and gingerly stepped out of the tub. She could barely walk. She toweled herself dry and slowly made her way to the bed. The nightgown still lay on the floor. It was ruined—and Natalie began to giggle. So was she! She sat down on the bed with a sharp intake of breath. It really hurt her . . . down there. Ira said it would go away in a few days—that it was always like that the first time. "Not to worry," he assured her. "In a few days you'll be good as new and we can pick up where we left off."

Natalie snuggled under the covers despite the discomfort of the rumpled, stained sheets. Had Ira been there, she would have liked to pick up where they left off right now, painful or not. Natalie heaved a contented sigh and fell instantly asleep. The phone rang a half hour later, and every half hour thereafter, but Natalie, dead to the world, heard nothing. If she had known the trauma that the unanswered phone caused Helen, she would, had she not been so sore, have kicked herself.

Natalie slept all day and at four-thirty, when Ira and her nephews returned, she awoke much refreshed, a wee bit less sore and purely happy. She dressed, opened the connecting doors and the four of them packed, chatting gaily between the rooms. They shut the last suitcase at five to five, gave a last look around and nostalgically closed the doors behind them. Natalie knew she would never forget the Disneyland Hotel. It was here, in Disneyland, that she had collected so many lovely childhood memories—and it was here, in Disneyland, that as an adult she had added one more, the loveliest memory of all, to her collection.

As they walked down the hall, Natalie again thought she heard the phone ring, but the door was locked, the elevator waiting. They descended to the lobby, where they checked out and had a bite to eat in the coffee shop. Everything was the same—the lobby still filled with people, the coffee shop still too noisy, the waitress who had taken their order last night still blonde and tired. But the Natalie who had arrived on Saturday was not the same Natalie who departed on Sunday. She was a different Natalie—inside and out. And the people who looked at them, who thought they were a lovely little family, would now be right, because now they were. Overnight, Natalie had, thanks to the benevolent God who always rewarded sinless people, and thanks to Helen, acquired two precious children and the best husband-to-be in all the no-longer-threatening world. Natalie had, in less than twenty-four hours, opened her eyes, opened her legs and become a woman. In a room in the hotel in the park that was built by a mouse.

Todd and Jeremy threw up on the way home despite the bottles of beer on the wall. "It was a mistake to feed them before driving," Natalie observed in a motherly way. Ira concurred and pulled off the freeway and into a carwash. They removed the luggage from the trunk and stood beside it while the car was cleaned and unsuccessfully defumed. "We won't get home now until seven-forty-eight," said Ira, checking his watch. He was off by only one minute. "I was off by only one minute," he informed Natalie as they parked in her driveway. Natalie nodded and smiled, proud of her accurate fiancé.

Helen, standing at the living-room window, her hand holding open the edge of the drapery, almost sobbed in relief as the car drew up. Ira shut off the headlights and a second later got out of the car. He walked around it and unlocked the trunk. He removed the luggage, closed the trunk and carried the bags to the doorstep. Todd and Jeremy tumbled out, laughing, and began running around in the grass. Helen waited, hardly breathing, so tense that her legs began to tremble. She heard Ira admonish the boys and saw them stop, nod and sit down on the step next to the suitcases. Then Ira walked to the passenger side of the car and opened the door. Helen's hand flew to her heart and began to pulse in rhythm with its pounding. She saw him lean in and gently help Natalie out. She saw him kiss her tenderly as she emerged. She saw them begin to walk to the front door. She saw the way Natalie walked. Helen's legs buckled and she fell into a chair near the window, where she put her hands over her face and burst into tears.

The doorbell rang and she heard Yuspeh push a kitchen chair out and begin to shuffle into the hall. For once her lips didn't tighten at Yuspeh's irritating habit of scraping the kitchen floor each time she stood up. The door was opened and excited voices filled the house. Helen, shaking and weeping, blew her nose and struggled to her feet. For a moment, she stood unsteadily, leaning against the chair, trying to bring herself under control. She took a deep, shuddering breath and wiped away the tears with the back of her hand. She straightened up and walked slowly to the hall, making a note to call the Temple first thing in the morning and reserve the chapel for the first available day. She wouldn't be completely at peace until she saw the ring on Natalie's finger. Marilyn could still call Ira. There was many a slip 'twixt the cup and the lip. But she didn't think so. Ira was an honorable man. Natalie could already even be pregnant. Helen smiled through her tears. She had done it. She had pulled it off.

Walking out of a dark room into the light made Helen's eyes blink. Her grandsons ran to her, and she bent to hug them, looking over their heads at Natalie and Ira. "Well," she said, straightening up, "I see a good time was had by all."

Unable to contain herself any longer, Natalie, stiff-legged and leaning slightly to her left, threw her arms around her mother. "Mama," she cried, "we're getting married."

"You better," muttered Yuspeh, leering at Ira.

Helen widened her eyes in feigned surprise. "Oh, how wonderful," she exclaimed beaming.

"We wanted you to be the first to know," grinned Ira, putting his arm around Helen's shoulders and hugging her.

"I've never been happier in my life," said Helen softly. "Mazel tov." She turned and looked fondly down at her grandsons. "Boys, you're going to have a new mommy now. Aunt Natalie. Aren't you happy?"

"Yay!" shouted the boys.

"Oh, Ira," she said, her eyes glistening. "You don't know what you've done for me. The two of you have given me a reason for living. Now maybe I can be happy again. Well," she said, linking an arm through each of theirs, "let's go into the kitchen. I just want to sit down and look at both of you."

They all walked into the kitchen and Helen disengaged her arms and went to the stove, where she turned on the light under the tea kettle. Ira pulled out Natalie's chair, and Yuspeh, already seated, watched her granddaughter cautiously lower herself onto the chair.

"So tell me," she asked innocently, "what made you two suddenly decide such a decision?"

"What difference does that make?" asked Helen sharply, returning to the table and giving her mother-in-law an angry look.

"Can't I ask a question?"

"It's very simple, Grandma," said Ira, "we just realized that we love each other."

"So what made you realize?"

"Mama," Helen cried in exasperation. "What does it matter what made them realize? It's enough that they did."

"Tell me, Natalie," asked Yuspeh, "you had a nice room?"

Natalie, the hard seat of the chair giving her great discomfort, sat with her legs crossed, on one side of her buttocks. The other buttock was lifted about an inch off the chair. "Very nice," said Natalie.

"You enjoyed?" asked Yuspeh.

"It was wonderful."

"You enjoyed also, Ira?"

"Very much, Grandma."

"Maybe even *too* much," said Yuspeh, eyeing Natalie's efforts to find a comfortable position.

The kettle began to whistle and Helen jumped up. "Who wants coffee, who wants tea?" she asked, hurrying to the stove and shutting it off.

"So our Natalie is getting married," marveled Yuspeh, "and so all of a sudden I can't catch mine breath, it's such a surprise." She turned all the way around in her chair and grinned wickedly at Helen, who was standing, her hands on her hips, waiting for beverage orders. "Aren't you surprised, Helen?" asked Yuspeh.

Helen ignored her. "Who wants coffee, who wants tea?"

"I want tea," said Yuspeh. "Give also a tea for Natalie, she looks a little to me pale."

"I'm just a bit tired," explained Natalie.

"Ira looks tired, too," observed Yuspeh. "Helen, bring Ira also a cup of tea."

From the den, where the boys had gone to watch television, came the sound of laughter.

"The boys aren't tired," remarked Yuspeh. "Maybe they slept better."

"I slept all day today," exclaimed Natalie.

"You should maybe have slept in the *night* . . . You would sit easier."

"Here's your tea, Mama. Drink it and stop talking so much." Helen pushed the hot cup into Yuspeh's hands. "Ira, go ask your sons if they want a glass of milk."

She sat down, taking another cup of tea off the tray and placing it before Natalie. The steam drifted up and into Natalie's face. Natalie took a teaspoonful, blew on it and sipped some off the spoon. She shifted in her chair, leaning now on her right side and accidentally tilting the spoon so that tea dripped onto the table. Quickly she put the spoon into her cup and wiped the spill with her napkin. Yuspeh's knowing glances were making her uneasy.

Ira returned, followed by Todd and Jeremy. "I'll take a raincheck on the tea, Mom," he said to Helen. "I want to get these weary travelers into bed."

"And not only them, I betcha," cackled Yuspeh.

Ira bent down and kissed Natalie's upturned face. "Sit," he told her. "I know where the door is. I'll call you at eleven thirty-one, right after the news." He put his lips close to her ear. "Now you work on getting rid of your sore bottom," he whispered. "Do I have to tell you why?"

Natalie smiled and blushed and gave Ira a quick peck on the lips. Somehow she was embarrassed under Grandma's keen, bright eyes.

As soon as Ira and the boys left, Yuspeh raised her cup and pointed it at Helen. "Helen," she said, "my congratulations to you."

"To Natalie, you mean."

"If I meant Natalie, I would say Natalie. To Natalie I wish a life with Ira of good luck, good sense and good children." She looked at Natalie playfully. "Good sexuals I think they already got, hey, Natashka?"

Again Natalie blushed, and Yuspeh, despite Helen's attempts to shush her, went on, "You remember, Natalie, how I'm always telling you should stand up straight?" Natalie nodded. "Well, you still don't stand perfect, but at least now you got a good reason. There's only one reason a girl can't sit and she walks like a sailboat . . . and piles it isn't."

"Stop it this minute," yelled Helen. "Leave the girl alone."

Natalie buried her eyes and nose in the teacup. She was too mortified to look up.

"What's the secret?" Yuspeh yelled back. "At sixteen, it's a secret. At thirty-one it's about time."

Natalie tilted her cup and took a long, hot swallow. Grandma was right. She had been a throwback—some people might even say a freak. But no more. She put down her cup and smiled at her grandmother. "I'm so happy," she said. "I've never been so happy in my entire life."

"A good way to be and a good way to stay. For this you can thank your mother."

"She doesn't have to thank me," cried Helen, "she has nothing to thank me for."

"I'm entitled to mine opinion," said Yuspeh, and smiled into her tea.

"I'm getting married," whispered Natalie, staring into space. "I can't believe it. I'm really getting married."

Helen reached for her daughter's hand. "I'm calling the Temple first thing in the morning," she said. "You'll have a beautiful wedding." She picked up Natalie's fingers and looked at them, one by one. "I always knew that some day your prince would come." She tugged and caressed Natalie's fingers, clucking at the rough-edged, bitten-down nails. Then she clasped the hand in hers, suddenly excited. "Why don't you call somebody and share your joy?" She closed her eyes and pretended to think. "I know," she said after a minute. "Why don't you call your sister Marilyn and tell her the good news . . . I just know how delighted she'll be for you."

Yuspeh stiffened and stared at the side of Helen's face. "For shame, Helen," she said in a low, reproving voice.

Helen ignored her and pressed Natalie's fingers. "Go on," she urged. "Call her."

Natalie looked at her doubtfully. "You think so?" she asked. "I was going to call everyone tomorrow."

"When I got engaged, I couldn't wait to spread the news." Helen reached over, and taking the telephone from the counter, placed it before her daughter. "Here," she said. "Call your sister and tell her you're marrying Ira."

Natalie picked up the receiver and began to dial. In the middle, she stopped and hung up again. "Ira was once Marilyn's husband—and now he's going to be mine," she said in a thoughtful voice. "When we were little girls, I used to get all her outgrown clothes . . . I'm *still* getting hand-me-downs from Marilyn."

"A husband is not an outgrown dress, Natalie. Stop comparing apples and pears and call."

"Call Phyllis," said Yuspeh, "or your Aunt Celia. Your Aunt Celia will be so surprised, she'll faint from it."

Eventually, Natalie called everyone. First, her sister Phyllis, who had had a nightgown she never wore, and second, her sister Marilyn, who had had a husband she never loved.

Natalie, who did with both what her sisters had not done with either, went upstairs, got into bed and waited for Ira to call.

Chapter

32

PHYLLIS HUNG UP THE PHONE and jumped to her feet. She ran, screaming her husband's name, through the hallway and into the bedroom, where he half-sat, half-lay on the bed, watching *Masterpiece Theatre* on television. "Neil," she panted, flopping down beside him, "you were right. You were right all along. She did it. She got her."

"Sshh," said Neil, "I want to watch this."

Phyllis sat back on her haunches, breathless and excited. "What I've got to tell you is better than what you're watching." She picked up the remote control and shut off the set.

"Dammit, Phyllis, cut that out." Neil lunged for the clicker, but Phyllis was faster and held it out of his reach. "Natalie just called," she said.

"Thank you for that stirring piece of news. Now may I have the clicker?"

"She's getting married."

Neil sat with his arms folded across his chest, staring at the blank screen of the television set. Without turning his head, he looked at his wife from the corners of his eyes. "You have just reaffirmed my belief in miracles. Now can I get on with my program?"

"Guess to who?"

"Whom."

"Guess to *whom*."

"Rock Hudson."

Disgusted, Phyllis held the clicker above his chest and dropped it. Neil grimaced and let it lie there. He turned his head and looked up at his wife reproachfully.

"That was dumb," he said, "you know I don't have disability insurance." Phyllis silently looked back at him. After a moment, Neil sighed in resignation. "Okay. Who?"

"Ira," said Phyllis, grinning from ear to ear.

Neil stared at her. "Ira?" he whispered in disbelief.

Phyllis nodded. "Uh-huh."

"But I thought he and Marilyn . . . you told me there was going to be a reconciliation."

"There *was*. Marilyn was going to call him."

"And?"

"He was away for the weekend, so she never got a chance to talk to him. When I called my grandmother, she told me he had taken the kids to Disneyland . . . what she didn't tell me was that he also took Natalie."

"Why would he take Natalie? He couldn't have been that desperate."

"When she tries, Natalie washes up pretty good. There's plenty worse than Natalie, I'll tell you," she said, offended.

"I wasn't talking about her looks. Natalie's a dud."

"Well—I guess Ira thinks different."

Neil shook his head and wrinkled his forehead. "I don't get it," he said.

"Grandma was very mysterious. She kept throwing innuendos at me, like she didn't want to tell me but she wanted me to guess. You know how she gets . . . like teasy, sly."

"What did she say?"

Phyllis pursed her lips and began imitating her grandmother. "Ira went away mit de boyss to de Disneyland all weekend . . .

end hees goink to hev dere som goot time, hi betcha . . . Netelie is ulso not hum." Then in her own voice, she continued, "But I never dreamed they were together."

Neil looked at her, then shook his head. "I still don't get it," he said. "Ira wouldn't just go off like that with Natalie. It doesn't make sense. I can see him taking the kids. But why Natalie? He was never interested in Natalie."

"Natalie and Ira have done that a lot, though. They're always taking the kids places."

"Yeah, but different, never for a weekend."

"It was a Writers' Guild weekend."

"But why bring Natalie? Ira could have brought someone else, or picked up something there . . ." Suddenly his head snapped up and he stared at his wife. "What did you mean before when you said, 'She did it, she got her'?" Slowly Phyllis nodded her head up and down.

"Your *mother?*" Neil whispered.

Phyllis nodded again.

Neil gaped at her. "Sita, Rama and Vishnu," he breathed. "She set him up . . . that old . . ." Neil stopped and slowly began to smile.

"Exactly," said Phyllis, smiling back.

"And she screwed Marilyn at the same time."

"Bingo."

"Holy healing hands," he marveled. Neil stood up and began to walk around the room, his head bent, his hands in the back pockets of his jeans. "But how?" he asked, suddenly coming to a halt and looking over at Phyllis. "How the hell did she do it?"

"That we'll probably never know."

"I wonder which motive took precedence," he mused, "the Ira-Natalie setup, or the shafting of Marilyn . . ."

Phyllis laughed softly. "That's another thing we'll never know."

Neil stood absolutely still, his face suddenly serious. He gazed deeply into his wife's eyes. "Phyllis," he said, a note of concern creeping into his voice, "you don't by any chance happen to take after your mother, do you?"

"No way, you jerk," she laughed. "Everybody always said I took after Grandma."

Neil turned and walked back to the bed. He lay down, picked up the remote and clicked on the set. "That bit of news doesn't exactly thrill me either," he informed her and turned up the volume.

"Tough," said Phyllis, giving him the finger.

She walked out of the bedroom and down the hall to the kitchen. She sat down at the Formica shelf that served as her desk, and looked at the phone. She frowned in concentration, wondering which one to call. She supposed she could have gotten the details out of Natalie—but then again Natalie might be too embarrassed to tell her, or too dumb. Grandma wasn't spilling anything. She preferred to keep people dangling and make them crazy. Helen? No. Her mother would deny having anything to do with it and get offended to boot. Celia, Phyllis was sure, knew nothing, or she would have told Marilyn. And Marilyn . . . well, Marilyn was strange. She had always been strange. She could go for days and days without talking to anybody . . . except for Daddy, of course. And it used to drive Helen bananas. She would say something to Marilyn, or tell her to do something, and Marilyn wouldn't answer—or even give any indication that she had heard. Helen would go berserk and chase after her with a broom. Once she threw all Marilyn's clothes out on the front lawn—but Phyllis couldn't remember what Marilyn had done in retaliation. Whatever, they went around and around. One of them would do the other a nasty, and then the other would do a nasty back. Well, now it was Marilyn's turn again. Phyllis picked up the phone and called her sister.

"Marilyn?"

"Yes."

"Hi, it's Phyllis."

"I know."

"So—how are you?"

"If you're trying to ascertain whether or not I've heard from Natalie, the answer is yes. I've heard from Natalie."

"Are you very upset?"

"I am upset."

"Well, I certainly don't blame you," Phyllis said, talking very fast, "especially now, when you were going to call Ira and all— the reconciliation and everything . . . uh . . . did you ever reach him?"

"No, I never reached him. Do you want to know if I *called* him?"

"Well, I was wondering . . ."

"Yes, I called him. He wasn't home, and the rest is history."

"Stop it, Marilyn. I want to know . . . I am concerned about how you must be feeling."

"How must I be feeling?"

Phyllis clucked in amazement. "Like shit."

"Well, you're wrong."

"But . . ."

"I wish Natalie every happiness."

"Well, I, uh, of course, you do. So do I."

"I wish Ira the same."

"Yes, well, so do I."

"I wish Helen Ritter cancer, or if there's anything else that's worse, I wish her that as well. Now you know how I feel. Good-bye, Phyllis. Thanks for calling." And Marilyn hung up, leaving Phyllis sitting with her mouth open, her hands sweating and the receiver pressing painfully against her ear.

Slowly she put down the phone. So Marilyn knew it was Helen. Of course she knew. Generally, at least when they were kids, whenever anything had happened to Marilyn, Helen usually had something to do with it.

Phyllis sat at her desk and doodled on her grocery list. Not a thing had changed. But cancer! Phyllis was well aware that there was no love lost between Helen and Marilyn. No love at all. What she hadn't known, that is until tonight, was the extent to which they hated each other. And the knowledge chilled her to the bone. How could a mother and a daughter hate each other so enormously? How could a mother and a daughter even hate each other at all? And how would it, if ever, end? She was glad she and Neil had no children. Phyllis smiled and drew a flower. She had an interesting life to look forward to—like a continuing soap opera, episode after episode, and each one of them filled with *Sturm und Drang*. No wonder Grandma was living so long. She also wanted to see how it would end.

Carefully Phyllis drew in two leaves, one on either side of the stem. Helen was a strange woman, too. Just as strange in her way as Marilyn was in hers. Other mothers at Helen's stage of the game had more ordinary projects. They worked at a job, or did fund-raising, or supported thrift shops, or volunteered to read to the blind or organized charity benefits. Things like that. But not Helen. Helen's children were her projects.

Suddenly Phyllis dropped her pencil. The flower lay half-petaled and pathetic, below "two bags bean sprouts, one loaf stone-ground whole wheat bread." Helen had, for the moment, finished off Marilyn. She had dealt with Natalie. "Krishna!" yelped Phyllis, sitting alone in an empty kitchen. "Help me, Krishna—because I'm next!" And she knew absolutely that as soon as Helen cleared up the details, when the wedding was over and Natalie and Ira off on their honeymoon, her mother would catch her breath and begin looking around for another project. And her eye would fall on Phyllis, the baby. Because she, Phyllis, was the only one left now.

What it would be, Phyllis had no idea. *That* it would be, she was sure. She stood up and pushed the chair under the desk. Then she walked back to the bedroom. She wanted to tell Neil about life—that it was an adventure—that they both would always have something to look forward to. And it would go on and on and on because everyone knows that with children, there's always something. And Helen was not one to sit around playing canasta when her children's lives needed fixing. Whether they wanted her to or not.

Chapter

33

SUNDAY HAD BEEN A DIFFICULT DAY for Marilyn. She spent the morning preparing a brief. Brenda called to say goodbye. She and Anthony were returning to Phoenix, but would be up again next month. Brenda told her that she had bumped into Sam Greenfield in Close Encounters, and he had asked Brenda how Marilyn was doing. "I told him you'd love to see him," said Brenda.

"What made you do that?" Marilyn asked, annoyed. "You know I'm planning to reconcile with Ira."

"Why?" Brenda had asked. "Why are you going back to someone you can't stand?"

"Because I need to be cared about."

"A lot of people care about you."

"A man, Brenda. I need to be loved by a man."

"But why Ira? You've never loved Ira."

"And I never will, Ira or anybody else. You didn't listen, Brenda. I said nothing about loving someone—I was talking about someone loving me."

"You've got a lousy attitude, Marilyn. You want something for nothing. You can't grow flowers without planting seeds."

"That's exactly why I'm calling Ira. He won't expect anything in return."

"You're making him out to be a jerk, Marilyn. He's really not."

Marilyn shrugged and her shoulder hit the mouthpiece of the phone. "He did it once before, if you recall."

"Yeah. I recall you went crazy with him."

"It's different now. I have my own life . . . and I don't have my father. Ira was redundant then—now he isn't."

"You don't know what you're missing, Marilyn."

Marilyn gave a short, cynical laugh. "If you mean love," she said, "I certainly do."

"To each her own," replied Brenda. "You want to crap up the rest of your life, be my guest. You want my opinion?"

"Not really."

"Fine. See you in a month . . . Marilyn?"

"Yes?"

"Flowers are pretty, Marilyn. They smell nice. Don't settle for a lot full of weeds. You know what happens to empty, weedy lots? Dogs go there to shit. *Arrivederci.*"

Marilyn had returned to her law journals and papers. When there was nothing more to do, she stood up, stretched and turned on the television set. However, Sunday was a bad TV day. At seven she called Ira, but there was no answer, so she switched on *Sixty Minutes*. Then she watched *All in the Family*. When that was over, she called Ira again. Still no answer. She went into the kitchen and made herself a scrambled egg and sat down with a magazine. She read an article about how to construct your own greenhouse and smiled. Brenda and her flowers. What was it about love and marriage that made women want to grow things? She, Marilyn, wanted neither to reap nor to sow. She had no use for flowers—or anything else that blazed briefly, withered, drooped and died.

At nine o'clock Natalie called, so excited she was barely coherent. But Marilyn understood completely. She understood that her mother, once again, had stuck it to her. She hung up the phone so rimed with hatred that she actually shivered. She was still frozen with fury when Phyllis called, and in an effort to warm herself, took a bath in water hot enough to make the bathroom walls begin to sweat and the mirrors steam and disappear. Her skin turned rosy with the heat, but the ice remained, and Marilyn went to bed unthawed. She dreamed she was an Aztec princess, beautiful, arrogant, indulged. She was dressed in filmy garments of turquoise, magenta, sun-yellow, rich green. Around her neck, waist, arms, and ankles gleamed heavy, ornate golden ornaments that proclaimed her rank. She drank, from jewel-encrusted cups, sweet velvety potions that left her sleepy and content. She lay on her back before the altar of her gods, receiving praise and hearing hymns and paeans to her glory. She lay there, proud and imperious, accepting the accolades and honors that were her due as if they were sweet-smelling flowers that were being flung upon her. It was only when she opened wide her half-closed eyes and saw the mad, fanatic smile of the high priestess and the glint of the curved blade as it flashed unerringly down toward her, that she finally understood. She opened her mouth to scream in disbelief, to protest, to deny, to plead, but before she could emit a sound it was already too late. Marilyn awoke shaking. She stared, unblinking, into the darkness, knowing full well that she hadn't really been dreaming at all.

Before work on Monday, she drove to Encino and knocked on her mother's door. Yuspeh answered, looked at her curiously and brought her into the kitchen, where Helen was talking on the phone, evidently making arrangements for hiring a group to play at Natalie's wedding reception. "No, no," Marilyn heard her say. "Six men is more than enough. I don't need an accordion player." Helen paused for a moment when she saw Marilyn, then looked away and continued with the conversation.

Marilyn glanced around the green-and-white kitchen—at the omnipresent, gleaming copper kettle permanently perched on the left rear burner of the stove when not in use. It was always brought forward to the left front burner if water needed to be boiled. She looked at the curtain covering the window over the sink, ever starched and pressed, white with little fuzzy green balls hanging four inches from the bottom, seeming to beg to be pulled. As a little girl she used to climb up on the counter, creep to the sink, reach out a naughty hand and pull off the tempting little balls, one at a time, until she was caught. Once she had given one to Phyllis, telling her it was candy. She smiled at the memory. Phyllis, infuriated by the deception, had come at her like a maddened kitten, fingers stiffened like claws, face contorted and snarling, mouth full of dry green fuzz. It had been worth the spankings, to pull off those little green balls.

But there must have been a million white, green-balled curtains, all exactly the same, because within a day or two after the denuding, there would be another curtain with the long row of balls completely intact. There were exactly twenty-four, Marilyn remembered.

And the plants. Helen had had Lenny build a shelf the length of the wall in the breakfast area, which was always called the breakfast area even though the family took all their meals there—unless they had company and ate in the dining room. Helen had filled the shelf with plants, and Papa had to build her another shelf beneath the first. That one, too, was soon filled. There were wall planters and floor planters and a corner baker's rack all filled with green, shiny-leafed plants, green spidery plants, tall ones, flat ones. On the wall opposite her father's hand-built shelves—well it was not really a wall, it was the back of the dish cabinet and stopped about three feet above the tile counter that separated the breakfast area from the kitchen—Helen had hung assorted copper molds; two fish molds, two Bundt molds, two gingerbread-men molds, a mold shaped like a star, another like an ear of corn. Marilyn, who had always sat in the chair that faced these molds, knew each indentation by heart.

Behind her waved the plants, framing her head in a green halo, like a living hat. She sat down there now, in the same seat she had occupied for all the years she had lived in this house, pulled an ashtray toward her and lit a cigarette. Smoking in the breakfast area always irritated Helen, though she never actually forbade it. She felt that the smoke was bad for the plants. Yuspeh sat down opposite her.

"So, how are you, Marilyn?" she asked.

"You know damn well how I am."

"Dot's true."

"You might have told me."

"For what? It would come out the same thing any ways."

Helen hung up the phone and walked over to the table. "See who's paying us a visit," Helen said to Yuspeh, then turned to Marilyn. "What can I do for you?"

"I'll have a cup of coffee, please—or tea, if it's more convenient."

"Certainly."

Helen walked to the stove, put the kettle on the front burner and turned it on. She took out three mugs and two tea bags. Then she put one tea bag back.

"You got a nice apartment?" asked Yuspeh.

"Very nice."

"You clean it yourself?"

"No."

Yuspeh nodded. "I knew dot," she said. "You would like a cookie? We got cookies, two kinds."

"No, thank you."

The kettle began to whistle and Helen filled the cups, put them on a tray and carried it to the table. She placed a cup before each of them and put the tray on the counter. Then she sat down.

"So," she said, "you decided to honor us with your presence. How come?"

"I haven't seen you for a long time," Marilyn answered. "I forgot what a real out-and-out miserable bitch looks like."

Helen stirred her tea. "You could have saved yourself a drive by looking in the mirror."

"I could have done a lot of things, and your opinions don't interest me. I'm not here to trade insults with you, although there's not an insult in the world that wouldn't apply. There's no use your insulting me, either. I've already had the biggest one of all. My father died, and you didn't."

Helen's lips tightened. "State your business and get out of my house," she hissed.

Marilyn took a drag on her cigarette, blew out the smoke and placed the cigarette on the lip of the ashtray. Yuspeh's eyes went from one face to the other, waiting.

"Well," said Helen impatiently, "what do you want?"

"How old was I when you began hating me?"

Helen sighed and shook her head. She picked up the spoon she had just used to stir her tea and put it back in her cup. Silently she began stirring again.

"Well?" asked Marilyn. "Can't you remember back that far?"

"I have no desire to continue this discussion, Marilyn. I have nothing to say to you."

"Good," said Yuspeh, breaking her silence. "A smart person, who I don't remember, said, 'You got nothing to say nice, it's better you say nothing.' Come, Marilyn, eat a cookie."

Marilyn looked at her mother. "We're both cursed," she whispered. "What kind of woman are you? What kind of mother would do to a child what you have done to me?"

"Me?" cried Helen. "You dare to talk about the kind of mother *I* am? I know all about you. I saw how you treated *your* children and how they were afraid of you." Helen laughed bitterly. "I know all about mothers like you. I had one."

She glared at Marilyn, breathing hard. Then with a conscious effort to control herself, she lifted her cup with shaking hands and took a long sip of tea. "The only decent thing you ever did," she said, putting down her cup, "was to divorce Ira and give him the children. I didn't realize it then, but I do now. Did you think I would sit back and watch you torture them all over again? Oh, no. I knew I had to stop you—and I did." She paused to catch her breath. "And there's not one thing you can do about it," she added triumphantly, "not one thing."

"Helen," said Yuspeh. "Enough. She wanted another chance. It's not a terrible thing to want another chance."

"Well, she isn't going to get another chance. I have seen to that. I fixed *her* wagon."

"Be quiet already, Helen," the old woman said sharply. "It's enough what you fixed. Don't be so happy in front of her about it."

Helen turned angrily to her mother-in-law. "You be quiet. You just sit there and keep your mouth shut. I don't have to put up with you, you know. This is my house!"

Slowly and deliberately, Yuspeh picked up her cup. "If you wouldn't mind, landlord, I finish mine tea. Then I pack." She put the cup to her lips and took a small sip.

"Just be quiet, Mama," Helen said shortly.

"Mine lips are zipped," replied Yuspeh.

Marilyn, sitting slumped in her seat, felt very tired. All she wanted now was to leave this house. She looked at Helen, and it was an effort just to turn her head.

"I always knew you hated me," she said quietly, "but I never really knew how much."

Helen closed her eyes for a moment and she, too, seemed to droop in her chair. "Neither did I," she said.

The three of them sat silently. Only Yuspeh continued to drink her tea.

Suddenly Helen put her hands on the sides of the chair and pushed herself up. "I'm very busy," she announced. "I have a wedding to make. And you know something, Marilyn?"

Surprised, Marilyn looked up.

"If your father were alive today, he would be very happy about Natalie's good fortune. My husband would agree with me that I did the right thing, and that it would be a heartless, thoughtless person who would want to sacrifice her sister's happiness for . . . for a selfish whim."

Abruptly Helen left the kitchen, and Marilyn heard her begin to climb the stairs. The weariness fled, and she felt a surge of rage so enormous that she could barely breathe.

She looked at Yuspeh, and the old woman stared back. As if sensing her intention, Yuspeh violently shook her head. "No."

But Marilyn knew what she had to do. She rose from her chair and walked to the large drawer where the tools were kept. From it she took Helen's garden shears. Then she walked back and stood before the shelves her father had built. Methodically, one after the other, she cut to pieces Helen's beloved plants. Yuspeh, her lips zipped, sat and watched the pile of stems and leaves grow on the kitchen floor. When she was done, Marilyn replaced the shears in the drawer. She looked around at the hacked-up plants and smiled bleakly. Then, almost as an afterthought, she walked to the sink, leaned over and ripped from the curtain all twenty-four of the little green fuzzy balls.

Chapter 34

SHE WALKED DOWN THE AISLE next to Phyllis, and when they reached the altar Phyllis went to the left, she to the right, flanking the rabbi, who was standing facing the guests who filled the seats in the small chapel. The doors at the back opened, and Ira, smiling and happy, started his walk, Neil beside him. At the altar they stopped, and Marilyn looked at her ex-husband and nodded. She felt more kindly toward him at this wedding, where he was marrying someone else, than she had at her own.

Neil stepped back and to the side, and Marilyn, looking down the aisle, watched the doors at the back open and Todd and Jeremy enter. They seemed very small and nervous, these little boys she had given birth to. Over their arms hung two little baskets filled with rose petals. Hesitantly they dipped their hands into the baskets, tossing petals as they marched. At the altar, they stopped, the baskets now empty, and walked over to stand next to Marilyn, throwing her shy looks from beneath their lashes. She put out her hand and patted them on their combed, bent little heads. Now that they were no longer her children, affection rose within her, and her hand lingered, gentle, upon their hair.

With a sweep of organ music, the doors opened once more, revealing Natalie and Helen, standing arm in arm. The guests turned around, craning their necks to get a view of the bride.

Natalie, in traditional white, veiled and elaborately coiffed, started her walk on the wrong foot, then with a hop-skip, righted her gaffe and continued slowly down the aisle next to her smiling, triumphant mother. She carried a white Bible, topped with white and mauve orchids. Around her neck hung a single strand of pearls, the diamond clasp in front. The Bible and bouquet trembled slightly in her unsteady hands, and as Marilyn watched, she saw Helen nudge the bride, and Natalie, with a slight start, straightened up.

As they reached the altar, Helen kissed her daughter and handed her to Ira. Then she went and stood next to Phyllis. Her eyes passed over Marilyn as though she were invisible, and she gave her grandsons a little wave. Ira and Natalie faced the rabbi, a tiny, bearded man who smiled benevolently up at them. Marilyn caught Natalie's eye and winked at her. She looked very nice, Marilyn thought, and so did Ira. They truly made a fine couple. Helen had been right after all. As the rabbi began his prayers, Marilyn's eyes roamed over the chapel. All the relatives were there, as well as many of Ira's clients. Her grandmother Yuspeh, looking ancient, hungry and bored, in light-blue lace, sat between Celia and Jack, clutching a silver plastic purse in her hands. She held it proudly, standing it on her lap and occasionally running her nail over its dull-sheened, textured fabric. She looked impatient, no doubt eager for the ceremony to be over so that she could begin foraging in the smorgasbord that waited, already set out, in the next room.

After that day when she had cleared the underbrush in her mother's kitchen, Marilyn, feeling that she had, with those same shears, also cut the ties binding her in hatred to the woman who had borne her, found herself surprisingly peaceful, almost content. It was as if her decision to cut herself off from love severed the bonds of hatred as well. She didn't hate Helen any more. She felt that she understood her at last, and forgave her. Celia had been right all along. It was Malka that Helen was getting back at—not Marilyn. Poor, confused Helen had simply mistaken one for the other. Marilyn was not particularly interested in the dynamics of separation; it was enough to know that detachment worked for her and gave her the peace and ease in which she was now becalmed. She had chopped up her mother's plants and recognized that it had been a symbolic act. Since then she had felt stronger, impenetrable, no longer threatened by unpredictable emotional assaults. For some people, love is treacherous rather than protective, painful rather than joyful, suffocating rather than freeing—and Marilyn recognized herself to be one of those people. She had loved once . . . and paid dearly for it.

By blocking her reconciliation with Ira, Helen had unwittingly done her a favor, and Marilyn smiled at the fact that it was no longer necessary for her to aggravate Helen by so informing her. Hatred was far too close to love, and Marilyn had cleansed herself of both emotions. She would never love, but she would become fond; never hate, merely become indifferent. There was nothing she possessed, either inside or out, that it would destroy her to lose. Marilyn Stillman was finally happy. Maybe she would even send Helen a Boston fern.

The rabbi stopped speaking and placed a cloth-wrapped glass on the floor in front of Ira. Ira raised his foot and brought it crashing down, shattering the glass. "Mazel tov!" everyone yelled, clapping, as he kissed his new wife. Marilyn bent toward her sons and whispered to them. "Your daddy is married," she said. "Be happy and go kiss your new momma." Todd looked at her warily. "Aren't you still our mother?" Marilyn smiled. "Just the mother who gave birth to you—now go and kiss the mother who will do all the rest." She gave them a gentle push toward Natalie and watched as her sons were kissed and hugged. Then they all walked, smiling and happy, up the aisle, family and friends leaving the pews to follow the bridal party to the reception hall.

Marilyn stood with her family on the receiving line, laughing, talking and greeting the guests. Table cards were picked up, the music began to play and people lined up, plates in hand, at the long hors d'oeuvres table. Marilyn laughed out loud as Yuspeh, overcome by the sight of the steaming chafing dish of stuffed cabbage, broke from the receiving line and all but ran, shoving aside those in her way, to grab a plate and push it demandingly at the waiter behind the table.

Marilyn walked over to where Ira and Natalie stood and kissed her sister. "I'm very happy for you, Nat," she said softly, "because you have everything you've always wanted."

Natalie, radiant, hugged her tightly. "Oh, Marilyn, thank you and I only hope that some day . . ."

"Shh," interrupted Marilyn, "I already have everything I want."

Ira leaned toward her and kissed her cheek. "Be happy, Marilyn," he said.

Marilyn smiled at him and nodded her head. "I am, Ira, I really finally am."

After an hour, the hors d'oeuvres table, now practically stripped, and stained and strewn with lumps and crumbs, was wheeled out, and the guests, checking their cards, began to seat themselves. Marilyn, on the dais with the family, sat waiting for Natalie and Ira to emerge from behind the band and dance for the first time together as man and wife. The music began, and everyone stood and applauded as the happy couple whirled around the dance floor. Then Helen was led out by her brother Murray and also began to dance. More applause as partners were switched, pairing Ira and Helen, Natalie and Murray. Neil and Phyllis, hand in hand, joined the dancers.

Marilyn looked down the row of now-empty chairs at Yuspeh, who was buttering a roll and eyeing the action on the dance floor. She put down her knife, took a bite and chewed diligently. Then she put down the roll and stood up. She walked off the dais and on to the floor. The band, seeing her there, switched from "Love Is a Many-Splendored Thing" to "Bei Mir Bist Du Schoen." Yuspeh lifted her skirt with one hand and raised the other, her forefinger pointing straight up. In perfect rhythm to the music, she began to turn, dip and bend, twirling her raised wrist and swirling her skirts. The other dancers stopped and formed a circle around her, clapping and urging her on. After a few minutes she stopped, acknowledged the applause with an arrogant toss of her head and walked back to her seat. She sat down, picked up her roll, sniffed it to see if the butter had gone rancid while she was off dancing and crammed it into her mouth. She sat there, her cheeks plumped with bread and her jaws pumping vigorously.

Feeling Marilyn's eyes upon her, she turned her head and regarded her granddaughter. She bent her head down and raised it again, quickly, as if to say, "Sue me, I'm a dancer." Marilyn smiled and nodded back. Celia waved to her from the relatives' table and motioned her over. "Later," mouthed Marilyn. Right now she just felt like sitting here, observing the results of her mother's diligent efforts against her.

The music stopped and tray-laden waitresses appeared at each table. Plates were placed, gravy was ladled, vegetables were spooned and roast beef tenderly laid before each guest. Wine was poured and the toasts began. "To my beautiful bride," said Ira, clinking his glass with Natalie's, "my darling sons, and my wonderful mother-in-law, twice over." "To my sister Helen," said Uncle Ben, "who never lets go of a good thing—and to Ira, whose motto is 'If at first you don't succeed, try the sister.' " The room filled with laughter and Ben continued, "And to our sweet Natalie, we all love you." Ben, red-faced and smiling, sat down amid loud applause.

Marilyn rose, her glass of champagne held high before her, and the room quieted. "This is a time," she said, "of ever-changing relationships—especially in *our* family. To my sister Natalie, my new brother and former husband, Ira, my sons and nephews, Todd and Jeremy, I give my sincere good wishes for health and happiness as well as my monogrammed towels and pillow slips. As Uncle Murray would say, 'Waste not, want not'— and I don't need them any more. And speaking of names," she went on over the laughter, "may we all soon be blessed with one who will do honor to the dearest . . ." Her voice broke. Her glass of champagne shook slightly, and a few drops leaped over the rim and dropped like tears on her hand. "To my Papa, Leonard Ritter," she said and draining her glass, tossed it over her shoulder. Then, picking up Phyllis's glass, she raised it high. "And to, I hope very soon, my new nephew, Leonard Ritter Stillman." This glass she also drained and tossed over her shoulder. Smiling, she turned to face Ira and Natalie. "I have just given you what I am sure will be a very pleasant assignment —so finish your dinner and start your homework."

Ira grinned, Natalie blushed, the band zoomed into a rousing rendition of "Oh Mein Papa" and Marilyn sat down to loud laughter and applause.

She glanced quickly at her watch. The wedding had begun at four, and it was now almost six. Marilyn looked around the room. Everyone seemed to be enjoying himself. People were laughing and talking. Natalie was dancing with Todd; Ira and Jeremy with Helen. Neil and Phyllis whispered in a corner. Once again, only she and Yuspeh were left at the table.

"Hi, Marilyn."

She looked up at Bo Baker. "Hello, Bo."

"Dance?"

"No, thanks. You're barely standing."

"Sho be it." Bo wandered off.

"Why you didn't dance with him?" asked Yuspeh.

"He was drunk."

"But he looks like a Jewish boy."

"He is."

Yuspeh clucked disapprovingly and wiped some crumbs off her purse. "I'm in trouble from you."

"Why?"

"Your mother is angry I didn't say nothing when you made such a hurricane in the kitchen."

"She told you to keep your mouth shut, didn't she?"

"Dot's what I said to her."

They looked at one another and grinned. At that moment, the band struck up "The Bride Cuts the Cake," and a huge three-tiered wedding cake was wheeled out. Everyone walked on to the dance floor and formed a circle around Ira and Natalie, watching as they sliced into the cake and fed each other a piece. Phyllis, standing next to Marilyn, had a disdainful look on her face. "That's so tacky," she murmured.

Natalie swallowed her cake and turned to face her well-wishers. "Get ready, all you singles," she trilled. "I'm going to throw the bouquet." She searched the crowd until she spied Marilyn. Then, smiling, she took her bouquet and threw it to her. Marilyn watched it arc through the air and come right at her. Although not a believer in omens, she was not about to take chances. Just as it reached her, thrown so accurately that had she held out her arms it would have fallen right into them, Marilyn stepped aside and the bouquet sailed through now-unoccupied space and landed on the floor. "Oohh," moaned the people, and then "Aahh," they cheered as Yuspeh scurried over and scooped it up.

Marilyn said her goodbyes, and as she hurried to the door, passed Helen, Neil and Phyllis deep in conversation. Noticing the uncomfortable looks on the faces of her sister and brother-in-law, she paused.

". . . so, I thought to myself," she heard Helen say with a smile, "Neil and Phyllis are bound to have a baby soon. They certainly should be thinking about it. It would really make my happiness complete." Neil and Phyllis looked at each other and Helen continued. "So again I thought to myself, why should Ira and I call in our loans? We know they've just taken over the store next door and are hard-pressed for cash . . . especially if they're thinking about having a baby."

"Uh, well," said Neil, "we don't really think . . ."

"Of course," interrupted Helen, "if you *don't* intend—well—it *has* been several years and the repayment date is long past due . . ."

Marilyn shook with silent laughter and skipped out the door. Let Helen play her little games, and let those she played with initiate their own strategies. She, Marilyn, was unaffected. Immune. Helen couldn't touch her any more, and Phyllis would have to fight her own battles.

But then again, perhaps Phyllis and Neil would appreciate

the offer of a loan. Hadn't Phyllis once said that sisters ought to stick together? Marilyn made a mental note to call Phyllis in the morning.

It was just beginning to get dark and the sky flamed a brilliant pink and orange. She stood for a moment, breathing deeply, the lemony scent of trees and grass delighting her nose. She ran to her car, and all through the drive home she sang along with the radio.

Epilogue

EIGHTEEN MONTHS AFTER NATALIE'S WEDDING, Marilyn had moved to a larger apartment and used the extra bedroom as a den-office. She dated frequently, whenever she pleased, having discovered that her desire for casual, noncommittal relationships that did not end in love or marriage was an attitude very attractive to men. Even when sex was involved, she never permitted a man to remain overnight in her bed. Marilyn liked her privacy. She liked to be alone. She had her career, she had money to spend—and because she needed no one and it was all the same to her if she went to the theater or a concert or a party escorted or with a girl friend or alone, she never *was* alone. The other single women with whom she had become friendly found her difficult to fathom and envied her ability to, as far as men were concerned, "take 'em or leave 'em." They envied even more the fact that guys fell all over themselves for Marilyn Stillman.

"What's your secret?" a new attorney in her office named Cookie Cohen once asked her. "You treat them like dirt and still the lines form."

"I don't demand that they love and/or marry me," Marilyn replied.

"Don't you ever want to marry again?" asked Cookie curiously.

"Absolutely not," replied Marilyn.

"But why?"

"Because," she said simply, "I do not want to have anyone *in* my life who is essential *to* my life."

"Why not?"

"Well, Cookie—that's a long story and I'd rather not go into it."

"What about when you're older and can't pick and choose the way you're doing now?"

"What about it?"

"You'll be all alone."

"How nice."

"You'll die alone."

"Oh, Cookie," said Marilyn. "Don't we all?"

Cookie looked at her for a long, long time. "You're like a man," she said at last. "You live like one, you think like one, your attitude is very masculine. Every eligible, single man I know is like you."

Shortly afterwards, Cookie left, still bewildered but feeling a strange mixture of pity and admiration.

Marilyn piled several folders in her attaché case and got ready to leave. She had shopping to do before she met Sam for dinner, and wanted to get it over with. It seemed to her she had bought nothing but baby presents lately. First Brenda had presented the world with Gina and James Santacroce—twins, of course. Leave it to Brenda, who claimed that (a) she had a lot of time to make up for, and (b) it was her nature to do things up really big. Then Natalie had popped, disappointing Helen and Marilyn, who had wanted a boy to name after Lenny. For some reason, and Marilyn was still curious, Natalie had named the baby Amber—after no one, at least no one Marilyn knew. And now she needed a shower gift for Phyllis, who was due in two months.

She clicked her case shut, told her secretary she was leaving and asked her to buzz the attendant to have her car ready. She smiled at the recollection of Phyllis making her pregnancy announcement. She had called her the evening of the day the rabbit died.

"I wanted you to be the sixth to know, Marilyn. I'm pregnant."

"You're *what?*"

"Pregnant. Expecting. Knocked up."

"Oh, Phyllis."

"Is that your way of saying congratulations?"

"But why? I lent you fifteen thousand dollars!"

Phyllis paused. "What really made you do that?" she asked. "I never did understand. All you ever told me was that you had a feeling that at this point in time perhaps a loan would come in handy."

"I overheard you and Neil talking to Mother at Natalie's wedding."

"Oh."

"Didn't you use the money to repay her?"

Phyllis was silent for a moment and then continued in a rush. "Well, we were going to, but the new addition cost so much more than we anticipated, and Neil put in a whole new line and . . . well . . . you know."

"I see," said Marilyn, smiling to herself. "At least you managed to hold out for over a year."

"That wasn't it at all, Marilyn. Neil and I feel ready for a child."

"Fine. Whatever you say. I hope it's a boy, to name for Papa."

"So do we."

"Are you honestly happy about it, Phyllis?"

"I'll answer that one after it's born."

The car was waiting in front of the office building when Marilyn emerged. She did her shopping two blocks away at the Century City Mall. She arrived home by six, showered and dressed and sat down in front of the television set. She watched the news and then *Newlywed Game,* marveling at how America had grown so great when, if *Newlywed Game* were any indication, so many of its citizens were so appallingly stupid.

Much later, after Sam had left, Marilyn read for half an hour and then shut off the light. Just before falling asleep, she blew a kiss to her father, who watched over her from his frame on the dresser.

She smiled at him and assured him she was fine—busy and as happy as being without him would permit. She looked at Malka and little Helen, who were now stuck with their family into the frame at the bottom of her father's picture. Even though neither one was looking at her and couldn't care less, Marilyn blew them a kiss too. She wished them peace, she wished them rest.

She wished them well.

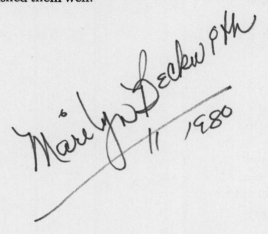

ABOUT THE AUTHOR

RHEA KOHAN is married to a television producer on the West Coast and has three children. They live in Los Angeles.